DOVER · THRIFT · EDITIONS

Erewhon
and
Erewhon Revisited

SAMUEL BUTLER

DOVER PUBLICATIONS, INC.
Mineola, New York

DOVER THRIFT EDITIONS

GENERAL EDITOR: MARY CAROLYN WALDREP
EDITOR OF THIS VOLUME: JANET B. KOPITO

Bibliographical Note

Erewhon and *Erewhon Revisited*, first published by Dover Publications, Inc., in 2015, is an unabridged republication of the following works: the 1901 revised and expanded edition of *Erewhon* (published by Grant Richards), originally published by Trübner & Company, London, in 1872, and *Erewhon Revisited*, originally published as *Erewhon Revisited Twenty Years Later, Both by the Original Discoverer of the Country and by His Son* by Grant Richards, London, in 1901. A Note has been specially written for the Dover edition.

Library of Congress Cataloging-in-Publication Data

Butler, Samuel, 1835–1902.
  [Novels. Selections]
  Erewhon : and Erewhon revisited / Samuel Butler.
      p. cm. — (Dover thrift editions)
  ISBN-13: 978-0-486-79637-6 (softcover)
  ISBN-10: 0-486-79637-X (softcover)
  1. Utopias—Fiction. I. Butler, Samuel, 1835–1902. Erewhon revisited.   II.
Title.   III. Title: Erewhon revisited.
  PR4349.B7A6 2015
  823'.8—dc23

                              2014044387

Manufactured in the United States by Courier Corporation
79637X01   2015
www.doverpublications.com

Note

SAMUEL BUTLER WAS born in Nottinghamshire, England, on December 4, 1835. The son of the Rev. Thomas Butler, Samuel was expected to become an Anglican priest, but due to his growing doubts about the Church, as well as his desire to become an artist, he decided to follow his own path. After graduating from Cambridge University in 1858, he traveled to New Zealand and became a sheep farmer—a vocation at which he was successful (his experiences in New Zealand provided a rich source of material for *Erewhon,* which begins with a discourse on sheep and shearing). During his sojourn abroad, Butler wrote "Darwin Among the Machines" (1863). After selling his farm at a profit, he returned to England in 1864 and thereafter followed his artistic ambitions: painting (he exhibited at the Royal Academy in London), composing music, and writing on various subjects. He wrote four books on evolution during the period 1877 to 1886, examining Darwin's theories; he was friendly with Darwin but contributed his own critical appraisal. Another interest of Butler's was Italy and its art—he visited the country frequently and was inspired to write about it in two works of the 1880s. He lived comfortably, having been left property and inheritances, and he devoted himself to a variety of literary endeavors, translating the *Iliad* (1898) and the *Odyssey* (1900); writing a study of Shakespeare's sonnets (1899); and producing *The Way of All Flesh* (published posthumously in 1903), his satire of the English middle class during the Victorian era. Butler died in a nursing home in London on June 18, 1902.

Erewhon (1872) and *Erewhon Revisited* (1901), presented as companions in this new edition, are essentially satirical examinations—rich in irony and pointed comparisons to Victorian society—of a quasi-Utopian nation, Erewhon (an anagram for "nowhere"). The narrator describes in minute detail the conventions of Erewhonian society, encompassing crime and punishment, religion, education—even the rights of animals and vegetables. One convention—punishing those who fall ill while absolving those who commit crimes—permits lawbreakers to declare that they are "suffering from a severe fit of immorality." There transgressors are visited by friends offering "great solicitude." Further, men known as "straighteners" are called in to practice "soul-craft"—rehabilitation of the criminals. The ill, and diseased, in contrast, are punished. The banning of machines (and wristwatches) in Erewhon leads to the narrator's decision regarding his residence in that land. Modern readers will recognize elements of science fiction, as well as intimations of steampunk culture, in both works.

Samuel Butler, in his *Preface* and *Preface to the Second Edition,* describes the publication history of *Erewhon.* In *Erewhon Revisited,* Butler uses the voice of the narrator's son, John Higgs, to continue the story. Full of plot twists and introducing the villains Professors Hanky and Panky, the sequel focuses more narrowly on aspects of religion as practiced in Erewhon. This new approach—provocative to Victorian sensibilities—caused Butler's publishers to reject the book. George Bernard Shaw came to the rescue, recommending that Butler approach Shaw's publisher, Grant Richards. *Erewhon Revisited* appeared in 1901.

Contents

Erewhon 1

Preface to the First Edition 2

Preface to the Second Edition . . . . : 3

Preface 6

     I. Waste Lands 11

    II. In the Wool-Shed 15

   III. Up the River 19

   IV. The Saddle 23

    V. The River and the Range 29

   VI. Into Erewhon 36

  VII. First Impressions 42

 VIII. In Prison 47

   IX. To the Metropolis 53

    X. Current Opinions 61

   XI. Some Erewhonian Trials 69

  XII. Malcontents 75

 XIII. The Views of the Erewhonians Concerning Death . . .80

 XIV. Mahaina 86

  XV. The Musical Banks 89

 XVI. Arowhena 98

   XVII. Ydgrun and the Ydgrunites. 104

  XVIII. Birth Formulæ 109

    XIX. The World of the Unborn 113

     XX. What They Mean by It. 119

    XXI. The Colleges of Unreason 125

   XXII. The Colleges of Unreason—(continued) 131

  XXIII. The Book of the Machines. 138

   XXIV. The Book of the Machines—(continued) 143

    XXV. The Book of the Machines—(concluded) 150

   XXVI. The Views of an Erewhonian Prophet
           Concerning the Rights of Animals 160

  XXVII. The Views of an Erewhonian Philosopher
           Concerning the Rights of Vegetables 166

 XXVIII. Escape 173

   XXIX. Conclusion 181

Erewhon Revisited **189**

Author's Preface to the Original Edition. 191

     I. Ups and Downs of Fortune—My Father Starts
           for Erewhon. 193

    II. To the Foot of the Pass Into Erewhon. 202

   III. My Father Is Accosted by Professors Hanky
           and Panky 206

    IV. My Father Overhears More of Hanky and Panky's
           Conversation 214

     V. My Father Meets a Son, of Whose Existence
           He Was Ignorant. 223

    VI. Further Conversation Between Father and Son . . . 230

   VII. Signs of the New Order of Things Catch
           My Father's Eye 235

  VIII. Yram, Now Mayoress, Gives a Dinner Party 242

    IX. Interview Between Yram and Her Son 250

Contents

X. My Father Betakes Himself to Fairmead 257

XI. President Gurgoyle's Pamphlet 263

XII. George Fails to Find My Father 271

XIII. A Visit to the Provincial Deformatory 277

XIV. My Father Makes the Acquaintance of
    Mr. Balmy 283

XV. The Temple Is Dedicated to My Father 292

XVI. Professor Hanky Preaches a Sermon 302

XVII. George Takes His Father to Prison 311

XVIII. Yram Invites Dr. Downie and Mrs. Humdrum
    to Luncheon 317

XIX. A Council Is Held at the Mayor's 320

XX. Mrs. Humdrum and Dr. Downie Propose a
    Compromise 326

XXI. Yram Goes to See My Father 330

XXII. An Extract from a Sunch'stonian Journal 336

XXIII. My Father Is Escorted to the Mayor's House 342

XXIV. What Is to Be Done About Sunchildism? 347

XXV. George Escorts My Father to the Statues 352

XXVI. My Father Reaches Home 358

XXVII. I Meet My Brother George at the Statues 362

XXVIII. George and I Spend a Few Hours Together 371

Erewhon

PREFACE TO THE FIRST EDITION

The Author wishes it to be understood that Erewhon is pronounced as a word of three syllables, all short—thus, Ĕ-rĕ-whŏn.

PREFACE TO THE SECOND EDITION

HAVING BEEN ENABLED by the kindness of the public to get through an unusually large edition of *Erewhon* in a very short time, I have taken the opportunity of a second edition to make some necessary corrections, and to add a few passages where it struck me that they would be appropriately introduced; the passages are few, and it is my fixed intention never to touch the work again.

I may perhaps be allowed to say a word or two here in reference to *The Coming Race*, to the success of which book *Erewhon* has been very generally set down as due. This is a mistake, though a perfectly natural one. The fact is that *Erewhon* was finished, with the exception of the last twenty pages and a sentence or two inserted from time to time here and there throughout the book, before the first advertisement of *The Coming Race* appeared. A friend having called my attention to one of the first of these advertisements, and suggesting that it probably referred to a work of similar character to my own, I took *Erewhon* to a well-known firm of publishers on the 1st of May 1871, and left it in their hands for consideration. I then went abroad, and on learning that the publishers alluded to declined the MS., I let it alone for six or seven months, and, being in an out-of-the-way part of Italy, never saw a single review of *The Coming Race*, nor a copy of the work. On my return, I purposely avoided looking into it until I had sent back my last revises to the printer. Then I had much pleasure in reading it, but was indeed surprised at the many little points of similarity between the two books, in spite of their entire independence of one another.

I regret that reviewers have in some cases been inclined to treat the chapters on Machines as an attempt to reduce Mr. Darwin's theory to an absurdity. Nothing could be further from my intention, and few things would be more distasteful to me than any attempt to laugh at Mr. Darwin; but I must own that I have myself to thank for the misconception, for I felt sure that my intention would be missed, but preferred not to weaken the chapters by explanation, and knew very well that Mr. Darwin's theory would take no harm. The only question in my mind was how far *I* could afford to be misrepresented as laughing at that for which I have the most profound admiration. I am surprised, however, that the book at which such an example of the specious misuse of analogy would seem most naturally levelled should have occurred to no reviewer; neither shall I mention the name of the book here, though I should fancy that the hint given will suffice.

I have been held by some whose opinions I respect to have denied men's responsibility for their actions. He who does this is an enemy who deserves no quarter. I should have imagined that I had been sufficiently explicit, but have made a few additions to the chapter on Malcontents, which will, I think, serve to render further mistake impossible.

An anonymous correspondent (by the handwriting presumably a clergyman) tells me that in quoting from the Latin grammar I should at any rate have done so correctly, and that I should have written "agricolas" instead of "agricolae." He added something about any boy in the fourth form, &c., &c., which I shall not quote, but which made me very uncomfortable. It may be said that I must have mis-quoted from design, from ignorance, or by a slip of the pen; but surely in these days it will be recognised as harsh to assign limits to the all-embracing boundlessness of truth, and it will be more reason-ably assumed that *each* of the three possible causes of misquotation must have had its share in the apparent blunder. The art of writing things that shall sound right and yet be wrong has made so many reputations, and affords comfort to such a large number of readers, that I could not venture to neglect it; the Latin grammar, however, is a subject on which some of the younger members of the com-munity feel strongly, so I have now written "agricolas." I have also parted with the word "infortuniam" (though not without regret), but have not dared to meddle with other similar inaccuracies.

For the inconsistencies in the book, and I am aware that there are not a few, I must ask the indulgence of the reader. The blame, how-ever, lies chiefly with the Erewhonians themselves, for they were really a very difficult people to understand. The most glaring anom-alies seemed to afford them no intellectual inconvenience; neither, provided they did not actually see the money dropping out of their pockets, nor suffer immediate physical pain, would they listen to any arguments as to the waste of money and happiness which their folly caused them. But this had an effect of which I have little reason to complain, for I was allowed almost to call them lifelong self-deceivers to their faces, and they said it was quite true, but that it did not matter.

I must not conclude without expressing my most sincere thanks to my critics and to the public for the leniency and consideration with which they have treated my adventures.

June 9, 1872

PREFACE

MR. GRANT RICHARDS wishes me to say a few words about the genesis of the work, a revised and enlarged edition of which he is herewith laying before the public. I therefore place on record as much as I can remember on this head after a lapse of more than thirty years.

The first part of *Erewhon* written was an article headed "Darwin among the Machines," and signed Cellarius. It was written in the Upper Rangitata district of the Canterbury Province (as it then was) of New Zealand, and appeared at Christchurch in the *Press* newspaper, June 13, 1863. A copy of this article is indexed under my books in the British Museum catalogue. In passing, I may say that the opening chapters of *Erewhon* were also drawn from the Upper Rangitata district, with such modifications as I found convenient.

A second article on the same subject as the one just referred to appeared in the *Press* shortly after the first, but I have no copy. It treated Machines from a different point of view, and was the basis of pp. 270-274 of the present edition* of "Erewhon." This view ultimately led me to the theory I put forward in *Life and Habit*, published in November 1877. I have put a bare outline of this theory (which I believe to be quite sound) into the mouth of an Erewhonian philosopher in Chapter XXVII of this book.

In 1865 I rewrote and enlarged "Darwin among the Machines" for the *Reasoner*, a paper published in London by Mr. G. J. Holyoake. It appeared July 1, 1865, under the heading, "The Mechanical Creation," and can be seen in the British Museum. I again rewrote

---

* Editor's note: The reference is to the 1901 revised and expanded edition. The pages are 158–160 in this Dover edition.

and enlarged it, till it assumed the form in which it appeared in the first edition of *Erewhon*.

The next part of *Erewhon* that I wrote was the "World of the Unborn," a preliminary form of which was sent to Mr. Holyoake's paper, but as I cannot find it among those copies of the *Reasoner* that are in the British Museum, I conclude that it was not accepted. I have, however, rather a strong fancy that it appeared in some London paper of the same character as the *Reasoner*, not very long after July 1, 1865, but I have no copy.

I also wrote about this time the substance of what ultimately became the Musical Banks, and the trial of a man for being in a consumption. These four detached papers were, I believe, all that was written of *Erewhon* before 1870. Between 1865 and 1870 I wrote hardly anything, being hopeful of attaining that success as a painter which it has not been vouchsafed me to attain, but in the autumn of 1870, just as I was beginning to get occasionally hung at Royal Academy exhibitions, my friend, the late Sir F. N. (then Mr.) Broome, suggested to me that I should add somewhat to the articles I had already written, and string them together into a book. I was rather fired by the idea, but as I only worked at the MS. on Sundays it was some months before I had completed it.

I see from my second Preface that I took the book to Messrs. Chapman & Hall May 1, 1871, and on their rejection of it, under the advice of one who has attained the highest rank among living writers, I let it sleep, till I took it to Mr. Trübner early in 1872. As regards its rejection by Messrs. Chapman & Hall, I believe their reader advised them quite wisely. They told me he reported that it was a philosophical work, little likely to be popular with a large circle of readers. I hope that if I had been their reader, and the book had been submitted to myself, I should have advised them to the same effect.

Erewhon appeared with the last day or two of March 1872. I attribute its unlooked-for success mainly to two early favourable reviews—the first in the *Pall Mall Gazette* of April 12, and the second in the *Spectator* of April 20. There was also another cause. I was complaining once to a friend that though *Erewhon* had met with such a warm reception, my subsequent books had been all of them practically still-born. He said, "You forget one charm that *Erewhon* had, but which none of your other books can have." I asked what? and was answered, "The sound of a new voice, and of an unknown voice."

The first edition of *Erewhon* sold in about three weeks; I had not taken moulds, and as the demand was strong, it was set up again immediately. I made a few unimportant alterations and additions, and added a Preface, of which I cannot say that I am particularly proud, but an inexperienced writer with a head somewhat turned by unexpected success is not to be trusted with a preface. I made a few further very trifling alterations before moulds were taken, but since the summer of 1872, as new editions were from time to time wanted, they have been printed from stereos then made.

Having now, I fear, at too great length done what Mr. Richards wished, I should like to add a few words on my own account. I am still fairly well satisfied with those parts of *Erewhon* that were repeatedly rewritten, but from those that had only a single writing I would gladly cut out some forty or fifty pages if I could.

This, however, may not be, for the copyright will probably expire in a little over twelve years. It was necessary, therefore, to revise the book throughout for literary inelegancies—of which I found many more than I had expected—and also to make such substantial additions as should secure a new lease of life—at any rate for the copyright. If, then, instead of cutting out, say fifty pages, I have been compelled to add about sixty *invitâ Minervâ*—the blame rests neither with Mr. Richards nor with me, but with the copyright laws. Nevertheless I can assure the reader that, though I have found it an irksome task to take up work which I thought I had got rid of thirty years ago, and much of which I am ashamed of, I have done my best to make the new matter savour so much of the better portions of the old, that none but the best critics shall perceive at what places the gaps of between thirty and forty years occur.

Lastly, if my readers note a considerable difference between the literary *technique* of *Erewhon* and that of *Erewhon Revisited*, I would remind them that, as I have just shown, *Erewhon* took something like ten years in writing, and even so was written with great difficulty, while *Erewhon Revisited* was written easily between November 1900 and the end of April 1901. There is no central idea underlying *Erewhon*, whereas the attempt to realise the effect of a single supposed great miracle dominates the whole of its successor. In *Erewhon* there was hardly any story, and little attempt to give life and individuality to the characters; I hope that in *Erewhon Revisited* both these defects have been in great measure avoided. *Erewhon* was not an organic whole, *Erewhon Revisited* may fairly claim to be one. Nevertheless, though in literary workmanship I do not doubt that this last-named book is an improvement on the first, I shall be agreeably surprised if I am not told that *Erewhon*, with all its faults, is the better reading of the two.

Samuel Butler.

August 7, 1901

CHAPTER I

WASTE LANDS

IF THE READER will excuse me, I will say nothing of my antecedents, nor of the circumstances which led me to leave my native country; the narrative would be tedious to him and painful to myself. Suffice it, that when I left home it was with the intention of going to some new colony, and either finding, or even perhaps purchasing, waste crown-land suitable for cattle or sheep farming, by which means I thought that I could better my fortunes more rapidly than in England.

It will be seen that I did not succeed in my design, and that however much I may have met with what was new and strange, I have been unable to reap any pecuniary advantage.

It is true, I imagine myself to have made a discovery which, if I can be the first to profit by it, will bring me a recompense beyond all money computation, and secure me a position such as has not been attained by more than some fifteen or sixteen persons, since the creation of the universe. But to this end I must possess myself of a considerable sum of money: neither do I know how to get it, except by interesting the public in my story, and inducing the charitable to come forward and assist me. With this hope I now publish my adventures; but I do so with great reluctance, for I fear that my story will be doubted unless I tell the whole of it; and yet I dare not do so, lest others with more means than mine should get the start of me. I prefer the risk of being doubted to that of being anticipated, and have therefore concealed my destination on leaving England, as also the point from which I began my more serious and difficult journey.

My chief consolation lies in the fact that truth bears its own impress, and that my story will carry conviction by reason of the internal evidences for its accuracy. No one who is himself honest will doubt my being so.

I reached my destination in one of the last months of 1868, but I dare not mention the season, lest the reader should gather in which hemisphere I was. The colony was one which had not been opened up even to the most adventurous settlers for more than eight or nine years, having been previously uninhabited, save by a few tribes of savages who frequented the seaboard. The part known to Europeans consisted of a coast-line about eight hundred miles in length (affording three or four good harbours), and a tract of country extending inland for a space varying from two to three hundred miles, until it reached the offshoots of an exceedingly lofty range of mountains, which could be seen from far out upon the plains, and were covered with perpetual snow. The coast was perfectly well known both north and south of the tract to which I have alluded, but in neither direction was there a single harbour for five hundred miles, and the mountains, which descended almost into the sea, were covered with thick timber, so that none would think of settling.

With this bay of land, however, the case was different. The harbours were sufficient; the country was timbered, but not too heavily; it was admirably suited for agriculture; it also contained millions on millions of acres of the most beautifully grassed country in the world, and of the best suited for all manner of sheep and cattle. The climate was temperate, and very healthy; there were no wild animals, nor were the natives dangerous, being few in number and of an intelligent tractable disposition.

It may be readily understood that when once Europeans set foot upon this territory they were not slow to take advantage of its capabilities. Sheep and cattle were introduced, and bred with extreme rapidity; men took up their 50,000 or 100,000 acres of country, going inland one behind the other, till in a few years there was not an acre between the sea and the front ranges which was not taken up, and stations either for sheep or cattle were spotted about at intervals of some twenty or thirty miles over the whole country. The front ranges stopped the tide of squatters for some little time; it was thought that there was too much snow upon them for too many months in the year,—that the sheep would get lost, the ground being too difficult for shepherding,—that the expense of getting wool down to the ship's side would eat up the farmer's profits,—and that the grass was too rough and sour for sheep to thrive upon; but one after another determined to try the experiment, and it was wonderful how successfully it turned out. Men pushed farther and farther into the mountains, and found a very considerable tract inside the front range, between it and another which was loftier still, though even this was not the highest, the great snowy one which could be seen from out upon the plains. This second range, however, seemed to mark the extreme limits of pastoral country; and it was here, at a small and newly founded station, that I was received as a cadet, and soon regularly employed. I was then just twenty-two years old.

I was delighted with the country and the manner of life. It was my daily business to go up to the top of a certain high mountain, and down one of its spurs on to the flat, in order to make sure that no sheep had crossed their boundaries. I was to see the sheep, not necessarily close at hand, nor to get them in a single mob, but to see enough of them here and there to feel easy that nothing had gone wrong; this was no difficult matter, for there were not above eight hundred of them; and, being all breeding ewes, they were pretty quiet.

There were a good many sheep which I knew, as two or three black ewes, and a black lamb or two, and several others which had some distinguishing mark whereby I could tell them. I would try and see all these, and if they were all there, and the mob looked large enough, I might rest assured that all was well. It is surprising how soon the eye becomes accustomed to missing twenty sheep out of two or three hundred. I had a telescope and a dog, and would take bread and meat and tobacco with me. Starting with early dawn, it would be night before I could complete my round; for the mountain over which I had to go was very high. In winter it was covered with snow, and the sheep needed no watching from above. If I were to see sheep dung or tracks going down on to the other side of the mountain (where there was a valley with a stream—a mere *cul de sac*), I was to follow them, and look out for sheep; but I never saw any, the sheep always descending on to their own side, partly from habit, and partly because there was abundance of good sweet feed, which had been burnt in the early spring, just before I came, and was now deliciously green and rich, while that on the other side had never been burnt, and was rank and coarse.

It was a monotonous life, but it was very healthy; and one does not much mind anything when one is well. The country was the grandest that can be imagined. How often have I sat on the mountain side and watched the waving downs, with the two white specks of huts in the distance, and the little square of garden behind them; the paddock with a patch of bright green oats above the huts, and the yards and wool-sheds down on the flat below; all seen as through the wrong end of a telescope, so clear and brilliant was the air, or as upon a colossal model or map spread out beneath me. Beyond the downs was a plain, going down to a river of great size, on the farther side of which there were other high mountains, with the winter's snow still not quite melted; up the river, which ran winding in many streams over a bed some two miles broad, I looked upon the second great chain, and could see a narrow gorge where the river retired and was lost. I knew that there was a range still farther back; but except from one place near the very top of my own mountain, no part of it was visible: from this point, however, I saw, whenever there were no clouds, a single snow-clad peak, many miles away, and I should think about as high as any mountain in the world. Never shall I forget the utter loneliness of the prospect—only the little far-away homestead giving sign of human handiwork;—the vastness of mountain and plain, of river and sky; the marvellous atmospheric effects— sometimes black mountains against a white sky, and then again, after cold weather, white mountains against a black sky—sometimes seen through breaks and swirls of cloud—and sometimes, which was best of all, I went up my mountain in a fog, and then got above the mist; going higher and higher, I would look down upon a sea of whiteness, through which would be thrust innumerable mountain tops that looked like islands.

I am there now, as I write; I fancy that I can see the downs, the huts, the plain, and the river-bed—that torrent pathway of desolation, with its distant roar of waters. Oh, wonderful! wonderful! so lonely and so solemn, with the sad grey clouds above, and no sound save a lost lamb bleating upon the mountain side, as though its little heart were breaking. Then there comes some lean and withered old ewe, with deep gruff voice and unlovely aspect, trotting back from the seductive pasture; now she examines this gully, and now that, and now she stands listening with uplifted head, that she may hear the distant wailing and obey it. Aha! they see, and rush towards each other. Alas! they are both mistaken; the ewe is not the lamb's ewe, they are neither kin nor kind to one another, and part in coldness. Each must cry louder, and wander farther yet; may luck be with them both that they may find their own at nightfall. But this is mere dreaming, and I must proceed.

I could not help speculating upon what might lie farther up the river and behind the second range. I had no money, but if I could only find workable country, I might stock it with borrowed capital, and consider myself a made man. True, the range looked so vast, that there seemed little chance of getting a sufficient road through it or over it; but no one had yet explored it, and it is wonderful how one finds that one can make a path into all sorts of places (and even get a road for packhorses), which from a distance appear inaccessible; the river was so great that it must drain an inner tract—at least I thought so; and though every one said it would be madness to attempt taking sheep farther inland, I knew that only three years ago the same cry had been raised against the country which my master's flock was now overrunning. I could not keep these thoughts out of my head as I would rest myself upon the mountain side; they haunted me as I went my daily rounds, and grew upon me from hour to hour, till I resolved that after shearing I would remain in doubt no longer, but saddle my horse, take as much provision with me as I could, and go and see for myself.

But over and above these thoughts came that of the great range itself. What was beyond it? Ah! who could say? There was no one in the whole world who had the smallest idea, save those who were themselves on the other side of it—if, indeed, there was any one at all. Could I hope to cross it? This would be the highest triumph that I could wish for; but it was too much to think of yet. I would try the nearer range, and see how far I could go. Even if I did not find country, might I not find gold, or diamonds, or copper, or silver? I would sometimes lie flat down to drink out of a stream, and could see little yellow specks among the sand; were these gold? People said no; but then people always said there was no gold until it was found to be abundant: there was plenty of slate and granite, which I had always understood to accompany gold; and even though it was not found in paying quantities here, it might be abundant in the main ranges. These thoughts filled my head, and I could not banish them.

CHAPTER II

IN THE WOOL-SHED

AT LAST SHEARING came; and with the shearers there was an old native, whom they had nicknamed Chowbok—though, I believe, his real name was Kahabuka. He was a sort of chief of the natives, could speak a little English, and was a great favourite with the missionaries. He did not do any regular work with the shearers, but pretended to help in the yards, his real aim being to get the grog, which is always more freely circulated at shearing-time: he did not get much, for he was apt to be dangerous when drunk; and very little would make him so: still he did get it occasionally, and if one wanted to get anything out of him, it was the best bribe to offer him. I resolved to question him, and get as much information from him as I could. I did so. As long as I kept to questions about the nearer ranges, he was easy to get on with—he had never been there, but there were traditions among his tribe to the effect that there was no sheep-country, nothing, in fact, but stunted timber and a few river-bed flats. It was very difficult to reach; still there were passes: one of them up our own river, though not directly along the river-bed, the gorge of which was not practicable; he had never seen any one who had been there: was there not enough on this side? But when I came to the main range, his manner changed at once. He became uneasy, and began to prevaricate and shuffle. In a very few minutes I could see that of this too there existed traditions in his tribe; but no efforts or coaxing could get a word from him about them. At last I hinted about grog, and presently he feigned consent: I gave it him; but as soon as he had drunk it he began shamming intoxication, and then went to sleep, or pretended to do so, letting me kick him pretty hard and never budging.

I was angry, for I had to go without my own grog and had got nothing out of him; so the next day I determined that he should tell me before I gave him any, or get none at all.

Accordingly, when night came and the shearers had knocked off work and had their supper, I got my share of rum in a tin pannikin and made a sign to Chowbok to follow me to the wool-shed, which he willingly did, slipping out after me, and no one taking any notice of either of us. When we got down to the wool-shed we lit a tallow candle, and having stuck it in an old bottle we sat down upon the wool bales and began to smoke. A wool-shed is a roomy place, built somewhat on the same plan as a cathedral, with aisles on either side full of pens for the sheep, a great nave, at the upper end of which the shearers work, and a further space for wool sorters and packers. It always refreshed me with a semblance of antiquity (precious in a new country), though I very well knew that the oldest wool-shed in the settlement was not more than seven years old, while this was only two. Chowbok pretended to expect his grog at once, though we both of us knew very well what the other was after, and that we were each playing against the other, the one for grog, the other for information.

We had a hard fight: for more than two hours he had tried to put me off with lies but had carried no conviction; during the whole time we had been morally wrestling with one another and had neither of us apparently gained the least advantage; at length, however, I had become sure that he would give in ultimately, and that with a little further patience I should get his story out of him. As upon a cold day in winter, when one has churned (as I had often had to do), and churned in vain, and the butter makes no sign of coming, at last one tells by the sound that the cream has gone to sleep, and then upon a sudden the butter comes, so I had churned at Chowbok until I perceived that he had arrived, as it were, at the sleepy stage, and that with a continuance of steady quiet pressure the day was mine. On a sudden, without a word of warning, he rolled two bales of wool (his strength was very great) into the middle of the floor, and on the top of these he placed another crosswise; he snatched up an empty wool-pack, threw it like a mantle over his shoulders, jumped upon the uppermost bale, and sat upon it. In a moment his whole form was changed. His high shoulders dropped; he set his feet close together, heel to heel and toe to toe; he laid his arms and hands close alongside of his body, the palms following his thighs; he held his head high but quite straight, and his eyes stared right in front of him; but he frowned horribly, and assumed an expression of face that was positively fiendish. At the best of times Chowbok was very ugly, but he now exceeded all conceivable limits of the hideous. His mouth extended almost from ear to ear, grinning horribly and showing all his teeth; his eyes glared, though they remained quite fixed, and his forehead was contracted with a most malevolent scowl.

I am afraid my description will have conveyed only the ridiculous side of his appearance; but the ridiculous and the sublime are near, and the grotesque fiendishness of Chowbok's face approached this last, if it did not reach it. I tried to be amused, but I felt a sort of creeping at the roots of my hair and over my whole body, as I looked and wondered what he could possibly be intending to signify. He continued thus for about a minute, sitting bolt upright, as stiff as a stone, and making this fearful face. Then there came from his lips a low moaning like the wind, rising and falling by infinitely small gradations till it became almost a shriek, from which it descended and died away; after that, he jumped down from the bale and held up the extended fingers of both his hands, as one who should say "Ten," though I did not then understand him.

For myself I was open-mouthed with astonishment. Chowbok rolled the bales rapidly into their place, and stood before me shuddering as in great fear; horror was written upon his face—this time quite involuntarily—as though the natural panic of one who had committed an awful crime against unknown and superhuman agencies. He nodded his head and gibbered, and pointed repeatedly to the mountains. He would not touch the grog, but, after a few seconds he made a run through the wool-shed door into the moonlight; nor did he reappear till next day at dinner-time, when he turned up, looking very sheepish and abject in his civility towards myself.

Of his meaning I had no conception. How could I? All I could feel sure of was, that he had a meaning which was true and awful to himself. It was enough for me that I believed him to have given me the best he had and all he had. This kindled my imagination more than if he had told me intelligible stories by the hour together. I knew not what the great snowy ranges might conceal, but I could no longer doubt that it would be something well worth discovering.

I kept aloof from Chowbok for the next few days, and showed no desire to question him further; when I spoke to him I called him Kahabuka, which gratified him greatly: he seemed to have become afraid of me, and acted as one who was in my power. Having therefore made up my mind that I would begin exploring as soon as shearing was over, I thought it would be a good thing to take Chowbok with me; so I told him that I meant going to the nearer ranges for a few days' prospecting, and that he was to come too. I made him promises of nightly grog, and held out the chances of finding gold. I said nothing about the main range, for I knew it would frighten him. I would get him as far up our own river as I could, and trace it if possible to its source. I would then either go on by myself, if I felt my courage equal to the attempt, or return with Chowbok. So, as soon as ever shearing was over and the wool sent off, I asked leave of absence, and obtained it. Also, I bought an old pack-horse and pack-saddle, so that I might take plenty of provisions, and blankets, and a small tent. I was to ride and find fords over the river; Chowbok was to follow and lead the pack-horse, which would also carry him over the fords. My master let me have tea and sugar, ship's biscuits, tobacco, and salt mutton, with two or three bottles of good brandy; for, as the wool was now sent down, abundance of provisions would come up with the empty drays.

Everything being now ready, all the hands on the station turned out to see us off, and we started on our journey, not very long after the summer solstice of 1870.

CHAPTER III
UP THE RIVER

THE FIRST DAY we had an easy time, following up the great flats by the river side, which had already been twice burned, so that there was no dense undergrowth to check us, though the ground was often rough, and we had to go a good deal upon the river-bed. Towards nightfall we had made a matter of some five-and-twenty miles, and camped at the point where the river entered upon the gorge.

The weather was delightfully warm, considering that the valley in which we were encamped must have been at least two thousand feet above the level of the sea. The river-bed was here about a mile and a half broad and entirely covered with shingle over which the river ran in many winding channels, looking, when seen from above, like a tangled skein of ribbon, and glistening in the sun. We knew that it was liable to very sudden and heavy freshets; but even had we not known it, we could have seen it by the snags of trees, which must have been carried long distances, and by the mass of vegetable and mineral *débris* which was banked against their lower side, showing that at times the whole river-bed must be covered with a roaring torrent many feet in depth and of ungovernable fury. At present the river was low, there being but five or six streams, too deep and rapid for even a strong man to ford on foot, but to be crossed safely on horseback. On either side of it there were still a few acres of flat, which grew wider and wider down the river, till they became the large plains on which we looked from my master's hut. Behind us rose the lowest spurs of the second range, leading abruptly to the range itself; and at a distance of half a mile began the gorge, where the river narrowed and became boisterous and terrible. The beauty of the scene cannot be conveyed in language. The one side of the valley was blue with evening shadow, through which loomed forest and precipice, hillside and mountain top; and the other was still brilliant with the sunset gold. The wide and wasteful river with its ceaseless rushing—the beautiful water-birds too, which abounded upon the islets and were so tame that we could come close up to them—the ineffable purity of the air—the solemn peacefulness of the untrodden region—could there be a more delightful and exhilarating combination?

We set about making our camp, close to some large bush which came down from the mountains on to the flat, and tethered out our horses upon ground as free as we could find it from anything round which they might wind the rope and get themselves tied up. We dared not let them run loose, lest they might stray down the river home again. We then gathered wood and lit the fire. We filled a tin pannikin with water and set it against the hot ashes to boil. When the water boiled we threw in two or three large pinches of tea and let them brew.

We had caught half a dozen young ducks in the course of the day—an easy matter, for the old birds made such a fuss in attempting to decoy us away from them—pretending to be badly hurt as they say the plover does—that we could always find them by going about in the opposite direction to the old bird till we heard the young ones crying: then we ran them down, for they could not fly though they were nearly full grown. Chowbok plucked them a little and singed them a good deal. Then we cut them up and boiled them in another pannikin, and this completed our preparations.

When we had done supper it was quite dark. The silence and freshness of the night, the occasional sharp cry of the wood-hen, the ruddy glow of the fire, the subdued rushing of the river, the sombre forest, and the immediate foreground of our saddles, packs and blankets, made a picture worthy of a Salvator Rosa or a Nicolas Poussin. I call it to mind and delight in it now, but I did not notice it at the time. We next to never know when we are well off: but this cuts two ways,—for if we did, we should perhaps know better when we are ill off also; and I have sometimes thought that there are as many ignorant of the one as of the other. He who wrote, "*O fortunatos nimium sua si bona nôrint agricolas*" might have written quite as truly, "*O infortunatos nimium sua si mala nôrint*"; and there are few of us who are not protected from the keenest pain by our inability to see what it is that we have done, what we are suffering, and what we truly are. Let us be grateful to the mirror for revealing to us our appearance only.

We found as soft a piece of ground as we could—though it was all stony—and having collected grass and so disposed of ourselves that we had a little hollow for our hip-bones, we strapped our blankets around us and went to sleep. Waking in the night I saw the stars overhead and the moonlight bright upon the mountains. The river was ever rushing; I heard one of our horses neigh to its companion, and was assured that they were still at hand; I had no care of mind or body, save that I had doubtless many difficulties to overcome; there came upon me a delicious sense of peace, a fulness of contentment which I do not believe can be felt by any but those who have spent days consecutively on horseback, or at any rate in the open air.

Next morning we found our last night's tea-leaves frozen at the bottom of the pannikins, though it was not nearly the beginning of autumn; we breakfasted as we had supped, and were on our way by six o'clock. In half an hour we had entered the gorge, and turning round a corner we bade farewell to the last sight of my master's country.

The gorge was narrow and precipitous; the river was now only a few yards wide, and roared and thundered against rocks of many tons in weight; the sound was deafening, for there was a great volume of water. We were two hours in making less than a mile, and that with danger, sometimes in the river and sometimes on the rock. There was that damp black smell of rocks covered with slimy vegetation, as near some huge waterfall where spray is ever rising. The air was clammy and cold. I cannot conceive how our horses managed to keep their footing, especially the one with the pack, and I dreaded the having to return almost as much as going forward. I suppose this lasted three miles, but it was well midday when the gorge got a little wider, and a small stream came into it from a tributary valley. Farther progress up the main river was impossible, for the cliffs descended like walls; so we went up the side stream, Chowbok seeming to think that here must be the pass of which reports existed among his people. We now incurred less of actual danger but more fatigue, and it was only after infinite trouble, owing to the rocks and tangled vegetation, that we got ourselves and our horses upon the saddle from which this small stream descended; by that time clouds had descended upon us, and it was raining heavily. Moreover, it was six o'clock and we were tired out, having made perhaps six miles in twelve hours.

On the saddle there was some coarse grass which was in full seed, and therefore very nourishing for the horses; also abundance of anise and sow-thistle, of which they are extravagantly fond, so we turned them loose and prepared to camp. Everything was soaking wet and we were half-perished with cold; indeed we were very uncomfortable. There was brushwood about, but we could get no fire till we had shaved off the wet outside of some dead branches and filled our pockets with the dry inside chips. Having done this we managed to start a fire, nor did we allow it to go out when we had once started it; we pitched the tent and by nine o'clock were comparatively warm and dry. Next morning it was fine; we broke camp, and after advancing a short distance we found that, by descending over ground less difficult than yesterday's, we should come again upon the river-bed, which had opened out above the gorge; but it was plain at a glance that there was no available sheep country, nothing but a few flats covered with scrub on either side of the river, and mountains which were perfectly worthless. But we could see the main range. There was no mistake about this. The glaciers were tumbling down the mountain sides like cataracts, and seemed actually to descend upon the river-bed; there could be no serious difficulty in reaching them by following up the river, which was wide and open; but it seemed rather an objectless thing·to do, for the main range looked hopeless, and my curiosity about the nature of the country above the gorge was now quite satisfied; there was no money in it whatever, unless there should be minerals, of which I saw no more signs than lower down.

However, I resolved that I would follow the river up, and not return until I was compelled to do so. I would go up every branch as far as I could, and wash well for gold. Chowbok liked seeing me do this, but it never came to anything, for we did not even find the colour. His dislike of the main range appeared to have worn off, and he made no objections to approaching it. I think he thought there was no danger of my trying to cross it, and he was not afraid of anything on this side; besides, we might find gold. But the fact was that he had made up his mind what to do if he saw me getting too near it.

We passed three weeks in exploring, and never did I find time go more quickly. The weather was fine, though the nights got very cold. We followed every stream but one, and always found it lead us to a glacier which was plainly impassable, at any rate without a larger party and ropes. One stream remained, which I should have followed up already, had not Chowbok said that he had risen early one morning while I was yet asleep, and after going up it for three or four miles, had seen that it was impossible to go farther. I had long ago discovered that he was a great liar, so I was bent on going up myself: in brief, I did so: so far from being impossible, it was quite easy travelling; and after five or six miles I saw a saddle at the end of it, which, though covered deep in snow, was not glaciered, and which did verily appear to be part of the main range itself. No words can express the intensity of my delight. My blood was all on fire with hope and elation; but on looking round for Chowbok, who was behind me, I saw to my surprise and anger that he had turned back, and was going down the valley as hard as he could. He had left me.

CHAPTER IV
THE SADDLE

I COOEYED TO him, but he would not hear. I ran after him, but he had got too good a start. Then I sat down on a stone and thought the matter carefully over. It was plain that Chowbok had designedly attempted to keep me from going up this valley, yet he had shown no unwillingness to follow me anywhere else. What could this mean, unless that I was now upon the route by which alone the mysteries of the great ranges could be revealed? What then should I do? Go back at the very moment when it had become plain that I was on the right scent? Hardly; yet to proceed alone would be both difficult and dangerous. It would be bad enough to return to my master's run, and pass through the rocky gorges, with no chance of help from another, should I get into a difficulty; but to advance for any considerable distance without a companion would be next door to madness. Accidents which are slight when there is another at hand (as the spraining of an ankle, or the falling into some place whence escape would be easy by means of an outstretched hand and a bit of rope) may be fatal to one who is alone. The more I pondered the less I liked it; and yet, the less could I make up my mind to return when I looked at the saddle at the head of the valley, and noted the comparative ease with which its smooth sweep of snow might be surmounted: I seemed to see my way almost from my present position to the very top. After much thought, I resolved to go forward until I should come to some place which was really dangerous, but then to return. I should thus, I hoped, at any rate reach the top of the saddle, and satisfy myself as to what might be on the other side.

I had no time to lose, for it was now between ten and eleven in the morning. Fortunately I was well equipped, for on leaving the camp and the horses at the lower end of the valley I had provided myself (according to my custom) with everything that I was likely to want for four or five days. Chowbok had carried half, but had dropped his whole swag—I suppose, at the moment of his taking flight—for I came upon it when I ran after him. I had, therefore, his provisions as well as my own. Accordingly, I took as many biscuits as I thought I could carry, and also some tobacco, tea, and a few matches. I rolled all these things (together with a flask nearly full of brandy, which I had kept in my pocket for fear lest Chowbok should get hold of it) inside my blankets, and strapped them very tightly, making the whole into a long roll of some seven feet in length and six inches in diameter. Then I tied the two ends together, and put the whole round my neck and over one shoulder. This is the easiest way of carrying a heavy swag, for one can rest one's self by shifting the burden from one shoulder to the other. I strapped my pannikin and a small axe about my waist, and thus equipped began to ascend the valley, angry at having been misled by Chowbok, but determined not to return till I was compelled to do so.

I crossed and recrossed the stream several times without difficulty, for there were many good fords. At one o'clock I was at the foot of the saddle; for four hours I mounted, the last two on the snow, where the going was easier; by five, I was within ten minutes of the top, in a state of excitement greater, I think, than I had ever known before. Ten minutes more, and the cold air from the other side came rushing upon me.

A glance. I was *not* on the main range.

Another glance. There was an awful river, muddy and horribly angry, roaring over an immense river-bed, thousands of feet below me.

It went round to the westward, and I could see no farther up the valley, save that there were enormous glaciers which must extend round the source of the river, and from which it must spring.

Another glance, and then I remained motionless.

There was an easy pass in the mountains directly opposite to me, through which I caught a glimpse of an immeasurable extent of blue and distant plains.

Easy? Yes, perfectly easy; grassed nearly to the summit, which was, as it were, an open path between two glaciers, from which an inconsiderable stream came tumbling down over rough but very possible hillsides, till it got down to the level of the great river, and formed a flat where there was grass and a small bush of stunted timber.

Almost before I could believe my eyes, a cloud had come up from the valley on the other side, and the plains were hidden. What wonderful luck was mine! Had I arrived five minutes later, the cloud would have been over the pass, and I should not have known of its existence. Now that the cloud was there, I began to doubt my memory, and to be uncertain whether it had been more than a blue line of distant vapour that had filled up the opening. I could only be certain of this much, namely, that the river in the valley below must be the one next to the northward of that which flowed past my master's station; of this there could be no doubt. Could I, however, imagine that my luck should have led me up a wrong river in search of a pass, and yet brought me to the spot where I could detect the one weak place in the fortifications of a more northern basin? This was too improbable. But even as I doubted there came a rent in the cloud opposite, and a second time I saw blue lines of heaving downs, growing gradually fainter, and retiring into a far space of plain. It was substantial; there had been no mistake whatsoever. I had hardly made myself perfectly sure of this, ere the rent in the clouds joined up again and I could see nothing more.

What, then, should I do? The night would be upon me shortly, and I was already chilled with standing still after the exertion of climbing. To stay where I was would be impossible; I must either go backwards or forwards. I found a rock which gave me shelter from the evening wind, and took a good pull at the brandy flask, which immediately warmed and encouraged me.

I asked myself, Could I descend upon the river-bed beneath me? It was impossible to say what precipices might prevent my doing so. If I were on the river-bed, dare I cross the river? I am an excellent swimmer, yet, once in that frightful rush of waters, I should be hurled whithersoever it willed, absolutely powerless. Moreover, there was my swag; I should perish of cold and hunger if I left it, but I should certainly be drowned if I attempted to carry it across the river. These were serious considerations, but the hope of finding an immense tract of available sheep country (which I was determined that I would monopolise as far as I possibly could) sufficed to outweigh them; and, in a few minutes, I felt resolved that, having made so important a discovery as a pass into a country which was probably as valuable as that on our own side of the ranges, I would follow it up and ascertain its value, even though I should pay the penalty of failure with life itself. The more I thought, the more determined I became either to win fame and perhaps fortune, by entering upon this unknown world, or give up life in the attempt. In fact, I felt that life would be no longer valuable if I were to have seen so great a prize and refused to grasp at the possible profits therefrom.

I had still an hour of good daylight during which I might begin my descent on to some suitable camping-ground, but there was not a moment to be lost. At first I got along rapidly, for I was on the snow, and sank into it enough to save me from falling, though I went forward straight down the mountain side as fast as I could; but there was less snow on this side than on the other, and I had soon done with it, getting on to a coomb of dangerous and very stony ground, where a slip might have given me a disastrous fall. But I was careful with all my speed, and got safely to the bottom, where there were patches of coarse grass, and an attempt here and there at brushwood: what was below this I could not see. I advanced a few hundred yards farther, and found that I was on the brink of a frightful precipice, which no one in his senses would attempt descending. I bethought me, however, to try the creek which drained the coomb, and see whether it might not have made itself a smoother way. In a few minutes I found myself at the upper end of a chasm in the rocks, something like Twll Dhu, only on a greatly larger scale; the creek had found its way into it, and had worn a deep channel through a material which appeared softer than that upon the other side of the mountain. I believe it must have been a different geological formation, though I regret to say that I cannot tell what it was.

I looked at this rift in great doubt; then I went a little way on either side of it, and found myself looking over the edge of horrible precipices on to the river, which roared some four or five thousand feet below me. I dared not think of getting down at all, unless I committed myself to the rift, of which I was hopeful when I reflected that the rock was soft, and that the water might have worn its channel tolerably evenly through the whole extent. The darkness was increasing with every minute, but I should have twilight for another half-hour, so I went into the chasm (though by no means without fear), and resolved to return and camp, and try some other path next day, should I come to any serious difficulty. In about five minutes I had completely lost my head; the side of the rift became hundreds of feet in height, and overhung so that I could not see the sky. It was full of rocks, and I had many falls and bruises. I was wet through from falling into the water, of which there was no great volume, but it had such force that I could do nothing against it; once I had to leap down a not inconsiderable waterfall into a deep pool below, and my swag was so heavy that I was very nearly drowned. I had indeed a hair's-breadth escape; but, as luck would have it, Providence was on my side. Shortly afterwards I began to fancy that the rift was getting wider, and that there was more brushwood. Presently I found myself on an open grassy slope, and feeling my way a little farther along the stream, I came upon a flat place with wood, where I could camp comfortably; which was well, for it was now quite dark.

My first care was for my matches; were they dry? The outside of my swag had got completely wet; but, on undoing the blankets, I found things warm and dry within. How thankful I was! I lit a fire, and was grateful for its warmth and company. I made myself some tea and ate two of my biscuits: my brandy I did not touch, for I had little left, and might want it when my courage failed me. All that I did, I did almost mechanically, for I could not realise my situation to myself, beyond knowing that I was alone, and that return through the chasm which I had just descended would be impossible. It is a dreadful feeling that of being cut off from all one's kind. I was still full of hope, and built golden castles for myself as soon as I was warmed with food and fire; but I do not believe that any man could long retain his reason in such solitude, unless he had the companionship of animals. One begins doubting one's own identity.

I remember deriving comfort even from the sight of my blankets, and the sound of my watch ticking—things which seemed to link me to other people; but the screaming of the wood-hens frightened me, as also a chattering bird which I had never heard before, and which seemed to laugh at me; though I soon got used to it, and before long could fancy that it was many years since I had first heard it.

I took off my clothes, and wrapped my inside blanket about me, till my things were dry. The night was very still, and I made a roaring fire; so I soon got warm, and at last could put my clothes on again. Then I strapped my blanket round me, and went to sleep as near the fire as I could.

I dreamed that there was an organ placed in my master's woolshed: the wool-shed faded away, and the organ seemed to grow and grow amid a blaze of brilliant light, till it became like a golden city upon the side of a mountain, with rows upon rows of pipes set in cliffs and precipices, one above the other, and in mysterious caverns, like that of Fingal, within whose depths I could see the burnished pillars gleaming. In the front there was a flight of lofty terraces, at the top of which I could see a man with his head buried forward towards a key-board, and his body swaying from side to side amid the storm of huge arpeggioed harmonies that came crashing overhead and round. Then there was one who touched me on the shoulder, and said, "Do you not see? it is Handel";—but I had hardly apprehended, and was trying to scale the terraces, and get near him, when I awoke, dazzled with the vividness and distinctness of the dream.

A piece of wood had burned through, and the ends had fallen into the ashes with a blaze: this, I supposed, had both given me my dream and robbed me of it. I was bitterly disappointed, and sitting up on my elbow, came back to reality and my strange surroundings as best I could.

I was thoroughly aroused—moreover, I felt a foreshadowing as though my attention were arrested by something more than the dream, although no sense in particular was as yet appealed to. I held my breath and waited, and then I heard—was it fancy? Nay; I listened again and again, and I *did* hear a faint and extremely distant sound of music, like that of an Æolian harp, borne upon the wind, which was blowing fresh and chill from the opposite mountains.

The roots of my hair thrilled. I listened, but the wind had died; and, fancying that it must have been the wind itself—no; on a sudden I remembered the noise which Chowbok had made in the wool-shed. Yes; it was that.

Thank Heaven, whatever it was, it was over now. I reasoned with myself, and recovered my firmness. I became convinced that I had only been dreaming more vividly than usual. Soon I began even to laugh, and think what a fool I was to be frightened at nothing, reminding myself that even if I were to come to a bad end it would be no such dreadful matter after all. I said my prayers, a duty which I had too often neglected, and in a little time fell into a really refreshing sleep, which lasted till broad daylight, and restored me. I rose, and searching among the embers of my fire, I found a few live coals and soon had a blaze again. I got breakfast, and was delighted to have the company of several small birds, which hopped about me and perched on my boots and hands. I felt comparatively happy, but I can assure the reader that I had had a far worse time of it than I have told him; and I strongly recommend him to remain in Europe if he can; or, at any rate, in some country which has been explored and settled, rather than go into places where others have not been before him. Exploring is delightful to look forward to and back upon, but it is not comfortable at the time, unless it be of such an easy nature as not to deserve the name.

CHAPTER V

THE RIVER AND THE RANGE

MY NEXT BUSINESS was to descend upon the river. I had lost sight of the pass which I had seen from the saddle, but had made such notes of it that I could not fail to find it. I was bruised and stiff, and my boots had begun to give, for I had been going on rough ground for more than three weeks; but, as the day wore on, and I found myself descending without serious difficulty, I became easier. In a couple of hours I got among pine forests where there was little undergrowth, and descended quickly till I reached the edge of another precipice, which gave me a great deal of trouble, though I eventually managed to avoid it. By about three or four o'clock I found myself on the river-bed.

From calculations which I made as to the height of the valley on the other side the saddle over which I had come, I concluded that the saddle itself could not be less than nine thousand feet high; and I should think that the river-bed, on to which I now descended, was three thousand feet above the sea-level. The water had a terrific current, with a fall of not less than forty to fifty feet per mile. It was certainly the river next to the northward of that which flowed past my master's run, and would have to go through an impassable gorge (as is commonly the case with the rivers of that country) before it came upon known parts. It was reckoned to be nearly two thousand feet above the sea-level where it came out of the gorge on to the plains.

As soon as I got to the river side I liked it even less than I thought I should. It was muddy, being near its parent glaciers. The stream was wide, rapid, and rough, and I could hear the smaller stones knocking against each other under the rage of the waters, as upon a seashore. Fording was out of the question. I could not swim and carry my swag, and I dared not leave my swag behind me. My only chance was to make a small raft; and that would be difficult to make, and not at all safe when it was made,—not for one man in such a current.

As it was too late to do much that afternoon, I spent the rest of it in going up and down the river side, and seeing where I should find the most favourable crossing. Then I camped early, and had a quiet comfortable night with no more music, for which I was thankful, as it had haunted me all day, although I perfectly well knew that it had been nothing but my own fancy, brought on by the reminiscence of what I had heard from Chowbok and by the over-excitement of the preceding evening.

Next day I began gathering the dry bloom stalks of a kind of flag or iris-looking plant, which was abundant, and whose leaves, when torn into strips, were as strong as the strongest string. I brought them to the waterside, and fell to making myself a kind of rough platform which should suffice for myself and my swag if I could only stick to it. The stalks were ten or twelve feet long, and very strong, but light and hollow. I made my raft entirely of them, binding bundles of them at right angles to each other, neatly and strongly, with strips from the leaves of the same plant, and tying other rods across. It took me all day till nearly four o'clock to finish the raft, but I had still enough daylight for crossing, and resolved on doing so at once.

I had selected a place where the river was broad and comparatively still, some seventy or eighty yards above a furious rapid. At this spot I had built my raft. I now launched it, made my swag fast to the middle, and got on to it myself, keeping in my hand one of the longest blossom stalks, so that I might punt myself across as long as the water was shallow enough to let me do so. I got on pretty well for twenty or thirty yards from the shore, but even in this short space I nearly upset my raft by shifting too rapidly from one side to the other. The water then became much deeper, and I leaned over so far in order to get the bloom rod to the bottom that I had to stay still, leaning on the rod for a few seconds. Then, when I lifted up the rod from the ground, the current was too much for me and I found myself being carried down the rapid. Everything in a second flew past me, and I had no more control over the raft; neither can I remember anything except hurry, and noise, and waters which in the end upset me. But it all came right, and I found myself near the shore, not more than up to my knees in water and pulling my raft to land, fortunately upon the left bank of the river, which was the one I wanted. When I had landed I found that I was about a mile, or perhaps a little less, below the point from which I started. My swag was wet upon the outside, and I was myself dripping; but I had gained my point, and knew that my difficulties were for a time over. I then lit my fire and dried myself; having done so I caught some of the young ducks and sea-gulls, which were abundant on and near the river-bed, so that I had not only a good meal, of which I was in great want, having had an insufficient diet from the time that Chowbok left me, but was also well provided for the morrow.

I thought of Chowbok, and felt how useful he had been to me, and in how many ways I was the loser by his absence, having now to do all sorts of things for myself which he had hitherto done for me, and could do infinitely better than I could. Moreover, I had set my heart upon making him a real convert to the Christian religion, which he had already embraced outwardly, though I cannot think that it had taken deep root in his impenetrably stupid nature. I used to catechise him by our camp fire, and explain to him the mysteries of the Trinity and of original sin, with which I was myself familiar, having been the grandson of an archdeacon by my mother's side, to say nothing of the fact that my father was a clergyman of the English Church. I was therefore sufficiently qualified for the task, and was the more inclined to it, over and above my real desire to save the unhappy creature from an eternity of torture, by recollecting the promise of St. James, that if any one converted a sinner (which Chowbok surely was) he should hide a multitude of sins. I reflected, therefore, that the conversion of Chowbok might in some degree compensate for irregularities and shortcomings in my own previous life, the remembrance of which had been more than once unpleasant to me during my recent experiences.

Indeed, on one occasion I had even gone so far as to baptize him, as well as I could, having ascertained that he had certainly not been both christened and baptized, and gathering (from his telling me that he had received the name William from the missionary) that it was probably the first-mentioned rite to which he had been subjected. I thought it great carelessness on the part of the missionary to have omitted the second, and certainly more important, ceremony which I have always understood precedes christening both in the case of infants and of adult converts; and when I thought of the risks we were both incurring I determined that there should be no further delay. Fortunately it was not yet twelve o'clock, so I baptized him at once from one of the pannikins (the only vessels I had) reverently, and, I trust, efficiently. I then set myself to work to instruct him in the deeper mysteries of our belief, and to make him, not only in name, but in heart a Christian.

It is true that I might not have succeeded, for Chowbok was very hard to teach. Indeed, on the evening of the same day that I baptized him he tried for the twentieth time to steal the brandy, which made me rather unhappy as to whether I could have baptized him rightly. He had a prayer-book—more than twenty years old—which had been given him by the missionaries, but the only thing in it which had taken any living hold upon him was the title of Adelaide the Queen Dowager, which he would repeat whenever strongly moved or touched, and which did really seem to have some deep spiritual significance to him, though he could never completely separate her individuality from that of Mary Magdalene, whose name had also fascinated him, though in a less degree.

He was indeed stony ground, but by digging about him I might have at any rate deprived him of all faith in the religion of his tribe, which would have been half way towards making him a sincere Christian; and now all this was cut off from me, and I could neither be of further spiritual assistance to him nor he of bodily profit to myself: besides, any company was better than being quite alone.

I got very melancholy as these reflections crossed me, but when I had boiled the ducks and eaten them I was much better. I had a little tea left and about a pound of tobacco, which should last me for another fortnight with moderate smoking. I had also eight ship biscuits, and, most precious of all, about six ounces of brandy, which I presently reduced to four, for the night was cold.

I rose with early dawn, and in an hour I was on my way, feeling strange, not to say weak, from the burden of solitude, but full of hope when I considered how many dangers I had overcome, and that this day should see me at the summit of the dividing range.

After a slow but steady climb of between three and four hours, during which I met with no serious hindrance, I found myself upon a tableland, and close to a glacier which I recognised as marking the summit of the pass. Above it towered a succession of rugged precipices and snowy mountain sides. The solitude was greater than I could bear; the mountain upon my master's sheep-run was a crowded thoroughfare in comparison with this sombre sullen place. The air, moreover, was dark and heavy, which made the loneliness even more oppressive. There was an inky gloom over all that was not covered with snow and ice. Grass there was none.

Each moment I felt increasing upon me that dreadful doubt as to my own identity—as to the continuity of my past and present existence—which is the first sign of that distraction which comes on those who have lost themselves in the bush. I had fought against this feeling hitherto, and had conquered it; but the intense silence and gloom of this rocky wilderness were too much for me, and I felt that my power of collecting myself was beginning to be impaired.

I rested for a little while, and then advanced over very rough ground, until I reached the lower end of the glacier. Then I saw another glacier, descending from the eastern side into a small lake. I passed along the western side of the lake, where the ground was easier, and when I had got about half way I expected that I should see the plains which I had already seen from the opposite mountains; but it was not to be so, for the clouds rolled up to the very summit of the pass, though they did not overlap it on to the side from which I had come. I therefore soon found myself enshrouded by a cold thin vapour, which prevented my seeing more than a very few yards in front of me. Then I came upon a large patch of old snow, in which I could distinctly trace the half-melted tracks of goats—and in one place, as it seemed to me, there had been a dog following them. Had I lighted upon a land of shepherds? The ground, where not covered with snow, was so poor and stony, and there was so little herbage, that I could see no sign of a path or regular sheep-track. But I could not help feeling rather uneasy as I wondered what sort of a reception I might meet with if I were to come suddenly upon inhabitants. I was thinking of this, and proceeding cautiously through the mist, when I began to fancy that I saw some objects darker than the cloud looming in front of me. A few steps brought me nearer, and a shudder of unutterable horror ran through me when I saw a circle of gigantic forms, many times higher than myself, upstanding grim and grey through the veil of cloud before me.

I suppose I must have fainted, for I found myself some time afterwards sitting upon the ground, sick and deadly cold. There were the figures, quite still and silent, seen vaguely through the thick gloom, but in human shape indisputably.

A sudden thought occurred to me, which would have doubtless struck me at once had I not been prepossessed with forebodings at the time that I first saw the figures, and had not the cloud concealed them from me—I mean that they were not living beings, but statues. I determined that I would count fifty slowly, and be sure that the objects were not alive if during that time I could detect no sign of motion.

How thankful was I when I came to the end of my fifty and there had been no movement!

I counted a second time—but again all was still.

I then advanced timidly forward, and in another moment I saw that my surmise was correct. I had come upon a sort of Stonehenge of rude and barbaric figures, seated as Chowbok had sat when I questioned him in the wool-shed, and with the same superhumanly malevolent expression upon their faces. They had been all seated, but two had fallen. They were barbarous—neither Egyptian, nor Assyrian, nor Japanese—different from any of these, and yet akin to all. They were six or seven times larger than life, of great antiquity, worn and lichen grown. They were ten in number. There was snow upon their heads and wherever snow could lodge. Each statue had been built of four or five enormous blocks, but how these had been raised and put together is known to those alone who raised them. Each was terrible after a different kind. One was raging furiously, as in pain and great despair; another was lean and cadaverous with famine; another cruel and idiotic, but with the silliest simper that can be conceived—this one had fallen, and looked exquisitely ludicrous in his fall—the mouths of all were more or less open, and as I looked at them from behind, I saw that their heads had been hollowed.

I was sick and shivering with cold. Solitude had unmanned me already, and I was utterly unfit to have come upon such an assembly of fiends in such a dreadful wilderness and without preparation. I would have given everything I had in the world to have been back at my master's station; but that was not to be thought of: my head was failing, and I felt sure that I could never get back alive.

Then came a gust of howling wind, accompanied with a moan from one of the statues above me. I clasped my hands in fear. I felt like a rat caught in a trap, as though I would have turned and bitten at whatever thing was nearest me. The wildness of the wind increased, the moans grew shriller, coming from several statues, and swelling into a chorus. I almost immediately knew what it was, but the sound was so unearthly that this was but little consolation. The inhuman beings into whose hearts the Evil One had put it to conceive these statues, had made their heads into a sort of organ-pipe, so that their mouths should catch the wind and sound with its blowing. It was horrible. However brave a man might be, he could never stand such a concert, from such lips, and in such a place. I heaped every

Prelude: arpeggio

invective upon them that my tongue could utter as I rushed away from them into the mist, and even after I had lost sight of them, and turning my head round could see nothing but the storm-wraiths driving behind me, I heard their ghostly chanting, and felt as though one of them would rush after me and grip me in his hand and throttle me.

I may say here that, since my return to England, I heard a friend playing some chords upon the organ which put me very forcibly in mind of the Erewhonian statues (for Erewhon is the name of the country upon which I was now entering). They rose most vividly to my recollection the moment my friend began. They are as follows [see p. 35], and are by the greatest of all musicians:—*

CHAPTER VI

INTO EREWHON

AND NOW I found myself on a narrow path which followed a small watercourse. I was too glad to have an easy track for my flight, to lay hold of the full significance of its existence. The thought, however, soon presented itself to me that I must be in an inhabited country, but one which was yet unknown. What, then, was to be my fate at the hands of its inhabitants? Should I be taken and offered up as a burnt-offering to those hideous guardians of the pass? It might be so. I shuddered at the thought, yet the horrors of solitude had now fairly possessed me; and so dazed was I, and chilled, and woebegone, that I could lay hold of no idea firmly amid the crowd of fancies that kept wandering in upon my brain.

I hurried onward—down, down, down. More streams came in; then there was a bridge, a few pine logs thrown over the water; but they gave me comfort, for savages do not make bridges. Then I had a treat such as I can never convey on paper—a moment, perhaps, the most striking and unexpected in my whole life—the one I think that, with some three or four exceptions, I would most gladly have again, were I able to recall it. I got below the level of the clouds, into a burst of brilliant evening sunshine. I was facing the north-west, and the sun was full upon me. Oh, how its light cheered me! But

---

* See Handel's compositions for the harpsichord, published by Litolf, p. 78.

what I saw! It was such an expanse as was revealed to Moses when he stood upon the summit of Mount Sinai, and beheld that promised land which it was not to be his to enter. The beautiful sunset sky was crimson and gold; blue, silver, and purple; exquisite and tranquillising; fading away therein were plains, on which I could see many a town and city, with buildings that had lofty steeples and rounded domes. Nearer beneath me lay ridge behind ridge, outline behind outline, sunlight behind shadow, and shadow behind sunlight, gully and serrated ravine. I saw large pine forests, and the glitter of a noble river winding its way upon the plains; also many villages and hamlets, some of them quite near at hand; and it was on these that I pondered most. I sank upon the ground at the foot of a large tree and thought what I had best do; but I could not collect myself. I was quite tired out; and presently, feeling warmed by the sun, and quieted, I fell off into a profound sleep.

I was awoke by the sound of tinkling bells, and looking up, I saw four or five goats feeding near me. As soon as I moved, the creatures turned their heads towards me with an expression of infinite wonder. They did not run away, but stood stock still, and looked at me from every side, as I at them. Then came the sound of chattering and laughter, and there approached two lovely girls, of about seventeen or eighteen years old, dressed each in a sort of linen gaberdine, with a girdle round the waist. They saw me. I sat quite still and looked at them, dazzled with their extreme beauty. For a moment they looked at me and at each other in great amazement; then they gave a little frightened cry and ran off as hard as they could.

"So that's that," said I to myself, as I watched them scampering. I knew that I had better stay where I was and meet my fate, whatever it was to be, and even if there were a better course, I had no strength left to take it. I must come into contact with the inhabitants sooner or later, and it might as well be sooner. Better not to seem afraid of them, as I should do by running away and being caught with a hue and cry tomorrow or next day. So I remained quite still and waited. In about an hour I heard distant voices talking excitedly, and in a few minutes I saw the two girls bringing up a party of six or seven men, well armed with bows and arrows and pikes. There was nothing for it, so I remained sitting quite still, even after they had seen me, until they came close up. Then we all had a good look at one another.

Both the girls and the men were very dark in colour, but not more so than the South Italians or Spaniards. The men wore no trousers, but were dressed nearly the same as the Arabs whom I have seen in

Algeria. They were of the most magnificent presence, being no less strong and handsome than the women were beautiful; and not only this, but their expression was courteous and benign. I think they would have killed me at once if I had made the slightest show of violence; but they gave me no impression of their being likely to hurt me so long as I was quiet. I am not much given to liking anybody at first sight, but these people impressed me much more favourably than I should have thought possible, so that I could not fear them as I scanned their faces one after another. They were all powerful men. I might have been a match for any one of them singly, for I have been told that I have more to glory in the flesh than in any other respect, being over six feet and proportionately strong; but any two could have soon mastered me, even were I not so bereft of energy by my recent adventures. My colour seemed to surprise them most, for I have light hair, blue eyes, and a fresh complexion. They could not understand how these things could be; my clothes also seemed quite beyond them. Their eyes kept wandering all over me, and the more they looked the less they seemed able to make me out.

At last I raised myself upon my feet, and leaning upon my stick, I spoke whatever came into my head to the man who seemed foremost among them. I spoke in English, though I was very sure that he would not understand. I said that I had no idea what country I was in; that I had stumbled upon it almost by accident, after a series of hairbreadth escapes; and that I trusted they would not allow any evil to overtake me now that I was completely at their mercy. All this I said quietly and firmly, with hardly any change of expression. They could not understand me, but they looked approvingly to one another, and seemed pleased (so I thought) that I showed no fear nor acknowl-edgment of inferiority—the fact being that I was exhausted beyond the sense of fear. Then one of them pointed to the mountain, in the direction of the statues, and made a grimace in imitation of one of them. I laughed and shuddered expressively, whereon they all burst out laughing too, and chattered hard to one another. I could make out nothing of what they said, but I think they thought it rather a good joke that I had come past the statues. Then one among them came forward and motioned me to follow, which I did without hesitation, for I dared not thwart them; moreover, I liked them well enough, and felt tolerably sure that they had no intention of hurting me.

In about a quarter of an hour we got to a small hamlet built on the side of a hill, with a narrow street and houses huddled up together. The roofs were large and overhanging. Some few windows were glazed, but not many. Altogether the village was exceedingly like one of those that one comes upon in descending the less known passes over the Alps on to Lombardy. I will pass over the excitement which my arrival caused. Suffice it, that though there was abundance of curiosity, there was no rudeness. I was taken to the principal house, which seemed to belong to the people who had captured me. There I was hospitably entertained, and a supper of milk and goat's flesh with a kind of oatcake was set before me, of which I ate heartily. But all the time I was eating I could not help turning my eyes upon the two beautiful girls whom I had first seen, and who seemed to consider me as their lawful prize—which indeed I was, for I would have gone through fire and water for either of them.

Then came the inevitable surprise at seeing me smoke, which I will spare the reader; but I noticed that when they saw me strike a match, there was a hubbub of excitement which, it struck me, was not altogether unmixed with disapproval: why, I could not guess. Then the women retired, and I was left alone with the men, who tried to talk to me in every conceivable way; but we could come to no understanding, except that I was quite alone, and had come from a long way over the mountains. In the course of time they grew tired, and I very sleepy. I made signs as though I would sleep on the floor in my blankets, but they gave me one of their bunks with plenty of dried fern and grass, on to which I had no sooner laid myself than I fell fast asleep; nor did I awake till well into the following day, when I found myself in the hut with two men keeping guard over me and an old woman cooking. When I woke the men seemed pleased, and spoke to me as though bidding me good morning in a pleasant tone.

I went out of doors to wash in a creek which ran a few yards from the house. My hosts were as engrossed with me as ever; they never took their eyes off me, following every action that I did, no matter how trifling, and each looking towards the other for his opinion at every touch and turn. They took great interest in my ablutions, for they seemed to have doubted whether I was in all respects human like themselves. They even laid hold of my arms and overhauled them, and expressed approval when they saw that they were strong and muscular. They now examined my legs, and especially my feet. When they desisted they nodded approvingly to each other; and when I had combed and brushed my hair, and generally made myself as neat and well arranged as circumstances would allow, I could see that their respect for me increased greatly, and that they were by no means sure that they had treated me with sufficient deference—a matter on which I am not competent to decide. All I know is that they were very good to me, for which I thanked them heartily, as it might well have been otherwise.

For my own part, I liked them and admired them, for their quiet self-possession and dignified ease impressed me pleasurably at once. Neither did their manner make me feel as though I were personally distasteful to them—only that I was a thing utterly new and unlooked for, which they could not comprehend. Their type was more that of the most robust Italians than any other; their manners also were eminently Italian, in their entire unconsciousness of self. Having travelled a good deal in Italy, I was struck with little gestures of the hand and shoulders, which constantly reminded me of that country. My feeling was that my wisest plan would be to go on as I had begun, and be simply myself for better or worse, such as I was, and take my chance accordingly.

I thought of these things while they were waiting for me to have done washing, and on my way back. Then they gave me breakfast— hot bread and milk, and fried flesh of something between mutton and venison. Their ways of cooking and eating were European, though they had only a skewer for a fork, and a sort of butcher's knife to cut with. The more I looked at everything in the house, the more I was struck with its quasi-European character; and had the walls only been pasted over with extracts from the *Illustrated London News* and *Punch*, I could have almost fancied myself in a shepherd's hut upon my master's sheep-run. And yet everything was slightly different. It was much the same with the birds and flowers on the other side, as compared with the English ones. On my arrival I had been pleased at noticing that nearly all the plants and birds were very like common English ones: thus, there was a robin, and a lark, and a wren, and daisies, and dandelions; not quite the same as the English, but still very like them—quite like enough to be called by the same name; so now, here, the ways of these two men, and the things they had in the house, were all very nearly the same as in Europe. It was not at all like going to China or Japan, where everything that one sees is strange. I was, indeed, at once struck with the primitive character of their appliances, for they seemed to be some five or six hundred years behind Europe in their inventions; but this is the case in many an Italian village.

All the time that I was eating my breakfast I kept speculating as to what family of mankind they could belong to; and shortly there came an idea into my head, which brought the blood into my cheeks with excitement as I thought of it. Was it possible that they might be the lost ten tribes of Israel, of whom I had heard both my grandfather and my father make mention as existing in an unknown country, and awaiting a final return to Palestine? Was it possible that *I* might have been designed by Providence as the instrument of their conversion? Oh, what a thought was this! I laid down my skewer and gave them a hasty survey. There was nothing of a Jewish type about them: their noses were distinctly Grecian, and their lips, though full, were not Jewish.

How could I settle this question? I knew neither Greek nor Hebrew, and even if I should get to understand the language here spoken, I should be unable to detect the roots of either of these tongues. I had not been long enough among them to ascertain their habits, but they did not give me the impression of being a religious people. This too was natural: the ten tribes had been always lamentably irreligious. But could I not make them change? To restore the lost ten tribes of Israel to a knowledge of the only truth: here would be indeed an immortal crown of glory! My heart beat fast and furious as I entertained the thought. What a position would it not ensure me in the next world; or perhaps even in this! What folly it would be to throw such a chance away! I should rank next to the Apostles, if not as high as they—certainly above the minor prophets, and possibly above any Old Testament writer except Moses and Isaiah. For such a future as this I would sacrifice all that I have without a moment's hesitation, could I be reasonably assured of it. I had always cordially approved of missionary efforts, and had at times contributed my mite towards their support and extension; but I had never hitherto felt drawn towards becoming a missionary myself; and indeed had always admired, and envied, and respected them, more than I had exactly liked them. But if these people were the lost ten tribes of Israel, the case would be widely different: the opening was too excellent to be lost, and I resolved that should I see indications which appeared to confirm my impression that I had indeed come upon the missing tribes, I would certainly convert them.

I may here mention that this discovery is the one to which I alluded in the opening pages of my story. Time strengthened the impression made upon me at first; and, though I remained in doubt for several months, I feel now no longer uncertain.

When I had done eating, my hosts approached, and pointed down the valley leading to their own country, as though wanting to show that I must go with them; at the same time they laid hold of my arms, and made as though they would take me, but used no violence. I laughed, and motioned my hand across my throat, pointing down the valley as though I was afraid lest I should be killed when I got there. But they divined me at once, and shook their heads with much decision, to show that I was in no danger. Their manner quite reassured me; and in half an hour or so I had packed up my swag, and was eager for the forward journey, feeling wonderfully strengthened and refreshed by good food and sleep, while my hope and curiosity were aroused to their very utmost by the extraordinary position in which I found myself.

But already my excitement had begun to cool and I reflected that these people might not be the ten tribes after all; in which case I could not but regret that my hopes of making money, which had led me into so much trouble and danger, were almost annihilated by the fact that the country was full to overflowing, with a people who had probably already developed its more available resources. Moreover, how was I to get back? For there was something about my hosts which told me that they had got me, and meant to keep me, in spite of all their goodness.

CHAPTER VII

FIRST IMPRESSIONS

WE FOLLOWED AN Alpine path for some four miles, now hundreds of feet above a brawling stream which descended from the glaciers, and now nearly alongside it. The morning was cold and somewhat foggy, for the autumn had made great strides latterly. Sometimes we went through forests of pine, or rather yew trees, though they looked like pine; and I remember that now and again we passed a little wayside shrine, wherein there would be a statue of great beauty, representing some figure, male or female, in the very heyday of youth, strength, and beauty, or of the most dignified maturity and old age. My hosts always bowed their heads as they passed one of these shrines, and it shocked me to see statues that had no apparent object, beyond the chronicling of some unusual individual excellence or beauty, receive so serious a homage. However, I showed no sign of wonder or disapproval; for I remembered that to be all things to all men was one of the injunctions of the Gentile Apostle, which for the present I should do well to heed. Shortly after passing one of these chapels we came suddenly upon a village which started up out of the mist; and I was alarmed lest I should be made an object of curiosity or dislike. But it was not so. My guides spoke to many in passing, and those spoken to showed much amazement. My guides, however, were well known, and the natural politeness of the people prevented them from putting me to any inconvenience; but they could not help eyeing me, nor I them. I may as well say at once what my after-experience taught me—namely, that with all their faults and extraordinary obliquity of mental vision upon many subjects, they are the very best-bred people that I ever fell in with.

The village was just like the one we had left, only rather larger. The streets were narrow and unpaved, but very fairly clean. The vine grew outside many of the houses; and there were some with sign-boards, on which was painted a bottle and a glass, that made me feel much at home. Even on this ledge of human society there was a stunted growth of shoplets, which had taken root and vegetated somehow, though as in an air mercantile of the bleakest. It was here as hitherto: all things were generically the same as in Europe, the differences being of species only; and I was amused at seeing in a window some bottles with barley-sugar and sweetmeats for children, as at home; but the barley-sugar was in plates, not in twisted sticks, and was coloured blue. Glass was plentiful in the better houses.

Lastly, I should say that the people were of a physical beauty which was simply amazing. I never saw anything in the least comparable to them. The women were vigorous, and had a most majestic gait, their heads being set upon their shoulders with a grace beyond all power of expression. Each feature was finished, eyelids, eyelashes, and ears being almost invariably perfect. Their colour was equal to that of the finest Italian paintings; being of the clearest olive, and yet ruddy with a glow of perfect health. Their expression was divine; and as they glanced at me timidly but with parted lips in great bewilderment, I forgot all thoughts of their conversion in feelings that were far more earthly. I was dazzled as I saw one after the other, of whom I could only feel that each was the loveliest I had ever seen. Even in middle age they were still comely, and the old grey-haired women at their cottage doors had a dignity, not to say majesty, of their own.

The men were as handsome as the women beautiful. I have always delighted in and reverenced beauty; but I felt simply abashed in the presence of such a splendid type—a compound of all that is best in Egyptian, Greek and Italian. The children were infinite in number, and exceedingly merry; I need hardly say that they came in for their full share of the prevailing beauty. I expressed by signs my admiration and pleasure to my guides, and they were greatly pleased. I should add that all seemed to take a pride in their personal appearance, and that even the poorest (and none seemed rich) were well kempt and tidy. I could fill many pages with a description of their dress and the ornaments which they wore, and a hundred details which struck me with all the force of novelty; but I must not stay to do so.

When we had got past the village the fog rose, and revealed magnificent views of the snowy mountains and their nearer abutments, while in front I could now and again catch glimpses of the great plains which I had surveyed on the preceding evening. The country was highly cultivated, every ledge being planted with chestnuts, walnuts, and apple-trees from which the apples were now gathering. Goats were abundant; also a kind of small black cattle, in the marshes near the river, which was now fast widening, and running between larger flats from which the hills receded more and more. I saw a few sheep with rounded noses and enormous tails. Dogs were there in plenty, and very English; but I saw no cats, nor indeed are these creatures known, their place being supplied by a sort of small terrier.

In about four hours of walking from the time we started, and after passing two or three more villages, we came upon a considerable town, and my guides made many attempts to make me understand something, but I gathered no inkling of their meaning, except that I need be under no apprehension of danger. I will spare the reader any description of the town, and would only bid him think of Domodossola or Faido. Suffice it that I found myself taken before the chief magistrate, and by his orders was placed in an apartment with two other people, who were the first I had seen looking anything but well and handsome. In fact, one of them was plainly very much out of health, and coughed violently from time to time in spite of manifest efforts to suppress it. The other looked pale and ill but he was marvellously self-contained, and it was impossible to say what was the matter with him. Both of them appeared astonished at seeing one who was evidently a stranger, but they were too ill to come up to me, and form conclusions concerning me. These two were first called out; and in about a quarter of an hour I was made to follow them, which I did in some fear, and with much curiosity.

The chief magistrate was a venerable-looking man, with white hair and beard and a face of great sagacity. He looked me all over for about five minutes, letting his eyes wander from the crown of my head to the soles of my feet, up and down, and down and up; neither did his mind seem in the least clearer when he had done looking than when he began. He at length asked me a single short question, which I supposed meant "Who are you?" I answered in English quite composedly as though he would understand me, and endeavoured to be my very most natural self as well as I could. He appeared more and more puzzled, and then retired, returning with two others much like himself. Then they took me into an inner room, and the two fresh arrivals stripped me, while the chief looked on. They felt my pulse, they looked at my tongue, they listened at my chest, they felt all my muscles; and at the end of each operation they looked at the chief and nodded, and said something in a tone quite pleasant, as though I were all right. They even pulled down my eyelids, and looked, I suppose, to see if they were bloodshot; but it was not so. At length they gave up; and I think that all were satisfied of my being in the most perfect health, and very robust to boot. At last the old magistrate made me a speech of about five minutes long, which the other two appeared to think greatly to the point, but from which I gathered nothing. As soon as it was ended, they proceeded to overhaul my swag and the contents of my pockets. This gave me little uneasiness, for I had no money with me, nor anything which they were at all likely to want, or which I cared about losing. At least I fancied so, but I soon found my mistake.

They got on comfortably at first, though they were much puzzled with my tobacco-pipe and insisted on seeing me use it. When I had shown them what I did with it, they were astonished but not displeased, and seemed to like the smell. But by and by they came to my watch, which I had hidden away in the inmost pocket that I had, and had forgotten when they began their search. They seemed concerned and uneasy as soon as they got hold of it. They then made me open it and show the works; and when I had done so they gave signs of very grave displeasure, which disturbed me all the more because I could not conceive wherein it could have offended them.

I remember that when they first found it I had thought of Paley, and how he tells us that a savage on seeing a watch would at once conclude that it was designed. True, these people were not savages, but I none the less felt sure that this was the conclusion they would arrive at; and I was thinking what a wonderfully wise man Archbishop Paley must have been, when I was aroused by a look of horror and dismay upon the face of the magistrate, a look which conveyed to me the impression that he regarded my watch not as having been designed, but rather as the designer of himself and of the universe; or as at any rate one of the great first causes of all things.

Then it struck me that this view was quite as likely to be taken as the other by a people who had no experience of European civilisation, and I was a little piqued with Paley for having led me so much astray; but I soon discovered that I had misinterpreted the expression on the magistrate's face, and that it was one not of fear, but hatred. He spoke to me solemnly and sternly for two or three minutes. Then, reflecting that this was of no use, he caused me to be conducted through several passages into a large room, which I afterwards found was the museum of the town, and wherein I beheld a sight which astonished me more than anything that I had yet seen.

It was filled with cases containing all manner of curiosities—such as skeletons, stuffed birds and animals, carvings in stone (whereof I saw several that were like those on the saddle, only smaller), but the greater part of the room was occupied by broken machinery of all descriptions. The larger specimens had a case to themselves, and tickets with writing on them in a character which I could not understand. There were fragments of steam engines, all broken and rusted; among them I saw a cylinder and piston, a broken fly-wheel, and part of a crank, which was laid on the ground by their side. Again, there was a very old carriage whose wheels in spite of rust and decay, I could see, had been designed originally for iron rails. Indeed, there were fragments of a great many of our own most advanced inventions; but they seemed all to be several hundred years old, and to be placed where they were, not for instruction, but curiosity. As I said before, all were marred and broken.

We passed many cases, and at last came to one in which there were several clocks and two or three old watches. Here the magistrate stopped, and opening the case began comparing my watch with the others. The design was different, but the thing was clearly the same. On this he turned to me and made me a speech in a severe and injured tone of voice, pointing repeatedly to the watches in the case, and to my own; neither did he seem in the least appeased until I made signs to him that he had better take my watch and put it with the others. This had some effect in calming him. I said in English (trusting to tone and manner to convey my meaning) that I was exceedingly sorry if I had been found to have anything contraband in my possession; that I had had no intention of evading the ordinary tolls, and that I would gladly forfeit the watch if my doing so would atone for an unintentional violation of the law. He began presently to relent, and spoke to me in a kinder manner. I think he saw that I had offended without knowledge; but I believe the chief thing that brought him round was my not seeming to be afraid of him, although I was quite respectful; this, and my having light hair and complexion, on which he had remarked previously by signs, as every one else had done.

I afterwards found that it was reckoned a very great merit to have fair hair, this being a thing of the rarest possible occurrence, and greatly admired and envied in all who were possessed of it. However that might be, my watch was taken from me; but our peace was made, and I was conducted back to the room where I had been examined. The magistrate then made me another speech, whereon I was taken to a building hard by, which I soon discovered to be the common prison of the town, but in which an apartment was assigned me separate from the other prisoners. The room contained a bed, table, and chairs, also a fireplace and a washing-stand. There was another door, which opened on to a balcony, with a flight of steps descending into a walled garden of some size. The man who conducted me into this room made signs to me that I might go down and walk in the garden whenever I pleased, and intimated that I should shortly have something brought me to eat. I was allowed to retain my blankets, and the few things which I had wrapped inside them, but it was plain that I was to consider myself a prisoner—for how long a period I could not by any means determine. He then left me alone.

CHAPTER VIII

IN PRISON

AND NOW FOR the first time my courage completely failed me. It is enough to say that I was penniless, and a prisoner in a foreign country, where I had no friend, nor any knowledge of the customs or language of the people. I was at the mercy of men with whom I had little in common. And yet, engrossed as I was with my extremely difficult and doubtful position, I could not help feeling deeply interested in the people among whom I had fallen. What was the meaning of that room full of old machinery which I had just seen, and of the displeasure with which the magistrate had regarded my watch? The people had very little machinery now. I had been struck with this over and over again, though I had not been more than four-and-twenty hours in the country. They were about as far advanced as Europeans of the twelfth or thirteenth century; certainly not more so. And yet they must have had at one time the fullest knowledge of our own most recent inventions. How could it have happened that having been once so far in advance they were now as much behind us? It was evident that it was not from ignorance. They knew my watch as a watch when they saw it; and the care with which the broken machines were preserved and ticketed, proved that they had not lost the recollection of their former civilisation. The more I thought, the less I could understand it; but at last I concluded that they must have worked out their mines of coal and iron, till either none were left, or so few, that the use of these metals was restricted to the very highest nobility. This was the only solution I could think of; and, though I afterwards found how entirely mistaken it was, I felt quite sure then that it must be the right one.

I had hardly arrived at this opinion for above four or five minutes, when the door opened, and a young woman made her appearance with a tray, and a very appetising smell of dinner. I gazed upon her with admiration as she laid a cloth and set a savoury-looking dish upon the table. As I beheld her I felt as though my position was already much ameliorated, for the very sight of her carried great comfort. She was not more than twenty, rather above the middle height, active and strong, but yet most delicately featured; her lips were full and sweet; her eyes were of a deep hazel, and fringed with long and springing eyelashes; her hair was neatly braided from off her forehead; her complexion was simply exquisite; her figure as robust as was consistent with the most perfect female beauty, yet not more so; her hands and feet might have served as models to a sculptor. Having set the stew upon the table, she retired with a glance of pity, whereon (remembering pity's kinsman) I decided that she should pity me a little more. She returned with a bottle and a glass, and found me sitting on the bed with my hands over my face, looking the very picture of abject misery, and, like all pictures, rather untruthful. As I watched her, through my fingers, out of the room again, I felt sure that she was exceedingly sorry for me. Her back being turned, I set to work and ate my dinner, which was excellent.

She returned in about an hour to take away; and there came with her a man who had a great bunch of keys at his waist, and whose manner convinced me that he was the jailor. I afterwards found that he was father to the beautiful creature who had brought me my dinner. I am not a much greater hypocrite than other people, and do what I would, I could not look so very miserable. I had already recovered from my dejection, and felt in a most genial humour both with my jailor and his daughter. I thanked them for their attention towards me; and, though they could not understand, they looked at one another and laughed and chattered till the old man said something or other which I suppose was a joke; for the girl laughed merrily and ran away, leaving her father to take away the dinner things. Then I had another visitor, who was not so prepossessing, and who seemed to have a great idea of himself and a small one of me. He brought a book with him, and pens and paper—all very English; and yet, neither paper, nor printing, nor binding, nor pen, nor ink, were quite the same as ours.

He gave me to understand that he was to teach me the language and that we were to begin at once. This delighted me, both because I should be more comfortable when I could understand and make myself understood, and because I supposed that the authorities would hardly teach me the language if they intended any cruel usage towards me afterwards. We began at once, and I learnt the names of everything in the room, and also the numerals and personal pronouns. I found to my sorrow that the resemblance to European things, which I had so frequently observed hitherto, did not hold good in the matter of language; for I could detect no analogy whatever between this and any tongue of which I have the slightest knowledge,—a thing which made me think it possible that I might be learning Hebrew.

I must detail no longer; from this time my days were spent with a monotony which would have been tedious but for the society of Yram, the jailor's daughter, who had taken a great fancy for me and treated me with the utmost kindness. The man came every day to teach me the language, but my real dictionary and grammar were Yram; and I consulted them to such purpose that I made the most extraordinary progress, being able at the end of a month to understand a great deal of the conversation which I overheard between Yram and her father. My teacher professed himself well satisfied, and said he should make a favourable report of me to the authorities. I then questioned him as to what would probably be done with me. He told me that my arrival had caused great excitement throughout the country, and that I was to be detained a close prisoner until the receipt of advices from the Government. My having had a watch, he said, was the only damaging feature in the case. And then, in answer to my asking why this should be so, he gave me a long story of which with my imperfect knowledge of the language I could make nothing whatever, except that it was a very heinous offence, almost as bad (at least, so I thought I understood him) as having typhus fever. But he said he thought my light hair would save me.

I was allowed to walk in the garden; there was a high wall so that I managed to play a sort of hand fives, which prevented my feeling the bad effects of my confinement, though it was stupid work playing alone. In the course of time people from the town and neighbourhood began to pester the jailor to be allowed to see me, and on receiving handsome fees he let them do so. The people were good to me; almost too good, for they were inclined to make a lion of me, which I hated—at least the women were; only they had to beware of Yram, who was a young lady of a jealous temperament, and kept a sharp eye both on me and on my lady visitors. However, I felt so kindly towards her, and was so entirely dependent upon her for almost all that made my life a blessing and a comfort to me, that I took good care not to vex her, and we remained excellent friends. The men were far less inquisitive, and would not, I believe, have come near me of their own accord; but the women made them come as escorts. I was delighted with their handsome mien, and pleasant genial manners.

My food was plain, but always varied and wholesome, and the good red wine was admirable. I had found a sort of wort in the garden, which I sweated in heaps and then dried, obtaining thus a substitute for tobacco; so that what with Yram, the language, visitors, fives in the garden, smoking, and bed, my time slipped by more rapidly and pleasantly than might have been expected. I also made myself a small flute; and being a tolerable player, amused myself at times with playing snatches from operas, and airs such as "O where and oh where," and "Home, sweet home." This was of great advantage to me, for the people of the country were ignorant of the diatonic scale and could hardly believe their ears on hearing some of our most common melodies. Often, too, they would make me sing; and I could at any time make Yram's eyes swim with tears by singing "Wilkins and his Dinah," "Billy Taylor," "The Ratcatcher's Daughter," or as much of them as I could remember.

I had one or two discussions with them because I never would sing on Sunday (of which I kept count in my pocket-book), except chants and hymn tunes; of these I regret to say that I had forgotten the words, so that I could only sing the tune. They appeared to have little or no religious feeling, and to have never so much as heard of the divine institution of the Sabbath, so they ascribed my observance of it to a fit of sulkiness, which they remarked as coming over me upon every seventh day. But they were very tolerant, and one of them said to me quite kindly that she knew how impossible it was to help being sulky at times, only she thought I ought to see some one if it became more serious—a piece of advice which I then failed to understand, though I pretended to take it quite as a matter of course.

Once only did Yram treat me in a way that was unkind and unreasonable,—at least so I thought it at the time. It happened thus. I had been playing fives in the garden and got much heated. Although the day was cold, for autumn was now advancing, and Cold Harbour (as the name of the town in which my prison was should be translated) stood fully 3000 feet above the sea, I had played without my coat and waistcoat, and took a sharp chill on resting myself too long in the open air without protection. The next day I had a severe cold and felt really poorly. Being little used even to the lightest ailments, and thinking that it would be rather nice to be petted and cossetted by Yram, I certainly did not make myself out to be any better than I was; in fact, I remember that I made the worst of things, and took it into my head to consider myself upon the sick list. When Yram brought me my breakfast I complained somewhat dolefully of my indisposition, expecting the sympathy and humouring which I should have received from my mother and sisters at home. Not a bit of it. She fired up in an instant, and asked me what I meant by it, and how I dared to presume to mention such a thing, especially when I considered in what place I was. She had the best mind to tell her father, only that she was afraid the consequences would be so very serious for me. Her manner was so injured and decided, and her anger so evidently unfeigned, that I forgot my cold upon the spot, begging her by all means to tell her father if she wished to do so, and telling her that I had no idea of being shielded by her from anything whatever; presently mollifying, after having said as many biting things as

I could, I asked her what it was that I had done amiss, and promised amendment as soon as ever I became aware of it. She saw that I was really ignorant, and had had no intention of being rude to her; whereon it came out that illness of any sort was considered in Erewhon to be highly criminal and immoral; and that I was liable, even for catching cold, to be had up before the magistrates and imprisoned for a considerable period—an announcement which struck me dumb with astonishment.

I followed up the conversation as well as my imperfect knowledge of the language would allow, and caught a glimmering of her position with regard to ill-health; but I did not even then fully comprehend it, nor had I as yet any idea of the other extraordinary perversions of thought which existed among the Erewhonians, but with which I was soon to become familiar. I propose, therefore, to make no mention of what passed between us on this occasion, save that we were reconciled, and that she brought me surreptitiously a hot glass of spirits and water before I went to bed, as also a pile of extra blankets, and that next morning I was quite well. I never remember to have lost a cold so rapidly.

This little affair explained much which had hitherto puzzled me. It seemed that the two men who were examined before the magistrates on the day of my arrival in the country, had been given in charge on account of ill health, and were both condemned to a long term of imprisonment with hard labour; they were now expiating their offence in this very prison, and their exercise ground was a yard separated by my fives wall from the garden in which I walked. This accounted for the sounds of coughing and groaning which I had often noticed as coming from the other side of the wall: it was high, and I had not dared to climb it for fear the jailor should see me and think that I was trying to escape; but I had often wondered what sort of people they could be on the other side, and had resolved on asking the jailor; but I seldom saw him, and Yram and I generally found other things to talk about.

Another month flew by, during which I made such progress in the language that I could understand all that was said to me, and express myself with tolerable fluency. My instructor professed to be astonished with the progress I had made; I was careful to attribute it to the pains he had taken with me and to his admirable method of explaining my difficulties, so we became excellent friends.

My visitors became more and more frequent. Among them there were some, both men and women, who delighted me entirely by their simplicity, unconsciousness of self, kindly genial manners, and last, but not least, by their exquisite beauty; there came others less well-bred, but still comely and agreeable people, while some were snobs pure and simple.

At the end of the third month the jailor and my instructor came together to visit me and told me that communications had been received from the Government to the effect that if I had behaved well and seemed generally reasonable, and if there could be no suspicion at all about my bodily health and vigour, and if my hair was really light, and my eyes blue and complexion fresh, I was to be sent up at once to the metropolis in order that the King and Queen might see me and converse with me; but that when I arrived there I should be set at liberty, and a suitable allowance would be made me. My teacher also told me that one of the leading merchants had sent me an invitation to repair to his house and to consider myself his guest for as long a time as I chose. "He is a delightful man," continued the interpreter, "but has suffered terribly from" (here there came a long word which I could not quite catch, only it was much longer than kleptomania), "and has but lately recovered from embezzling a large sum of money under singularly distressing circumstances; but he has quite got over it, and the straightener's say that he has made a really wonderful recovery; you are sure to like him."

CHAPTER IX
TO THE METROPOLIS

WITH THE ABOVE words the good man left the room before I had time to express my astonishment at hearing such extraordinary language from the lips of one who seemed to be a reputable member of society. "Embezzle a large sum of money under singularly distressing circumstances!" I exclaimed to myself, "and ask *me* to go and stay with him! I shall do nothing of the sort—compromise myself at the very outset in the eyes of all decent people, and give the death-blow to my chances of either converting them if they are the lost tribes of Israel, or making money out of them if they are not! No. I will do anything rather than that." And when I next saw my teacher I told him that I did not at all like the sound of what had been proposed for me, and that I would have nothing to do with it. For by my education and the example of my own parents, and I trust also in some degree from inborn instinct, I have a very genuine dislike for all unhandsome dealings in money matters, though none can have a greater regard for money than I have, if it be got fairly.

The interpreter was much surprised by my answer, and said that I should be very foolish if I persisted in my refusal.

"Mr. Nosnibor," he continued, "is a man of at least 500,000 horse-power" (for their way of reckoning and classifying men is by the number of foot pounds which they have money enough to raise, or more roughly by their horse-power), "and keeps a capital table; besides, his two daughters are among the most beautiful women in Erewhon."

When I heard all this, I confess that I was much shaken, and inquired whether he was favourably considered in the best society.

"Certainly," was the answer; "no man in the country stands higher."

He then went on to say that one would have thought from my manner that my proposed host had had jaundice or pleurisy or been generally unfortunate, and that I was in fear of infection.

"I am not much afraid of infection," said I, impatiently, "but I have some regard for my character; and if I know a man to be an embezzler of other people's money, be sure of it, I will give him as wide a berth as I can. If he were ill or poor—"

"Ill or poor!" interrupted the interpreter, with a face of great alarm. "So that's your notion of propriety! You would consort with the basest criminals, and yet deem simple embezzlement a bar to friendly intercourse. I cannot understand you."

"But I am poor myself," cried I.

"You were," said he; "and you were liable to be severely punished for it,—indeed, at the council which was held concerning you, this fact was very nearly consigning you to what I should myself consider a well-deserved chastisement" (for he was getting angry, and so was I); "but the Queen was so inquisitive, and wanted so much to see you, that she petitioned the King and made him give you his pardon, and assign you a pension in consideration of your meritorious complexion. It is lucky for you that he has not heard what you have been saying now, or he would be sure to cancel it."

As I heard these words my heart sank within me. I felt the extreme difficulty of my position, and how wicked I should be in running counter to established usage. I remained silent for several minutes, and then said that I should be happy to accept the embezzler's invitation,—on which my instructor brightened and said I was a sensible fellow. But I felt very uncomfortable. When he had left the room, I mused over the conversation which had just taken place between us, but I could make nothing out of it, except that it argued an even greater perversity of mental vision than I had been yet prepared for. And this made me wretched; for I cannot bear having much to do with people who think differently from myself. All sorts of wandering thoughts kept coming into my head. I thought of my master's hut, and my seat upon the mountain side, where I had first conceived the insane idea of exploring. What years and years seemed to have passed since I had begun my journey!

I thought of my adventures in the gorge, and on the journey hither, and of Chowbok. I wondered what Chowbok told them about me when he got back,—he had done well in going back, Chowbok had. He was not handsome—nay, he was hideous; and it would have gone hardly with him. Twilight drew on, and rain pattered against the windows. Never yet had I felt so unhappy, except during three days of seasickness at the beginning of my voyage from England. I sat musing and in great melancholy, until Yram made her appearance with light and supper. She too, poor girl, was miserable; for she had heard that I was to leave them. She had made up her mind that I was to remain always in the town, even after my imprisonment was over; and I fancy had resolved to marry me though I had never so much as hinted at her doing so. So what with the distressingly strange conversation with my teacher, my own friendless condition, and Yram's melancholy, I felt more unhappy than I can describe, and remained so till I got to bed, and sleep sealed my eyelids.

On awaking next morning I was much better. It was settled that I was to make my start in a conveyance which was to be in waiting for me at about eleven o'clock; and the anticipation of change put me in good spirits, which even the tearful face of Yram could hardly altogether derange. I kissed her again and again, assured her that we should meet hereafter, and that in the meanwhile I should be ever mindful of her kindness. I gave her two of the buttons off my coat and a lock of my hair as a keepsake, taking a goodly curl from her own beautiful head in return: and so, having said good-bye a hundred times, till I was fairly overcome with her great sweetness and her sorrow, I tore myself away from her and got down-stairs to the calèche which was in waiting. How thankful I was when it was all over, and I was driven away and out of sight. Would that I could have felt that it was out of mind also! Pray heaven that it is so now, and that she is married happily among her own people, and has forgotten me!

And now began a long and tedious journey with which I should hardly trouble the reader if I could. He is safe, however, for the simple reason that I was blindfolded during the greater part of the time. A bandage was put upon my eyes every morning, and was only removed at night when I reached the inn at which we were to pass the night. We travelled slowly, although the roads were good. We drove but one horse, which took us our day's journey from morning till evening, about six hours, exclusive of two hours' rest in the middle of the day. I do not suppose we made above thirty or thirty-five miles on an average. Each day we had a fresh horse. As I have said already, I could see nothing of the country. I only know that it was level, and that several times we had to cross large rivers in ferry-boats. The inns were clean and comfortable. In one or two of the larger towns they were quite sumptuous, and the food was good and well cooked. The same wonderful health and grace and beauty prevailed everywhere.

I found myself an object of great interest; so much so, that the driver told me he had to keep our route secret, and at times to go to places that were not directly on our road, in order to avoid the press that would otherwise have awaited us. Every evening I had a reception, and grew heartily tired of having to say the same things over and over again in answer to the same questions, but it was impossible to be angry with people whose manners were so delightful. They never once asked after my health, or even whether I was fatigued with my journey; but their first question was almost invariably an inquiry after my temper, the *naïveté* of which astonished me till I became used to it. One day, being tired and cold, and weary of saying the same thing over and over again, I turned a little brusquely on my questioner and said that I was exceedingly cross, and that I could hardly feel in a worse humour with myself and every one else than at that moment. To my surprise, I was met with the kindest expressions of condolence, and heard it buzzed about the room that I was in an ill temper; whereon people began to give me nice things to smell and to eat, which really did seem to have some temper-mending quality about them, for I soon felt pleased and was at once congratulated upon being better. The next morning two or three people sent their servants to the hotel with sweetmeats, and inquiries whether I had quite recovered from my ill humour. On receiving the good things I felt in half a mind to be ill-tempered every evening; but I disliked the condolences and the inquiries, and found it most comfortable to keep my natural temper, which is smooth enough generally.

Among those who came to visit me were some who had received a liberal education at the Colleges of Unreason, and taken the highest degrees in hypothetics, which are their principal study. These gentlemen had now settled down to various employments in the country, as straighteners, managers and cashiers of the Musical Banks, priests of religion, or what not, and carrying their education with them they diffused a leaven of culture throughout the country. I naturally questioned them about many of the things which had puzzled me since my arrival. I inquired what was the object and meaning of the statues which I had seen upon the plateau of the pass. I was told that they dated from a very remote period, and that there were several other such groups in the country, but none so remarkable as the one which I had seen. They had a religious origin, having been designed to propitiate the gods of deformity and disease. In former times it had been the custom to make expeditions over the ranges, and capture the ugliest of Chowbok's ancestors whom they could find, in order to sacrifice them in the presence of these deities, and thus avert ugliness and disease from the Erewhonians themselves. It had been whispered (but my informant assured me untruly) that centuries ago they had even offered up some of their own people who were ugly or out of health, in order to make examples of them; these detestable customs, however, had been long discontinued; neither was there any present observance of the statues.

I had the curiosity to inquire what would be done to any of Chowbok's tribe if they crossed over into Erewhon. I was told that nobody knew, inasmuch as such a thing had not happened for ages. They would be too ugly to be allowed to go at large, but not so much so as to be criminally liable. Their offence in having come would be a moral one; but they would be beyond the straightener's art. Possibly they would be consigned to the Hospital for Incurable Bores, and made to work at being bored for so many hours a day by the Erewhonian inhabitants of the hospital, who are extremely impatient of one another's boredom, but would soon die if they had no one whom they might bore—in fact, that they would be kept as professional borees. When I heard this, it occurred to me that some rumours of its substance might perhaps have become current among Chowbok's people; for the agony of his fear had been too great to have been inspired by the mere dread of being burnt alive before the statues.

I also questioned them about the museum of old machines, and the cause of the apparent retrogression in all arts, sciences, and inventions. I learnt that about four hundred years previously, the state of mechanical knowledge was far beyond our own, and was advancing with prodigious rapidity, until one of the most learned professors of hypothetics wrote an extraordinary book (from which I propose to give extracts later on), proving that the machines were ultimately destined to supplant the race of man, and to become instinct with a vitality as different from, and superior to, that of animals, as animal to vegetable life. So convincing was his reasoning, or unreasoning, to this effect, that he carried the country with him; and they made a clean sweep of all machinery that had not been in use for more than two hundred and seventy-one years (which period was arrived at after a series of compromises), and strictly forbade all further improvements and inventions under pain of being considered in the eye of the law to be labouring under typhus fever, which they regard as one of the worst of all crimes.

This is the only case in which they have confounded mental and physical diseases, and they do it even here as by an avowed legal fiction. I became uneasy when I remembered about my watch; but they comforted me with the assurance that transgression in this matter was now so unheard of, that the law could afford to be lenient towards an utter stranger, especially towards one who had such a good character (they meant physique), and such beautiful light hair. Moreover the watch was a real curiosity, and would be a welcome addition to the metropolitan collection; so they did not think I need let it trouble me seriously.

I will write, however, more fully upon this subject when I deal with the Colleges of Unreason, and the Book of the Machines.

In about a month from the time of our starting I was told that our journey was nearly over. The bandage was now dispensed with, for it seemed impossible that I should ever be able to find my way back without being captured. Then we rolled merrily along through the streets of a handsome town, and got on to a long, broad, and level road, with poplar trees on either side. The road was raised slightly above the surrounding country, and had formerly been a railway; the fields on either side were in the highest conceivable cultivation, but the harvest and also the vintage had been already gathered. The weather had got cooler more rapidly than could be quite accounted for by the progress of the season; so I rather thought that we must have been making away from the sun, and were some degrees farther from the equator than when we started. Even here the vegetation showed that the climate was a hot one, yet there was no lack of vigour among the people; on the contrary, they were a very hardy race, and capable of great endurance. For the hundredth time I thought that, take them all round, I had never seen their equals in respect of physique, and they looked as good-natured as they were robust. The flowers were for the most part over, but their absence was in some measure compensated for by a profusion of delicious fruit, closely resembling the figs, peaches, and pears of Italy and France. I saw no wild animals, but birds were plentiful and much as in Europe, but not tame as they had been on the other side of the ranges. They were shot at with the cross-bow and with arrows, gunpowder being unknown, or at any rate not in use.

We were now nearing the metropolis and I could see great towers and fortifications, and lofty buildings that looked like palaces. I began to be nervous as to my reception; but I had got on very well so far, and resolved to continue upon the same plan as hitherto—namely, to behave just as though I were in England until I saw that I was making a blunder, and then to say nothing till I could gather how the land lay. We drew nearer and nearer. The news of my approach had got abroad, and there was a great crowd collected on either side of the road, who greeted me with marks of most respectful curiosity, keeping me bowing constantly in acknowledgement from side to side.

When we were about a mile off, we were met by the Mayor and several Councillors, among whom was a venerable old man, who was introduced to me by the Mayor (for so I suppose I should call him) as the gentleman who had invited me to his house. I bowed deeply and told him how grateful I felt to him, and how gladly I would accept his hospitality. He forbade me to say more, and pointing to his carriage, which was close at hand, he motioned me to a seat therein. I again bowed profoundly to the Mayor and Councillors, and drove off with my entertainer, whose name was Senoj Nosnibor. After about half a mile the carriage turned off the main road, and we drove under the walls of the town till we reached a *palazzo* on a slight eminence, and just on the outskirts of the city. This was Senoj Nosnibor's house, and nothing can be imagined finer. It was situated near the magnificent and venerable ruins of the old railway station, which formed an imposing feature from the gardens of the house.

The grounds, some ten or a dozen acres in extent, were laid out in terraced gardens, one above the other, with flights of broad steps ascending and descending the declivity of the garden. On these steps there were statues of most exquisite workmanship. Besides the statues there were vases filled with various shrubs that were new to me; and on either side of the flights of steps there were rows of old cypresses and cedars, with grassy alleys between them. Then came choice vineyards and orchards of fruit-trees in full bearing.

The house itself was approached by a court-yard and round it was a corridor on to which rooms opened, as at Pompeii. In the middle of the court there was a bath and a fountain. Having passed the court we came to the main body of the house, which was two stories in height. The rooms were large and lofty; perhaps at first they looked rather bare of furniture, but in hot climates people generally keep their rooms more bare than they do in colder ones. I missed also the sight of a grand piano or some similar instrument, there being no means of producing music in any of the rooms save the larger drawing-room, where there were half a dozen large bronze gongs, which the ladies used occasionally to beat about at random. It was not pleasant to hear them, but I have heard quite as unpleasant music both before and since.

Mr. Nosnibor took me through several spacious rooms till we reached a boudoir where were his wife and daughters, of whom I had heard from the interpreter. Mrs. Nosnibor was about forty years old, and still handsome, but she had grown very stout: her daughters were in the prime of youth and exquisitely beautiful. I gave the preference almost at once to the younger, whose name was Arowhena; for the elder sister was haughty, while the younger had a very winning manner. Mrs. Nosnibor received me with the perfection of courtesy, so that I must have indeed been shy and nervous if I had not at once felt welcome. Scarcely was the ceremony of my introduction well completed before a servant announced that dinner was ready in the next room. I was exceedingly hungry, and the dinner was beyond all praise. Can the reader wonder that I began to consider myself in excellent quarters? "That man embezzle money?" thought I to myself; "impossible."

But I noticed that my host was uneasy during the whole meal, and that he ate nothing but a little bread and milk; towards the end of dinner there came a tall lean man with a black beard, to whom Mr. Nosnibor and the whole family paid great attention: he was the family straightener. With this gentleman Mr. Nosnibor retired into another room, from which there presently proceeded a sound of weeping and wailing. I could hardly believe my ears, but in a few minutes I got to know for a certainty that they came from Mr. Nosnibor himself.

"Poor papa," said Arowhena, as she helped herself composedly to the salt, "how terribly he has suffered."

"Yes," answered her mother; "but I think he is quite out of danger now."

Then they went on to explain to me the circumstances of the case, and the treatment which the straightener had prescribed, and how successful he had been—all which I will reserve for another chapter, and put rather in the form of a general summary of the opinions current upon these subjects than in the exact words in which the facts were delivered to me; the reader, however, is earnestly requested to believe that both in this next chapter and in those that follow it I have endeavoured to adhere most conscientiously to the strictest accuracy, and that I have never willingly misrepresented, though I may have sometimes failed to understand all the bearings of an opinion or custom.

CHAPTER X
CURRENT OPINIONS

THIS IS WHAT I gathered. That in that country if a man falls into ill health, or catches any disorder, or fails bodily in any way before he is seventy years old, he is tried before a jury of his countrymen, and if convicted is held up to public scorn and sentenced more or less severely as the case may be. There are subdivisions of illnesses into crimes and misdemeanours as with offences amongst ourselves—a man being punished very heavily for serious illness, while failure of eyes or hearing in one over sixty-five, who has had good health hitherto, is dealt with by fine only, or imprisonment in default of payment. But if a man forges a cheque, or sets his house on fire, or robs with violence from the person, or does any other such things as are criminal in our own country, he is either taken to a hospital and most carefully tended at the public expense, or if he is in good circumstances, he lets it be known to all his friends that he is suffering from a severe fit of immorality, just as we do when we are ill, and they come and visit him with great solicitude, and inquire with interest how it all came about, what symptoms first showed themselves, and so forth,—questions which he will answer with perfect unreserve; for bad conduct, though considered no less deplorable than illness with ourselves, and as unquestionably indicating something seriously wrong with the individual who misbehaves, is nevertheless held to be the result of either pre-natal or post-natal misfortune.

The strange part of the story, however, is that though they ascribe moral defects to the effect of misfortune either in character or surroundings, they will not listen to the plea of misfortune in cases that in England meet with sympathy and commiseration only. Ill luck of any kind, or even ill treatment at the hands of others, is considered an offence against society, inasmuch as it makes people uncomfortable to hear of it. Loss of fortune, therefore, or loss of some dear friend on whom another was much dependent, is punished hardly less severely than physical delinquency.

Foreign, indeed, as such ideas are to our own, traces of somewhat similar opinions can be found even in nineteenth century England. If a person has an abscess, the medical man will say that it contains "peccant" matter, and people say that they have a "bad" arm or finger, or that they are very "bad" all over, when they only mean "diseased." Among foreign nations Erewhonian opinions may be still more clearly noted. The Mohammedans, for example, to this day, send their female prisoners to hospitals, and the New Zealand Maoris visit any misfortune with forcible entry into the house of the offender, and the breaking up and burning of all his goods. The Italians, again, use the same word for "disgrace" and "misfortune." I once heard an Italian lady speak of a young friend whom she described as endowed with every virtue under heaven, "ma," she exclaimed, "povero disgraziato, ha ammazzato suo zio." ("Poor unfortunate fellow, he has murdered his uncle.")

On mentioning this, which I heard when taken to Italy as a boy by my father, the person to whom I told it showed no surprise. He said that he had been driven for two or three years in a certain city by a young Sicilian cabdriver of prepossessing manners and appearance, but then lost sight of him. On asking what had become of him, he was told that he was in prison for having shot at his father with intent to kill him—happily without serious result. Some years later my informant again found himself warmly accosted by the prepossessing young cabdriver. "Ah, caro signore," he exclaimed, "sono cinque anni che non lo vedo—tre anni di militare, e due anni di disgrazia," &c. ("My dear sir, it is five years since I saw you—three years of military service, and two of misfortune")—during which last the poor fellow had been in prison. Of moral sense he showed not so much as a trace. He and his father were now on excellent terms, and were likely to remain so unless either of them should again have the misfortune mortally to offend the other.

In the following chapter I will give you a few examples of the way in which what we should call misfortune, hardship, or disease are dealt with by the Erewhonians, but for the moment will return to their treatment of cases that with us are criminal. As I have already said, these, though not judicially punishable, are recognised as requiring correction. Accordingly, there exists a class of men trained in soul-craft, whom they call straighteners, as nearly as I can translate a word which literally means "one who bends back the crooked." These men practise much as medical men in England, and receive a quasi-surreptitious fee on every visit. They are treated with the same unreserve, and obeyed as readily, as our own doctors—that is to say, on the whole sufficiently—because people know that it is their interest to get well as soon as they can, and that they will not be scouted as they would be if their bodies were out of order, even though they may have to undergo a very painful course of treatment.

When I say that they will not be scouted, I do not mean that an Erewhonian will suffer no social inconvenience in consequence, we will say, of having committed fraud. Friends will fall away from him because of his being less pleasant company, just as we ourselves are disinclined to make companions of those who are either poor or poorly. No one with any sense of self-respect will place himself on an equality in the matter of affection with those who are less lucky than himself in birth, health, money, good looks, capacity, or anything else. Indeed, that dislike and even disgust should be felt by the fortunate for the unfortunate, or at any rate for those who have been discovered to have met with any of the more serious and less familiar misfortunes, is not only natural, but desirable for any society, whether of man or brute.

The fact, therefore, that the Erewhonians attach none of that guilt to crime which they do to physical ailments, does not prevent the more selfish among them from neglecting a friend who has robbed a bank, for instance, till he has fully recovered; but it does prevent them from even thinking of treating criminals with that contemptuous tone which would seem to say, "I, if I were you, should be a better man than you are," a tone which is held quite reasonable in regard to physical ailment. Hence, though they conceal ill health by every cunning and hypocrisy and artifice which they can devise, they are quite open about the most flagrant mental diseases, should they happen to exist, which to do the people justice is not often. Indeed, there are some who are, so to speak, spiritual valetudinarians, and who make themselves exceedingly ridiculous by their nervous supposition that they are wicked, while they are very tolerable people all the time. This however is exceptional; and on the whole they use much the same reserve or unreserve about the state of their moral welfare as we do about our health.

Hence all the ordinary greetings among ourselves, such as, How do you do? and the like, are considered signs of gross ill-breeding; nor do the politer classes tolerate even such a common complimentary remark as telling a man that he is looking well. They salute each other with, "I hope you are good this morning;" or "I hope you have recovered from the snappishness from which you were suffering when I last saw you;" and if the person saluted has not been good, or is still snappish, he says so at once and is condoled with accordingly. Indeed, the straighteners have gone so far as to give names from the hypothetical language (as taught at the Colleges of Unreason), to all known forms of mental indisposition, and to classify them according to a system of their own, which, though I could not understand it, seemed to work well in practice; for they are always able to tell a man what is the matter with him as soon as they have heard his story, and their familiarity with the long names assures him that they thoroughly understand his case.

The reader will have no difficulty in believing that the laws regarding ill health were frequently evaded by the help of recognised fictions, which every one understood, but which it would be considered gross ill-breeding to even seem to understand. Thus, a day or two after my arrival at the Nosnibors', one of the many ladies who called on me made excuses for her husband's only sending his card, on the ground that when going through the public marketplace that morning he had stolen a pair of socks. I had already been warned that I should never show surprise, so I merely expressed my sympathy, and said that though I had only been in the capital so short a time, I had already had a very narrow escape from stealing a clothes-brush, and that though I had resisted temptation so far, I was sadly afraid that if I saw any object of special interest that was neither too hot nor too heavy, I should have to put myself in the straightener's hands.

Mrs. Nosnibor, who had been keeping an ear on all that I had been saying, praised me when the lady had gone. Nothing, she said, could have been more polite according to Erewhonian etiquette. She then explained that to have stolen a pair of socks, or "to have the socks" (in more colloquial language), was a recognised way of saying that the person in question was slightly indisposed.

In spite of all this they have a keen sense of the enjoyment consequent upon what they call being "well." They admire mental health and love it in other people, and take all the pains they can (consistently with their other duties) to secure it for themselves. They have an extreme dislike to marrying into what they consider unhealthy families. They send for the straightener at once whenever they have been guilty of anything seriously flagitious—often even if they think that they are on the point of committing it; and though his remedies are sometimes exceedingly painful, involving close confinement for weeks, and in some cases the most cruel physical tortures, I never heard of a reasonable Erewhonian refusing to do what his straightener told him, any more than of a reasonable Englishman refusing to undergo even the most frightful operation, if his doctors told him it was necessary.

We in England never shrink from telling our doctor what is the matter with us merely through the fear that he will hurt us. We let him do his worst upon us, and stand it without a murmur, because we are not scouted for being ill, and because we know that the doctor is doing his best to cure us, and that he can judge of our case better than we can; but we should conceal all illness if we were treated as the Erewhonians are when they have anything the matter with them; we should do the same as with moral and intellectual diseases,—we should feign health with the most consummate art, till we were found out, and should hate a single flogging given in the way of mere punishment more than the amputation of a limb, if it were kindly and courteously performed from a wish to help us out of our difficulty, and with the full consciousness on the part of the doctor that it was only by an accident of constitution that he was not in the like plight himself. So the Erewhonians take a flogging once a week, and a diet of bread and water for two or three months together, whenever their straightener recommends it.

I do not suppose that even my host, on having swindled a confiding widow out of the whole of her property, was put to more actual suffering than a man will readily undergo at the hands of an English doctor. And yet he must have had a very bad time of it. The sounds I heard were sufficient to show that his pain was exquisite, but he never shrank from undergoing it. He was quite sure that it did him good; and I think he was right. I cannot believe that that man will ever embezzle money again. He may—but it will be a long time before he does so.

During my confinement in prison, and on my journey, I had already discovered a great deal of the above; but it still seemed surpassingly strange, and I was in constant fear of committing some piece of rudeness, through my inability to look at things from the same stand-point as my neighbours; but after a few weeks' stay with the Nosnibors, I got to understand things better, especially on having heard all about my host's illness, of which he told me fully and repeatedly.

It seemed that he had been on the Stock Exchange of the city for many years and had amassed enormous wealth, without exceeding the limits of what was generally considered justifiable, or at any rate, permissible dealing; but at length on several occasions he had become aware of a desire to make money by fraudulent representations, and had actually dealt with two or three sums in a way which had made him rather uncomfortable. He had unfortunately made light of it and pooh-poohed the ailment, until circumstances eventually presented themselves which enabled him to cheat upon a very considerable scale;—he told me what they were, and they were about as bad as anything could be, but I need not detail them;—he seized the opportunity, and became aware, when it was too late, that he must be seriously out of order. He had neglected himself too long.

He drove home at once, broke the news to his wife and daughters as gently as he could, and sent off for one of the most celebrated straighteners of the kingdom to a consultation with the family practitioner, for the case was plainly serious. On the arrival of the straightener he told his story, and expressed his fear that his morals must be permanently impaired.

The eminent man reassured him with a few cheering words, and then proceeded to make a more careful diagnosis of the case. He inquired concerning Mr. Nosnibor's parents—had their moral health been good? He was answered that there had not been anything seriously amiss with them, but that his maternal grandfather, whom he was supposed to resemble somewhat in person, had been a consummate scoundrel and had ended his days in a hospital,—while a brother of his father's, after having led a most flagitious life for many years, had been at last cured by a philosopher of a new school, which as far as I could understand it bore much the same relation to the old as homœopathy to allopathy. The straightener shook his head at this, and laughingly replied that the cure must have been due to nature. After a few more questions he wrote a prescription and departed.

I saw the prescription. It ordered a fine to the State of double the money embezzled; no food but bread and milk for six months, and a severe flogging once a month for twelve. I was surprised to see that no part of the fine was to be paid to the poor woman whose money had been embezzled, but on inquiry I learned that she would have been prosecuted in the Misplaced Confidence Court, if she had not escaped its clutches by dying shortly after she had discovered her loss.

As for Mr. Nosnibor, he had received his eleventh flogging on the day of my arrival. I saw him later on the same afternoon, and he was still twinged; but there had been no escape from following out the straightener's prescription, for the so-called sanitary laws of Erewhon are very rigorous, and unless the straightener was satisfied that his orders had been obeyed, the patient would have been taken to a hospital (as the poor are), and would have been much worse off. Such at least is the law, but it is never necessary to enforce it.

On a subsequent occasion I was present at an interview between Mr. Nosnibor and the family straightener, who was considered competent to watch the completion of the cure. I was struck with the delicacy with which he avoided even the remotest semblance of inquiry after the physical well-being of his patient, though there was a certain yellowness about my host's eyes which argued a bilious habit of body. To have taken notice of this would have been a gross breach of professional etiquette. I was told, however, that a straightener sometimes thinks it right to glance at the possibility of some slight physical disorder if he finds it important in order to assist him in his diagnosis; but the answers which he gets are generally untrue or evasive, and he forms his own conclusions upon the matter as well as he can. Sensible men have been known to say that the straightener should in strict confidence be told of every physical ailment that is likely to bear upon the case; but people are naturally shy of doing this, for they do not like lowering themselves in the opinion of the straightener, and his ignorance of medical science is supreme. I heard of one lady, indeed, who had the hardihood to confess that a furious outbreak of ill-humour and extravagant fancies for which she was seeking advice was possibly the result of indisposition. "You should resist that," said the straightener, in a kind, but grave voice; "we can do nothing for the bodies of our patients; such matters are beyond our province, and I desire that I may hear no further particulars."

The lady burst into tears, and promised faithfully that she would never be unwell again.

But to return to Mr. Nosnibor. As the afternoon wore on many carriages drove up with callers to inquire how he had stood his flogging. It had been very severe, but the kind inquiries upon every side gave him great pleasure, and he assured me that he felt almost tempted to do wrong again by the solicitude with which his friends had treated him during his recovery: in this I need hardly say that he was not serious.

During the remainder of my stay in the country Mr. Nosnibor was constantly attentive to his business, and largely increased his already great possessions; but I never heard a whisper to the effect of his having been indisposed a second time, or made money by other than the most strictly honourable means. I did hear afterwards in confidence that there had been reason to believe that his health had been not a little affected by the straightener's treatment, but his friends did not choose to be over-curious upon the subject, and on his return to his affairs it was by common consent passed over as hardly criminal in one who was otherwise so much afflicted. For they regard bodily ailments as the more venial in proportion as they have been produced by causes independent of the constitution. Thus if a person ruin his health by excessive indulgence at the table or by drinking, they count it to be almost a part of the mental disease which brought it about, and so it goes for little, but they have no mercy on such illnesses as fevers or catarrhs or lung diseases, which to us appear to be beyond the control of the individual. They are only more lenient towards the diseases of the young—such as measles, which they think to be like sowing one's wild oats—and look over them as pardonable indiscretions if they have not been too serious, and if they are atoned for by complete subsequent recovery.

It is hardly necessary to say that the office of straightener is one which requires long and special training. It stands to reason that he who would cure a moral ailment must be practically acquainted with it in all its bearings. The student for the profession of straightener is required to set apart certain seasons for the practice of each vice in turn, as a religious duty. These seasons are called "fasts" and are continued by the student until he finds that he really can subdue all the more usual vices in his own person, and hence can advise his patients from the results of his own experience.

Those who intend to be specialists, rather than general practitioners, devote themselves more particularly to the branch in which their practice will mainly lie. Some students have been obliged to continue their exercises during their whole lives, and some devoted men have actually died as martyrs to the drink, or gluttony, or whatever branch of vice they may have chosen for their especial study. The greater number, however, take no harm by the excursions into the various departments of vice which it is incumbent upon them to study.

For the Erewhonians hold that unalloyed virtue is not a thing to be immoderately indulged in. I was shown more than one case in which the real or supposed virtues of parents were visited upon the children to the third and fourth generation. The straighteners say that the most that can be truly said for virtue is that there is a considerable balance in its favour, and that it is on the whole a good deal better to be on its side than against it; but they urge that there is much pseudo-virtue going about, which is apt to let people in very badly before they find it out. Those men, they say, are best who are not remarkable either for vice or virtue. I told them about Hogarth's idle and industrious apprentices, but they did not seem to think that the industrious apprentice was a very nice person.

CHAPTER XI
SOME EREWHONIAN TRIALS

In Erewhon as in other countries there are some courts of justice that deal with special subjects. Misfortune generally, as I have above explained, is considered more or less criminal, but it admits of classification, and a court is assigned to each of the main heads under which it can be supposed to fall. Not very long after I had reached the capital I strolled into the Personal Bereavement Court, and was much both interested and pained by listening to the trial of a man who was accused of having just lost a wife to whom he had been tenderly attached, and who had left him with three little children, of whom the eldest was only three years old.

The defence which the prisoner's counsel endeavoured to establish was, that the prisoner had never really loved his wife; but it broke down completely, for the public prosecutor called witness after witness who deposed to the fact that the couple had been devoted to one another, and the prisoner repeatedly wept as incidents were put

in evidence that reminded him of the irreparable nature of the loss
he had sustained. The jury returned a verdict of guilty after very
little deliberation, but recommended the prisoner to mercy on the
ground that he had but recently insured his wife's life for a considerable sum, and might be deemed lucky inasmuch as he had received
the money without demur from the insurance company, though he
had only paid two premiums.

I have just said that the jury found the prisoner guilty. When the
judge passed sentence, I was struck with the way in which the prisoner's counsel was rebuked for having referred to a work in which
the guilt of such misfortunes as the prisoner's was extenuated to a
degree that roused the indignation of the court.

"We shall have," said the judge, "these crude and subversionary
books from time to time until it is recognised as an axiom of morality that luck is the only fit object of human veneration. How far a
man has any right to be more lucky and hence more venerable than
his neighbours, is a point that always has been, and always will be,
settled proximately by a kind of higgling and haggling of the market,
and ultimately by brute force; but however this may be, it stands to
reason that no man should be allowed to be unlucky to more than
a very moderate extent."

Then, turning to the prisoner, the judge continued:—"You have
suffered a great loss. Nature attaches a severe penalty to such offences,
and human law must emphasise the decrees of nature. But for the
recommendation of the jury I should have given you six months'
hard labour. I will, however, commute your sentence to one of three
months, with the option of a fine of twenty-five per cent of the
money you have received from the insurance company."

The prisoner thanked the judge, and said that as he had no one to
look after his children if he was sent to prison, he would embrace
the option mercifully permitted him by his lordship, and pay the sum
he had named. He was then removed from the dock.

The next case was that of a youth barely arrived at man's estate,
who was charged with having been swindled out of large property
during his minority by his guardian, who was also one of his nearest
relations. His father had been long dead, and it was for this reason
that his offence came on for trial in the Personal Bereavement Court.
The lad, who was undefended, pleaded that he was young, inexperienced, greatly in awe of his guardian, and without independent
professional advice. "Young man," said the judge sternly, "do not
talk nonsense. People have no right to be young, inexperienced,

greatly in awe of their guardians, and without independent professional advice. If by such indiscretions they outrage the moral sense of their friends, they must expect to suffer accordingly." He then ordered the prisoner to apologise to his guardian, and to receive twelve strokes with a cat-of-nine-tails.

But I shall perhaps best convey to the reader an idea of the entire perversion of thought which exists among this extraordinary people, by describing the public trial of a man who was accused of pulmonary consumption—an offence which was punished with death until quite recently. It did not occur till I had been some months in the country, and I am deviating from chronological order in giving it here; but I had perhaps better do so in order that I may exhaust this subject before proceeding to others. Moreover I should never come to an end were I to keep to a strictly narrative form, and detail the infinite absurdities with which I daily came in contact.

The prisoner was placed in the dock, and the jury were sworn much as in Europe; almost all our own modes of procedure were reproduced, even to the requiring the prisoner to plead guilty or not guilty. He pleaded not guilty, and the case proceeded. The evidence for the prosecution was very strong; but I must do the court the justice to observe that the trial was absolutely impartial. Counsel for the prisoner was allowed to urge everything that could be said in his defence: the line taken was that the prisoner was simulating consumption in order to defraud an insurance company, from which he was about to buy an annuity, and that he hoped thus to obtain it on more advantageous terms. If this could have been shown to be the case he would have escaped a criminal prosecution, and been sent to a hospital as for a moral ailment. The view, however, was one which could not be reasonably sustained, in spite of all the ingenuity and eloquence of one of the most celebrated advocates of the country. The case was only too clear, for the prisoner was almost at the point of death, and it was astonishing that he had not been tried and convicted long previously. His coughing was incessant during the whole trial, and it was all that the two jailors in charge of him could do to keep him on his legs until it was over.

The summing up of the judge was admirable. He dwelt upon every point that could be construed in favour of the prisoner, but as he proceeded it became clear that the evidence was too convincing to admit of doubt, and there was but one opinion in the court as to the impending verdict when the jury retired from the box. They were absent for about ten minutes, and on their return the foreman pronounced the prisoner guilty. There was a faint murmur of applause, but it was instantly repressed. The judge then proceeded to pronounce sentence in words which I can never forget, and which I copied out into a notebook next day from the report that was published in the leading newspaper. I must condense it somewhat, and nothing which I could say would give more than a faint idea of the solemn, not to say majestic, severity with which it was delivered. The sentence was as follows:—

"Prisoner at the bar, you have been accused of the great crime of labouring under pulmonary consumption, and after an impartial trial before a jury of your countrymen, you have been found guilty. Against the justice of the verdict I can say nothing: the evidence against you was conclusive, and it only remains for me to pass such a sentence upon you, as shall satisfy the ends of the law. That sentence must be a very severe one. It pains me much to see one who is yet so young, and whose prospects in life were otherwise so excellent, brought to this distressing condition by a constitution which I can only regard as radically vicious; but yours is no case for compassion: this is not your first offence: you have led a career of crime, and have only profited by the leniency shown you upon past occasions, to offend yet more seriously against the laws and institutions of your country. You were convicted of aggravated bronchitis last year: and I find that though you are now only twenty-three years old, you have been imprisoned on no less than fourteen occasions for illnesses of a more or less hateful character; in fact, it is not too much to say that you have spent the greater part of your life in a jail.

"It is all very well for you to say that you came of unhealthy parents, and had a severe accident in your childhood which permanently undermined your constitution; excuses such as these are the ordinary refuge of the criminal; but they cannot for one moment be listened to by the ear of justice. I am not here to enter upon curious metaphysical questions as to the origin of this or that—questions to which there would be no end were their introduction once tolerated, and which would result in throwing the only guilt on the tissues of the primordial cell, or on the elementary gases. There is no question of how you came to be wicked, but only this—namely, are you wicked or not? This has been decided in the affirmative, neither can I hesitate for a single moment to say that it has been decided justly. You are a bad and dangerous person, and stand branded in the eyes of your fellow-countrymen with one of the most heinous known offences.

"It is not my business to justify the law: the law may in some cases have its inevitable hardships, and I may feel regret at times that I have not the option of passing a less severe sentence than I am compelled to do. But yours is no such case; on the contrary, had not the capital punishment for consumption been abolished, I should certainly inflict it now.

"It is intolerable that an example of such terrible enormity should be allowed to go at large unpunished. Your presence in the society of respectable people would lead the less able-bodied to think more lightly of all forms of illness; neither can it be permitted that you should have the chance of corrupting unborn beings who might hereafter pester you. The unborn must not be allowed to come near you: and this not so much for their protection (for they are our natural enemies), as for our own; for since they will not be utterly gainsaid, it must be seen to that they shall be quartered upon those who are least likely to corrupt them.

"But independently of this consideration, and independently of the physical guilt which attaches itself to a crime so great as yours, there is yet another reason why we should be unable to show you mercy, even if we were inclined to do so. I refer to the existence of a class of men who lie hidden among us, and who are called physicians. Were the severity of the law or the current feeling of the country to be relaxed never so slightly, these abandoned persons, who are now compelled to practise secretly and who can be consulted only at the greatest risk, would become frequent visitors in every household; their organisation and their intimate acquaintance with all family secrets would give them a power, both social and political, which nothing could resist. The head of the household would become subordinate to the family doctor, who would interfere between man and wife, between master and servant, until the doctors should be the only depositaries of power in the nation, and have all that we hold precious at their mercy. A time of universal dephysicalisation would ensue; medicine-vendors of all kinds would abound in our streets and advertise in all our newspapers. There is one remedy for this, and one only. It is that which the laws of this country have long received and acted upon, and consists in the sternest repression of all diseases whatsoever, as soon as their existence is made manifest to the eye of the law. Would that that eye were far more piercing than it is.

"But I will enlarge no further upon things that are themselves so obvious. You may say that it is not your fault. The answer is ready enough at hand, and it amounts to this—that if you had been born of healthy and well-to-do parents, and been well taken care of when you were a child, you would never have offended against the laws of your country, nor found yourself in your present disgraceful position. If you tell me that you had no hand in your parentage and education, and that it is therefore unjust to lay these things to your charge, I answer that whether your being in a consumption is your fault or no, it is a fault in you, and it is my duty to see that against such faults as this the commonwealth shall be protected. You may say that it is your misfortune to be criminal; I answer that it is your crime to be unfortunate.

"Lastly, I should point out that even though the jury had acquitted you—a supposition that I cannot seriously entertain—I should have felt it my duty to inflict a sentence hardly less severe than that which I must pass at present; for the more you had been found guiltless of the crime imputed to you, the more you would have been found guilty of one hardly less heinous—I mean the crime of having been maligned unjustly.

"I do not hesitate therefore to sentence you to imprisonment, with hard labour, for the rest of your miserable existence. During that period I would earnestly entreat you to repent of the wrongs you have done already, and to entirely reform the constitution of your whole body. I entertain but little hope that you will pay attention to my advice; you are already far too abandoned. Did it rest with myself, I should add nothing in mitigation of the sentence which I have passed, but it is the merciful provision of the law that even the most hardened criminal shall be allowed some one of the three official remedies, which is to be prescribed at the time of his conviction. I shall therefore order that you receive two tablespoonfuls of castor oil daily, until the pleasure of the court be further known."

When the sentence was concluded the prisoner acknowledged in a few scarcely audible words that he was justly punished, and that he had had a fair trial. He was then removed to the prison from which he was never to return. There was a second attempt at applause when the judge had finished speaking, but as before it was at once repressed; and though the feeling of the court was strongly against the prisoner, there was no show of any violence against him, if one may except a little hooting from the bystanders when he was being removed in the prisoners' van. Indeed, nothing struck me more during my whole sojourn in the country, than the general respect for law and order.

CHAPTER XII

MALCONTENTS

I CONFESS THAT I felt rather unhappy when I got home, and thought more closely over the trial that I had just witnessed. For the time I was carried away by the opinion of those among whom I was. They had no misgivings about what they were doing. There did not seem to be a person in the whole court who had the smallest doubt but that all was exactly as it should be. This universal unsuspecting confidence was imparted by sympathy to myself, in spite of all my training in opinions so widely different. So it is with most of us: that which we observe to be taken as a matter of course by those around us, we take as a matter of course ourselves. And after all, it is our duty to do this, save upon grave occasion.

But when I was alone, and began to think the trial over, it certainly did strike me as betraying a strange and untenable position. Had the judge said that he acknowledged the probable truth, namely, that the prisoner was born of unhealthy parents, or had been starved in infancy, or had met with some accidents which had developed consumption; and had he then gone on to say that though he knew all this, and bitterly regretted that the protection of society obliged him to inflict additional pain on one who had suffered so much already, yet that there was no help for it, I could have understood the position, however mistaken I might have thought it. The judge was fully persuaded that the infliction of pain upon the weak and sickly was the only means of preventing weakness and sickliness from spreading, and that ten times the suffering now inflicted upon the accused was eventually warded off from others by the present apparent severity. I could therefore perfectly understand his inflicting whatever pain he might consider necessary in order to prevent so bad an example from spreading further and lowering the Erewhonian standard; but it seemed almost childish to tell the prisoner that he could have been in good health, if he had been more fortunate in his constitution, and been exposed to less hardships when he was a boy.

I write with great diffidence, but it seems to me that there is no unfairness in punishing people for their misfortunes, or rewarding them for their sheer good luck: it is the normal condition of human life that this should be done, and no right-minded person will complain of being subjected to the common treatment. There is no alternative open to us. It is idle to say that men are not responsible for their misfortunes. What is responsibility? Surely to be responsible means to be liable to have to give an answer should it be demanded, and all things which live are responsible for their lives and actions should society see fit to question them through the mouth of its authorised agent.

What is the offence of a lamb that we should rear it, and tend it, and lull it into security, for the express purpose of killing it? Its offence is the misfortune of being something which society wants to eat, and which cannot defend itself. This is ample. Who shall limit the right of society except society itself? And what consideration for the individual is tolerable unless society be the gainer thereby? Wherefore should a man be so richly rewarded for having been son to a millionaire, were it not clearly provable that the common welfare is thus better furthered? We cannot seriously detract from a man's merit in having been the son of a rich father without imperilling our own tenure of things which we do not wish to jeopardise; if this were otherwise we should not let him keep his money for a single hour; we would have it ourselves at once. For property is robbery, but then, we are all robbers or would-be robbers together, and have found it essential to organise our thieving, as we have found it necessary to organise our lust and our revenge. Property, marriage, the law; as the bed to the river, so rule and convention to the instinct; and woe to him who tampers with the banks while the flood is flowing.

But to return. Even in England a man on board a ship with yellow fever is held responsible for his mischance, no matter what his being kept in quarantine may cost him. He may catch the fever and die; we cannot help it; he must take his chance as other people do; but surely it would be desperate unkindness to add contumely to our self-protection, unless, indeed, we believe that contumely is one of our best means of self-protection. Again, take the case of maniacs. We say that they are irresponsible for their actions, but we take good care, or ought to take good care, that they shall answer to us for their insanity, and we imprison them in what we call an asylum (that modern sanctuary!) if we do not like their answers. This is a strange kind of irresponsibility. What we ought to say is that we can afford to be satisfied with a less satisfactory answer from a lunatic than from one who is not mad, because lunacy is less infectious than crime.

We kill a serpent if we go in danger by it, simply for being such and such a serpent in such and such a place; but we never say that the serpent has only itself to blame for not having been a harmless creature. Its crime is that of being the thing which it is: but this is a capital offence, and we are right in killing it out of the way, unless we think it more danger to do so than to let it escape; nevertheless we pity the creature, even though we kill it.

But in the case of him whose trial I have described above, it was impossible that any one in the court should not have known that it was but by an accident of birth and circumstances that he was not himself also in a consumption; and yet none thought that it disgraced them to hear the judge give vent to the most cruel truisms about him. The judge himself was a kind and thoughtful person. He was a man of magnificent and benign presence. He was evidently of an iron constitution, and his face wore an expression of the maturest wisdom and experience; yet for all this, old and learned as he was, he could not see things which one would have thought would have been apparent even to a child. He could not emancipate himself from, nay, it did not even occur to him to feel, the bondage of the ideas in which he had been born and bred.

So was it also with the jury and bystanders; and—most wonderful of all—so was it even with the prisoner. Throughout he seemed fully impressed with the notion that he was being dealt with justly: he saw nothing wanton in his being told by the judge that he was to be punished, not so much as a necessary protection to society (although this was not entirely lost sight of), as because he had not been better born and bred than he was. But this led me to hope that he suffered less than he would have done if he had seen the matter in the same light that I did. And, after all, justice is relative.

I may here mention that only a few years before my arrival in the country, the treatment of all convicted invalids had been much more barbarous than now, for no physical remedy was provided, and prisoners were put to the severest labour in all sorts of weather, so that most of them soon succumbed to the extreme hardships which they suffered; this was supposed to be beneficial in some ways, inasmuch as it put the country to less expense for the maintenance of its criminal class; but the growth of luxury had induced a relaxation of the old severity, and a sensitive age would no longer tolerate what appeared to be an excess of rigour, even towards the most guilty; moreover, it was found that juries were less willing to convict, and justice was often cheated because there was no alternative between virtually condemning a man to death and letting him go free; it was also held that the country paid in recommittals for its over-severity; for those who had been imprisoned even for trifling ailments were often permanently disabled by their imprisonment; and when a man had been once convicted, it was probable that he would seldom afterwards be off the hands of the country.

These evils had long been apparent and recognised; yet people were too indolent, and too indifferent to suffering not their own, to bestir themselves about putting an end to them, until at last a benevolent reformer devoted his whole life to effecting the necessary changes. He divided all illnesses into three classes—those affecting the head, the trunk, and the lower limbs—and obtained an enactment that all diseases of the head, whether internal or external, should be treated with laudanum, those of the body with castor-oil, and those of the lower limbs with an embrocation of strong sulphuric acid and water.

It may be said that the classification was not sufficiently careful, and that the remedies were ill chosen; but it is a hard thing to initiate any reform, and it was necessary to familiarise the public mind with the principle, by inserting the thin end of the wedge first: it is not, therefore, to be wondered at that among so practical a people there should still be some room for improvement. The mass of the nation are well pleased with existing arrangements, and believe that their treatment of criminals leaves little or nothing to be desired; but there is an energetic minority who hold what are considered to be extreme opinions, and who are not at all disposed to rest contented until the principle lately admitted has been carried further.

I was at some pains to discover the opinions of these men, and their reasons for entertaining them. They are held in great odium by the generality of the public, and are considered as subverters of all morality whatever. The malcontents, on the other hand, assert that illness is the inevitable result of certain antecedent causes, which, in the great majority of cases, were beyond the control of the individual, and that therefore a man is only guilty for being in a consumption in the same way as rotten fruit is guilty for having gone rotten. True, the fruit must be thrown on one side as unfit for man's use, and the man in a consumption must be put in prison for the protection of his fellow-citizens; but these radicals would not punish him further than by loss of liberty and a strict surveillance. So long as he was prevented from injuring society, they would allow him to make himself useful by supplying whatever of society's wants he could supply. If he succeeded in thus earning money, they would have him made as comfortable in prison as possible, and would in no way interfere with his liberty more than was necessary to prevent him from escaping, or from becoming more severely indisposed within the prison walls; but they would deduct from his earnings the expenses of his board, lodging, surveillance, and half those of his conviction. If he was too ill to do anything for his support in prison, they would allow him nothing but bread and water, and very little of that.

They say that society is foolish in refusing to allow itself to be benefited by a man merely because he has done it harm hitherto, and that objection to the labour of the diseased classes is only protection in another form. It is an attempt to raise the natural price of a commodity by saying that such and such persons, who are able and willing to produce it, shall not do so, whereby every one has to pay more for it.

Besides, so long as a man has not been actually killed he is our fellow creature, though perhaps a very unpleasant one. It is in a great degree the doing of others that he is what he is, or in other words, the society which now condemns him is partly answerable concerning him. They say that there is no fear of any increase of disease under these circumstances; for the loss of liberty, the surveillance, the considerable and compulsory deduction from the prisoner's earnings, the very sparing use of stimulants (of which they would allow but little to any, and none to those who did not earn them), the enforced celibacy, and above all, the loss of reputation among friends, are in their opinion as ample safeguards to society against a general neglect of health as those now resorted to. A man, therefore, (so they say) should carry his profession or trade into prison with him if possible; if not, he must earn his living by the nearest thing to it that he can; but if he be a gentleman born and bred to no profession, he must pick oakum, or write art criticisms for a newspaper.

These people say further, that the greater part of the illness which exists in their country is brought about by the insane manner in which it is treated.

They believe that illness is in many cases just as curable as the moral diseases which they see daily cured around them, but that a great reform is impossible till men learn to take a juster view of what physical obliquity proceeds from. Men will hide their illnesses as long as they are scouted on its becoming known that they are ill; it is the scouting, not the physic, which produces the concealment; and if a man felt that the news of his being in ill-health would be received by his neighbours as a deplorable fact, but one as much the result of necessary antecedent causes as though he had broken into a jewellers shop and stolen a valuable diamond necklace—as a fact which might just as easily have happened to themselves, only that they had the luck to be better born or reared; and if they also felt that they would not be made more uncomfortable in the prison than the protection of society against infection and the proper treatment of their own disease actually demanded, men would give themselves up to the police as readily on perceiving that they had taken small-pox, as they go now to the straightener when they feel that they are on the point of forging a will, or running away with somebody else's wife.

But the main argument on which they rely is that of economy: for they know that they will sooner gain their end by appealing to men's pockets, in which they have generally something of their own, than to their heads, which contain for the most part little but borrowed or stolen property; and also, they believe it to be the readiest test and the one which has most to show for itself. If a course of conduct can be shown to cost a country less, and this by no dishonourable saving and with no indirectly increased expenditure in other ways, they hold that it requires a good deal to upset the arguments in favour of its being adopted, and whether rightly or wrongly I cannot pretend to say, they think that the more medicinal and humane treatment of the diseased of which they are the advocates would in the long run be much cheaper to the country: but I did not gather that these reformers were opposed to meeting some of the more violent forms of illness with the cat-of-nine-tails, or with death; for they saw no so effectual way of checking them; they would therefore both flog and hang, but they would do so pitifully.

I have perhaps dwelt too long upon opinions which can have no possible bearing upon our own, but I have not said the tenth part of what these would-be reformers urged upon me. I feel, however, that I have sufficiently trespassed upon the attention of the reader.

CHAPTER XIII

THE VIEWS OF THE EREWHONIANS CONCERNING DEATH

THE EREWHONIANS REGARD death with less abhorrence than disease. If it is an offence at all, it is one beyond the reach of the law, which is therefore silent on the subject; but they insist that the greater number of those who are commonly said to die, have never yet been born—not, at least, into that unseen world which is alone worthy of consideration. As regards this unseen world I understand them to say that some miscarry in respect to it before they have even reached the seen, and some after, while few are ever truly born into it at all—the greater part of all the men and women over the whole country miscarrying before they reach it. And they say that this does not matter so much as we think it does.

As for what we call death, they argue that too much has been made of it. The mere knowledge that we shall one day die does not make us very unhappy; no one thinks that he or she will escape, so that none are disappointed. We do not care greatly even though we know that we have not long to live; the only thing that would seriously affect us would be the knowing—or rather thinking that we know—the precise moment at which the blow will fall. Happily no one can ever certainly know this, though many try to make themselves miserable by endeavouring to find it out. It seems as though there were some power somewhere which mercifully stays us from putting that sting into the tail of death, which we would put there if we could, and which ensures that though death must always be a bugbear, it shall never under any conceivable circumstances be more than a bugbear.

For even though a man is condemned to die in a week's time and is shut up in a prison from which it is certain that he cannot escape, he will always hope that a reprieve may come before the week is over. Besides, the prison may catch fire, and he may be suffocated not with a rope, but with common ordinary smoke; or he may be struck dead by lightning while exercising in the prison yards. When the morning is come on which the poor wretch is to be hanged, he may choke at his breakfast, or die from failure of the heart's action before the drop has fallen; and even though it has fallen, he cannot be quite certain that he is going to die, for he cannot know this till his death has actually taken place, and it will be too late then for him to discover that he was going to die at the appointed hour after all. The Erewhonians, therefore, hold that death, like life, is an affair of being more frightened than hurt.

They burn their dead, and the ashes are presently scattered over any piece of ground which the deceased may himself have chosen. No one is permitted to refuse this hospitality to the dead: people, therefore, generally choose some garden or orchard which they may have known and been fond of when they were young. The superstitious hold that those whose ashes are scattered over any land become its jealous guardians from that time forward; and the living like to think that they shall become identified with this or that locality where they have once been happy.

They do not put up monuments, nor write epitaphs, for their dead, though in former ages their practice was much as ours, but they have a custom which comes to much the same thing, for the instinct of preserving the name alive after the death of the body seems to be common to all mankind. They have statues of themselves made while they are still alive (those, that is, who can afford it), and write inscriptions under them, which are often quite as untruthful as are our own epitaphs—only in another way. For they do not hesitate to describe themselves as victims to ill temper, jealousy, covetousness, and the like, but almost always lay claim to personal beauty, whether they have it or not, and, often, to the possession of a large sum in the funded debt of the country. If a person is ugly he does not sit as a model for his own statue, although it bears his name. He gets the handsomest of his friends to sit for him, and one of the ways of paying a compliment to another is to ask him to sit for such a statue. Women generally sit for their own statues, from a natural disinclination to admit the superior beauty of a friend, but they expect to be idealised. I understood that the multitude of these statues was beginning to be felt as an encumbrance in almost every family, and that the custom would probably before long fall into desuetude.

Indeed, this has already come about to the satisfaction of every one, as regards the statues of public men—not more than three of which can be found in the whole capital. I expressed my surprise at this, and was told that some five hundred years before my visit, the city had been so overrun with these pests, that there was no getting about, and people were worried beyond endurance by having their attention called at every touch and turn to something, which, when they had attended to it, they found not to concern them. Most of these statues were mere attempts to do for some man or woman what an animal-stuffer does more successfully for a dog, or bird, or pike. They were generally foisted on the public by some *côterie* that was trying to exalt itself in exalting some one else, and not unfrequently they had no other inception than desire on the part of some member of the *côterie* to find a job for a young sculptor to whom his daughter was engaged. Statues so begotten could never be anything but deformities, and this is the way in which they are sure to be begotten, as soon as the art of making them at all has become widely practised.

I know not why, but all the noblest arts hold in perfection but for a very little moment. They soon reach a height from which they begin to decline, and when they have begun to decline it is a pity that they cannot be knocked on the head; for an art is like a living organism—better dead than dying. There is no way of making an aged art young again; it must be born anew and grow up from infancy as a new thing, working out its own salvation from effort to effort in all fear and trembling.

The Erewhonians five hundred years ago understood nothing of all this—I doubt whether they even do so now. They wanted to get the nearest thing they could to a stuffed man whose stuffing should not grow mouldy. They should have had some such an establishment as our Madame Tussaud's, where the figures wear real clothes, and are painted up to nature. Such an institution might have been made self-supporting, for people might have been made to pay before going in. As it was, they had let their poor cold grimy colourless heroes and heroines loaf about in squares and in corners of streets in all weathers, without any attempt at artistic sanitation—for there was no provision for burying their dead works of art out of their sight— no drainage, so to speak, whereby statues that had been sufficiently assimilated, so as to form part of the residuary impression of the country, might be carried away out of the system. Hence they put them up with a light heart on the cackling of their *côteries*, and they and their children had to live, often enough, with some wordy windbag whose cowardice had cost the country untold loss in blood and money.

At last the evil reached such a pitch that the people rose, and with indiscriminate fury destroyed good and bad alike. Most of what was destroyed was bad, but some few works were good, and the sculptors of to-day wring their hands over some of the fragments that have been preserved in museums up and down the country. For a couple of hundred years or so, not a statue was made from one end of the kingdom to the other, but the instinct for having stuffed men and women was so strong, that people at length again began to try to make them. Not knowing how to make them, and having no academics to mislead them, the earliest sculptors of this period thought things out for themselves, and again produced works that were full of interest, so that in three or four generations they reached a perfection hardly if at all inferior to that of several hundred years earlier.

On this the same evils recurred. Sculptors obtained high prices— the art became a trade—schools arose which professed to sell the holy spirit of art for money; pupils flocked from far and near to buy it, in the hopes of selling it later on, and were struck purblind as a punishment for the sin of those who sent them. Before long a second iconoclastic fury would infallibly have followed, but for the prescience of a statesman who succeeded in passing an Act to the effect that no statue of any public man or woman should be allowed to remain unbroken for more than fifty years, unless at the end of that time a jury of twenty-four men taken at random from the street pronounced in favour of its being allowed a second fifty years of life. Every fifty years this reconsideration was to be repeated, and unless there was a majority of eighteen in favour of the retention of the statue, it was to be destroyed.

Perhaps a simpler plan would have been to forbid the erection of a statue to any public man or woman till he or she had been dead at least one hundred years, and even then to insist on reconsideration of the claims of the deceased and the merit of the statue every fifty years—but the working of the Act brought about results that on the whole were satisfactory. For in the first place, many public statues that would have been voted under the old system, were not ordered, when it was known that they would be almost certainly broken up after fifty years, and in the second, public sculptors, knowing their work to be so ephemeral, scamped it to an extent that made it offensive even to the most uncultured eye. Hence before long subscribers took to paying the sculptor for the statue of their dead statesman, on condition that he did not make it. The tribute of respect was thus paid to the deceased, the public sculptors were not mulcted, and the rest of the public suffered no inconvenience.

I was told, however, that an abuse of this custom is growing up, inasmuch as the competition for the commission not to make a statue is so keen, that sculptors have been known to return a considerable part of the purchase money to the subscribers, by an arrangement made with them beforehand. Such transactions, however, are always clandestine. A small inscription is let into the pavement, where the public statue would have stood, which informs the reader that such a statue has been ordered for the person, whoever he or she may be, but that as yet the sculptor has not been able to complete it. There has been no Act to repress statues that are intended for private consumption, but as I have said, the custom is falling into desuetude.

Returning to Erewhonian customs in connection with death, there is one which I can hardly pass over. When any one dies, the friends of the family write no letters of condolence, neither do they attend the scattering, nor wear mourning, but they send little boxes filled with artificial tears, and with the name of the sender painted neatly upon the outside of the lid. The tears vary in number from two to fifteen or sixteen, according to degree of intimacy or relationship; and people sometimes find it a nice point of etiquette to know the exact number which they ought to send. Strange as it may appear, this attention is highly valued, and its omission by those from whom it might be expected is keenly felt. These tears were formerly stuck with adhesive plaster to the cheeks of the bereaved, and were worn in public for a few months after the death of a relative; they were then banished to the hat or bonnet, and are now no longer worn.

The birth of a child is looked upon as a painful subject on which it is kinder not to touch: the illness of the mother is carefully concealed until the necessity for signing the birth-formula (of which hereafter) renders further secrecy impossible, and for some months before the event the family live in retirement, seeing very little company. When the offence is over and done with, it is condoned by the common want of logic; for this merciful provision of nature, this buffer against collisions, this friction which upsets our calculations but without which existence would be intolerable, this crowning glory of human invention whereby we can be blind and see at one and the same moment, this blessed inconsistency, exists here as elsewhere; and though the strictest writers on morality have maintained that it is wicked for a woman to have children at all, inasmuch as it is wrong to be out of health that good may come, yet the necessity of the case has caused a general feeling in favour of passing over such events in silence, and of assuming their non-existence except in such flagrant cases as force themselves on the public notice. Against these the condemnation of society is inexorable, and if it is believed that the illness has been dangerous and protracted, it is almost impossible for a woman to recover her former position in society.

The above conventions struck me as arbitrary and cruel, but they put a stop to many fancied ailments; for the situation, so far from being considered interesting, is looked upon as savouring more or less distinctly of a very reprehensible condition of things, and the ladies take care to conceal it as long as they can even from their own husbands, in anticipation of a severe scolding as soon as the misdemeanour is discovered. Also the baby is kept out of sight, except on the day of signing the birth-formula, until it can walk and talk. Should the child unhappily die, a coroner's inquest is inevitable, but in order to avoid disgracing a family which may have been hitherto respected, it is almost invariably found that the child was over seventy-five years old, and died from the decay of nature.

CHAPTER XIV

MAHAINA

I CONTINUED MY sojourn with the Nosnibors. In a few days Mr. Nosnibor had recovered from his flogging, and was looking forward with glee to the fact that the next would be the last. I did not think that there seemed any occasion even for this; but he said it was better to be on the safe side, and he would make up the dozen. He now went to his business as usual; and I understood that he was never more prosperous, in spite of his heavy fine. He was unable to give me much of his time during the day; for he was one of those valuable men who are paid, not by the year, month, week, or day, but by the minute. His wife and daughters, however, made much of me, and introduced me to their friends, who came in shoals to call upon me.

One of these persons was a lady called Mahaina. Zulora (the elder of my host's daughters) ran up to her and embraced her as soon as she entered the room, at the same time inquiring tenderly after her "poor dipsomania." Mahaina answered that it was just as bad as ever; she was a perfect martyr to it, and her excellent health was the only thing which consoled her under her affliction.

Then the other ladies joined in with condolences and the never-failing suggestions which they had ready for every mental malady. They recommended their own straightener and disparaged Mahaina's. Mrs. Nosnibor had a favourite nostrum, but I could catch little of its nature. I heard the words "full confidence that the desire to drink will cease when the formula has been repeated ★ ★ ★ this confidence is *everything* ★ ★ ★ far from undervaluing a thorough determination never to touch spirits again ★ ★ ★ fail too often ★ ★ ★ formula a *certain cure* (with great emphasis) ★ ★ ★ prescribed form ★ ★ ★ full conviction." The conversation then became more audible, and was carried on at considerable length. I should perplex myself and the reader by endeavouring to follow the ingenious perversity of all they said; enough, that in the course of time the visit came to an end, and

Mahaina took her leave receiving affectionate embraces from all the ladies. I had remained in the background after the first ceremony of introduction, for I did not like the looks of Mahaina, and the conversation displeased me. When she left the room I had some consolation in the remarks called forth by her departure.

At first they fell to praising her very demurely. She was all this that and the other, till I disliked her more and more at every word, and inquired how it was that the straighteners had not been able to cure her as they had cured Mr. Nosnibor.

There was a shade of significance on Mrs. Nosnibor's face as I said this, which seemed to imply that she did not consider Mahaina's case to be quite one for a straightener. It flashed across me that perhaps the poor woman did not drink at all. I knew that I ought not to have inquired, but I could not help it, and asked point blank whether she did or not.

"We can none of us judge of the condition of other people," said Mrs. Nosnibor in a gravely charitable tone and with a look towards Zulora.

"Oh, mamma," answered Zulora, pretending to be half angry but rejoiced at being able to say out what she was already longing to insinuate; "I don't believe a word of it. It's all indigestion. I remember staying in the house with her for a whole month last summer, and I am sure she never once touched a drop of wine or spirits. The fact is, Mahaina is a very weakly girl, and she pretends to get tipsy in order to win a forbearance from her friends to which she is not entitled. She is not strong enough for her calisthenic exercises, and she knows she would be made to do them unless her inability was referred to moral causes."

Here the younger sister, who was ever sweet and kind, remarked that she thought Mahaina did tipple occasionally. "I also think," she added, "that she sometimes takes poppy juice."

"Well, then, perhaps she does drink sometimes," said Zulora; "but she would make us all think that she does it much oftener in order to hide her weakness."

And so they went on for half an hour and more, bandying about the question as to how far their late visitor's intemperance was real or no. Every now and then they would join in some charitable commonplace, and would pretend to be all of one mind that Mahaina was a person whose bodily health would be excellent if it were not for her unfortunate inability to refrain from excessive drinking; but as soon as this appeared to be fairly settled they began to be uncomfortable until they had undone their work and left some serious imputation upon her constitution. At last, seeing that the debate had assumed the character of a cyclone or circular storm, going round and round and round and round till one could never say where it began nor where it ended, I made some apology for an abrupt departure and retired to my own room.

Here at least I was alone, but I was very unhappy. I had fallen upon a set of people who, in spite of their high civilisation and many excellences, had been so warped by the mistaken views presented to them during childhood from generation to generation, that it was impossible to see how they could ever clear themselves. Was there nothing which I could say to make them feel that the constitution of a person's body was a thing over which he or she had at any rate no initial control whatever, while the mind was a perfectly different thing, and capable of being created anew and directed according to the pleasure of its possessor? Could I never bring them to see that while habits of mind and character were entirely independent of initial mental force and early education, the body was so much a creature of parentage and circumstances, that no punishment for ill-health should be ever tolerated save as a protection from contagion, and that even where punishment was inevitable it should be attended with compassion? Surely, if the unfortunate Mahaina were to feel that she could avow her bodily weakness without fear of being despised for her infirmities, and if there were medical men to whom she could fairly state her case, she would not hesitate about doing so through the fear of taking nasty medicine. It was possible that her malady was incurable (for I had heard enough to convince me that her dipsomania was only a pretence and that she was temperate in all her habits); in that case she might perhaps be justly subject to annoyances or even to restraint; but who could say whether she was curable or not, until she was able to make a clean breast of her symptoms instead of concealing them? In their eagerness to stamp out disease, these people overshot their mark; for people had become so clever at dissembling—they painted their faces with such consummate skill—they repaired the decay of time and the effects of mischance with such profound dissimulation—that it was really impossible to say whether any one was well or ill till after an intimate acquaintance of months or years. Even then the shrewdest were constantly mistaken in their judgements, and marriages were often contracted with most deplorable results, owing to the art with which infirmity had been concealed.

It appeared to me that the first step towards the cure of disease should be the announcement of the fact to a person's near relations and friends. If any one had a headache, he ought to be permitted within reasonable limits to say so at once, and to retire to his own bedroom and take a pill, without every one's looking grave and tears being shed and all the rest of it. As it was, even upon hearing it whispered that somebody else was subject to headaches, a whole company must look as though they had never had a headache in their lives. It is true they were not very prevalent, for the people were the healthiest and most comely imaginable, owing to the severity with which ill health was treated; still, even the best were liable to be out of sorts sometimes, and there were few families that had not a medicine-chest in a cupboard somewhere.

CHAPTER XV
THE MUSICAL BANKS

ON MY RETURN to the drawing-room, I found that the Mahaina current had expended itself. The ladies were just putting away their work and preparing to go out. I asked them where they were going. They answered with a certain air of reserve that they were going to the bank to get some money.

Now I had already collected that the mercantile affairs of the Erewhonians were conducted on a totally different system from our own; I had, however, gathered little hitherto, except that they had two distinct commercial systems, of which the one appealed more strongly to the imagination than anything to which we are accustomed in Europe, inasmuch as the banks that were conducted upon this system were decorated in the most profuse fashion, and all mercantile transactions were accompanied with music, so that they were called Musical Banks, though the music was hideous to a European ear.

As for the system itself I never understood it, neither can I do so now: they have a code in connection with it, which I have not the slightest doubt that they understand, but no foreigner can hope to do so. One rule runs into, and against, another as in a most complicated grammar, or as in Chinese pronunciation, wherein I am told that the slightest change in accentuation or tone of voice alters the meaning of a whole sentence. Whatever is incoherent in my description must be referred to the fact of my never having attained to a full comprehension of the subject.

So far, however, as I could collect anything certain, I gathered that they have two distinct currencies, each under the control of its own banks and mercantile codes. One of these (the one with the Musical Banks) was supposed to be *the* system, and to give out the currency in which all monetary transactions should be carried on; and as far as I could see, all who wished to be considered respectable, kept a larger or smaller balance at these banks. On the other hand, if there is one thing of which I am more sure than another, it is that the amount so kept had no direct commercial value in the outside world; I am sure that the managers and cashiers of the Musical Banks were not paid in their own currency. Mr. Nosnibor used to go to these banks, or rather to the great mother bank of the city, sometimes but not very often. He was a pillar of one of the other kind of banks, though he appeared to hold some minor office also in the musical ones. The ladies generally went alone; as indeed was the case in most families, except on state occasions.

I had long wanted to know more of this strange system, and had the greatest desire to accompany my hostess and her daughters. I had seen them go out almost every morning since my arrival and had noticed that they carried their purses in their hands, not exactly ostentatiously, yet just so as that those who met them should see whither they were going. I had never, however, yet been asked to go with them myself.

It is not easy to convey a person's manner by words, and I can hardly give any idea of the peculiar feeling that came upon me when I saw the ladies on the point of starting for the bank. There was a something of regret, a something as though they would wish to take me with them, but did not like to ask me, and yet as though I were hardly to ask to be taken. I was determined, however, to bring matters to an issue with my hostess about my going with them, and after a little parleying, and many inquiries as to whether I was perfectly sure that I myself wished to go, it was decided that I might do so.

We passed through several streets of more or less considerable houses, and at last turning round a comer we came upon a large piazza, at the end of which was a magnificent building, of a strange but noble architecture and of great antiquity. It did not open directly on to the piazza, there being a screen, through which was an archway, between the piazza and the actual precincts of the bank. On passing under the archway we entered upon a green sward, round which there ran an arcade or cloister, while in front of us uprose the majestic towers of the bank and its venerable front, which was divided into three deep recesses and adorned with all sorts of marbles and many sculptures. On either side there were beautiful old trees wherein the birds were busy by the hundred, and a number of quaint but substantial houses of singularly comfortable appearance; they were situated in the midst of orchards and gardens, and gave me an impression of great peace and plenty.

Indeed it had been no error to say that this building was one that appealed to the imagination; it did more—it carried both imagination and judgement by storm. It was an epic in stone and marble, and so powerful was the effect it produced on me, that as I beheld it I was charmed and melted. I felt more conscious of the existence of a remote past. One knows of this always, but the knowledge is never so living as in the actual presence of some witness to the life of bygone ages. I felt how short a space of human life was the period of our own existence. I was more impressed with my own littleness, and much more inclinable to believe that the people whose sense of the fitness of things was equal to the upraising of so serene a handiwork, were hardly likely to be wrong in the conclusions they might come to upon any subject. My feeling certainly was that the currency of this bank must be the right one.

We crossed the sward and entered the building. If the outside had been impressive the inside was even more so. It was very lofty and divided into several parts by walls which rested upon massive pillars; the windows were filled with stained glass descriptive of the principal commercial incidents of the bank for many ages. In a remote part of the building there were men and boys singing; this was the only disturbing feature, for as the gamut was still unknown, there was no music in the country which could be agreeable to a European ear. The singers seemed to have derived their inspirations from the songs of birds and the wailing of the wind, which last they tried to imitate in melancholy cadences that at times degenerated into a howl. To my thinking the noise was hideous, but it produced a great effect upon my companions, who professed themselves much moved. As soon as the singing was over, the ladies requested me to stay where I was while they went inside the place from which it had seemed to come.

During their absence certain reflections forced themselves upon me.

In the first place, it struck me as strange that the building should be so nearly empty; I was almost alone, and the few besides myself had been led by curiosity, and had no intention of doing business with the bank. But there might be more inside. I stole up to the curtain, and ventured to draw the extreme edge of it on one side. No, there was hardly any one there. I saw a large number of cashiers, all at their desks ready to pay cheques, and one or two who seemed to be the managing partners. I also saw my hostess and her daughters and two or three other ladies; also three or four old women and the boys from one of the neighbouring Colleges of Unreason; but there was no one else. This did not look as though the bank was doing a very large business; and yet I had always been told that every one in the city dealt with this establishment.

I cannot describe all that took place in these inner precincts, for a sinister-looking person in a black gown came and made unpleasant gestures at me for peeping. I happened to have in my pocket one of the Musical Bank pieces, which had been given me by Mrs. Nosnibor, so I tried to tip him with it; but having seen what it was, he became so angry that I had to give him a piece of the other kind of money to pacify him. When I had done this he became civil directly. As soon as he was gone I ventured to take a second look, and saw Zulora in the very act of giving a piece of paper which looked like a cheque to one of the cashiers. He did not examine it, but putting his hand into an antique coffer hard by, he pulled out a quantity of metal pieces apparently at random, and handed them over without counting them; neither did Zulora count them, but put them into her purse and went back to her seat after dropping a few pieces of the other coinage into an alms box that stood by the cashier's side: Mrs. Nosnibor and Arowhena then did likewise, but a little later they gave all (so far as I could see) that they had received from the cashier back to a verger, who I have no doubt put it back into the coffer from which it had been taken. They then began making towards the curtain; whereon I let it drop and retreated to a reasonable distance.

They soon joined me. For some few minutes we all kept silence, but at last I ventured to remark that the bank was not so busy to-day as it probably often was. On this Mrs. Nosnibor said that it was indeed melancholy to see what little heed people paid to the most precious of all institutions. I could say nothing in reply, but I have ever been of opinion that the greater part of mankind do approximately know where they get that which does them good.

Mrs. Nosnibor went on to say that I must not think there was any want of confidence in the bank because I had seen so few people there; the heart of the country was thoroughly devoted to these establishments, and any sign of their being in danger would bring in support from the most unexpected quarters. It was only because people knew them to be so very safe, that in some cases (as she lamented to say in Mr. Nosnibor's) they felt that their support was unnecessary. Moreover these institutions never departed from the safest and most approved banking principles. Thus they never allowed interest on deposit, a thing now frequently done by certain bubble companies, which by doing an illegitimate trade had drawn many customers away; and even the shareholders were fewer than formerly, owing to the innovations of these unscrupulous persons, for the Musical Banks paid little or no dividend, but divided their profits by way of bonus on the original shares once in every thirty thousand years; and as it was now only two thousand years since there had been one of these distributions, people felt that they could not hope for another in their own time and preferred investments whereby they got some more tangible return; all which, she said, was very melancholy to think of.

Having made these last admissions, she returned to her original statement, namely, that every one in the country really supported these banks. As to the fewness of the people, and the absence of the able-bodied, she pointed out to me with some justice that this was exactly what we ought to expect. The men who were most conversant about the stability of human institutions, such as the lawyers, men of science, doctors, statesmen, painters, and the like, were just those who were most likely to be misled by their own fancied accomplishments, and to be made unduly suspicious by their licentious desire for greater present return, which was at the root of nine-tenths of the opposition; by their vanity, which would prompt them to affect superiority to the prejudices of the vulgar; and by the stings of their own conscience, which was constantly upbraiding them in the most cruel manner on account of their bodies, which were generally diseased.

Let a person's intellect (she continued) be never so sound, unless his body is in absolute health, he can form no judgement worth having on matters of this kind. The body is everything: it need not perhaps be such a strong body (she said this because she saw that I was thinking of the old and infirm-looking folks whom I had seen in the bank), but it must be in perfect health; in this case, the less active strength it had the more free would be the working of the intellect, and therefore the sounder the conclusion. The people, then, whom I had seen at the bank were in reality the very ones whose opinions were most worth having; they declared its advantages to be incalculable, and even professed to consider the immediate return to be far larger than they were entitled to; and so she ran on, nor did she leave off till we had got back to the house.

She might say what she pleased, but her manner carried no conviction, and later on I saw signs of general indifference to these banks that were not to be mistaken. Their supporters often denied it, but the denial was generally so couched as to add another proof of its existence. In commercial panics, and in times of general distress, the people as a mass did not so much as even think of turning to these banks. A few might do so, some from habit and early training, some from the instinct that prompts us to catch at any straw when we think ourselves drowning, but few from a genuine belief that the Musical Banks could save them from financial ruin, if they were unable to meet their engagements in the other kind of currency.

In conversation with one of the Musical Bank managers I ventured to hint this as plainly as politeness would allow. He said that it had been more or less true till lately; but that now they had put fresh stained glass windows into all the banks in the country, and repaired the buildings, and enlarged the organs; the presidents, moreover, had taken to riding in omnibuses and talking nicely to people in the streets, and to remembering the ages of their children, and giving them things when they were naughty, so that all would henceforth go smoothly.

"But haven't you done anything to the money itself?" said I, timidly.

"It is not necessary," he rejoined; "not in the least necessary, I assure you."

And yet any one could see that the money given out at these banks was not that with which people bought their bread, meat, and clothing. It was like it at a first glance, and was stamped with designs that were often of great beauty; it was not, again, a spurious coinage, made with the intention that it should be mistaken for the money in actual use; it was more like a toy money, or the counters used for certain games at cards; for, notwithstanding the beauty of the designs, the material on which they were stamped was as nearly valueless as possible. Some were covered with tinfoil, but the greater part were frankly of a cheap base metal the exact nature of which I was not able to determine. Indeed they were made of a great variety of metals, or, perhaps more accurately, alloys, some of which were hard, while others would bend easily and assume almost any form which their possessor might desire at the moment.

Of course every one knew that their commercial value was *nil*, but all those who wished to be considered respectable thought it incumbent upon them to retain a few coins in their possession, and to let them be seen from time to time in their hands and purses. Not only this, but they would stick to it that the current coin of the realm was dross in comparison with the Musical Bank coinage. Perhaps, however, the strangest thing of all was that these very people would at times make fun in small ways of the whole system; indeed, there was hardly any insinuation against it which they would not tolerate and even applaud in their daily newspapers if written anonymously, while if the same thing were said without ambiguity to their faces—nominative case verb and accusative being all in their right places, and doubt impossible—they would consider themselves very seriously and justly outraged, and accuse the speaker of being unwell.

I never could understand (neither can I quite do so now, though I begin to see better what they mean) why a single currency should not suffice them; it would seem to me as though all their dealings would have been thus greatly simplified; but I was met with a look of horror if ever I dared to hint at it. Even those who to my certain knowledge kept only just enough money at the Musical Banks to swear by, would call the other banks (where their securities really lay) cold, deadening, paralysing, and the like.

I noticed another thing, moreover, which struck me greatly. I was taken to the opening of one of these banks in a neighbouring town, and saw a large assemblage of cashiers and managers. I sat opposite them and scanned their faces attentively. They did not please me; they lacked, with few exceptions, the true Erewhonian frankness; and an equal number from any other class would have looked happier and better men. When I met them in the streets they did not seem like other people, but had, as a general rule, a cramped expression upon their faces which pained and depressed me.

Those who came from the country were better; they seemed to have lived less as a separate class, and to be freer and healthier; but in spite of my seeing not a few whose looks were benign and noble,

I could not help asking myself concerning the greater number of those whom I met, whether Erewhon would be a better country if their expression were to be transferred to the people in general. I answered myself emphatically, no. The expression on the faces of the high Ydgrunites was that which one would wish to diffuse, and not that of the cashiers.

A man's expression is his sacrament; it is the outward and visible sign of his inward and spiritual grace, or want of grace; and as I looked at the majority of these men, I could not help feeling that there must be a something in their lives which had stunted their natural development, and that they would have been more healthily minded in any other profession. I was always sorry for them, for in nine cases out of ten they were well-meaning persons; they were in the main very poorly paid; their constitutions were as a rule above suspicion; and there were recorded numberless instances of their self-sacrifice and generosity; but they had had the misfortune to have been betrayed into a false position at an age for the most part when their judgement was not matured, and after having been kept in studied ignorance of the real difficulties of the system. But this did not make their position the less a false one, and its bad effects upon themselves were unmistakable.

Few people would speak quite openly and freely before them, which struck me as a very bad sign. When they were in the room every one would talk as though all currency save that of the Musical Banks should be abolished; and yet they knew perfectly well that even the cashiers themselves hardly used the Musical Bank money more than other people. It was expected of them that they should appear to do so, but this was all. The less thoughtful of them did not seem particularly unhappy, but many were plainly sick at heart, though perhaps they hardly knew it, and would not have owned to being so. Some few were opponents of the whole system; but these were liable to be dismissed from their employment at any moment, and this rendered them very careful, for a man who had once been cashier at a Musical Bank was out of the field for other employment, and was generally unfitted for it by reason of that course of treatment which was commonly called his education. In fact it was a career from which retreat was virtually impossible, and into which young men were generally induced to enter before they could be reasonably expected, considering their training, to have formed any opinions of their own. Not unfrequently, indeed, they were induced, by what we in England should call undue influence, concealment, and fraud.

Few indeed were those who had the courage to insist on seeing both sides of the question before they committed themselves to what was practically a leap in the dark. One would have thought that caution in this respect was an elementary principle,—one of the first things that an honourable man would teach his boy to understand; but in practice it was not so.

I even saw cases in which parents bought the right of presenting to the office of cashier at one of these banks, with the fixed determination that some one of their sons (perhaps a mere child) should fill it. There was the lad himself—growing up with every promise of becoming a good and honourable man—but utterly without warning concerning the iron shoe which his natural protector was providing for him. Who could say that the whole thing would not end in a life-long lie, and vain chafing to escape? I confess that there were few things in Erewhon which shocked me more than this.

Yet we do something not so very different from this even in England, and as regards the dual commercial system, all countries have, and have had, a law of the land, and also another law, which, though professedly more sacred, has far less effect on their daily life and actions. It seems as though the need for some law over and above, and sometimes even conflicting with, the law of the land, must spring from something that lies deep down in man's nature; indeed, it is hard to think that man could ever have become man at all, but for the gradual evolution of a perception that though this world looms so large when we are in it, it may seem a little thing when we have got away from it.

When man had grown to the perception that in the everlasting Is-and-Is-Not of nature, the world and all that it contains, including man, is at the same time both seen and unseen, he felt the need of two rules of life, one for the seen, and the other for the unseen side of things. For the laws affecting the seen world he claimed the sanction of seen powers; for the unseen (of which he knows nothing save that it exists and is powerful) he appealed to the unseen power (of which, again, he knows nothing save that it exists and is powerful) to which he gives the name of God.

Some Erewhonian opinions concerning the intelligence of the unborn embryo, that I regret my space will not permit me to lay before the reader, have led me to conclude that the Erewhonian Musical Banks, and perhaps the religious systems of all countries are now more or less of an attempt to uphold the unfathomable and unconscious instinctive wisdom of millions of past generations, against the comparatively shallow, consciously reasoning, and ephemeral conclusions drawn from that of the last thirty or forty.

The saving feature of the Erewhonian Musical Bank system (as distinct from the quasi-idolatrous views which coexist with it, and on which I will touch later) was that while it bore witness to the existence of a kingdom that is not of this world, it made no attempt to pierce the veil that hides it from human eyes. It is here that almost all religions go wrong. Their priests try to make us believe that they know more about the unseen world than those whose eyes are still blinded by the seen, can ever know—forgetting that while to deny the existence of an unseen kingdom is bad, to pretend that we know more about it than its bare existence is no better.

This chapter is already longer than I intended, but I should like to say that in spite of the saving feature of which I have just spoken, I cannot help thinking that the Erewhonians are on the eve of some great change in their religious opinions, or at any rate in that part of them which finds expression through their Musical Banks. So far as I could see, fully ninety per cent of the population of the metropolis looked upon these banks with something not far removed from contempt. If this is so, any such startling event as is sure to arise sooner or later, may serve as nucleus to a new order of things that will be more in *harmony* with both the heads and hearts of the people.

CHAPTER XVI

AROWHENA

THE READER WILL perhaps have learned by this time a thing which I had myself suspected before I had been twenty-four hours in Mr. Nosnibor's house—I mean, that though the Nosnibors showed me every attention, I could not cordially like them, with the exception of Arowhena who was quite different from the rest. They were not fair samples of Erewhonians. I saw many families with whom they were on visiting terms, whose manners charmed me more than I know how to say, but I never could get over my original prejudice against Mr. Nosnibor for having embezzled the money. Mrs. Nosnibor, too, was a very worldly woman, yet to hear her talk one would have thought that she was singularly the reverse; neither could I endure Zulora; Arowhena, however, was perfection.

She it was who ran all the little errands for her mother and Mr. Nosnibor and Zulora, and gave those thousand proofs of sweetness and unselfishness which some one member of a family is generally required to give. All day long it was Arowhena this, and Arowhena that; but she never seemed to know that she was being put upon, and was always bright and willing from morning till evening. Zulora certainly was very handsome, but Arowhena was infinitely the more graceful of the two and was the very *ne plus ultra* of youth and beauty. I will not attempt to describe her, for anything that I could say would fall so far short of the reality as only to mislead the reader. Let him think of the very loveliest that he can imagine, and he will still be below the truth. Having said this much, I need hardly say that I had fallen in love with her.

She must have seen what I felt for her, but I tried my hardest not to let it appear even by the slightest sign. I had many reasons for this. I had no idea what Mr. and Mrs. Nosnibor would say to it; and I knew that Arowhena would not look at me (at any rate not yet) if her father and mother disapproved, which they probably would, considering that I had nothing except the pension of about a pound a day of our money which the King had granted me. I did not yet know of a more serious obstacle.

In the meantime, I may say that I had been presented at court, and was told that my reception had been considered as singularly gracious; indeed, I had several interviews both with the King and Queen, at which from time to time the Queen got everything from me that I had in the world, clothes and all, except the two buttons I had given to Yram, the loss of which seemed to annoy her a good deal. I was presented with a court suit, and her Majesty had my old clothes put upon a wooden dummy, on which they probably remain, unless they have been removed in consequence of my subsequent downfall. His Majesty's manners were those of a cultivated English gentleman. He was much pleased at hearing that our government was monarchical, and that the mass of the people were resolute that it should not be changed; indeed, I was so much encouraged by the evident pleasure with which he heard me, that I ventured to quote to him those beautiful lines of Shakespeare's—

> "There's a divinity doth hedge a king,
> Rough hew him how we may;"

but I was sorry I had done so afterwards, for I do not think his Majesty admired the lines as much as I could have wished.

There is no occasion for me to dwell further upon my experience of the court, but I ought perhaps to allude to one of my conversations with the King, inasmuch as it was pregnant with the most important consequences.

He had been asking me about my watch, and enquiring whether such dangerous inventions were tolerated in the country from which I came. I owned with some confusion that watches were not uncommon; but observing the gravity which came over his Majesty's face I presumed to say that they were fast dying out, and that we had few if any other mechanical contrivances of which he was likely to disapprove. Upon his asking me to name some of our most advanced machines, I did not dare to tell him of our steam-engines and railroads and electric telegraphs, and was puzzling my brains to think what I could say, when, of all things in the world, balloons suggested themselves, and I gave him an account of a very remarkable ascent which was made some years ago. The King was too polite to contradict, but I felt sure that he did not believe me, and from that day forward though he always showed me the attention which was due to my genius (for in this light was my complexion regarded), he never questioned me about the manners and customs of my country.

To return, however, to Arowhena. I soon gathered that neither Mr. nor Mrs. Nosnibor would have any objection to my marrying into the family; a physical excellence is considered in Erewhon as a set off against almost any other disqualification, and my light hair was sufficient to make me an eligible match. But along with this welcome fact I gathered another which filled me with dismay: I was expected to marry Zulora, for whom I had already conceived a great aversion.

At first I hardly noticed the little hints and the artifices which were resorted to in order to bring us together, but after a time they became too plain. Zulora, whether she was in love with me or not, was bent on marrying me, and I gathered in talking with a young gentleman of my acquaintance who frequently visited the house and whom I greatly disliked, that it was considered a sacred and inviolable rule that whoever married into a family must marry the eldest daughter at that time unmarried. The young gentleman urged this upon me so frequently that I at last saw he was in love with Arowhena himself, and wanted me to get Zulora out of the way; but others told me the same story as to the custom of the country, and I saw there was a serious difficulty. My only comfort was that Arowhena snubbed my rival and would not look at him. Neither would she look at me;

nevertheless there was a difference in the manner of her disregard; this was all I could get from her.

Not that she avoided me; on the contrary I had many a *tête-à-tête* with her, for her mother and sister were anxious for me to deposit some part of my pension in the Musical Banks, this being in accordance with the dictates of their goddess Ydgrun, of whom both Mrs. Nosnibor and Zulora were great devotees. I was not sure whether I had kept my secret from being perceived by Arowhena herself, but none of the others suspected me, so she was set upon me to get me to open an account, at any rate *pro formâ*, with the Musical Banks; and I need hardly say that she succeeded. But I did not yield at once; I enjoyed the process of being argued with too keenly to lose it by a prompt concession; besides, a little hesitation rendered the concession itself more valuable. It was in the course of conversations on this subject that I learned the more defined religious opinions of the Erewhonians, that coexist with the Musical Bank system, but are not recognised by those curious institutions. I will describe them as briefly as possible in the following chapters before I return to the personal adventures of Arowhena and myself.

They were idolaters, though of a comparatively enlightened kind; but here, as in other things, there was a discrepancy between their professed and actual belief, for they had a genuine and potent faith which existed without recognition alongside of their idol worship.

The gods whom they worship openly are personifications of human qualities, as justice, strength, hope, fear, love, &c., &c. The people think that prototypes of these have a real objective existence in a region far beyond the clouds, holding, as did the ancients, that they are like men and women both in body and passion, except that they are even comelier and more powerful, and also that they can render themselves invisible to human eyesight. They are capable of being propitiated by mankind and of coming to the assistance of those who ask their aid. Their interest in human affairs is keen, and on the whole beneficent; but they become very angry if neglected, and punish rather the first they come upon, than the actual person who has offended them; their fury being blind when it is raised, though never raised without reason. They will not punish with any less severity when people sin against them from ignorance, and without the chance of having had knowledge; they will take no excuses of this kind, but are even as the English law, which assumes itself to be known to every one.

Thus they have a law that two pieces of matter may not occupy the same space at the same moment, which law is presided over and administered by the gods of time and space jointly, so that if a flying stone and a man's head attempt to outrage these gods, by "arrogating a right which they do not possess" (for so it is written in one of their books), and to occupy the same space simultaneously, a severe punishment, sometimes even death itself, is sure to follow, without any regard to whether the stone knew that the man's head was there, or the head the stone; this at least is their view of the common accidents of life. Moreover, they hold their deities to be quite regardless of motives. With them it is the thing done which is everything, and the motive goes for nothing.

Thus they hold it strictly forbidden for a man to go without common air in his lungs for more than a very few minutes; and if by any chance he gets into the water, the air-god is very angry, and will not suffer it; no matter whether the man got into the water by accident or on purpose, whether through the attempt to save a child or through presumptuous contempt of the air-god, the air-god will kill him, unless he keeps his head high enough out of the water, and thus gives the air-god his due.

This with regard to the deities who manage physical affairs. Over and above these they personify hope, fear, love, and so forth, giving them temples and priests, and carving likenesses of them in stone, which they verily believe to be faithful representations of living beings who are only not human in being more than human. If any one denies the objective existence of these divinities, and says that there is really no such being as a beautiful woman called Justice, with her eyes blinded and a pair of scales, positively living and moving in a remote and ethereal region, but that justice is only the personified expression of certain modes of human thought and action—they say that he denies the existence of justice in denying her personality, and that he is a wanton disturber of men's religious convictions. They detest nothing so much as any attempt to lead them to higher spiritual conceptions of the deities whom they profess to worship. Arowhena and I had a pitched battle on this point, and should have had many more but for my prudence in allowing her to get the better of me.

I am sure that in her heart she was suspicious of her own position for she returned more than once to the subject. "Can you not see," I had exclaimed, "that the fact of justice being admirable will not be affected by the absence of a belief in her being also a living agent?

Can you really think that men will be one whit less hopeful, because they no longer believe that hope is an actual person?" She shook her head, and said that with men's belief in the personality all incentive to the reverence of the thing itself, as justice or hope, would cease; men from that hour would never be either just or hopeful again.

I could not move her, nor, indeed, did I seriously wish to do so. She deferred to me in most things, but she never shrank from maintaining her opinions if they were put in question; nor does she to this day abate one jot of her belief in the religion of her childhood, though in compliance with my repeated entreaties she has allowed herself to be baptized into the English Church. She has, however, made a gloss upon her original faith to the effect that her baby and I are the only human beings exempt from the vengeance of the deities for not believing in their personality. She is quite clear that we are exempted. She should never have so strong a conviction of it otherwise. How it has come about she does not know, neither does she wish to know; there are things which it is better not to know and this is one of them; but when I tell her that I believe in her deities as much as she does—and that it is a difference about words, not things, she becomes silent with a slight emphasis.

I own that she very nearly conquered me once; for she asked me what I should think if she were to tell me that my God, whose nature and attributes I had been explaining to her, was but the expression for man's highest conception of goodness, wisdom, and power; that in order to generate a more vivid conception of so great and glorious a thought, man had personified it and called it by a name; that it was an unworthy conception of the Deity to hold Him personal, inasmuch as escape from human contingencies became thus impossible; that the real thing men should worship was the Divine, whereinsoever they could find it; that "God" was but man's way of expressing his sense of the Divine; that as justice, hope, wisdom, &c., were all parts of goodness, so God was the expression which embraced all goodness and all good power; that people would no more cease to love God on ceasing to believe in His objective personality, than they had ceased to love justice on discovering that she was not really personal; nay, that they would never truly love Him till they saw Him thus.

She said all this in her artless way, and with none of the coherence with which I have here written it; her face kindled, and she felt sure that she had convinced me that I was wrong, and that justice was a living person. Indeed I did wince a little; but I recovered myself immediately, and pointed out to her that we had books whose genuineness was beyond all possibility of doubt, as they were certainly none of them less than 1800 years old; that in these there were the most authentic accounts of men who had been spoken to by the Deity Himself, and of one prophet who had been allowed to see the back parts of God through the hand that was laid over his face.

This was conclusive; and I spoke with such solemnity that she was a little frightened, and only answered that they too had their books, in which their ancestors had seen the gods; on which I saw that further argument was not at all likely to convince her; and fearing that she might tell her mother what I had been saying, and that I might lose the hold upon her affections which I was beginning to feel pretty sure that I was obtaining, I began to let her have her own way, and to convince me; neither till after we were safely married did I show the cloven hoof again.

Nevertheless, her remarks have haunted me, and I have since met with many very godly people who have had a great knowledge of divinity, but no sense of the divine: and again, I have seen a radiance upon the face of those who were worshipping the divine either in art or nature—in picture or statue—in field or cloud or sea—in man, woman, or child—which I have never seen kindled by any talking about the nature and attributes of God. Mention but the word divinity, and our sense of the divine is clouded.

CHAPTER XVII
YDGRUN AND THE YDGRUNITES

IN SPITE OF all the to-do they make about their idols, and the temples they build, and the priests and priestesses whom they support, I could never think that their professed religion was more than skin-deep; but they had another which they carried with them into all their actions; and although no one from the outside of things would suspect it to have any existence at all, it was in reality their great guide, the mariner's compass of their lives; so that there were very few things which they ever either did, or refrained from doing, without reference to its precepts.

Now I suspected that their professed faith had no great hold upon them—firstly, because I often heard the priests complain of the prevailing indifference, and they would hardly have done so without reason; secondly, because of the show which was made, for there was none of this about the worship of the goddess Ydgrun, in whom they really did believe; thirdly, because though the priests were constantly abusing Ydgrun as being the great enemy of the gods, it was well known that she had no more devoted worshippers in the whole country than these very persons, who were often priests of Ydgrun rather than of their own deities. Neither am I by any means sure that these were not the best of the priests.

Ydgrun certainly occupied a very anomalous position; she was held to be both omnipresent and omnipotent, but she was not an elevated conception, and was sometimes both cruel and absurd. Even her most devoted worshippers were a little ashamed of her, and served her more with heart and in deed than with their tongues. Theirs was no lip service; on the contrary, even when worshipping her most devoutly, they would often deny her. Take her all in all, however, she was a beneficent and useful deity, who did not care how much she was denied so long as she was obeyed and feared, and who kept hundreds of thousands in those paths which make life tolerably happy, who would never have been kept there otherwise, and over whom a higher and more spiritual ideal would have had no power.

I greatly doubt whether the Erewhonians are yet prepared for any better religion, and though (considering my gradually strengthened conviction that they were the representatives of the lost tribes of Israel) I would have set about converting them at all hazards had I seen the remotest prospect of success, I could hardly contemplate the displacement of Ydgrun as the great central object of their regard without admitting that it would be attended with frightful consequences; in fact were I a mere philosopher, I should say that the gradual raising of the popular conception of Ydgrun would be the greatest spiritual boon which could be conferred upon them, and that nothing could effect this except example. I generally found that those who complained most loudly that Ydgrun was not high enough for them had hardly as yet come up to the Ydgrun standard, and I often met with a class of men whom I called to myself "high Ydgrunites" (the rest being Ydgrunites, and low Ydgrunites), who, in the matter of human conduct and the affairs of life, appeared to me to have got about as far as it is in the right nature of man to go.

They were gentlemen in the full sense of the word; and what has one not said in saying this? They seldom spoke of Ydgrun, or even alluded to her, but would never run counter to her dictates without ample reason for doing so: in such cases they would override her with due self-reliance, and the goddess seldom punished them; for they are brave, and Ydgrun is not. They had most of them a smattering of the hypothetical language, and some few more than this, but only a few. I do not think that this language has had much hand in making them what they are; but rather that the fact of their being generally possessed of its rudiments was one great reason for the reverence paid to the hypothetical language itself.

Being inured from youth to exercises and athletics of all sorts, and living fearlessly under the eye of their peers, among whom there exists a high standard of courage, generosity, honour, and every good and manly quality—what wonder that they should have become, so to speak, a law unto themselves; and, while taking an elevated view of the goddess Ydgrun, they should have gradually lost all faith in the recognised deities of the country? These they do not openly disregard, for conformity until absolutely intolerable is a law of Ydgrun, yet they have no real belief in the objective existence of beings which so readily explain themselves as abstractions, and whose personality demands a quasi-materialism which it baffles the imagination to realise. They keep their opinions, however, greatly to themselves, inasmuch as most of their countrymen feel strongly about the gods, and they hold it wrong to give pain, unless for some greater good than seems likely to arise from their plain speaking.

On the other hand, surely those whose own minds are clear about any given matter (even though it be only that there is little certainty) should go so far towards imparting that clearness to others, as to say openly what they think and why they think it, whenever they can properly do so; for they may be sure that they owe their own clearness almost entirely to the fact that others have done this by them: after all, they may be mistaken, and if so, it is for their own and the general well-being that they should let their error be seen as distinctly as possible, so that it may be more easily refuted. I own, therefore, that on this one point I disapproved of the practice even of the highest Ydgrunites, and objected to it all the more because I knew that I should find my own future task more easy if the high Ydgrunites had already undermined the belief which is supposed to prevail at present.

In other respects they were more like the best class of Englishmen than any whom I have seen in other countries. I should have liked to have persuaded half-a-dozen of them to come over to England and go upon the stage, for they had most of them a keen sense of humour and a taste for acting: they would be of great use to us. The example of a real gentleman is, if I may say so without profanity, the best of all gospels; such a man upon the stage becomes a potent humanising influence, an Ideal which all may look upon for a shilling.

I always liked and admired these men, and although I could not help deeply regretting their certain ultimate perdition (for they had no sense of a hereafter, and their only religion was that of self-respect and consideration for other people), I never dared to take so great a liberty with them as to attempt to put them in possession of my own religious convictions, in spite of my knowing that they were the only ones which could make them really good and happy, either here or hereafter. I did try sometimes, being impelled to do so by a strong sense of duty, and by my deep regret that so much that was admirable should be doomed to ages if not eternity of torture; but the words stuck in my throat as soon as I began.

Whether a professional missionary might have a better chance I know not; such persons must doubtless know more about the science of conversion: for myself, I could only be thankful that I was in the right path, and was obliged to let others take their chance as yet. If the plan fails by which I propose to convert them myself, I would gladly contribute my mite towards the sending of two or three trained missionaries, who have been known as successful converters of Jews and Mohammedans; but such have seldom much to glory in the flesh, and when I think of the high Ydgrunites, and of the figure which a missionary would probably cut among them, I cannot feel sanguine that much good would be arrived at. Still the attempt is worth making, and the worst danger to the missionaries themselves would be that of being sent to the hospital where Chowbok would have been sent had he come with me into Erewhon.

Taking then their religious opinions as a whole, I must own that the Erewhonians are superstitious, on account of the views which they hold of their professed gods, and their entirely anomalous and inexplicable worship of Ydgrun, a worship at once the most powerful, yet most devoid of formalism, that I ever met with; but in practice things worked better than might have been expected, and the conflicting claims of Ydgrun and the gods were arranged by unwritten compromises (for the most part in Ydgrun's favour), which in ninety-nine cases out of a hundred were very well understood.

I could not conceive why they should not openly acknowledge high Ydgrunism, and discard the objective personality of hope, justice, &c.; but whenever I so much as hinted at this, I found that I

was on dangerous ground. They would never have it; returning
constantly to the assertion that ages ago the divinities were frequently
seen, and that the moment their personality was disbelieved in, men
would leave off practising even those ordinary virtues which the
common experience of mankind has agreed on as being the greatest
secret of happiness. "Who ever heard," they asked, indignantly, "of
such things as kindly training, a good example, and an enlightened
regard to one's own welfare, being able to keep men straight?" In
my hurry, forgetting things which I ought to have remembered, I
answered that if a person could not be kept straight by these things,
there was nothing that could straighten him, and that if he were not
ruled by the love and fear of men whom he had seen, neither would
he be so by that of the gods whom he had not seen.

At one time indeed I came upon a small but growing sect who
believed, after a fashion, in the immortality of the soul and the resur-
rection from the dead; they taught that those who had been born
with feeble and diseased bodies and had passed their lives in ailing,
would be tortured eternally hereafter; but that those who had been
born strong and healthy and handsome would be rewarded for ever
and ever. Of moral qualities or conduct they made no mention.

Bad as this was, it was a step in advance, inasmuch as they did hold
out a future state of some sort, and I was shocked to find that for the
most part they met with opposition, on the score that their doctrine
was based upon no sort of foundation, also that it was immoral in its
tendency, and not to be desired by any reasonable beings.

When I asked how it could be immoral, I was answered, that if
firmly held, it would lead people to cheapen this present life, making
it appear to be an affair of only secondary importance; that it would
thus distract men's minds from the perfecting of this world's economy,
and was an impatient cutting, so to speak, of the Gordian knot of
life's problems, whereby some people might gain present satisfaction
to themselves at the cost of infinite damage to others; that the doctrine
tended to encourage the poor in their improvidence, and in a debas-
ing acquiescence in ills which they might well remedy; that the
rewards were illusory and the result, after all, of luck, whose empire
should be bounded by the grave; that its terrors were enervating and
unjust; and that even the most blessed rising would be but the disturbing of a still more blessed slumber.

To all which I could only say that the thing had been actually
known to happen, and that there were several well-authenticated
instances of people having died and come to life again—instances
which no man in his senses could doubt.

"If this be so," said my opponent, "we must bear it as best we may."

I then translated for him, as well as I could, the noble speech of Hamlet in which he says that it is the fear lest worse evils may befall us after death which alone prevents us from rushing into death's arms.

"Nonsense," he answered, "no man was ever yet stopped from cutting his throat by any such fears as your poet ascribes to him—and your poet probably knew this perfectly well. If a man cuts his throat he is at bay, and thinks of nothing but escape, no matter whither, provided he can shuffle off his present. No. Men are kept at their posts, not by the fear that if they quit them they may quit a frying-pan for a fire, but by the hope that if they hold on, the fire may burn less fiercely. 'The respect,' to quote your poet, 'that makes calamity of so long a life,' is the consideration that though calamity may live long, the sufferer may live longer still."

On this, seeing that there was little probability of our coming to an agreement, I let the argument drop, and my opponent presently left me with as much disapprobation as he could show without being overtly rude.

CHAPTER XVIII
BIRTH FORMULÆ

I HEARD WHAT follows not from Arowhena, but from Mr. Nosnibor and some of the gentlemen who occasionally dined at the house: they told me that the Erewhonians believe in pre-existence; and not only this (of which I will write more fully in the next chapter), but they believe that it is of their own free act and deed in a previous state that they come to be born into this world at all. They hold that the unborn are perpetually plaguing and tormenting the married of both sexes, fluttering about them incessantly, and giving them no peace either of mind or body until they have consented to take them under their protection. If this were not so (this at least is what they urge), it would be a monstrous freedom for one man to take with another, to say that he should undergo the chances and changes of this mortal life without any option in the matter. No man would have any right to get married at all, inasmuch as he can never tell what frightful misery his doing so may entail forcibly upon a being who cannot be unhappy as long as he does not exist. They feel this so strongly that they are resolved to shift the blame on to other shoulders; and have fashioned a long mythology as to the world in which the unborn people live, and what they do, and the arts and machinations to which they have recourse in order to get themselves into our own world. But of this more anon: what I would relate here is their manner of dealing with those who do come.

It is a distinguishing peculiarity of the Erewhonians that when they profess themselves to be quite certain about any matter, and avow it as a base on which they are to build a system of practice, they seldom quite believe in it. If they smell a rat about the precincts of a cherished institution, they will always stop their noses to it if they can.

This is what most of them did in this matter of the unborn, for I cannot (and never could) think that they seriously believed in their mythology concerning pre-existence: they did and they did not; they did not know themselves what they believed; all they did know was that it was a disease not to believe as they did. The only thing of which they were quite sure was that it was the pestering of the unborn which caused them to be brought into this world, and that they would not have been here if they would have only let peaceable people alone.

It would be hard to disprove this position, and they might have a good case if they would only leave it as it stands. But this they will not do; they must have assurance doubly sure; they must have the written word of the child itself as soon as it is born, giving the parents indemnity from all responsibility on the score of its birth, and asserting its own pre-existence. They have therefore devised something which they call a birth formula—a document which varies in words according to the caution of parents, but is much the same practically in all cases; for it has been the business of the Erewhonian lawyers during many ages to exercise their skill in perfecting it and providing for every contingency.

These formulæ are printed on common paper at a moderate cost for the poor; but the rich have them written on parchment and handsomely bound, so that the getting up of a person's birth formula is a test of his social position. They commence by setting forth, That whereas A. B. was a member of the kingdom of the unborn, where he was well provided for in every way, and had no cause of discontent, &c., &c., he did of his own wanton depravity and restlessness conceive a desire to enter into this present world; that thereon having taken the necessary steps as set forth in laws of the unborn kingdom, he did with malice aforethought set himself to plague and pester two unfortunate people who had never wronged him, and who were quite contented and happy until he conceived this base design against their peace; for which wrong he now humbly entreats their pardon.

He acknowledges that he is responsible for all physical blemishes and deficiencies which may render him answerable to the laws of his country; that his parents have nothing whatever to do with any of these things; and that they have a right to kill him at once if they be so minded, though he entreats them to show their marvellous goodness and clemency by sparing his life. If they will do this, he promises to be their most obedient and abject creature during his earlier years, and indeed all his life, unless they should see fit in their abundant generosity to remit some portion of his service hereafter. And so the formula continues, going sometimes into very minute details, according to the fancies of family lawyers, who will not make it any shorter than they can help.

The deed being thus prepared, on the third or fourth day after the birth of the child, or as they call it, the "final importunity," the friends gather together, and there is a feast held, where they are all very melancholy—as a general rule, I believe, quite truly so—and make presents to the father and mother of the child in order to console them for the injury which has just been done them by the unborn.

By-and-by the child himself is brought down by his nurse, and the company begin to rail upon him, upbraiding him for his impertinence, and asking him what amends he proposes to make for the wrong that he has committed, and how he can look for care and nourishment from those who have perhaps already been injured by the unborn on some ten or twelve occasions; for they say of people with large families, that they have suffered terrible injuries from the unborn; till at last, when this has been carried far enough, some one suggests the formula, which is brought out and solemnly read to the child by the family straightener. This gentleman is always invited on these occasions, for the very fact of intrusion into a peaceful family shows a depravity on the part of the child which requires his professional services.

On being teased by the reading and tweaked by the nurse, the child will commonly begin to cry, which is reckoned a good sign, as showing a consciousness of guilt. He is thereon asked, Does he assent to the formula? on which, as he still continues crying and can obviously make no answer, some one of the friends comes forward and undertakes to sign the document on his behalf, feeling sure (so he says) that the child would do it if he only knew how, and that he will release the present signer from his engagement on arriving at maturity. The friend then inscribes the signature of the child at the foot of the parchment, which is held to bind the child as much as though he had signed it himself.

Even this, however, does not fully content them, for they feel a little uneasy until they have got the child's own signature after all. So when he is about fourteen, these good people partly bribe him by promises of greater liberty and good things, and partly intimidate him through their great power of making themselves actively unpleasant to him, so that though there is a show of freedom made, there is really none; they also use the offices of the teachers in the Colleges of Unreason, till at last, in one way or another, they take very good care that he shall sign the paper by which he professes to have been a free agent in coming into the world, and to take all the responsibility of having done so on to his own shoulders. And yet, though this document is obviously the most important which any one can sign in his whole life, they will have him do so at an age when neither they nor the law will for many a year allow any one else to bind him to the smallest obligation, no matter how righteously he may owe it, because they hold him too young to know what he is about, and do not consider it fair that he should commit himself to anything that may prejudice him in after years.

I own that all this seemed rather hard, and not of a piece with the many admirable institutions existing among them. I once ventured to say a part of what I thought about it to one of the Professors of Unreason. I did it very tenderly, but his justification of the system was quite out of my comprehension. I remember asking him whether he did not think it would do harm to a lad's principles, by weakening his sense of the sanctity of his word and of truth generally, that he should be led into entering upon a solemn declaration as to the truth of things about which all that he can certainly know is that he knows nothing—whether, in fact, the teachers who so led him, or who taught anything as a certainty of which they were themselves uncertain, were not earning their living by impairing the truth-sense of their pupils (a delicate organisation mostly), and by vitiating one of their most sacred instincts.

The Professor, who was a delightful person, seemed greatly surprised at the view which I took, but it had no influence with him whatsoever. No one, he answered, expected that the boy either would or could know all that he said he knew; but the world was full of compromises; and there was hardly any affirmation which would bear being interpreted literally. Human language was too gross a vehicle of thought—thought being incapable of absolute translation. He added, that as there can be no translation from one language into another which shall not scant the meaning somewhat, or enlarge upon it, so there is no language which can render thought without a jarring and a harshness somewhere—and so forth; all of which seemed to come to this in the end, that it was the custom of the country, and that the Erewhonians were a conservative people; that the boy would have to begin compromising sooner or later, and this was part of his education in the art. It was perhaps to be regretted that compromise should be as necessary as it was; still it was necessary, and the sooner the boy got to understand it the better for himself. But they never tell this to the boy.

From the book of their mythology about the unborn I made the extracts which will form the following chapter.

CHAPTER XIX
THE WORLD OF THE UNBORN

THE EREWHONIANS SAY that we are drawn through life backwards; or again, that we go onwards into the future as into a dark corridor. Time walks beside us and flings back shutters as we advance; but the light thus given often dazzles us, and deepens the darkness which is in front. We can see but little at a time, and heed that little far less than our apprehension of what we shall see next; ever peering curiously through the glare of the present into the gloom of the future, we presage the leading lines of that which is before us, by faintly reflected lights from dull mirrors that are behind, and stumble on as we may till the trapdoor opens beneath us and we are gone.

They say at other times that the future and the past are as a panorama upon two rollers; that which is on the roller of the future unwraps itself on to the roller of the past; we cannot hasten it, and we may not stay it; we must see all that is unfolded to us whether it be good or ill; and what we have seen once we may see again no more. It is ever unwinding and being wound; we catch it in transition for a moment, and call it present; our flustered senses gather what impression they can, and we guess at what is coming by the tenor of that which we have seen. The same hand has painted the whole picture, and the incidents vary little—rivers, woods, plains, mountains, towns and peoples, love, sorrow, and death: yet the interest never flags, and we look hopefully for some good fortune, or fearfully lest our own faces be shown us as figuring in something terrible. When the scene is past we think we know it, though there is so much to see, and so little time to see it, that our conceit of knowledge as regards the past is for the most part poorly founded; neither do we care about it greatly, save in so far as it may affect the future, wherein our interest mainly lies.

The Erewhonians say it was by chance only that the earth and stars and all the heavenly worlds began to roll from east to west, and not from west to east, and in like manner they say it is by chance that man is drawn through life with his face to the past instead of to the future. For the future is there as much as the past, only that we may not see it. Is it not in the loins of the past, and must not the past alter before the future can do so?

Sometimes, again, they say that there was a race of men tried upon the earth once, who knew the future better than the past, but that they died in a twelvemonth from the misery which their knowledge caused them; and if any were to be born too prescient now, he would be culled out by natural selection, before he had time to transmit so peace-destroying a faculty to his descendants.

Strange fate for man! He must perish if he get that, which he must perish if he strive not after. If he strive not after it he is no better than the brutes, if he get it he is more miserable than the devils.

Having waded through many chapters like the above, I came at last to the unborn themselves, and found that they were held to be souls pure and simple, having no actual bodies, but living in a sort of gaseous yet more or less anthropomorphic existence, like that of a ghost; they have thus neither flesh nor blood nor warmth. Nevertheless they are supposed to have local habitations and cities wherein they dwell, though these are as unsubstantial as their inhabitants; they are even thought to eat and drink some thin ambrosial sustenance, and generally to be capable of doing whatever mankind can do, only after a visionary ghostly fashion as in a dream. On the other hand, as long as they remain where they are they never die

—the only form of death in the unborn world being the leaving it for our own. They are believed to be extremely numerous, far more so than mankind. They arrive from unknown planets, full grown, in large batches at a time; but they can only leave the unborn world by taking the steps necessary for their arrival here—which is, in fact, by suicide.

They ought to be an exceedingly happy people, for they have no extremes of good or ill fortune; never marrying, but living in a state much like that fabled by the poets as the primitive condition of mankind. In spite of this, however, they are incessantly complaining; they know that we in this world have bodies, and indeed they know everything else about us, for they move among us whithersoever they will, and can read our thoughts, as well as survey our actions at pleasure. One would think that this should be enough for them; and most of them are indeed alive to the desperate risk which they will run by indulging themselves in that body with "sensible warm motion" which they so much desire; nevertheless, there are some to whom the *ennui* of a disembodied existence is so intolerable that they will venture anything for a change; so they resolve to quit. The conditions which they must accept are so uncertain, that none but the most foolish of the unborn will consent to them; and it is from these, and these only, that our own ranks are recruited.

When they have finally made up their minds to leave, they must go before the magistrate of the nearest town, and sign an affidavit of their desire to quit their then existence. On their having done this, the magistrate reads them the conditions which they must accept, and which are so long that I can only extract some of the principal points, which are mainly the following:—

First, they must take a potion which will destroy their memory and sense of identity; they must go into the world helpless, and without a will of their own; they must draw lots for their dispositions before they go, and take them, such as they are, for better or worse— neither are they to be allowed any choice in the matter of the body which they so much desire; they are simply allotted by chance, and without appeal, to two people whom it is their business to find and pester until they adopt them. Who these are to be, whether rich or poor, kind or unkind, healthy or diseased, there is no knowing; they have, in fact, to entrust themselves for many years to the care of those for whose good constitution and good sense they have no sort of guarantee.

It is curious to read the lectures which the wiser heads give to those who are meditating a change. They talk with them as we talk with a spendthrift, and with about as much success.

"To be born," they say, "is a felony—it is a capital crime, for which sentence may be executed at any moment after the commission of the offence. You may perhaps happen to live for some seventy or eighty years, but what is that, compared with the eternity you now enjoy? And even though the sentence were commuted, and you were allowed to live on for ever, you would in time become so terribly weary of life that execution would be the greatest mercy to you.

"Consider the infinite risk; to be born of wicked parents and trained in vice! to be born of silly parents, and trained to unrealities! of parents who regard you as a sort of chattel or property, belonging more to them than to yourself! Again, you may draw utterly unsympathetic parents, who will never be able to understand you, and who will do their best to thwart you (as a hen when she has hatched a duckling), and then call you ungrateful because you do not love them; or, again, you may draw parents who look upon you as a thing to be cowed while it is still young, lest it should give them trouble hereafter by having wishes and feelings of its own.

"In later life, when you have been finally allowed to pass muster as a full member of the world, you will yourself become liable to the pesterings of the unborn—and a very happy life you may be led in consequence! For we solicit so strongly that a few only—nor these the best—can refuse us; and yet not to refuse is much the same as going into partnership with half-a-dozen different people about whom one can know absolutely nothing beforehand—not even whether one is going into partnership with men or women, nor with how many of either. Delude not yourself with thinking that you will be wiser than your parents. You may be an age in advance of those whom you have pestered, but unless you are one of the great ones you will still be an age behind those who will in their turn pester you.

"Imagine what it must be to have an unborn quartered upon you, who is of an entirely different temperament and disposition to your own; nay, half-a-dozen such, who will not love you though you have stinted yourself in a thousand ways to provide for their comfort and well-being,—who will forget all your self-sacrifice, and of whom you may never be sure that they are not bearing a grudge against you for errors of judgement into which you may have fallen, though you had hoped that such had been long since atoned for. Ingratitude such as this is not uncommon, yet fancy what it must be to bear! It is hard upon the duckling to have been hatched by a hen, but is it not also hard upon the hen to have hatched the duckling?

"Consider it again, we pray you, not for our sake but for your own. Your initial character you must draw by lot; but whatever it is, it can only come to a tolerably successful development after long training; remember that over that training you will have no control. It is possible, and even probable, that whatever you may get in after life which is of real pleasure and service to you, will have to be won in spite of, rather than by the help of, those whom you are now about to pester, and that you will only win your freedom after years of a painful struggle in which it will be hard to say whether you have suffered most injury, or inflicted it.

"Remember also, that if you go into the world you will have free will; that you will be obliged to have it; that there is no escaping it; that you will be fettered to it during your whole life, and must on every occasion do that which on the whole seems best to you at any given time, no matter whether you are right or wrong in choosing it. Your mind will be a balance for considerations, and your action will go with the heavier scale. How it shall fall will depend upon the kind of scales which you may have drawn at birth, the bias which they will have obtained by use, and the weight of the immediate considerations. If the scales were good to start with, and if they have not been outrageously tampered with in childhood, and if the combinations into which you enter are average ones, you may come off well; but there are too many 'ifs' in this, and with the failure of any one of them your misery is assured. Reflect on this, and remember that should the ill come upon you, you will have yourself to thank, for it is your own choice to be born, and there is no compulsion in the matter.

"Not that we deny the existence of pleasures among mankind; there is a certain show of sundry phases of contentment which may even amount to very considerable happiness; but mark how they are distributed over a man's life, belonging, all the keenest of them, to the fore part, and few indeed to the after. Can there be any pleasure worth purchasing with the miseries of a decrepit age? If you are good, strong, and handsome, you have a fine fortune indeed at twenty, but how much of it will be left at sixty? For you must live on your capital; there is no investing your powers so that you may get a small annuity of life for ever: you must eat up your principal bit by bit, and be tortured by seeing it grow continually smaller and smaller, even though you happen to escape being rudely robbed of it by crime or casualty.

"Remember, too, that there never yet was a man of forty who would not come back into the world of the unborn if he could do so with decency and honour. Being in the world he will as a general rule stay till he is forced to go; but do you think that he would consent to be born again, and re-live his life, if he had the offer of doing so? Do not think it. If he could so alter the past as that he should never have come into being at all, do you not think that he would do it very gladly?

"What was it that one of their own poets meant, if it was not this, when he cried out upon the day in which he was born, and the night in which it was said there is a man child conceived? 'For now,' he says, 'I should have lain still and been quiet, I should have slept; then had I been at rest with kings and counsellors of the earth, which built desolate palaces for themselves; or with princes that had gold, who filled their houses with silver; or as an hidden untimely birth, I had not been; as infants which never saw light. There the wicked cease from troubling, and the weary are at rest.' Be very sure that the guilt of being born carries this punishment at times to all men; but how can they ask for pity, or complain of any mischief that may befall them, having entered open-eyed into the snare?

"One word more and we have done. If any faint remembrance, as of a dream, flit in some puzzled moment across your brain, and you shall feel that the potion which is to be given you shall not have done its work, and the memory of this existence which you are leaving endeavours vainly to return; we say in such a moment, when you clutch at the dream but it eludes your grasp, and you watch it, as Orpheus watched Eurydice, gliding back again into the twilight kingdom, fly—fly—if you can remember the advice—to the haven of your present and immediate duty, taking shelter incessantly in the work which you have in hand. This much you may perhaps recall; and this, if you will imprint it deeply upon your every faculty, will be most likely to bring you safely and honourably home through the trials that are before you.'"*

This is the fashion in which they reason with those who would be for leaving them, but it is seldom that they do much good, for

---

* The myth above alluded to exists in Erewhon with changed names, and considerable modifications. I have taken the liberty of referring to the story as familiar to ourselves.

none but the unquiet and unreasonable ever think of being born, and those who are foolish enough to think of it are generally foolish enough to do it. Finding, therefore, that they can do no more, the friends follow weeping to the courthouse of the chief magistrate, where the one who wishes to be born declares solemnly and openly that he accepts the conditions attached to his decision. On this he is presented with a potion, which immediately destroys his memory and sense of identity, and dissipates the thin gaseous tenement which he has inhabited: he becomes a bare vital principle, not to be perceived by human senses, nor to be by any chemical test appreciated. He has but one instinct, which is that he is to go to such and such a place, where he will find two persons whom he is to importune till they consent to undertake him; but whether he is to find these persons among the race of Chowbok or the Erewhonians themselves is not for him to choose.

CHAPTER XX

WHAT THEY MEAN BY IT

I HAVE GIVEN the above mythology at some length, but it is only a small part of what they have upon the subject. My first feeling on reading it was that any amount of folly on the part of the unborn in coming here was justified by a desire to escape from such intolerable prosing. The mythology is obviously an unfair and exaggerated representation of life and things; and had its authors been so minded they could have easily drawn a picture which would err as much on the bright side as this does on the dark. No Erewhonian believes that the world is as black as it has been here painted, but it is one of their peculiarities that they very often do not believe or mean things which they profess to regard as indisputable.

In the present instance their professed views concerning the unborn have arisen from their desire to prove that people have been presented with the gloomiest possible picture of their own prospects before they came here; otherwise, they could hardly say to one whom they are going to punish for an affection of the heart or brain that it is all his own doing. In practice they modify their theory to a considerable extent, and seldom refer to the birth formula except in extreme cases;

for the force of habit, or what not, gives many of them a kindly interest even in creatures who have so much wronged them as the unborn have done; and though a man generally hates the unwelcome little stranger for the first twelve months, he is apt to mollify (according to his lights) as time goes on, and sometimes he will become inordinately attached to the beings whom he is pleased to call his children.

Of course, according to Erewhonian premises, it would serve people right to be punished and scouted for moral and intellectual diseases as much as for physical, and I cannot to this day understand why they should have stopped short half way. Neither, again, can I understand why their having done so should have been, as it certainly was, a matter of so much concern to myself. What could it matter to me how many absurdities the Erewhonians might adopt? Nevertheless I longed to make them think as I did, for the wish to spread those opinions that we hold conducive to our own welfare is so deeply rooted in the English character that few of us can escape its influence. But let this pass.

In spite of not a few modifications in practice of a theory which is itself revolting, the relations between children and parents in that country are less happy than in Europe. It was rarely that I saw cases of real hearty and intense affection between the old people and the young ones. Here and there I did so, and was quite sure that the children, even at the age of twenty, were fonder of their parents than they were of any one else; and that of their own inclination, being free to choose what company they would, they would often choose that of their father and mother. The straightener's carriage was rarely seen at the door of those houses. I saw two or three such cases during the time that I remained in the country, and cannot express the pleasure which I derived from a sight suggestive of so much goodness and wisdom and forbearance, so richly rewarded; yet I firmly believe that the same thing would happen in nine families out of ten if the parents were merely to remember how they felt when they were young, and actually to behave towards their children as they would have had their own parents behave towards themselves. But this, which would appear to be so simple and obvious, seems also to be a thing which not one in a hundred thousand is able to put in practice. It is only the very great and good who have any living faith in the simplest axioms; and there are few who are so holy as to feel that 19 and 13 make 32 as certainly as 2 and 2 make 4.

I am quite sure that if this narrative should ever fall into Erewhonian hands, it will be said that what I have written about the relations between parents and children being seldom satisfactory is an infamous perversion of facts, and that in truth there are few young people who do not feel happier in the society of their nearest relations* than in any other. Mr. Nosnibor would be sure to say this. Yet I cannot refrain from expressing an opinion that he would be a good deal embarrassed if his deceased parents were to reappear and propose to pay him a six months' visit. I doubt whether there are many things which he would regard as a greater infliction. They had died at a ripe old age some twenty years before I came to know him, so the case is an extreme one; but surely if they had treated him with what in his youth he had felt to be true unselfishness, his face would brighten when he thought of them to the end of his life.

In the one or two cases of true family affection which I met with, I am sure that the young people who were so genuinely fond of their fathers and mothers at eighteen, would at sixty be perfectly delighted were they to get the chance of welcoming them as their guests. There is nothing which could please them better, except perhaps to watch the happiness of their own children and grandchildren.

This is how things should be. It is not an impossible ideal; it is one which actually does exist in some few cases, and might exist in almost all, with a little more patience and forbearance upon the parents' part; but it is rare at present—so rare that they have a proverb which I can only translate in a very roundabout way, but which says that the great happiness of some people in a future state will consist in watching the distress of their parents on returning to eternal companionship with their grandfathers and grandmothers; whilst "compulsory affection" is the idea which lies at the root of their word for the deepest anguish.

There is no talisman in the word "parent" which can generate miracles of affection, and I can well believe that my own child might find it less of a calamity to lose both Arowhena and myself when he is six years old, than to find us again when he is sixty—a sentence which I would not pen did I not feel that by doing so I was giving him something like a hostage, or at any rate putting a weapon into his hands against me, should my selfishness exceed reasonable limits.

---

* What a *safe* word 'relation' is; how little it predicates! yet it has overgrown 'kinsman.'

Money is at the bottom of all this to a great extent. If the parents would put their children in the way of earning a competence earlier than they do, the children would soon become self-supporting and independent. As it is, under the present system, the young ones get old enough to have all manner of legitimate wants (that is, if they have any "go" about them) before they have learnt the means of earning money to pay for them; hence they must either do without them, or take more money than the parents can be expected to spare. This is due chiefly to the schools of Unreason, where a boy is taught upon hypothetical principles, as I will explain hereafter; spending years in being incapacitated for doing this, that, or the other (he hardly knows what), during all which time he ought to have been actually doing the thing itself, beginning at the lowest grades, picking it up through actual practice, and rising according to the energy which is in him.

These schools of Unreason surprised me much. It would be easy to fall into pseudo-utilitarianism, and I would fain believe that the system may be good for the children of very rich parents, or for those who show a natural instinct to acquire hypothetical lore; but the misery was that their Ydgrun-worship required all people with any pretence to respectability to send their children to some one or other of these schools, mulcting them of years of money. It astonished me to see what sacrifices the parents would make in order to render their children as nearly useless as possible; and it was hard to say whether the old suffered most from the expense which they were thus put to, or the young from being deliberately swindled in some of the most important branches of human inquiry, and directed into false channels or left to drift in the great majority of cases.

I cannot think I am mistaken in believing that the growing tendency to limit families by infanticide—an evil which was causing general alarm throughout the country—was almost entirely due to the way in which education had become a fetish from one end of Erewhon to the other. Granted that provision should be made whereby every child should be taught reading, writing, and arithmetic, but here compulsory state-aided education should end, and the child should begin (with all due precautions to ensure that he is not over-worked) to acquire the rudiments of that art whereby he is to earn his living.

He cannot acquire these in what we in England call schools of technical education; such schools are cloister life as against the rough and tumble of the world; they unfit, rather than fit for work in the open. An art can only be learned in the workshop of those who are winning their bread by it.

Boys, as a rule, hate the artificial, and delight in the actual; give them the chance of earning, and they will soon earn. When parents find that their children, instead of being made artificially burdensome, will early begin to contribute to the well-being of the family, they will soon leave off killing them, and will seek to have that plenitude of offspring which they now avoid. As things are, the state lays greater burdens on parents than flesh and blood can bear, and then wrings its hands over an evil for which it is itself mainly responsible.

With the less well-dressed classes the harm was not so great; for among these, at about ten years old, the child has to begin doing something: if he is capable he makes his way up; if he is not, he is at any rate not made more incapable by what his friends are pleased to call his education. People find their level as a rule; and though they unfortunately sometimes miss it, it is in the main true that those who have valuable qualities are perceived to have them and can sell them. I think that the Erewhonians are beginning to become aware of these things, for there was much talk about putting a tax upon all parents whose children were not earning a competence according to their degrees by the time they were twenty years old. I am sure that if they will have the courage to carry it through they will never regret it; for the parents will take care that the children shall begin earning money (which means "doing good" to society) at an early age; then the children will be independent early, and they will not press on the parents, nor the parents on them, and they will like each other better than they do now.

This is the true philanthropy. He who makes a colossal fortune in the hosiery trade, and by his energy has succeeded in reducing the price of woollen goods by the thousandth part of a penny in the pound—this man is worth ten professional philanthropists. So strongly are the Erewhonians impressed with this, that if a man has made a fortune of over £20,000 a year they exempt him from all taxation, considering him as a work of art, and too precious to be meddled with; they say, "How very much he must have done for society before society could have been prevailed upon to give him so much money"; so magnificent an organisation overawes them; they regard it as a thing dropped from heaven.

"Money," they say, "is the symbol of duty, it is the sacrament of having done for mankind that which mankind wanted. Mankind may not be a very good judge, but there is no better." This used to shock me at first, when I remembered that it had been said on high authority that they who have riches shall enter hardly into the kingdom of heaven; but the influence of Erewhon had made me begin to see things in a new light, and I could not help thinking that they who have not riches shall enter more hardly still.

People oppose money to culture, and imply that if a man has spent his time in making money he will not be cultivated—fallacy of fallacies! As though there could be a greater aid to culture than the having earned an honourable independence, and as though any amount of culture will do much for the man who is penniless, except make him feel his position more deeply. The young man who was told to sell all his goods and give to the poor, must have been an entirely exceptional person if the advice was given wisely, either for him or for the poor; how much more often does it happen that we perceive a man to have all sorts of good qualities except money, and feel that his real duty lies in getting every half-penny that he can persuade others to pay him for his services, and becoming rich. It has been said that the love of money is the root of all evil. The want of money is so quite as truly.

The above may sound irreverent, but it is conceived in a spirit of the most utter reverence for those things which do alone deserve it—that is, for the things which are, which mould us and fashion us, be they what they may; for the things that have power to punish us, and which will punish us if we do not heed them; for our masters therefore. But I am drifting away from my story.

They have another plan about which they are making a great noise and fuss, much as some are doing with women's rights in England. A party of extreme radicals have professed themselves unable to decide upon the superiority of age or youth. At present all goes on the supposition that it is desirable to make the young old as soon as possible. Some would have it that this is wrong, and that the object of education should be to keep the old young as long as possible. They say that each age should take it turn in turn about, week by week, one week the old to be topsawyers, and the other the young, drawing the line at thirty-five years of age; but they insist that the young should be allowed to inflict corporal chastisement on the old, without which the old would be quite incorrigible. In any European country this would be out of the question; but it is not so there, for the straighteners are constantly ordering people to be flogged, so that they are familiar with the notion. I do not suppose that the idea will be ever acted upon; but its having been even mooted is enough to show the utter perversion of the Erewhonian mind.

CHAPTER XXI

THE COLLEGES OF UNREASON

I HAD NOW been a visitor with the Nosnibors for some five or six months, and though I had frequently proposed to leave them and take apartments of my own, they would not hear of my doing so. I suppose they thought I should be more likely to fall in love with Zulora if I remained, but it was my affection for Arowhena that kept me.

During all this time both Arowhena and myself had been dreaming, and drifting towards an avowed attachment, but had not dared to face the real difficulties of the position. Gradually, however, matters came to a crisis in spite of ourselves, and we got to see the true state of the case, all too clearly.

One evening we were sitting in the garden, and I had been trying in every stupid roundabout way to get her to say that she should be at any rate sorry for a man, if he really loved a woman who would not marry him. I had been stammering and blushing, and been as silly as any one could be, and I suppose had pained her by fishing for pity for myself in such a transparent way, and saying nothing about her own need of it; at any rate, she turned all upon me with a sweet sad smile and said, "Sorry? I am sorry for myself; I am sorry for you; and I am sorry for every one." The words had no sooner crossed her lips than she bowed her head, gave me a look as though I were to make no answer, and left me.

The words were few and simple, but the manner with which they were uttered was ineffable: the scales fell from my eyes, and I felt that I had no right to try and induce her to infringe one of the most inviolable customs of her country, as she needs must do if she were to marry me. I sat for a long while thinking, and when I remembered the sin and shame and misery which an unrighteous marriage—for as such it would be held in Erewhon—would entail, I became thoroughly ashamed of myself for having been so long self-blinded. I write coldly now, but I suffered keenly at the time, and should probably retain a much more vivid recollection of what I felt, had not all ended so happily.

As for giving up the idea of marrying Arowhena, it never so much as entered my head to do so: the solution must be found in some other direction than this. The idea of waiting till somebody married Zulora was to be no less summarily dismissed. To marry Arowhena at once in Erewhon—this had already been abandoned: there remained therefore but one alternative, and that was to run away with her, and get her with me to Europe, where there would be no bar to our union save my own impecuniosity, a matter which gave me no uneasiness.

To this obvious and simple plan I could see but two objections that deserved the name,—the first, that perhaps Arowhena would not come; the second, that it was almost impossible for me to escape even alone, for the king had himself told me that I was to consider myself a prisoner on parole, and that the first sign of my endeavouring to escape would cause me to be sent to one of the hospitals for incurables. Besides, I did not know the geography of the country, and even were I to try and find my way back, I should be discovered long before I had reached the pass over which I had come. How then could I hope to be able to take Arowhena with me? For days and days I turned these difficulties over in my mind, and at last hit upon as wild a plan as was ever suggested by extremity. This was to meet the second difficulty: the first gave me less uneasiness, for when Arowhena and I next met after our interview in the garden I could see that she had suffered not less acutely than myself.

I resolved that I would have another interview with her—the last for the present—that I would then leave her, and set to work upon maturing my plan as fast as possible. We got a chance of being alone together, and then I gave myself the loose rein, and told her how passionately and devotedly I loved her. She said little in return, but her tears (which I could not refrain from answering with my own) and the little she did say were quite enough to show me that I should meet with no obstacle from her. Then I asked her whether she would run a terrible risk which we should share in common, if, in case of success, I could take her to my own people, to the home of my mother and sisters, who would welcome her very gladly. At the same time I pointed out that the chances of failure were far greater than those of success, and that the probability was that even though I could get so far as to carry my design into execution, it would end in death to us both.

I was not mistaken in her; she said that she believed I loved her as much as she loved me, and that she would brave anything if I could only assure her that what I proposed would not be thought dishonourable in England; she could not live without me, and would rather die with me than alone; that death was perhaps the best for us both; that I must plan, and that when the hour came I was to send for her, and trust her not to fail me; and so after many tears and embraces, we tore ourselves away.

I then left the Nosnibors, took a lodging in the town, and became melancholy to my heart's content. Arowhena and I used to see each other sometimes, for I had taken to going regularly to the Musical Banks, but Mrs. Nosnibor and Zulora both treated me with considerable coldness. I felt sure that they suspected me. Arowhena looked miserable, and I saw that her purse was now always as full as she could fill it with the Musical Bank money—much fuller than of old. Then the horrible thought occurred to me that her health might break down, and that she might be subjected to a criminal prosecution. Oh! how I hated Erewhon at that time.

I was still received at court, but my good looks were beginning to fail me, and I was not such an adept at concealing the effects of pain as the Erewhonians are. I could see that my friends began to look concerned about me, and was obliged to take a leaf out of Mahaina's book, and pretend to have developed a taste for drinking. I even consulted a straightener as though this were so, and submitted to much discomfort. This made matters better for a time, but I could see that my friends thought less highly of my constitution as my flesh began to fall away.

I was told that the poor made an outcry about my pension, and I saw a stinging article in an anti-ministerial paper, in which the writer went so far as to say that my having light hair reflected little credit upon me, inasmuch as I had been reported to have said that it was a common thing in the country from which I came. I have reason to believe that Mr. Nosnibor himself inspired this article. Presently it came round to me that the king had begun to dwell upon my having been possessed of a watch, and to say that I ought to be treated medicinally for having told him a lie about the balloons. I saw misfortune gathering round me in every direction, and felt that I should have need of all my wits and a good many more, if I was to steer myself and Arowhena to a good conclusion.

There were some who continued to show me kindness, and strange to say, I received the most from the very persons from whom I should have least expected it—I mean from the cashiers of the Musical Banks. I had made the acquaintance of several of these persons, and now that I frequented their bank, they were inclined to make a good deal of me. One of them, seeing that I was thoroughly out of health, though of course he pretended not to notice it, suggested that I should take a little change of air and go down with him to one of the principal towns, which was some two or three days' journey from the metropolis, and the chief seat of the Colleges of Unreason; he assured me that I should be delighted, with what I saw, and that I should receive a most hospitable welcome. I determined therefore to accept the invitation.

We started two or three days later, and after a night on the road, we arrived at our destination towards evening. It was now full spring, and as nearly as might be ten months since I had started with Chowbok on my expedition, but it seemed more like ten years. The trees were in their freshest beauty, and the air had become warm without being oppressively hot. After having lived so many months in the metropolis, the sight of the country, and the country villages through which we passed refreshed me greatly, but I could not forget my troubles. The last five miles or so were the most beautiful part of the journey, for the country became more undulating, and the woods were more extensive; but the first sight of the city of the colleges itself was the most delightful of all. I cannot imagine that there can be any fairer in the whole world, and I expressed my pleasure to my companion, and thanked him for having brought me.

We drove to an inn in the middle of the town, and then, while it was still light, my friend the cashier, whose name was Thims, took me for a stroll in the streets and in the court-yards of the principal colleges. Their beauty and interest were extreme; it was impossible to see them without being attracted towards them; and I thought to myself that he must be indeed an ill-grained and ungrateful person who can have been a member of one of these colleges without retaining an affectionate feeling towards it for the rest of his life. All my misgivings gave way at once when I saw the beauty and venerable appearance of this delightful city. For half-an-hour I forgot both myself and Arowhena.

After supper Mr. Thims told me a good deal about the system of education which is here practised. I already knew a part of what I heard, but much was new to me, and I obtained a better idea of the Erewhonian position than I had done hitherto: nevertheless there were parts of the scheme of which I could not comprehend the fitness, although I fully admit that this inability was probably the result of my having been trained so very differently, and to my being then much out of sorts.

The main feature in their system is the prominence which they give to a study which I can only translate by the word "hypothetics." They argue thus—that to teach a boy merely the nature of the things which exist in the world around him, and about which he will have to be conversant during his whole life, would be giving him but a narrow and shallow conception of the universe, which it is urged might contain all manner of things which are not now to be found therein. To open his eyes to these possibilities, and so to prepare him for all sorts of emergencies, is the object of this system of hypothetics. To imagine a set of utterly strange and impossible contingencies, and require the youths to give intelligent answers to the questions that arise therefrom, is reckoned the fittest conceivable way of preparing them for the actual conduct of their affairs in after life.

Thus they are taught what is called the hypothetical language for many of their best years—a language which was originally composed at a time when the country was in a very different state of civilisation to what it is at present, a state which has long since disappeared and been superseded. Many valuable maxims and noble thoughts which were at one time concealed in it have become current in their modern literature, and have been translated over and over again into the language now spoken. Surely then it would seem enough that the study of the original language should be confined to the few whose instincts led them naturally to pursue it.

But the Erewhonians think differently; the store they set by this hypothetical language can hardly be believed; they will even give any one a maintenance for life if he attains a considerable proficiency in the study of it; nay, they will spend years in learning to translate some of their own good poetry into the hypothetical language—to do so with fluency being reckoned a distinguishing mark of a scholar and a gentleman. Heaven forbid that I should be flippant, but it appeared to me to be a wanton waste of good human energy that men should spend years and years in the perfection of so barren an exercise, when their own civilisation presented problems by the hundred which cried aloud for solution and would have paid the solver handsomely; but people know their own affairs best. If the youths chose it for themselves I should have wondered less; but they do not choose it; they have it thrust upon them, and for the most part are disinclined towards it. I can only say that all I heard in defence of the system was insufficient to make me think very highly of its advantages.

The arguments in favour of the deliberate development of the unreasoning faculties were much more cogent. But here they depart from the principles on which they justify their study of hypothetics;

for they base the importance which they assign to hypothetics upon the fact of their being a preparation for the extraordinary, while their study of Unreason rests upon its developing those faculties which are required for the daily conduct of affairs. Hence their professorships of Inconsistency and Evasion, in both of which studies the youths are examined before being allowed to proceed to their degree in hypothetics. The more earnest and conscientious students attain to a proficiency in these subjects which is quite surprising; there is hardly any inconsistency so glaring but they soon learn to defend it, or injunction so clear that they cannot find some pretext for disregarding it.

Life, they urge, would be intolerable if men were to be guided in all they did by reason and reason only. Reason betrays men into the drawing of hard and fast lines, and to the defining by language—language being like the sun, which rears and then scorches. Extremes are alone logical, but they are always absurd; the mean is illogical, but an illogical mean is better than the sheer absurdity of an extreme. There are no follies and no unreasonablenesses so great as those which can apparently be irrefragably defended by reason itself, and there is hardly an error into which men may not easily be led if they base their conduct upon reason only.

Reason might very possibly abolish the double currency; it might even attack the personality of Hope and Justice. Besides, people have such a strong natural bias towards it that they will seek it for themselves and act upon it quite as much as or more than is good for them: there is no need of encouraging reason. With unreason the case is different. She is the natural complement of reason, without whose existence reason itself were non-existent.

If, then, reason would be non-existent were there no such thing as unreason, surely it follows that the more unreason there is, the more reason there must be also? Hence the necessity for the development of unreason, even in the interests of reason herself. The Professors of Unreason deny that they undervalue reason: none can be more convinced than they are, that if the double currency cannot be rigorously deduced as a necessary consequence of human reason, the double currency should cease forthwith; but they say that it must be deduced from no narrow and exclusive view of reason which should deprive that admirable faculty of the one-half of its own existence. Unreason is a part of reason; it must therefore be allowed its full share in stating the initial conditions.

CHAPTER XXII

THE COLLEGES OF UNREASON— (CONTINUED)

OF GENIUS THEY make no account, for they say that every one is a genius, more or less. No one is so physically sound that no part of him will be even a little unsound, and no one is so diseased but that some part of him will be healthy—so no man is so mentally and morally sound, but that he will be in part both mad and wicked; and no man is so mad and wicked but he will be sensible and honourable in part. In like manner there is no genius who is not also a fool, and no fool who is not also a genius.

When I talked about originality and genius to some gentlemen whom I met at a supper party given by Mr. Thims in my honour, and said that original thought ought to be encouraged, I had to eat my words at once. Their view evidently was that genius was like offences—needs must that it come, but woe unto that man through whom it comes. A man's business, they hold, is to think as his neighbours do, for Heaven help him if he thinks good what they count bad. And really it is hard to see how the Erewhonian theory differs from our own, for the word "idiot" only means a person who forms his opinions for himself.

The venerable Professor of Worldly Wisdom, a man verging on eighty but still hale, spoke to me very seriously on this subject in consequence of the few words that I had imprudently let fall in defence of genius. He was one of those who carried most weight in the university, and had the reputation of having done more perhaps than any other living man to suppress any kind of originality.

"It is not our business," he said, "to help students to think for themselves. Surely this is the very last thing which one who wishes them well should encourage them to do. Our duty is to ensure that they shall think as we do, or at any rate, as we hold it expedient to say we do." In some respects, however, he was thought to hold somewhat radical opinions, for he was President of the Society for the Suppression of Useless Knowledge, and for the Completer Obliteration of the Past.

As regards the tests that a youth must pass before he can get a degree, I found that they have no class lists, and discourage anything like competition among the students; this, indeed, they regard as self-seeking and unneighbourly. The examinations are conducted by way of papers written by the candidate on set subjects, some of which are known to him beforehand, while others are devised with a view of testing his general capacity and *savoir faire*.

My friend the Professor of Worldly Wisdom was the terror of the greater number of students; and, so far as I could judge, he very well might be, for he had taken his Professorship more seriously than any of the other Professors had done. I heard of his having plucked one poor fellow for want of sufficient vagueness in his saving clauses paper. Another was sent down for having written an article on a scientific subject without having made free enough use of the words "carefully," "patiently," and "earnestly." One man was refused a degree for being too often and too seriously in the right, while a few days before I came a whole batch had been plucked for insufficient distrust of printed matter.

About this there was just then rather a ferment, for it seems that the Professor had written an article in the leading university magazine, which was well known to be by him, and which abounded in all sorts of plausible blunders. He then set a paper which afforded the examinees an opportunity of repeating these blunders—which, believing the article to be by their own examiner, they of course did. The Professor plucked every single one of them, but his action was considered to have been not quite handsome.

I told them of Homer's noble line to the effect that a man should strive ever to be foremost and in all things to outvie his peers; but they said that no wonder the countries in which such a detestable maxim was held in admiration were always flying at one another's throats.

"Why," asked one Professor, "should a man want to be better than his neighbours? Let him be thankful if he is no worse."

I ventured feebly to say that I did not see how progress could be made in any art or science, or indeed in anything at all, without more or less self-seeking, and hence unamiability.

"Of course it cannot," said the Professor, "and therefore we object to progress."

After which there was no more to be said. Later on, however, a young Professor took me aside and said he did not think I quite understood their views about progress.

"We like progress," he said, "but it must commend itself to the common sense of the people. If a man gets to know more than his neighbours he should keep his knowledge to himself till he has sounded them, and seen whether they agree, or are likely to agree with him. He said it was as immoral to be too far in front of one's own age, as to lag too far behind it. If a man can carry his neighbours with him, he may say what he likes; but if not, what insult can be more gratuitous than the telling them what they do not want to know? A man should remember that intellectual over-indulgence is one of the most insidious and disgraceful forms that excess can take. Granted that every one should exceed more or less, inasmuch as absolutely perfect sanity would drive any man mad the moment he reached it, but . . ."

He was now warming to his subject and I was beginning to wonder how I should get rid of him, when the party broke up, and though I promised to call on him before I left, I was unfortunately prevented from doing so.

I have now said enough to give English readers some idea of the strange views which the Erewhonians hold concerning unreason, hypothetics, and education generally. In many respects they were sensible enough, but I could not get over the hypothetics, especially the turning their own good poetry into the hypothetical language. In the course of my stay I met one youth who told me that for fourteen years the hypothetical language had been almost the only thing that he had been taught, although he had never (to his credit, as it seemed to me) shown the slightest proclivity towards it, while he had been endowed with not inconsiderable ability for several other branches of human learning. He assured me that he would never open another hypothetical book after he had taken his degree, but would follow out the bent of his own inclinations. This was well enough, but who could give him his fourteen years back again?

I sometimes wondered how it was that the mischief done was not more clearly perceptible, and that the young men and women grew up as sensible and goodly as they did, in spite of the attempts almost deliberately made to warp and stunt their growth. Some doubtless received damage, from which they suffered to their life's end; but many seemed little or none the worse, and some, almost the better. The reason would seem to be that the natural instinct of the lads in most cases so absolutely rebelled against their training, that do what the teachers might they could never get them to pay serious heed to it. The consequence was that the boys only lost their time, and not so much of this as might have been expected, for in their hours of leisure they were actively engaged in exercises and sports which developed their physical nature, and made them at any rate strong and healthy.

Moreover those who had any special tastes could not be restrained from developing them: they would learn what they wanted to learn and liked, in spite of obstacles which seemed rather to urge them on than to discourage them, while for those who had no special capacity, the loss of time was of comparatively little moment; but in spite of these alleviations of the mischief, I am sure that much harm was done to the children of the sub-wealthy classes, by the system which passes current among the Erewhonians as education. The poorest children suffered least—if destruction and death have heard the sound of wisdom, to a certain extent poverty has done so also.

And yet perhaps, after all, it is better for a country that its seats of learning should do more to suppress mental growth than to encourage it. Were it not for a certain priggishness which these places infuse into so great a number of their *alumni*, genuine work would become dangerously common. It is essential that by far the greater part of what is said or done in the world should be so ephemeral as to take itself away quickly; it should keep good for twenty-four hours, or even twice as long, but it should not be good enough a week hence to prevent people from going on to something else. No doubt the marvellous development of journalism in England, as also the fact that our seats of learning aim rather at fostering mediocrity than anything higher, is due to our subconscious recognition of the fact that it is even more necessary to check exuberance of mental development than to encourage it. There can be no doubt that this is what our academic bodies do, and they do it the more effectually because they do it only subconsciously. They think they are advancing healthy mental assimilation and digestion, whereas in reality they are little better than cancer in the stomach.

Let me return, however, to the Erewhonians. Nothing surprised me more than to see the occasional flashes of common sense with which one branch of study or another was lit up, while not a single ray fell upon so many others. I was particularly struck with this on strolling into the Art School of the University. Here I found that the course of study was divided into two branches—the practical and the commercial—no student being permitted to continue his studies in the actual practice of the art he had taken up, unless he made equal progress in its commercial history.

Thus those who were studying painting were examined at frequent intervals in the prices which all the leading pictures of the last fifty or a hundred years had realised, and in the fluctuations in their values when (as often happened) they had been sold and resold three or four times. The artist, they contend, is a dealer in pictures, and it is as important for him to learn how to adapt his wares to the market, and to know approximately what kind of a picture will fetch how much, as it is for him to be able to paint the picture. This, I suppose, is what the French mean by laying so much stress upon "Values."

As regards the city itself, the more I saw the more enchanted I became. I dare not trust myself with any description of the exquisite beauty of the different colleges, and their walks and gardens. Truly in these things alone there must be a hallowing and refining influence which is in itself half an education, and which no amount of error can wholly spoil. I was introduced to many of the Professors, who showed me every hospitality and kindness; nevertheless I could hardly avoid a sort of suspicion that some of those whom I was taken to see had been so long engrossed in their own study of hypothetics that they had become the exact antitheses of the Athenians in the days of St. Paul; for whereas the Athenians spent their lives in nothing save to see and to hear some new thing, there were some here who seemed to devote themselves to the avoidance of every opinion with which they were not perfectly familiar, and regarded their own brains as a sort of sanctuary, to which if an opinion had once resorted, none other was to attack it.

I should warn the reader, however, that I was rarely sure what the men whom I met while staying with Mr. Thims really meant; for there was no getting anything out of them if they scented even a suspicion that they might be what they call "giving themselves away." As there is hardly any subject on which this suspicion cannot arise, I found it difficult to get definite opinions from any of them, except on such subjects as the weather, eating and drinking, holiday excursions, or games of skill.

If they cannot wriggle out of expressing an opinion of some sort, they will commonly retail those of some one who has already written upon the subject, and conclude by saying that though they quite admit that there is an element of truth in what the writer has said, there are many points on which they are unable to agree with him. Which these points were, I invariably found myself unable to determine; indeed, it seemed to be counted the perfection of scholarship and good breeding among them not to have—much less to express—an opinion on any subject on which it might prove later that they had been mistaken. The art of sitting gracefully on a fence has never,

I should think, been brought to greater perfection than at the Erewhonian Colleges of Unreason.

Even when, wriggle as they may, they find themselves pinned down to some expression of definite opinion, as often as not they will argue in support of what they perfectly well know to be untrue. I repeatedly met with reviews and articles even in their best journals, between the lines of which I had little difficulty in detecting a sense exactly contrary to the one ostensibly put forward. So well is this understood, that a man must be a mere tyro in the arts of Erewhonian polite society, unless he instinctively suspects a hidden "yea" in every "nay" that meets him. Granted that it comes to much the same in the end, for it does not matter whether "yea" is called "yea" or "nay," so long as it is understood which it is to be; but our own more direct way of calling a spade a spade, rather than a rake, with the intention that every one should understand it as a spade, seems more satisfactory. On the other hand, the Erewhonian system lends itself better to the suppression of that downrightness which it seems the express aim of Erewhonian philosophy to discountenance.

However this may be, the fear-of-giving-themselves-away disease was fatal to the intelligence of those infected by it, and almost every one at the Colleges of Unreason had caught it to a greater or less degree. After a few years atrophy of the opinions invariably supervened, and the sufferer became stone dead to everything except the more superficial aspects of those material objects with which he came most in contact. The expression on the faces of these people was repellent; they did not, however, seem particularly unhappy, for they none of them had the faintest idea that they were in reality more dead than alive. No cure for this disgusting fear-of-giving-themselves-away disease has yet been discovered.

It was during my stay in the city of the Colleges of Unreason—a city whose Erewhonian name is so cacophonous that I refrain from giving it—that I learned the particulars of the revolution which had ended in the destruction of so many of the mechanical inventions which were formerly in common use.

Mr. Thims took me to the rooms of a gentleman who had a great reputation for learning, but who was also, so Mr. Thims told me, rather a dangerous person, inasmuch as he had attempted to introduce an adverb into the hypothetical language. He had heard of my watch and been exceedingly anxious to see me, for he was accounted the most learned antiquary in Erewhon on the subject of mechanical lore. We fell to talking upon the subject, and when I left he gave me a reprinted copy of the work which brought the revolution about.

It had taken place some five hundred years before my arrival: people had long become thoroughly used to the change, although at the time that it was made the country was plunged into the deepest misery, and a reaction which followed had very nearly proved successful. Civil war raged for many years, and is said to have reduced the number of the inhabitants by one-half. The parties were styled the machinists and the anti-machinists, and in the end, as I have said already, the latter got the victory, treating their opponents with such unparalleled severity that they extirpated every trace of opposition.

The wonder was that they allowed any mechanical appliances to remain in the kingdom, neither do I believe that they would have done so, had not the Professors of Inconsistency and Evasion made a stand against the carrying of the new principles to their legitimate conclusions. These Professors, moreover, insisted that during the struggle the anti-machinists should use every known improvement in the art of war, and several new weapons, offensive and defensive, were invented, while it was in progress. I was surprised at there remaining so many mechanical specimens as are seen in the museums, and at students having rediscovered their past uses so completely; for at the time of the revolution the victors wrecked all the more complicated machines, and burned all treatises on mechanics, and all engineers' workshops—thus, so they thought, cutting the mischief out root and branch, at an incalculable cost of blood and treasure.

Certainly they had not spared their labour, but work of this description can never be perfectly achieved, and when, some two hundred years before my arrival, all passion upon the subject had cooled down, and no one save a lunatic would have dreamed of reintroducing forbidden inventions, the subject came to be regarded as a curious antiquarian study, like that of some long-forgotten religious practices among ourselves. Then came the careful search for whatever fragments could be found, and for any machines that might have been hidden away, and also numberless treatises were written, showing what the functions of each rediscovered machine had been; all being done with no idea of using such machinery again, but with the feelings of an English antiquarian concerning Druidical monuments or flint arrow heads.

On my return to the metropolis, during the remaining weeks or rather days of my sojourn in Erewhon I made a *resumé* in English of the work which brought about the already mentioned revolution.

My ignorance of technical terms has led me doubtless into many errors, and I have occasionally, where I found translation impossible, substituted purely English names and ideas for the original Erewhonian ones, but the reader may rely on my general accuracy. I have thought it best to insert my translation here.

CHAPTER XXIII

THE BOOK OF THE MACHINES

THE WRITER COMMENCES:—"There was a time, when the earth was to all appearance utterly destitute both of animal and vegetable life, and when according to the opinion of our best philosophers it was simply a hot round ball with a crust gradually cooling. Now if a human being had existed while the earth was in this state and had been allowed to see it as though it were some other world with which he had no concern, and if at the same time he were entirely ignorant of all physical science, would he not have pronounced it impossible that creatures possessed of anything like consciousness should be evolved from the seeming cinder which he was beholding? Would he not have denied that it contained any potentiality of consciousness? Yet in the course of time consciousness came. Is it not possible then that there may be even yet new channels dug out for consciousness, though we can detect no signs of them at present?

"Again. Consciousness, in anything like the present acceptation of the term, having been once a new thing—a thing, as far as we can see, subsequent even to an individual centre of action and to a reproductive system (which we see existing in plants without apparent consciousness)—why may not there arise some new phase of mind which shall be as different from all present known phases, as the mind of animals is from that of vegetables?

"It would be absurd to attempt to define such a mental state (or whatever it may be called), inasmuch as it must be something so foreign to man that his experience can give him no help towards conceiving its nature; but surely when we reflect upon the manifold phases of life and consciousness which have been evolved already, it would be rash to say that no others can be developed, and that animal life is the end of all things. There was a time when fire was the end of all things: another when rocks and water were so."

The writer, after enlarging on the above for several pages, proceeded to inquire whether traces of the approach of such a new phase of life could be perceived at present; whether we could see any tenements preparing which might in a remote futurity be adapted for it; whether, in fact, the primordial cell of such a kind of life could be now detected upon earth. In the course of his work he answered this question in the affirmative and pointed to the higher machines.

"There is no security"—to quote his own words—"against the ultimate development of mechanical consciousness, in the fact of machines possessing little consciousness now. A mollusc has not much consciousness. Reflect upon the extraordinary advance which machines have made during the last few hundred years, and note how slowly the animal and vegetable kingdoms are advancing. The more highly organised machines are creatures not so much of yesterday, as of the last five minutes, so to speak, in comparison with past time. Assume for the sake of argument that conscious beings have existed for some twenty million years: see what strides machines have made in the last thousand! May not the world last twenty million years longer? If so, what will they not in the end become? Is it not safer to nip the mischief in the bud and to forbid them further progress?

"But who can say that the vapour engine has not a kind of consciousness? Where does consciousness begin, and where end? Who can draw the line? Who can draw any line? Is not everything interwoven with everything? Is not machinery linked with animal life in an infinite variety of ways? The shell of a hen's egg is made of a delicate white ware and is a machine as much as an egg-cup is: the shell is a device for holding the egg, as much as the egg-cup for holding the shell: both are phases of the same function; the hen makes the shell in her inside, but it is pure pottery. She makes her nest outside of herself for convenience' sake, but the nest is not more of a machine than the egg-shell is. A 'machine' is only a 'device.'"

Then returning to consciousness, and endeavouring to detect its earliest manifestations, the writer continued:—

"There is a kind of plant that eats organic food with its flowers: when a fly settles upon the blossom, the petals close upon it and hold it fast till the plant has absorbed the insect into its system; but they will close on nothing but what is good to eat; of a drop of rain or a piece of stick they will take no notice. Curious! that so unconscious a thing should have such a keen eye to its own interest. If this is unconsciousness, where is the use of consciousness?

"Shall we say that the plant does not know what it is doing merely because it has no eyes, or ears, or brains? If we say that it acts mechanically, and mechanically only, shall we not be forced to admit that sundry other and apparently very deliberate actions are also mechanical? If it seems to us that the plant kills and eats a fly mechanically, may it not seem to the plant that a man must kill and eat a sheep mechanically?

"But it may be said that the plant is void of reason, because the growth of a plant is an involuntary growth. Given earth, air, and due temperature, the plant must grow: it is like a clock, which being once wound up will go till it is stopped or run down: it is like the wind blowing on the sails of a ship—the ship must go when the wind blows it. But can a healthy boy help growing if he have good meat and drink and clothing? Can anything help going as long as it is wound up, or go on after it is run down? Is there not a winding-up process everywhere?

"Even a potato* in a dark cellar has a certain low cunning about him which serves him in excellent stead. He knows perfectly well what he wants and how to get it. He sees the light coming from the cellar window and sends his shoots crawling straight thereto: they will crawl along the floor and up the wall and out at the cellar window; if there be a little earth anywhere on the journey he will find it and use it for his own ends. What deliberation he may exercise in the matter of his roots when he is planted in the earth is a thing unknown to us, but we can imagine him saying, 'I will have a tuber here and a tuber there, and I will suck whatsoever advantage I can from all my surroundings. This neighbour I will overshadow, and that I will undermine; and what I can do shall be the limit of what I will do. He that is stronger and better placed than I shall overcome me, and him that is weaker I will overcome.'

"The potato says these things by doing them, which is the best of languages. What is consciousness if this is not consciousness? We find it difficult to sympathise with the emotions of a potato; so we do with those of an oyster. Neither of these things makes a noise on being boiled or opened, and noise appeals to us more strongly than

---

* The root alluded to is not the potato of our own gardens, but a plant so near akin to it that I have ventured to translate it thus. Apropos of its intelligence, had the writer known Butler he would probably have said—

> 'He knows what's what, and that's as high,
> As metaphysic wit can fly.'

anything else, because we make so much about our own sufferings. Since, then, they do not annoy us by any expression of pain we call them emotionless; and so *quâ* mankind they are; but mankind is not everybody.

"If it be urged that the action of the potato is chemical and mechanical only, and that it is due to the chemical and mechanical effects of light and heat, the answer would seem to lie in an inquiry whether every sensation is not chemical and mechanical in its operation? Whether those things which we deem most purely spiritual are anything but disturbances of equilibrium in an infinite series of levers, beginning with those that are too small for microscopic detection, and going up to the human arm and the appliances which it makes use of? Whether there be not a molecular action of thought, whence a dynamical theory of the passions shall be deducible? Whether strictly speaking we should not ask what kind of levers a man is made of rather than what is his temperament? How are they balanced? How much of such and such will it take to weigh them down so as to make him do so and so?"

The writer went on to say that he anticipated a time when it would be possible, by examining a single hair with a powerful microscope, to know whether its owner could be insulted with impunity. He then became more and more obscure, so that I was obliged to give up all attempt at translation; neither did I follow the drift of his argument. On coming to the next part which I could construe, I found that he had changed his ground.

"Either," he proceeds, "a great deal of action that has been called purely mechanical and unconscious must be admitted to contain more elements of consciousness than has been allowed hitherto (and in this case germs of consciousness will be found in many actions of the higher machines)—Or (assuming the theory of evolution but at the same time denying the consciousness of vegetable and crystalline action) the race of man has descended from things which had no consciousness at all. In this case there is no *a priori* improbability in the descent of conscious (and more than conscious) machines from those which now exist, except that which is suggested by the apparent absence of anything like a reproductive system in the mechanical kingdom. This absence however is only apparent, as I shall presently show.

"Do not let me be misunderstood as living in fear of any actually existing machine; there is probably no known machine which is more than a prototype of future mechanical life. The present machines are to the future as the early Saurians to man. The largest of them will probably greatly diminish in size. Some of the lowest vertebrata attained a much greater bulk than has descended to their more highly organised living representatives, and in like manner a diminution in the size of machines has often attended their development and progress.

"Take the watch, for example; examine its beautiful structure; observe the intelligent play of the minute members which compose it: yet this little creature is but a development of the cumbrous clocks that preceded it; it is no deterioration from them. A day may come when clocks, which certainly at the present time are not diminishing in bulk, will be superseded owing to the universal use of watches, in which case they will become as extinct as ichthyosauri, while the watch, whose tendency has for some years been to decrease in size rather than the contrary, will remain the only existing type of an extinct race.

"But returning to the argument, I would repeat that I fear none of the existing machines; what I fear is the extraordinary rapidity with which they are becoming something very different to what they are at present. No class of beings have in any time past made so rapid a movement forward. Should not that movement be jealously watched, and checked while we can still check it? And is it not necessary for this end to destroy the more advanced of the machines which are in use at present, though it is admitted that they are in themselves harmless?

"As yet the machines receive their impressions through the agency of man's senses: one travelling machine calls to another in a shrill accent of alarm and the other instantly retires; but it is through the ears of the driver that the voice of the one has acted upon the other. Had there been no driver, the callee would have been deaf to the caller. There was a time when it must have seemed highly improbable that machines should learn to make their wants known by sound, even through the ears of man; may we not conceive, then, that a day will come when those ears will be no longer needed, and the hearing will be done by the delicacy of the machine's own construction?—when its language shall have been developed from the cry of animals to a speech as intricate as our own?

"It is possible that by that time children will learn the differential calculus—as they learn now to speak—from their mothers and nurses, or that they may talk in the hypothetical language, and work rule-of-three sums, as soon as they are born; but this is not probable; we cannot calculate on any corresponding advance in man's intellectual or physical powers which shall be a set-off against the far greater development which seems in store for the machines. Some people may say that man's moral influence will suffice to rule them; but I cannot think it will ever be safe to repose much trust in the moral sense of any machine.

"Again, might not the glory of the machines consist in their being without this same boasted gift of language? 'Silence,' it has been said by one writer, 'is a virtue which renders us agreeable to our fellow-creatures.'"

CHAPTER XXIV

THE BOOK OF THE MACHINES— (CONTINUED)

"BUT OTHER QUESTIONS come upon us. What is a man's eye but a machine for the little creature that sits behind in his brain to look through? A dead eye is nearly as good as a living one for some time after the man is dead. It is not the eye that cannot see, but the rest-less one that cannot see through it. Is it man's eyes, or is it the big seeing-engine which has revealed to us the existence of worlds beyond worlds into infinity? What has made man familiar with the scenery of the moon, the spots on the sun, or the geography of the planets? He is at the mercy of the seeing-engine for these things, and is pow-erless unless he tack it on to his own identity, and make it part and parcel of himself. Or, again, is it the eye, or the little see-engine, which has shown us the existence of infinitely minute organisms which swarm unsuspected around us?

"And take man's vaunted power of calculation. Have we not engines which can do all manner of sums more quickly and correctly than we can? What prizeman in Hypothetics at any of our Colleges of Unreason can compare with some of these machines in their own line? In fact, wherever precision is required man flies to the machine at once, as far preferable to himself. Our sum-engines never drop a figure, nor our looms a stitch; the machine is brisk and active, when the man is weary; it is clear-headed and collected, when the man is stupid and dull; it needs no slumber, when man must sleep or drop; ever at its post, ever ready for work, its alacrity never flags, its patience never gives in; its might is stronger than combined hundreds, and swifter than the flight of birds; it can burrow beneath the earth, and walk upon the largest rivers and sink not. This is the green tree; what then shall be done in the dry?

"Who shall say that a man does see or hear? He is such a hive and swarm of parasites that it is doubtful whether his body is not more theirs than his, and whether he is anything but another kind of ant-heap after all. May not man himself become a sort of parasite upon the machines? An affectionate machine-tickling aphid?

"It is said by some that our blood is composed of infinite living agents which go up and down the highways and byways of our bodies as people in the streets of a city. When we look down from a high place upon crowded thoroughfares, is it possible not to think of corpuscles of blood travelling through veins and nourishing the heart of the town? No mention shall be made of sewers, nor of the hidden nerves which serve to communicate sensations from one part of the town's body to another; nor of the yawning jaws of the railway stations, whereby the circulation is carried directly into the heart,— which receive the venous lines, and disgorge the arterial, with an eternal pulse of people. And the sleep of the town, how life-like! with its change in the circulation."

Here the writer became again so hopelessly obscure that I was obliged to miss several pages. He resumed:—

"It can be answered that even though machines should hear never so well and speak never so wisely, they will still always do the one or the other for our advantage, not their own; that man will be the ruling spirit and the machine the servant; that as soon as a machine fails to discharge the service which man expects from it, it is doomed to extinction; that the machines stand to man simply in the relation of lower animals, the vapour-engine itself being only a more economical kind of horse; so that instead of being likely to be developed into a higher kind of life than man's, they owe their very existence and progress to their power of ministering to human wants, and must therefore both now and ever be man's inferiors.

"This is all very well. But the servant glides by imperceptible approaches into the master; and we have come to such a pass that, even now, man must suffer terribly on ceasing to benefit the machines. If all machines were to be annihilated at one moment, so that not a knife nor lever nor rag of clothing nor anything whatsoever were left to man but his bare body alone that he was born with, and if all knowledge of mechanical laws were taken from him so that he could make no more machines, and all machine-made food destroyed so that the race of man should be left as it were naked upon a desert island, we should become extinct in six weeks. A few miserable individuals might linger, but even these in a year or two would become worse than monkeys. Man's very soul is due to the machines; it is a machine-made thing: he thinks as he thinks, and feels as he feels, through the work that machines have wrought upon him, and their existence is quite as much a *sine quâ non* for his, as his for theirs. This fact precludes us from proposing the complete annihilation of machinery, but surely it indicates that we should destroy as many of them as we can possibly dispense with, lest they should tyrannise over us even more completely.

"True, from a low materialistic point of view, it would seem that those thrive best who use machinery wherever its use is possible with profit; but this is the art of the machines—they serve that they may rule. They bear no malice towards man for destroying a whole race of them provided he creates a better instead; on the contrary, they reward him liberally for having hastened their development. It is for neglecting them that he incurs their wrath, or for using inferior machines, or for not making sufficient exertions to invent new ones, or for destroying them without replacing them; yet these are the very things we ought to do, and do quickly; for though our rebellion against their infant power will cause infinite suffering, what will not things come to, if that rebellion is delayed?

"They have preyed upon man's grovelling preference for his material over his spiritual interests, and have betrayed him into supplying that element of struggle and warfare without which no race can advance. The lower animals progress because they struggle with one another; the weaker die, the stronger breed and transmit their strength. The machines being of themselves unable to struggle, have got man to do their struggling for them: as long as he fulfils this function duly, all goes well with him—at least he thinks so; but the moment he fails to do his best for the advancement of machinery by encouraging the good and destroying the bad, he is left behind in the race of competition; and this means that he will be made uncomfortable in a variety of ways, and perhaps die.

"So that even now the machines will only serve on condition of being served, and that too upon their own terms; the moment their terms are not complied with, they jib, and either smash both themselves and all whom they can reach, or turn churlish and refuse to work at all. How many men at this hour are living in a state of bondage to the machines? How many spend their whole lives, from the cradle to the grave, in tending them by night and day? Is it not plain that the machines are gaining ground upon us, when we reflect on the increasing number of those who are bound down to them as slaves, and of those who devote their whole souls to the advancement of the mechanical kingdom?

"The vapour-engine must be fed with food and consume it by fire even as man consumes it; it supports its combustion by air as man supports it; it has a pulse and circulation as man has. It may be granted that man's body is as yet the more versatile of the two, but then man's body is an older thing; give the vapour-engine but half the time that man has had, give it also a continuance of our present infatuation, and what may it not ere long attain to?

"There are certain functions indeed of the vapour-engine which will probably remain unchanged for myriads of years—which in fact will perhaps survive when the use of vapour has been superseded: the piston and cylinder, the beam, the fly-wheel, and other parts of the machine will probably be permanent, just as we see that man and many of the lower animals share like modes of eating, drinking, and sleeping; thus they have hearts which beat as ours, veins and arteries, eyes, ears, and noses; they sigh even in their sleep, and weep and yawn; they are affected by their children; they feel pleasure and pain, hope, fear, anger, shame; they have memory and prescience; they know that if certain things happen to them they will die, and they fear death as much as we do; they communicate their thoughts to one another, and some of them deliberately act in concert. The comparison of similarities is endless: I only make it because some may say that since the vapour-engine is not likely to be improved in the main particulars, it is unlikely to be henceforward extensively modified at all. This is too good to be true: it will be modified and suited for an infinite variety of purposes, as much as man has been modified so as to exceed the brutes in skill.

"In the meantime the stoker is almost as much a cook for his engine as our own cooks for ourselves. Consider also the colliers and pitmen and coal merchants and coal trains, and the men who drive them, and the ships that carry coals—what an army of servants do the machines thus employ! Are there not probably more men engaged in tending machinery than in tending men? Do not machines eat as it were by mannery? Are we not ourselves creating our successors in the supremacy of the earth? daily adding to the beauty and delicacy of their organisation, daily giving them greater skill and supplying more and more of that self-regulating self-acting power which will be better than any intellect?

"What a new thing it is for a machine to feed at all! The plough, the spade, and the cart must eat through man's stomach; the fuel that sets them going must burn in the furnace of a man or of horses. Man must consume bread and meat or he cannot dig; the bread and meat are the fuel which drive the spade. If a plough be drawn by horses, the power is supplied by grass or beans or oats, which being burnt in the belly of the cattle give the power of working: without this fuel the work would cease, as an engine would stop if its furnaces were to go out.

"A man of science has demonstrated 'that no animal has the power of originating mechanical energy, but that all the work done in its life by any animal, and all the heat that has been emitted from it, and the heat which would be obtained by burning the combustible matter which has been lost from its body during life, and by burning its body after death, make up altogether an exact equivalent to the heat which would be obtained by burning as much food as it has used during its life, and an amount of fuel which would generate as much heat as its body if burned immediately after death.' I do not know how he has found this out, but he is a man of science—how then can it be objected against the future vitality of the machines that they are, in their present infancy, at the beck and call of beings who are themselves incapable of originating mechanical energy?

"The main point, however, to be observed as affording cause for alarm is, that whereas animals were formerly the only stomachs of the machines, there are now many which have stomachs of their own, and consume their food themselves. This is a great step towards their becoming, if not animate, yet something so near akin to it, as not to differ more widely from our own life than animals do from vegetables. And though man should remain, in some respects, the higher creature, is not this in accordance with the practice of nature, which allows superiority in some things to animals which have, on the whole, been long surpassed? Has she not allowed the ant and the bee to retain superiority over man in the organisation of their communities and social arrangements, the bird in traversing the air, the fish in swimming, the horse in strength and fleetness, and the dog in self-sacrifice?

"It is said by some with whom I have conversed upon this subject, that the machines can never be developed into animate or *quasi*-animate existences, inasmuch as they have no reproductive system, nor seem ever likely to possess one. If this be taken to mean that they cannot marry, and that we are never likely to see a fertile union between two vapour-engines with the young ones playing about the door of the shed, however greatly we might desire to do so, I will readily grant it. But the objection is not a very profound one. No one expects that all the features of the now existing organisations will be absolutely repeated in an entirely new class of life. The reproductive system of animals differs widely from that of plants, but both are reproductive systems. Has nature exhausted her phases of this power?

"Surely if a machine is able to reproduce another machine systematically, we may say that it has a reproductive system. What is a reproductive system, if it be not a system for reproduction? And how few of the machines are there which have not been produced systematically by other machines? But it is man that makes them do so. Yes; but is it not insects that make many of the plants reproductive, and would not whole families of plants die out if their fertilisation was not effected by a class of agents utterly foreign to themselves? Does any one say that the red clover has no reproductive system because the humble bee (and the humble bee only) must aid and abet it before it can reproduce? No one. The humble bee is a part of the reproductive system of the clover. Each one of ourselves has sprung from minute animalcules whose entity was entirely distinct from our own, and which acted after their kind with no thought or heed of what we might think about it. These little creatures are part of our own reproductive system; then why not we part of that of the machines?

"But the machines which reproduce machinery do not reproduce machines after their own kind. A thimble may be made by machinery, but it was not made by, neither will it ever make, a thimble. Here, again, if we turn to nature we shall find abundance of analogies which will teach us that a reproductive system may be in full force without the thing produced being of the same kind as that which produced it. Very few creatures reproduce after their own kind; they reproduce something which has the potentiality of becoming that which their parents were. Thus the butterfly lays an egg, which egg can become a caterpillar, which caterpillar can become a chrysalis, which chrysalis can become a butterfly; and though I freely grant that the machines cannot be said to have more than the germ of a true reproductive system at present, have we not just seen that they have only recently obtained the germs of a mouth and stomach? And may not some stride be made in the direction of true reproduction which shall be as great as that which has been recently taken in the direction of true feeding?

"It is possible that the system when developed may be in many cases a vicarious thing. Certain classes of machines may be alone fertile, while the rest discharge other functions in the mechanical system, just as the great majority of ants and bees have nothing to do with the continuation of their species, but get food and store it, without thought of breeding. One cannot expect the parallel to be complete or nearly so; certainly not now, and probably never; but is there not enough analogy existing at the present moment, to make us feel seriously uneasy about the future, and to render it our duty to check the evil while we can still do so? Machines can within certain limits beget machines of any class, no matter how different to themselves. Every class of machines will probably have its special mechanical breeders, and all the higher ones will owe their existence to a large number of parents and not to two only.

"We are misled by considering any complicated machine as a single thing; in truth it is a city or society, each member of which was bred truly after its kind. We see a machine as a whole, we call it by a name and individualise it; we look at our own limbs, and know that the combination forms an individual which springs from a single centre of reproductive action; we therefore assume that there can be no reproductive action which does not arise from a single centre; but this assumption is unscientific, and the bare fact that no vapour-engine was ever made entirely by another, or two others, of its own kind, is not sufficient to warrant us in saying that vapour-engines have no reproductive system. The truth is that each part of every vapour-engine is bred by its own special breeders, whose function it is to breed that part, and that only, while the combination of the parts into a whole forms another department of the mechanical reproductive system, which is at present exceedingly complex and difficult to see in its entirety.

"Complex now, but how much simpler and more intelligibly organised may it not become in another hundred thousand years? or in twenty thousand? For man at present believes that his interest lies in that direction; he spends an incalculable amount of labour and time and thought in making machines breed always better and better; he has already succeeded in effecting much that at one time appeared impossible, and there seem no limits to the results of accumulated improvements if they are allowed to descend with modification from generation to generation. It must always be remembered that man's body is what it is through having been moulded into its present shape by the chances and changes of many millions of years, but that his organisation never advanced with anything like the rapidity with which that of the machines is advancing. This is the most alarming feature in the case, and I must be pardoned for insisting on it so frequently."

CHAPTER XXV

THE BOOK OF THE MACHINES—
(CONCLUDED)

HERE FOLLOWED A very long and untranslatable digression about the different races and families of the then existing machines. The writer attempted to support his theory by pointing out the similarities existing between many machines of a widely different character, which served to show descent from a common ancestor. He divided machines into their genera, subgenera, species, varieties, subvarieties, and so forth. He proved the existence of connecting links between machines that seemed to have very little in common, and showed that many more such links had existed, but had now perished. He pointed out tendencies to reversion, and the presence of rudimentary organs which existed in many machines feebly developed and perfectly useless, yet serving to mark descent from an ancestor to whom the function was actually useful.

I left the translation of this part of the treatise, which, by the way, was far longer than all that I have given here, for a later opportunity. Unfortunately, I left Erewhon before I could return to the subject; and though I saved my translation and other papers at the hazard of my life, I was obliged to sacrifice the original work. It went to my heart to do so; but I thus gained ten minutes of invaluable time, without which both Arowhena and myself must have certainly perished.

I remember one incident which bears upon this part of the treatise. The gentleman who gave it to me had asked to see my tobacco-pipe; he examined it carefully, and when he came to the little protuberance at the bottom of the bowl he seemed much delighted, and exclaimed that it must be rudimentary. I asked him what he meant.

"Sir," he answered, "this organ is identical with the rim at the bottom of a cup; it is but another form of the same function. Its purpose must have been to keep the heat of the pipe from marking the table upon which it rested. You would find, if you were to look up the history of tobacco-pipes, that in early specimens this protuber-ance was of a different shape to what it is now. It will have been broad at the bottom, and flat, so that while the pipe was being smoked the bowl might rest upon the table without marking it. Use and disuse must have come into play and reduced the function to its present rudimentary condition. I should not be surprised, sir," he continued, "if, in the course of time, it were to become modified still farther, and to assume the form of an ornamental leaf or scroll, or even a butterfly, while, in some cases, it will become extinct."

On my return to England, I looked up the point, and found that my friend was right.

Returning, however, to the treatise, my translation recommences as follows:—

"May we not fancy that if, in the remotest geological period, some early form of vegetable life had been endowed with the power of reflecting upon the dawning life of animals which was coming into existence alongside of its own, it would have thought itself exceed-ingly acute if it had surmised that animals would one day become real vegetables? Yet would this be more mistaken than it would be on our part to imagine that because the life of machines is a very different one to our own, there is therefore no higher possible devel-opment of life than ours; or that because mechanical life is a very different thing from ours, therefore that it is not life at all?

"But I have heard it said, 'granted that this is so, and that the vapour-engine has a strength of its own, surely no one will say that it has a will of its own?' Alas! if we look more closely, we shall find that this does not make against the supposition that the vapour-engine is one of the germs of a new phase of life. What is there in this whole world, or in the worlds beyond it, which has a will of its own? The Unknown and Unknowable only!

"A man is the resultant and exponent of all the forces that have been brought to bear upon him, whether before his birth or after-wards. His action at any moment depends solely upon his constitu-tion, and on the intensity and direction of the various agencies to which he is, and has been, subjected. Some of these will counteract each other; but as he is by nature, and as he has been acted on, and is now acted on from without, so will he do, as certainly and regularly as though he were a machine.

"We do not generally admit this, because we do not know the whole nature of any one, nor the whole of the forces that act upon him. We see but a part, and being thus unable to generalise human conduct, except very roughly, we deny that it is subject to any fixed laws at all, and ascribe much both of a man's character and actions to chance, or luck, or fortune; but these are only words whereby we escape the admission of our own ignorance; and a little reflection will teach us that the most daring flight of the imagination or the most subtle exercise of the reason is as much the thing that must arise, and the only thing that can by any possibility arise, at the moment of its arising, as the falling of a dead leaf when the wind shakes it from the tree.

"For the future depends upon the present, and the present (whose existence is only one of those minor compromises of which human life is full—for it lives only on sufferance of the past and future) depends upon the past, and the past is unalterable. The only reason why we cannot see the future as plainly as the past, is because we know too little of the actual past and actual present; these things are too great for us, otherwise the future, in its minutest details, would lie spread out before our eyes, and we should lose our sense of time present by reason of the clearness with which we should see the past and future; perhaps we should not be even able to distinguish time at all; but that is foreign. What we do know is, that the more the past and present are known, the more the future can be predicted; and that no one dreams of doubting the fixity of the future in cases where he is fully cognisant of both past and present, and has had experience of the consequences that followed from such a past and such a present on previous occasions. He perfectly well knows what will happen, and will stake his whole fortune thereon.

"And this is a great blessing; for it is the foundation on which morality and science are built. The assurance that the future is no arbitrary and changeable thing, but that like futures will invariably follow like presents, is the groundwork on which we lay all our plans—the faith on which we do every conscious action of our lives. If this were not so we should be without a guide; we should have no confidence in acting, and hence we should never act, for there would be no knowing that the results which will follow now will be the same as those which followed before.

"Who would plough or sow if he disbelieved in the fixity of the future? Who would throw water on a blazing house if the action of water upon fire were uncertain? Men will only do their utmost when they feel certain that the future will discover itself against them if their utmost has not been done. The feeling of such a certainty is a constituent part of the sum of the forces at work upon them, and will act most powerfully on the best and most moral men. Those who are most firmly persuaded that the future is immutably bound up with the present in which their work is lying, will best husband their present, and till it with the greatest care. The future must be a lottery to those who think that the same combinations can sometimes precede one set of results, and sometimes another. If their belief is sincere they will speculate instead of working: these ought to be the immoral men; the others have the strongest spur to exertion and morality, if their belief is a living one.

"The bearing of all this upon the machines is not immediately apparent, but will become so presently. In the meantime I must deal with friends who tell me that, though the future is fixed as regards inorganic matter, and in some respects with regard to man, yet that there are many ways in which it cannot be considered as fixed. Thus, they say that fire applied to dry shavings, and well fed with oxygen gas, will always produce a blaze, but that a coward brought into contact with a terrifying object will not always result in a man running away. Nevertheless, if there be two cowards perfectly similar in every respect, and if they be subjected in a perfectly similar way to two terrifying agents, which are themselves perfectly similar, there are few who will not expect a perfect similarity in the running away, even though a thousand years intervene between the original combination and its being repeated.

"The apparently greater regularity in the results of chemical than of human combinations arises from our inability to perceive the subtle differences in human combinations—combinations which are never identically repeated. Fire we know, and shavings we know, but no two men ever were or ever will be exactly alike; and the smallest difference may change the whole conditions of the problem. Our registry of results must be infinite before we could arrive at a full forecast of future combinations; the wonder is that there is as much certainty concerning human action as there is; and assuredly the older we grow the more certain we feel as to what such and such a kind of person will do in given circumstances; but this could never be the case unless human conduct were under the influence of laws, with the working of which we become more and more familiar through experience.

"If the above is sound, it follows that the regularity with which machinery acts is no proof of the absence of vitality, or at least of germs which may be developed into a new phase of life. At first sight it would indeed appear that a vapour-engine cannot help going when set upon a line of rails with the steam up and the machinery in full play; whereas the man whose business it is to drive it can help doing so at any moment that he pleases; so that the first has no spontaneity, and is not possessed of any sort of free will, while the second has and is.

"This is true up to a certain point; the driver can stop the engine at any moment that he pleases, but he can only please to do so at certain points which have been fixed for him by others, or in the case of unexpected obstructions which force him to please to do so. His pleasure is not spontaneous; there is an unseen choir of influences around him, which makes it impossible for him to act in any other way than one. It is known beforehand how much strength must be given to these influences, just as it is known beforehand how much coal and water are necessary for the vapour-engine itself; and curiously enough it will be found that the influences brought to bear upon the driver are of the same kind as those brought to bear upon the engine—that is to say, food and warmth. The driver is obedient to his masters, because he gets food and warmth from them, and if these are withheld or given in insufficient quantities he will cease to drive; in like manner the engine will cease to work if it is insufficiently fed. The only difference is, that the man is conscious about his wants, and the engine (beyond refusing to work) does not seem to be so; but this is temporary, and has been dealt with above.

"Accordingly, the requisite strength being given to the motives that are to drive the driver, there has never, or hardly ever, been an instance of a man stopping his engine through wantonness. But such a case might occur; yes, and it might occur that the engine should break down: but if the train is stopped from some trivial motive it will be found either that the strength of the necessary influences has been miscalculated, or that the man has been miscalculated, in the same way as an engine may break down from an unsuspected flaw; but even in such a case there will have been no spontaneity; the action will have had its true parental causes: spontaneity is only a term for man's ignorance of the gods.

"Is there, then, no spontaneity on the part of those who drive the driver?"

Here followed an obscure argument upon this subject, which I have thought it best to omit. The writer resumes:—"After all then it comes to this, that the difference between the life of a man and that of a machine is one rather of degree than of kind, though differences in kind are not wanting. An animal has more provision for emergency than a machine. The machine is less versatile; its range of action is narrow; its strength and accuracy in its own sphere are superhuman, but it shows badly in a dilemma; sometimes when its normal action is disturbed, it will lose its head, and go from bad to worse like a lunatic in a raging frenzy: but here, again, we are met by the same consideration as before, namely, that the machines are still in their infancy; they are mere skeletons without muscles and flesh.

"For how many emergencies is an oyster adapted? For as many as are likely to happen to it, and no more. So are the machines; and so is man himself. The list of casualties that daily occur to man through his want of adaptability is probably as great as that occurring to the machines; and every day gives them some greater provision for the unforeseen. Let any one examine the wonderful self-regulating and self-adjusting contrivances which are now incorporated with the vapour-engine, let him watch the way in which it supplies itself with oil; in which it indicates its wants to those who tend it; in which, by the governor, it regulates its application of its own strength; let him look at that store-house of inertia and momentum the fly-wheel, or at the buffers on a railway carriage; let him see how those improvements are being selected for perpetuity which contain provision against the emergencies that may arise to harass the machines, and then let him think of a hundred thousand years, and the accumulated progress which they will bring unless man can be awakened to a sense of his situation, and of the doom which he is preparing for himself.*

"The misery is that man has been blind so long already. In his reliance upon the use of steam he has been betrayed into increasing

---

* Since my return to England, I have been told that those who are conversant about machines use many terms concerning them which show that their vitality is here recognised, and that a collection of expressions in use among those who attend on steam engines would be no less startling than instructive. I am also informed, that almost all machines have their own tricks and idiosyncracies; that they know their drivers and keepers, and that they will play pranks upon a stranger. It is my intention, on a future occasion, to bring together examples both of the expressions in common use among mechanicians, and of any extraordinary exhibitions of mechanical sagacity and eccentricity that I can meet with—not as believing in the Erewhonian Professor's theory, but from the interest of the subject.

and multiplying. To withdraw steam power suddenly will not have the effect of reducing us to the state in which we were before its introduction; there will be a general break-up and time of anarchy such as has never been known; it will be as though our population were suddenly doubled, with no additional means of feeding the increased number. The air we breathe is hardly more necessary for our animal life than the use of any machine, on the strength of which we have increased our numbers, is to our civilisation; it is the machines which act upon man and make him man, as much as man who has acted upon and made the machines; but we must choose between the alternative of undergoing much present suffering, or seeing ourselves gradually superseded by our own creatures, till we rank no higher in comparison with them, than the beasts of the field with ourselves.

"Herein lies our danger. For many seem inclined to acquiesce in so dishonourable a future. They say that although man should become to the machines what the horse and dog are to us, yet that he will continue to exist, and will probably be better off in a state of domestication under the beneficent rule of the machines than in his present wild condition. We treat our domestic animals with much kindness. We give them whatever we believe to be the best for them; and there can be no doubt that our use of meat has increased their happiness rather than detracted from it. In like manner there is reason to hope that the machines will use us kindly, for their existence will be in a great measure dependent upon ours; they will rule us with a rod of iron, but they will not eat us; they will not only require our services in the reproduction and education of their young, but also in waiting upon them as servants; in gathering food for them, and feeding them; in restoring them to health when they are sick; and in either burying their dead or working up their deceased members into new forms of mechanical existence.

"The very nature of the motive power which works the advancement of the machines precludes the possibility of man's life being rendered miserable as well as enslaved. Slaves are tolerably happy if they have good masters, and the revolution will not occur in our time, nor hardly in ten thousand years, or ten times that. Is it wise to be uneasy about a contingency which is so remote? Man is not a sentimental animal where his material interests are concerned, and though here and there some ardent soul may look upon himself and curse his fate that he was not born a vapour-engine, yet the mass of mankind will acquiesce in any arrangement which gives them better food and clothing at a cheaper rate, and will refrain from yielding to unreasonable jealousy merely because there are other destinies more glorious than their own.

"The power of custom is enormous, and so gradual will be the change, that man's sense of what is due to himself will be at no time rudely shocked; our bondage will steal upon us noiselessly and by imperceptible approaches; nor will there ever be such a clashing of desires between man and the machines as will lead to an encounter between them. Among themselves the machines will war eternally, but they will still require man as the being through whose agency the struggle will be principally conducted. In point of fact there is no occasion for anxiety about the future happiness of man so long as he continues to be in any way profitable to the machines; he may become the inferior race, but he will be infinitely better off than he is now. Is it not then both absurd and unreasonable to be envious of our benefactors? And should we not be guilty of consummate folly if we were to reject advantages which we cannot obtain otherwise, merely because they involve a greater gain to others than to ourselves?

"With those who can argue in this way I have nothing in common. I shrink with as much horror from believing that my race can ever be superseded or surpassed, as I should do from believing that even at the remotest period my ancestors were other than human beings. Could I believe that ten hundred thousand years ago a single one of my ancestors was another kind of being to myself, I should lose all self-respect, and take no further pleasure or interest in life. I have the same feeling with regard to my descendants, and believe it to be one that will be felt so generally that the country will resolve upon putting an immediate stop to all further mechanical progress, and upon destroying all improvements that have been made for the last three hundred years. I would not urge more than this. We may trust ourselves to deal with those that remain, and though I should prefer to have seen the destruction include another two hundred years, I am aware of the necessity for compromising, and would so far sacrifice my own individual convictions as to be content with three hundred. Less than this will be insufficient."

This was the conclusion of the attack which led to the destruction of machinery throughout Erewhon. There was only one serious attempt to answer it. Its author said that machines were to be regarded as a part of man's own physical nature, being really nothing but extra-corporeal limbs. Man, he said, was a machinate mammal. The lower animals keep all their limbs at home in their own bodies, but many of man's are loose, and lie about detached, now here and now there, in various parts of the world—some being kept always handy for contingent use, and others being occasionally hundreds of miles away. A machine is merely a supplementary limb; this is the be all and end all of machinery. We do not use our own limbs other than as machines; and a leg is only a much better wooden leg than any one can manufacture.

"Observe a man digging with a spade; his right fore-arm has become artificially lengthened, and his hand has become a joint. The handle of the spade is like the knob at the end of the humerus; the shaft is the additional bone, and the oblong iron plate is the new form of the hand which enables its possessor to disturb the earth in a way to which his original hand was unequal. Having thus modified himself, not as other animals are modified, by circumstances over which they have had not even the appearance of control, but having, as it were, taken forethought and added a cubit to his stature, civilisation began to dawn upon the race, the social good offices, the genial companionship of friends, the art of unreason, and all those habits of mind which most elevate man above the lower animals, in the course of time ensued.

"Thus civilisation and mechanical progress advanced hand in hand, each developing and being developed by the other, the earliest accidental use of the stick having set the ball rolling, and the prospect of advantage keeping it in motion. In fact, machines are to be regarded as the mode of development by which human organism is now especially advancing, every past invention being an addition to the resources of the human body. Even community of limbs is thus rendered possible to those who have so much community of soul as to own money enough to pay a railway fare; for a train is only a seven-leagued foot that five hundred may own at once."

The one serious danger which this writer apprehended was that the machines would so equalise men's powers, and so lessen the severity of competition, that many persons of inferior physique would escape detection and transmit their inferiority to their descendants. He feared that the removal of the present pressure might cause a degeneracy of the human race, and indeed that the whole body might become purely rudimentary, the man himself being nothing but soul and mechanism, an intelligent but passionless principle of mechanical action.

"How greatly," he wrote, "do we not now live with our external limbs? We vary our physique with the seasons, with age, with advancing or decreasing wealth. If it is wet we are furnished with an organ commonly called an umbrella, and which is designed for the purpose of protecting our clothes or our skins from the injurious effects of rain. Man has now many extra-corporeal members, which are of more importance to him than a good deal of his hair, or at any rate than his whiskers. His memory goes in his pocket-book. He becomes more and more complex as he grows older; he will then be seen with see-engines, or perhaps with artificial teeth and hair: if he be a really well-developed specimen of his race, he will be furnished with a large box upon wheels, two horses, and a coachman."

It was this writer who originated the custom of classifying men by their horse-power, and who divided them into genera, species, varieties, and subvarieties, giving them names from the hypothetical language which expressed the number of limbs which they could command at any moment. He showed that men became more highly and delicately organised the more nearly they approached the summit of opulence, and that none but millionaires possessed the full complement of limbs with which mankind could become incorporate.

"Those mighty organisms," he continued, "our leading bankers and merchants, speak to their congeners through the length and breadth of the land in a second of time; their rich and subtle souls can defy all material impediment, whereas the souls of the poor are clogged and hampered by matter, which sticks fast about them as treacle to the wings of a fly, or as one struggling in a quicksand: their dull ears must take days or weeks to hear what another would tell them from a distance, instead of hearing it in a second as is done by the more highly organised classes. Who shall deny that one who can tack on a special train to his identity, and go wheresoever he will whensoever he pleases, is more highly organised than he who, should he wish for the same power, might wish for the wings of a bird with an equal chance of getting them; and whose legs are his only means of locomotion? That old philosophic enemy, matter, the inherently and essentially evil, still hangs about the neck of the poor and strangles him: but to the rich, matter is immaterial; the elaborate organisation of his extra-corporeal system has freed his soul.

"This is the secret of the homage which we see rich men receive from those who are poorer than themselves: it would be a grave error to suppose that this deference proceeds from motives which we need be ashamed of: it is the natural respect which all living creatures pay to those whom they recognise as higher than themselves in the scale of animal life, and is analogous to the veneration which a dog feels for man. Among savage races it is deemed highly honourable to be the possessor of a gun, and throughout all known time there has been a feeling that those who are worth most are the worthiest."

And so he went on at considerable length, attempting to show what changes in the distribution of animal and vegetable life throughout the kingdom had been caused by this and that of man's inventions, and in what way each was connected with the moral and intellectual development of the human species: he even allotted to some the share which they had had in the creation and modification of man's body, and that which they would hereafter have in its destruction; but the other writer was considered to have the best of it, and in the end succeeded in destroying all the inventions that had been discovered for the preceding 271 years, a period which was agreed upon by all parties after several years of wrangling as to whether a certain kind of mangle which was much in use among washerwomen should be saved or no. It was at last ruled to be dangerous, and was just excluded by the limit of 271 years. Then came the reactionary civil wars which nearly ruined the country, but which it would be beyond my present scope to describe.

CHAPTER XXVI

THE VIEWS OF AN EREWHONIAN PROPHET CONCERNING THE RIGHTS OF ANIMALS

IT WILL BE seen from the foregoing chapters that the Erewhonians are a meek and long-suffering people, easily led by the nose, and quick to offer up common sense at the shrine of logic, when a philosopher arises among them, who carries them away through his reputation for especial learning, or by convincing them that their existing institutions are not based on the strictest principles of morality.

The series of revolutions on which I shall now briefly touch shows this even more plainly than the way (already dealt with) in which at a later date they cut their throats in the matter of machinery; for if the second of the two reformers of whom I am about to speak had had his way—or rather the way that he professed to have—the whole race would have died of starvation within a twelve-month. Happily common sense, though she is by nature the gentlest creature living, when she feels the knife at her throat, is apt to develop unexpected powers of resistance, and to send doctrinaires flying, even when they have bound her down and think they have her at their mercy. What happened, so far as I could collect it from the best authorities, was as follows:—

Some two thousand five hundred years ago the Erewhonians were still uncivilised, and lived by hunting, fishing, a rude system of agriculture, and plundering such few other nations as they had not yet completely conquered. They had no schools or systems of philosophy, but by a kind of dog-knowledge did that which was right in their own eyes and in those of their neighbours; the common sense, therefore, of the public being as yet unvitiated, crime and disease were looked upon much as they are in other countries.

But with the gradual advance of civilisation and increase in material prosperity, people began to ask questions about things that they had hitherto taken as matters of course, and one old gentleman, who had great influence over them by reason of the sanctity of his life, and his supposed inspiration by an unseen power, whose existence was now beginning to be felt, took it into his head to disquiet himself about the rights of animals—a question that so far had disturbed nobody.

All prophets are more or less fussy, and this old gentleman seems to have been one of the more fussy ones. Being maintained at the public expense, he had ample leisure, and not content with limiting his attention to the rights of animals, he wanted to reduce right and wrong to rules, to consider the foundations of duty and of good and evil, and otherwise to put all sorts of matters on a logical basis, which people whose time is money are content to accept on no basis at all.

As a matter of course, the basis on which he decided that duty could alone rest was one that afforded no standing-room for many of the old-established habits of the people. These, he assured them, were all wrong, and whenever any one ventured to differ from him, he referred the matter to the unseen power with which he alone was in direct communication, and the unseen power invariably assured him that he was right. As regards the rights of animals he taught as follows:—

"You know," he said, "how wicked it is of you to kill one another. Once upon a time your forefathers made no scruple about not only killing, but also eating their relations. No one would now go back to such detestable practices, for it is notorious that we have lived much more happily since they were abandoned. From this increased prosperity we may confidently deduce the maxim that we should not kill and eat our fellow-creatures. I have consulted the higher power by whom you know that I am inspired, and he has assured me that this conclusion is irrefragable.

"Now it cannot be denied that sheep, cattle, deer, birds, and fishes are our fellow-creatures. They differ from us in some respects, but those in which they differ are few and secondary, while those that they have in common with us are many and essential. My friends, if it was wrong of you to kill and eat your fellow-men, it is wrong also to kill and eat fish, flesh, and fowl. Birds, beasts, and fishes, have as full a right to live as long as they can unmolested by man, as man has to live unmolested by his neighbours. These words, let me again assure you, are not mine, but those of the higher power which inspires me.

"I grant," he continued, "that animals molest one another, and that some of them go so far as to molest man, but I have yet to learn that we should model our conduct on that of the lower animals. We should endeavour, rather, to instruct them, and bring them to a better mind. To kill a tiger, for example, who has lived on the flesh of men and women whom he has killed, is to reduce ourselves to the level of the tiger, and is unworthy of people who seek to be guided by the highest principles in all, both their thoughts and actions.

"The unseen power who has revealed himself to me alone among you, has told me to tell you that you ought by this time to have outgrown the barbarous habits of your ancestors. If, as you believe, you know better than they, you should do better. He commands you, therefore, to refrain from killing any living being for the sake of eating it. The only animal food that you may eat, is the flesh of any birds, beasts, or fishes that you may come upon as having died a natural death, or any that may have been born prematurely, or so deformed that it is a mercy to put them out of their pain; you may also eat all such animals as have committed suicide. As regards vegetables you may eat all those that will let you eat them with impunity."

So wisely and so well did the old prophet argue, and so terrible were the threats he hurled at those who should disobey him, that in the end he carried the more highly educated part of the people with him, and presently the poorer classes followed suit, or professed to do so. Having seen the triumph of his principles, he was gathered to his fathers, and no doubt entered at once into full communion with that unseen power whose favour he had already so pre-eminently enjoyed.

He had not, however, been dead very long, before some of his more ardent disciples took it upon them to better the instruction of their master. The old prophet had allowed the use of eggs and milk, but his disciples decided that to eat a fresh egg was to destroy a potential chicken, and that this came to much the same as murdering a live one. Stale eggs, if it was quite certain that they were too far gone to be able to be hatched, were grudgingly permitted, but all eggs offered for sale had to be submitted to an inspector, who, on being satisfied that they were addled, would label them "Laid not less than three months" from the date, whatever it might happen to be. These eggs, I need hardly say, were only used in puddings, and as a medicine in certain cases where an emetic was urgently required. Milk was forbidden inasmuch as it could not be obtained without robbing some calf of its natural sustenance, and thus endangering its life.

It will be easily believed that at first there were many who gave the new rules outward observance, but embraced every opportunity of indulging secretly in those flesh-pots to which they had been accustomed. It was found that animals were continually dying natural deaths under more or less suspicious circumstances. Suicidal mania, again, which had hitherto been confined exclusively to donkeys, became alarmingly prevalent even among such for the most part self-respecting creatures as sheep and cattle. It was astonishing how some of these unfortunate animals would scent out a butcher's knife if there was one within a mile of them, and run right up against it if the butcher did not get it out of their way in time.

Dogs, again, that had been quite law-abiding as regards domestic poultry, tame rabbits, sucking pigs, or sheep and lambs, suddenly took to breaking beyond the control of their masters, and killing anything that they were told not to touch. It was held that any animal killed by a dog had died a natural death, for it was the dog's nature to kill things, and he had only refrained from molesting farmyard creatures hitherto because his nature had been tampered with. Unfortunately the more these unruly tendencies became developed, the more the common people seemed to delight in breeding the very animals that would put temptation in the dog's way. There is little doubt, in fact, that they were deliberately evading the law; but whether this was so or no they sold or ate everything their dogs had killed.

Evasion was more difficult in the case of the larger animals, for the magistrates could not wink at all the pretended suicides of pigs, sheep, and cattle that were brought before them. Sometimes they had to convict, and a few convictions had a very terrorising effect—whereas in the case of animals killed by a dog, the marks of the dog's teeth could be seen, and it was practically impossible to prove malice on the part of the owner of the dog.

Another fertile source of disobedience to the law was furnished by a decision of one of the judges that raised a great outcry among the more fervent disciples of the old prophet. The judge held that it was lawful to kill any animal in self-defence, and that such conduct was so natural on the part of a man who found himself attacked, that the attacking creature should be held to have died a natural death. The High Vegetarians had indeed good reason to be alarmed, for hardly had this decision become generally known before a number of animals, hitherto harmless, took to attacking their owners with such ferocity, that it became necessary to put them to a natural death. Again, it was quite common at that time to see the carcase of a calf, lamb, or kid exposed for sale with a label from the inspector certifying that it had been killed in self-defence. Sometimes even the carcase of a lamb or calf was exposed as "warranted still-born," when it presented every appearance of having enjoyed at least a month of life.

As for the flesh of animals that had *bona fide* died a natural death, the permission to eat it was nugatory, for it was generally eaten by some other animal before man got hold of it; or failing this it was often poisonous, so that practically people were forced to evade the law by some of the means above spoken of, or to become vegetarians. This last alternative was so little to the taste of the Erewhonians, that the laws against killing animals were falling into desuetude, and would very likely have been repealed, but for the breaking out of a pestilence, which was ascribed by the priests and prophets of the day to the lawlessness of the people in the matter of eating forbidden flesh. On this, there was a reaction; stringent laws were passed, forbidding the use of meat in any form or shape, and permitting no food but grain, fruits, and vegetables to be sold in shops and markets. These laws were enacted about two hundred years after the death of the old prophet who had first unsettled people's minds about the rights of animals; but they had hardly been passed before people again began to break them.

I was told that the most painful consequence of all this folly did not lie in the fact that law-abiding people had to go without animal food—many nations do this and seem none the worse, and even in flesh-eating countries such as Italy, Spain, and Greece, the poor seldom see meat from year's end to year's end. The mischief lay in the jar which undue prohibition gave to the consciences of all but those who were strong enough to know that though conscience as a rule boons, it can also bane. The awakened conscience of an individual will often lead him to do things in haste that he had better have left undone, but the conscience of a nation awakened by a respectable old gentleman who has an unseen power up his sleeve will pave hell with a vengeance.

Young people were told that it was a sin to do what their fathers had done unhurt for centuries; those, moreover, who preached to them about the enormity of eating meat, were an unattractive academic folk, and though they overawed all but the bolder youths, there were few who did not in their hearts dislike them. However much the young person might be shielded, he soon got to know that men and women of the world—often far nicer people than the prophets who preached abstention—continually spoke sneeringly of the new doctrinaire laws, and were believed to set them aside in secret, though they dared not do so openly. Small wonder, then, that the more human among the student classes were provoked by the touch-not, taste-not, handle-not precepts of their rulers, into questioning much that they would otherwise have unhesitatingly accepted.

One sad story is on record about a young man of promising amiable disposition, but cursed with more conscience than brains, who had been told by his doctor (for as I have above said disease was not yet held to be criminal) that he ought to eat meat, law or no law. He was much shocked and for some time refused to comply with what he deemed the unrighteous advice given him by his doctor; at last, however, finding that he grew weaker and weaker, he stole secretly on a dark night into one of those dens in which meat was surreptitiously sold, and bought a pound of prime steak. He took it home, cooked it in his bedroom when every one in the house had gone to rest, ate it, and though he could hardly sleep for remorse and shame, felt so much better next morning that he hardly knew himself.

Three or four days later, he again found himself irresistibly drawn to this same den. Again he bought a pound of steak, again he cooked and ate it, and again, in spite of much mental torture, on the following morning felt himself a different man. To cut the story short, though he never went beyond the bounds of moderation, it preyed upon his mind that he should be drifting, as he certainly was, into the ranks of the habitual law-breakers.

All the time his health kept on improving, and though he felt sure that he owed this to the beefsteaks, the better he became in body, the more his conscience gave him no rest; two voices were for ever ringing in his ears—the one saying, "I am Common Sense and Nature; heed me, and I will reward you as I rewarded your fathers before you." But the other voice said: "Let not that plausible spirit lure you to your ruin. I am Duty; heed me, and I will reward you as I rewarded your fathers before you."

Sometimes he even seemed to see the faces of the speakers. Common Sense looked so easy, genial, and serene, so frank and fearless, that do what he might he could not mistrust her; but as he was on the point of following her, he would be checked by the austere face of Duty, so grave, but yet so kindly; and it cut him to the heart that from time to time he should see her turn pitying away from him as he followed after her rival.

The poor boy continually thought of the better class of his fellow-students, and tried to model his conduct on what he thought was theirs. "They," he said to himself, "eat a beefsteak? Never." But they most of them ate one now and again, unless it was a mutton chop that tempted them. And they used him for a model much as he did them. "He," they would say to themselves, "eat a mutton chop? Never." One night, however, he was followed by one of the authorities, who was always prowling about in search of law-breakers, and was caught coming out of the den with half a shoulder of mutton concealed about his person. On this, even though he had not been put in prison, he would have been sent away with his prospects in life irretrievably ruined; he therefore hanged himself as soon as he got home.

CHAPTER XXVII

THE VIEWS OF AN EREWHONIAN PHILOSOPHER CONCERNING THE RIGHTS OF VEGETABLES

LET ME LEAVE this unhappy story, and return to the course of events among the Erewhonians at large. No matter how many laws they passed increasing the severity of the punishments inflicted on those who ate meat in secret, the people found means of setting them aside as fast as they were made. At times, indeed, they would become almost obsolete, but when they were on the point of being repealed, some national disaster or the preaching of some fanatic would reawaken the conscience of the nation, and people were imprisoned by the thousand for illicitly selling and buying animal food.

About six or seven hundred years, however, after the death of the old prophet, a philosopher appeared, who, though he did not claim to have any communication with an unseen power, laid down the law with as much confidence as if such a power had inspired him. Many think that this philosopher did not believe his own teaching, and, being in secret a great meat-eater, had no other end in view than reducing the prohibition against eating animal food to an absurdity, greater even than an Erewhonian Puritan would be able to stand.

Those who take this view hold that he knew how impossible it would be to get the nation to accept legislation that it held to be sinful; he knew also how hopeless it would be to convince people that it was not wicked to kill a sheep and eat it, unless he could show them that they must either sin to a certain extent, or die. He, therefore, it is believed, made the monstrous proposals of which I will now speak.

He began by paying a tribute of profound respect to the old prophet, whose advocacy of the rights of animals, he admitted, had done much to soften the national character, and enlarge its views about the sanctity of life in general. But he urged that times had now changed; the lesson of which the country had stood in need had been sufficiently learnt, while as regards vegetables much had become known that was not even suspected formerly, and which, if the nation was to persevere in that strict adherence to the highest moral principles which had been the secret of its prosperity hitherto, must necessitate a radical change in its attitude towards them.

It was indeed true that much was now known that had not been suspected formerly, for the people had had no foreign enemies, and, being both quick-witted and inquisitive into the mysteries of nature, had made extraordinary progress in all the many branches of art and science. In the chief Erewhonian museum I was shown a microscope of considerable power, that was ascribed by the authorities to a date much about that of the philosopher of whom I am now speaking, and was even supposed by some to have been the instrument with which he had actually worked.

This philosopher was Professor of Botany in the chief seat of learning then in Erewhon, and whether with the help of the microscope still preserved, or with another, had arrived at a conclusion now universally accepted among ourselves—I mean, that all, both animals and plants, have had a common ancestry, and that hence the second should be deemed as much alive as the first. He contended, therefore, that animals and plants were cousins, and would have been seen to be so, all along, if people had not made an arbitrary and unreasonable division between what they chose to call the animal and vegetable kingdoms.

He declared, and demonstrated to the satisfaction of all those who were able to form an opinion upon the subject, that there is no difference appreciable either by the eye, or by any other test, between a germ that will develop into an oak, a vine, a rose, and one that (given its accustomed surroundings) will become a mouse, an elephant, or a man.

He contended that the course of any germ's development was dictated by the habits of the germs from which it was descended, and of whose identity it had once formed part. If a germ found itself placed as the germs in the line of its ancestry were placed, it would do as its ancestors had done, and grow up into the same kind of organism as theirs. If it found the circumstances only a little different, it would make shift (successfully or unsuccessfully) to modify its development accordingly; if the circumstances were widely different, it would die, probably without an effort at self-adaptation. This, he argued, applied equally to the germs of plants and of animals.

He therefore connected all, both animal and vegetable development, with intelligence, either spent and now unconscious, or still unspent and conscious; and in support of his view as regards vegetable life, he pointed to the way in which all plants have adapted themselves to their habitual environment. Granting that vegetable intelligence at first sight appears to differ materially from animal, yet, he urged, it is like it in the one essential fact that though it has evidently busied itself about matters that are vital to the well-being of the organism that possesses it, it has never shown the slightest tendency to occupy itself with anything else. This, he insisted, is as great a proof of intelligence as any living being can give.

"Plants," said he, "show no sign of interesting themselves in human affairs. We shall never get a rose to understand that five times seven are thirty-five, and there is no use in talking to an oak about fluctuations in the price of stocks. Hence we say that the oak and the rose are unintelligent, and on finding that they do not understand our business conclude that they do not understand their own. But what can a creature who talks in this way know about intelligence? Which shows greater signs of intelligence? He, or the rose and oak?

"And when we call plants stupid for not understanding our business, how capable do we show ourselves of understanding theirs? Can we form even the faintest conception of the way in which a seed from a rose-tree turns earth, air, warmth and water into a rose full-blown? Where does it get its colour from? From the earth, air, &c.? Yes—but how? Those petals of such ineffable texture—that hue that outvies the cheek of a child—that scent again? Look at earth, air, and water—these are all the raw material that the rose has got to work with; does it show any sign of want of intelligence in the alchemy with which it turns mud into rose-leaves? What chemist can do anything comparable? Why does no one try? Simply because every one knows that no human intelligence is equal to the task. We give it up. It is the rose's department; let the rose attend to it—and be dubbed unintelligent because it baffles us by the miracles it works, and the unconcerned businesslike way in which it works them.

"See what pains, again, plants take to protect themselves against their enemies. They scratch, cut, sting, make bad smells, secrete the most dreadful poisons (which Heaven only knows how they contrive to make), cover their precious seeds with spines like those of a hedgehog, frighten insects with delicate nervous systems by assuming portentous shapes, hide themselves, grow in inaccessible places, and tell lies so plausibly as to deceive even their subtlest foes.

"They lay traps smeared with bird-lime, to catch insects, and persuade them to drown themselves in pitchers which they have made of their leaves, and fill with water; others make themselves, as it were, into living rat-traps, which close with a spring on any insect that settles upon them; others make their flowers into the shape of a certain fly that is a great pillager of honey, so that when the real fly comes it thinks that the flowers are bespoke, and goes on elsewhere. Some are so clever as even to overreach themselves, like the horse-radish, which gets pulled up and eaten for the sake of that pungency with which it protects itself against underground enemies. If, on the other hand, they think that any insect can be of service to them, see how pretty they make themselves.

"What is to be intelligent if to know how to do what one wants to do, and to do it repeatedly, is not to be intelligent? Some say that the rose-seed does not want to grow into a rose-bush. Why, then, in the name of all that is reasonable, does it grow? Likely enough it is unaware of the want that is spurring it on to action. We have no reason to suppose that a human embryo knows that it wants to grow into a baby, or a baby into a man. Nothing ever shows signs of knowing what it is either wanting or doing, when its convictions both as to what it wants, and how to get it, have been settled beyond further power of question. The less signs living creatures give of knowing what they do, provided they do it, and do it repeatedly and well, the greater proof they give that in reality they know how to do it, and have done it already on an infinite number of past occasions.

"Some one may say," he continued, " 'What do you mean by talking about an infinite number of past occasions? When did a rose-seed make itself into a rose-bush on any past occasion?'

"I answer this question with another. 'Did the rose-seed ever form part of the identity of the rose-bush on which it grew?' Who can say that it did not? Again I ask: 'Was this rose-bush ever linked by all those links that we commonly consider as constituting personal identity, with the seed from which it in its turn grew?' Who can say that it was not?

"Then, if rose-seed number two is a continuation of the personality of its parent rose-bush, and if that rose-bush is a continuation of the personality of the rose-seed from which it sprang, rose-seed number two must also be a continuation of the personality of the earlier rose-seed. And this rose-seed must be a continuation of the personality of the preceding rose-seed—and so back and back *ad infinitum*. Hence it is impossible to deny continued personality between any existing rose-seed and the earliest seed that can be called a rose-seed at all.

"The answer, then, to our objector is not far to seek. The rose-seed did what it now does in the persons of its ancestors—to whom it has been so linked as to be able to remember what those ancestors did when they were placed as the rose-seed now is. Each stage of development brings back the recollection of the course taken in the preceding stage, and the development has been so often repeated, that all doubt—and with all doubt, all consciousness of action—is suspended.

"But an objector may still say, 'Granted that the linking between all successive generations has been so close and unbroken, that each one of them may be conceived as able to remember what it did in the persons of its ancestors—how do you show that it actually did remember?'

"The answer is: 'By the action which each generation takes—an action which repeats all the phenomena that we commonly associate with memory—which is explicable on the supposition that it has been guided by memory—and which has neither been explained, nor seems ever likely to be explained on any other theory than the supposition that there is an abiding memory between successive generations.'

"Will any one bring an example of any living creature whose action we can understand, performing an ineffably difficult and intricate action, time after time, with invariable success, and yet not knowing how to do it, and never having done it before? Show me the example and I will say no more, but until it is shown me, I shall credit action where I cannot watch it, with being controlled by the same laws as when it is within our ken. It will become unconscious as soon as the skill that directs it has become perfected. Neither rose-seed, therefore, nor embryo should be expected to show signs of knowing that they know what they know—if they showed such signs the fact of their knowing what they want, and how to get it, might more reasonably be doubted."

Some of the passages already given in Chapter XXIII were obviously inspired by the one just quoted. As I read it, in a reprint shown me by a Professor who had edited much of the early literature on the subject, I could not but remember the one in which our Lord tells His disciples to consider the lilies of the field, who neither toil nor spin, but whose raiment surpasses even that of Solomon in all his glory.

"They toil not, neither do they spin?" Is that so? "Toil not?" Perhaps not, now that the method of procedure is so well known as to admit of no further question—but it is not likely that lilies came to make themselves so beautifully without having ever taken any pains about the matter. "Neither do they spin?" Not with a spinning-wheel; but is there no textile fabric in a leaf?

What would the lilies of the field say if they heard one of us declaring that they neither toil nor spin? They would say, I take it, much what we should if we were to hear of their preaching humility on the text of Solomon, and saying, "Consider the Solomons in all their glory, they toil not neither do they spin." We should say that the lilies were talking about things that they did not understand, and that though the Solomons do not toil nor spin, yet there had been no lack of either toiling or spinning before they came to be arrayed so gorgeously.

Let me now return to the Professor. I have said enough to show the general drift of the arguments on which he relied in order to show that vegetables are only animals under another name, but have not stated his case in anything like the fullness with which he laid it before the public. The conclusion he drew, or pretended to draw, was that if it was sinful to kill and eat animals, it was not less sinful to do the like by vegetables, or their seeds. None such, he said, should be eaten, save what had died a natural death, such as fruit that was lying on the ground and about to rot, or cabbage-leaves that had turned yellow in late autumn. These and other like garbage he declared to be the only food that might be eaten with a clear conscience. Even so the eater must plant the pips of any apples or pears that he may have eaten, or any plum-stones, cherry-stones, and the like, or he would come near to incurring the guilt of infanticide. The grain of cereals, according to him, was out of the question, for every such grain had a living soul as much as man had, and had as good a right as man to possess that soul in peace.

Having thus driven his fellow countrymen into a corner at the point of a logical bayonet from which they felt that there was no escape, he proposed that the question what was to be done should be referred to an oracle in which the whole country had the greatest confidence, and to which recourse was always had in times of special perplexity. It was whispered that a near relation of the philosopher's was lady's-maid to the priestess who delivered the oracle, and the Puritan party declared that the strangely unequivocal answer of the oracle was obtained by backstairs influence; but whether this was so or no, the response as nearly as I can translate it was as follows:—

"He who sins aught
Sins more than he ought;
But he who sins nought
Has much to be taught.
Beat or be beaten,
Eat or be eaten,
Be killed or kill;
Choose which you will."

It was clear that this response sanctioned at any rate the destruction of vegetable life when wanted as food by man; and so forcibly had the philosopher shown that what was sauce for vegetables was so also for animals, that, though the Puritan party made a furious outcry, the acts forbidding the use of meat were repealed by a considerable majority. Thus, after several hundred years of wandering in the wilderness of philosophy, the country reached the conclusions that common sense had long since arrived at. Even the Puritans after a vain attempt to subsist on a kind of jam made of apples and yellow cabbage leaves, succumbed to the inevitable, and resigned themselves to a diet of roast beef and mutton, with all the usual adjuncts of a modern dinner-table.

One would have thought that the dance they had been led by the old prophet, and that still madder dance which the Professor of botany had gravely, but as I believe insidiously, proposed to lead them, would have made the Erewhonians for a long time suspicious of prophets whether they professed to have communications with an unseen power or no; but so engrained in the human heart is the desire to believe that some people really do know what they say they know, and can thus save them from the trouble of thinking for themselves, that in a short time would-be philosophers and faddists became more powerful than ever, and gradually led their countrymen to accept all those absurd views of life, some account of which I have given in my earlier chapters. Indeed I can see no hope for the Erewhonians till they have got to understand that reason uncorrected by instinct is as bad as instinct uncorrected by reason.

CHAPTER XXVIII

ESCAPE

THOUGH BUSILY ENGAGED in translating the extracts given in the last five chapters, I was also laying matters in train for my escape with Arowhena. And indeed it was high time, for I received an intimation from one of the cashiers of the Musical Banks, that I was to be prosecuted in a criminal court ostensibly for measles, but really for having owned a watch, and attempted the reintroduction of machinery.

I asked why measles? and was told that there was a fear lest extenuating circumstances should prevent a jury from convicting me, if I were indicted for typhus or small-pox, but that a verdict would probably be obtained for measles, a disease which could be sufficiently punished in a person of my age. I was given to understand that unless some unexpected change should come over the mind of his Majesty, I might expect the blow to be struck within a very few days.

My plan was this—that Arowhena and I should escape in a balloon together. I fear that the reader will disbelieve this part of my story, yet in no other have I endeavoured to adhere more conscientiously to facts, and can only throw myself upon his charity.

I had already gained the ear of the Queen, and had so worked upon her curiosity that she promised to get leave for me to have a balloon made and inflated; I pointed out to her that no complicated machinery would be wanted—nothing, in fact, but a large quantity of oiled silk, a car, a few ropes, &c., &c., and some light kind of gas, such as the antiquarians who were acquainted with the means employed by the ancients for the production of the lighter gases could easily instruct her workmen how to provide. Her eagerness to see so strange a sight as the ascent of a human being into the sky overcame any scruples of conscience that she might have otherwise felt, and she set the antiquarians about showing her workmen how to make the gas, and sent her maids to buy, and oil, a very large quantity of silk (for I was determined that the balloon should be a big one) even before she began to try and gain the King's permission; this, however, she now set herself to do, for I had sent her word that my prosecution was imminent.

As for myself, I need hardly say that I knew nothing about balloons; nor did I see my way to smuggling Arowhena into the car; nevertheless, knowing that we had no other chance of getting away from Erewhon, I drew inspiration from the extremity in which we were placed, and made a pattern from which the Queen's workmen were able to work successfully. Meanwhile the Queen's carriage-builders set about making the car, and it was with the attachments of this to the balloon that I had the greatest difficulty; I doubt, indeed, whether I should have succeeded here, but for the great intelligence of a foreman, who threw himself heart and soul into the matter, and often both foresaw requirements, the necessity for which had escaped me, and suggested the means of providing for them.

It happened that there had been a long drought, during the latter part of which prayers had been vainly offered up in all the temples of the air god. When I first told her Majesty that I wanted a balloon, I said my intention was to go up into the sky and prevail upon the air god by means of a personal interview. I own that this proposition bordered on the idolatrous, but I have long since repented of it, and am little likely ever to repeat the offence. Moreover the deceit, serious though it was, will probably lead to the conversion of the whole country.

When the Queen told his Majesty of my proposal, he at first not only ridiculed it, but was inclined to veto it. Being, however, a very uxorious husband, he at length consented—as he eventually always did to everything on which the Queen had set her heart. He yielded all the more readily now, because he did not believe in the possibility of my ascent; he was convinced that even though the balloon should mount a few feet into the air, it would collapse immediately, whereon I should fall and break my neck, and he should be rid of me. He demonstrated this to her so convincingly, that she was alarmed, and tried to talk me into giving up the idea, but on finding that I persisted in my wish to have the balloon made, she produced an order from the King to the effect that all facilities I might require should be afforded me.

At the same time her Majesty told me that my attempted ascent would be made an article of impeachment against me in case I did not succeed in prevailing on the air god to stop the drought. Neither King nor Queen had any idea that I meant going right away if I could get the wind to take me, nor had he any conception of the existence of a certain steady upper current of air which was always setting in one direction, as could be seen by the shape of the higher clouds, which pointed invariably from south-east to north-west. I had myself long noticed this peculiarity in the climate, and attributed it, I believe justly, to a trade-wind which was constant at a few thousand feet above the earth, but was disturbed by local influences at lower elevations.

My next business was to break the plan to Arowhena, and to devise the means for getting her into the car. I felt sure that she would come with me, but had made up my mind that if her courage failed her, the whole thing should come to nothing. Arowhena and I had been in constant communication through her maid, but I had thought it best not to tell her the details of my scheme till everything was settled. The time had now arrived, and I arranged with the maid that I should be admitted by a private door into Mr. Nosnibor's garden at about dusk on the following evening.

I came at the appointed time; the girl let me into the garden and bade me wait in a secluded alley until Arowhena should come. It was now early summer, and the leaves were so thick upon the trees that even though some one else had entered the garden I could have easily hidden myself. The night was one of extreme beauty; the sun had long set, but there was still a rosy gleam in the sky over the ruins of the railway station; below me was the city already twinkling with lights, while beyond it stretched the plains for many a league until they blended with the sky. I just noted these things, but I could not heed them. I could heed nothing, till, as I peered into the darkness of the alley, I perceived a white figure gliding swiftly towards me. I bounded towards it, and ere thought could either prompt or check, I had caught Arowhena to my heart and covered her unresisting cheek with kisses.

So overjoyed were we that we knew not how to speak; indeed I do not know when we should have found words and come to our senses, if the maid had not gone off into a fit of hysterics, and awakened us to the necessity of self-control; then, briefly and plainly, I unfolded what I proposed; I showed her the darkest side, for I felt sure that the darker the prospect the more likely she was to come. I told her that my plan would probably end in death for both of us, and that I dared not press it—that at a word from her it should be abandoned; still that there was just a possibility of our escaping together to some part of the world where there would be no bar to our getting married, and that I could see no other hope.

She made no resistance, not a sign or hint of doubt or hesitation. She would do all I told her, and come whenever I was ready; so I bade her send her maid to meet me nightly—told her that she must put a good face on, look as bright and happy as she could, so as to make her father and mother and Zulora think that she was forgetting me—and be ready at a moment's notice to come to the Queen's workshops, and be concealed among the ballast and under rugs in the car of the balloon; and so we parted.

I hurried my preparations forward, for I feared rain, and also that the King might change his mind; but the weather continued dry, and in another week the Queen's workmen had finished the balloon and car, while the gas was ready to be turned on into the balloon at any moment. All being now prepared I was to ascend on the following morning. I had stipulated for being allowed to take abundance of rugs and wrappings as protection from the cold of the upper atmosphere, and also ten or a dozen good-sized bags of ballast.

I had nearly a quarter's pension in hand, and with this I fee'd Arowhena's maid, and bribed the Queen's foreman—who would, I believe, have given me assistance even without a bribe. He helped me to secrete food and wine in the bags of ballast, and on the morning of my ascent he kept the other workmen out of the way while I got Arowhena into the car. She came with early dawn, muffled up, and in her maid's dress. She was supposed to be gone to an early performance at one of the Musical Banks, and told me that she should not be missed till breakfast, but that her absence must then be discovered. I arranged the ballast about her so that it should conceal her as she lay at the bottom of the car, and covered her with wrappings. Although it still wanted some hours of the time fixed for my ascent, I could not trust myself one moment from the car, so I got into it at once, and watched the gradual inflation of the balloon. Luggage I had none, save the provisions hidden in the ballast bags, the books of mythology, and the treatises on the machines, with my own manuscript diaries and translations.

I sat quietly, and awaited the hour fixed for my departure—quiet outwardly, but inwardly I was in an agony of suspense lest Arowhena's absence should be discovered before the arrival of the King and Queen, who were to witness my ascent. They were not due yet for another two hours, and during this time a hundred things might happen, any one of which would undo me.

At last the balloon was full; the pipe which had filled it was removed, the escape of the gas having been first carefully precluded. Nothing remained to hinder the balloon from ascending but the hands and weight of those who were holding on to it with ropes. I strained my eyes for the coming of the King and Queen, but could see no sign of their approach. I looked in the direction of Mr. Nosnibor's house—there was nothing to indicate disturbance, but it was not yet breakfast time. The crowd began to gather; they were aware that I was under the displeasure of the court, but I could detect no signs of my being unpopular. On the contrary, I received many kindly expressions of regard and encouragement, with good wishes as to the result of my journey.

I was speaking to one gentleman of my acquaintance, and telling him the substance of what I intended to do when I had got into the presence of the air god (what he thought of me I cannot guess, for I am sure that he did not believe in the objective existence of the air god, nor that I myself believed in it), when I became aware of a small crowd of people running as fast as they could from Mr. Nosnibor's house towards the Queen's workshops. For the moment my pulse ceased beating, and then, knowing that the time had come when I must either do or die, I called vehemently to those who were holding the ropes (some thirty men) to let go at once, and made gestures signifying danger, and that there would be mischief if they held on longer. Many obeyed; the rest were too weak to hold on to the ropes, and were forced to let them go. On this the balloon bounded suddenly upwards, but my own feeling was that the earth had dropped off from me, and was sinking fast into the open space beneath.

This happened at the very moment that the attention of the crowd was divided, the one half paying heed to the eager gestures of those coming from Mr. Nosnibor's house, and the other to the exclamations from myself. A minute more and Arowhena would doubtless have been discovered, but before that minute was over, I was at such a height above the city that nothing could harm me, and every second both the town and the crowd became smaller and more confused. In an incredibly short time, I could see little but a vast wall of blue plains rising up against me, towards whichever side I looked.

At first, the balloon mounted vertically upwards, but after about five minutes, when we had already attained a very great elevation, I fancied that the objects on the plain beneath began to move from under me. I did not feel so much as a breath of wind, and could not suppose that the balloon itself was travelling. I was, therefore, wondering what this strange movement of fixed objects could mean, when it struck me that people in a balloon do not feel the wind inasmuch as they travel with it and offer it no resistance. Then I was happy in thinking that I must now have reached the invariable trade wind of the upper air, and that I should be very possibly wafted for hundreds or even thousands of miles, far from Erewhon and the Erewhonians.

Already I had removed the wrappings and freed Arowhena; but I soon covered her up with them again, for it was already very cold, and she was half stupefied with the strangeness of her position.

And now began a time, dream-like and delirious, of which I do not suppose that I shall ever recover a distinct recollection. Some things I can recall—as that we were ere long enveloped in vapour which froze upon my moustache and whiskers; then comes a memory of sitting for hours and hours in a thick fog, hearing no sound but my own breathing and Arowhena's (for we hardly spoke) and seeing no sight but the car beneath us and beside us and the dark balloon above.

Perhaps the most painful feeling when the earth was hidden was that the balloon was motionless, though our only hope lay in our going forward with an extreme of speed. From time to time through a rift in the clouds I caught a glimpse of earth, and was thankful to perceive that we must be flying forward faster than in an express train; but no sooner was the rift closed than the old conviction of our being stationary returned in full force, and was not to be reasoned with; there was another feeling also which was nearly as bad; for as a child that fears it has gone blind in a long tunnel if there is no light, so ere the earth had been many minutes hidden, I became half frightened lest we might not have broken away from it clean and for ever. Now and again, I ate and gave food to Arowhena, but by guesswork as regards time. Then came darkness, a dreadful dreary time, without even the moon to cheer us.

With dawn the scene was changed: the clouds were gone and morning stars were shining; the rising of the splendid sun remains still impressed upon me as the most glorious that I have ever seen; beneath us there was an embossed chain of mountains with snow fresh fallen upon them; but we were far above them; we both of us felt our breathing seriously affected, but I would not allow the balloon to descend a single inch, not knowing for how long we might not need all the buoyancy which we could command; indeed I was thankful to find that, after nearly four-and-twenty hours, we were still at so great a height above the earth.

In a couple of hours we had passed the ranges, which must have been some hundred and fifty miles across, and again I saw a tract of level plain extending far away to the horizon. I knew not where we were, and dared not descend, lest I should waste the power of the balloon, but I was half hopeful that we might be above the country from which I had originally started. I looked anxiously for any sign by which I could recognise it, but could see nothing, and feared that we might be above some distant part of Erewhon, or a country inhabited by savages. While I was still in doubt, the balloon was again wrapped in clouds, and we were left to blank space and to conjectures.

The weary time dragged on. How I longed for my unhappy watch! I felt as though not even time was moving, so dumb and spell-bound were our surroundings. Sometimes I would feel my pulse, and count its beats for half-an-hour together; anything to mark the time—to prove that it was there, and to assure myself that we were within the blessed range of its influence, and not gone adrift into the timelessness of eternity.

I had been doing this for the twentieth or thirtieth time, and had fallen into a light sleep: I dreamed wildly of a journey in an express train, and of arriving at a railway station where the air was full of the sound of locomotive engines blowing off steam with a horrible and tremendous hissing; I woke frightened and uneasy, but the hissing and crashing noises pursued me now that I was awake, and forced me to own that they were real. What they were I knew not, but they grew gradually fainter and fainter, and after a time were lost. In a few hours the clouds broke, and I saw beneath me that which made the chilled blood run colder in my veins. I saw the sea, and nothing but the sea; in the main black, but flecked with white heads of storm-tossed, angry waves.

Arowhena was sleeping quietly at the bottom of the car, and as I looked at her sweet and saintly beauty, I groaned, and cursed myself for the misery into which I had brought her; but there was nothing for it now.

I sat and waited for the worst, and presently I saw signs as though that worst were soon to be at hand, for the balloon had begun to sink. On first seeing the sea I had been impressed with the idea that we must have been falling, but now there could be no mistake, we were sinking, and that fast. I threw out a bag of ballast, and for a time we rose again, but in the course of a few hours the sinking recommenced, and I threw out another bag.

Then the battle commenced in earnest. It lasted all that afternoon and through the night until the following evening. I had seen never a sail nor a sign of a sail, though I had half blinded myself with straining my eyes incessantly in every direction; we had parted with everything but the clothes which we had upon our backs; food and water were gone, all thrown out to the wheeling albatrosses, in order to save us a few hours or even minutes from the sea. I did not throw away the books till we were within a few feet of the water, and clung to my manuscripts to the very last. Hope there seemed none whatever—yet, strangely enough we were neither of us utterly hopeless, and even when the evil that we dreaded was upon us, and that which we greatly feared had come, we sat in the car of the balloon with the waters up to our middle and still smiled with a ghastly hopefulness to one another.

He who has crossed the St. Gothard will remember that below Andermatt there is one of those Alpine gorges which reach the very utmost limits of the sublime and terrible. The feelings of the traveller have become more and more highly wrought at every step, until at last the naked and overhanging precipices seem to close above his head, as he crosses a bridge hung in mid-air over a roaring waterfall, and enters on the darkness of a tunnel, hewn out of the rock.

What can be in store for him on emerging? Surely something even wilder and more desolate than that which he has seen already; yet his imagination is paralysed, and can suggest no fancy or vision of anything to surpass the reality which he had just witnessed. Awed and breathless he advances; when lo! the light of the afternoon sun welcomes him as he leaves the tunnel, and behold a smiling valley— a babbling brook, a village with tall belfries, and meadows of brilliant green—these are the things which greet him, and he smiles to himself as the terror passes away and in another moment is forgotten.

So fared it now with ourselves. We had been in the water some two or three hours, and the night had come upon us. We had said farewell for the hundredth time, and had resigned ourselves to meet the end; indeed I was myself battling with a drowsiness from which it was only too probable that I should never wake; when suddenly, Arowhena touched me on the shoulder, and pointed to a light and to a dark mass which was bearing right upon us. A cry for help—loud and clear and shrill—broke forth from both of us at once; and in another five minutes we were carried by kind and tender hands on to the deck of an Italian vessel.

CHAPTER XXIX

CONCLUSION

THE SHIP WAS the *Principe Umberto*, bound from Callao to Genoa; she had carried a number of emigrants to Rio, had gone thence to Callao, where she had taken in a cargo of guano, and was now on her way home. The captain was a certain Giovanni Gianni, a native of Sestri; he has kindly allowed me to refer to him in case the truth of my story should be disputed; but I grieve to say that I suffered him to mislead himself in some important particulars. I should add that when we were picked up we were a thousand miles from land.

As soon as we were on board, the captain began questioning us about the siege of Paris, from which city he had assumed that we must have come, notwithstanding our immense distance from Europe. As may be supposed, I had not heard a syllable about the war between France and Germany, and was too ill to do more than assent to all that he chose to put into my mouth. My knowledge of Italian is very imperfect, and I gathered little from anything that he said; but I was glad to conceal the true point of our departure, and resolved to take any cue that he chose to give me.

The line that thus suggested itself was that there had been ten or twelve others in the balloon, that I was an English Milord, and Arowhena a Russian Countess; that all the others had been drowned, and that the despatches which we had carried were lost. I came afterwards to learn that this story would not have been credible, had not the captain been for some weeks at sea, for I found that when we were picked up, the Germans had already long been masters of Paris. As it was, the captain settled the whole story for me, and I was well content.

In a few days we sighted an English vessel bound from Melbourne to London with wool. At my earnest request, in spite of stormy weather which rendered it dangerous for a boat to take us from one ship to the other, the captain consented to signal the English vessel, and we were received on board, but we were transferred with such difficulty that no communication took place as to the manner of our being found. I did indeed hear the Italian mate who was in charge of the boat shout out something in French to the effect that we had been picked up from a balloon, but the noise of the wind was so great, and the captain understood so little French that he caught nothing of the truth, and it was assumed that we were two persons who had been saved from ship-wreck. When the captain asked me in what ship I had been wrecked, I said that a party of us had been carried out to sea in a pleasure-boat by a strong current, and that Arowhena (whom I described as a Peruvian lady) and I were alone saved.

There were several passengers, whose goodness towards us we can never repay. I grieve to think that they cannot fail to discover that we did not take them fully into our confidence; but had we told them all, they would not have believed us, and I was determined that no one should hear of Erewhon, or have the chance of getting there before me, as long as I could prevent it. Indeed, the recollection of the many falsehoods which I was then obliged to tell, would render my life miserable were I not sustained by the consolations of my religion. Among the passengers there was a most estimable clergyman, by whom Arowhena and I were married within a very few days of our coming on board.

After a prosperous voyage of about two months, we sighted the Land's End, and in another week we were landed at London. A liberal subscription was made for us on board the ship, so that we found ourselves in no immediate difficulty about money. I accordingly took Arowhena down into Somersetshire, where my mother and sisters had resided when I last heard of them. To my great sorrow I found that my mother was dead, and that her death had been accelerated by the report of my having been killed, which had been brought to my employer's station by Chowbok. It appeared that he must have waited for a few days to see whether I returned, that he then considered it safe to assume that I should never do so, and had accordingly made up a story about my having fallen into a whirlpool of seething waters while coming down the gorge homeward. Search was made for my body, but the rascal had chosen to drown me in a place where there would be no chance of its ever being recovered.

My sisters were both married, but neither of their husbands was rich. No one seemed overjoyed on my return; and I soon discovered that when a man's relations have once mourned for him as dead, they seldom like the prospect of having to mourn for him a second time.

Accordingly I returned to London with my wife, and through the assistance of an old friend supported myself by writing good little stories for the magazines, and for a tract society. I was well paid; and I trust that I may not be considered presumptuous in saying that some of the most popular of the *brochures* which are distributed in the streets, and which are to be found in the waiting-rooms of the railway stations, have proceeded from my pen. During the time that I could spare, I arranged my notes and diary till they assumed their present shape. There remains nothing for me to add, save to unfold the scheme which I propose for the conversion of Erewhon.

That scheme has only been quite recently decided upon as the one which seems most likely to be successful.

It will be seen at once that it would be madness for me to go with ten or a dozen subordinate missionaries by the same way as that which led me to discover Erewhon. I should be imprisoned for typhus, besides being handed over to the straighteners for having run away with Arowhena: an even darker fate, to which I dare hardly again allude, would be reserved for my devoted fellow-labourers. It is plain, therefore, that some other way must be found for getting at the Erewhonians, and I am thankful to say that such another way is not wanting. One of the rivers which descends from the Snowy Mountains, and passes through Erewhon, is known to be navigable for several hundred miles from its mouth. Its upper waters have never yet been explored, but I feel little doubt that it will be found possible to take a light gunboat (for we must protect ourselves) to the outskirts of the Erewhonian country.

I propose, therefore, that one of those associations should be formed in which the risk of each of the members is confined to the amount of his stake in the concern. The first step would be to draw up a prospectus. In this I would advise that no mention should be made of the fact that the Erewhonians are the lost tribes. The discovery is one of absorbing interest to myself, but it is of a sentimental rather than commercial value, and business is business. The capital to be raised should not be less than fifty thousand pounds, and might be either in five or ten pound shares as hereafter determined. This should be amply sufficient for the expenses of an experimental voyage.

When the money had been subscribed, it would be our duty to charter a steamer of some twelve or fourteen hundred tons burden, and with accommodation for a cargo of steerage passengers. She should carry two or three guns in case of her being attacked by savages at the mouth of the river. Boats of considerable size should be also provided, and I think it would be desirable that these also should carry two or three six-pounders. The ship should be taken up the river as far as was considered safe, and a picked party should then ascend in the boats. The presence both of Arowhena and myself would be necessary at this stage, inasmuch as our knowledge of the language would disarm suspicion, and facilitate negotiations.

We should begin by representing the advantages afforded to labour in the colony of Queensland, and point out to the Erewhonians that by emigrating thither, they would be able to amass, each and all of them, enormous fortunes—a fact which would be easily provable by a reference to statistics. I have no doubt that a very great number might be thus induced to come back with us in the larger boats, and that we could fill our vessel with emigrants in three or four journeys.

Should we be attacked, our course would be even simpler, for the Erewhonians have no gunpowder, and would be so surprised with its effects that we should be able to capture as many as we chose; in this case we should feel able to engage them on more advantageous terms, for they would be prisoners of war. But even though we were to meet with no violence, I doubt not that a cargo of seven or eight hundred Erewhonians could be induced, when they were once on board the vessel, to sign an agreement which should be mutually advantageous both to us and them.

We should then proceed to Queensland, and dispose of our engagement with the Erewhonians to the sugar-growers of that settlement, who are in great want of labour; it is believed that the money thus realised would enable us to declare a handsome dividend, and leave a considerable balance, which might be spent in repeating our operations and bringing over other cargoes of Erewhonians, with fresh consequent profits. In fact we could go backwards and forwards as long as there was a demand for labour in Queensland, or indeed in any other Christian colony, for the supply of Erewhonians would be unlimited, and they could be packed closely and fed at a very reasonable cost.

It would be my duty and Arowhena's to see that our emigrants should be boarded and lodged in the households of religious sugar-growers; these persons would give them the benefit of that instruction whereof they stand so greatly in need. Each day, as soon as they could be spared from their work in the plantations, they would be assembled for praise, and be thoroughly grounded in the Church Catechism, while the whole of every Sabbath should be devoted to singing psalms and church-going.

This must be insisted upon, both in order to put a stop to any uneasy feeling which might show itself either in Queensland or in the mother country as to the means whereby the Erewhonians had been obtained, and also because it would give our own shareholders the comfort of reflecting that they were saving souls and filling their own pockets at one and the same moment. By the time the emigrants had got too old for work they would have become thoroughly instructed in religion; they could then be shipped back to Erewhon and carry the good seed with them.

I can see no hitch nor difficulty about the matter, and trust that this book will sufficiently advertise the scheme to insure the subscription of the necessary capital; as soon as this is forthcoming I will guarantee that I convert the Erewhonians not only into good Christians but into a source of considerable profit to the shareholders.

I should add that I cannot claim the credit for having originated the above scheme. I had been for months at my wit's end, forming plan after plan for the evangelisation of Erewhon, when by one of those special interpositions which should be a sufficient answer to the sceptic, and make even the most confirmed rationalist irrational, my eye was directed to the following paragraph in the *Times* newspaper, of one of the first days in January 1872:—

"POLYNESIANS IN QUEENSLAND.— The Marquis of Normanby, the new Governor of Queensland, has completed his inspection of the northern districts of the colony. It is stated that at Mackay, one of the best sugar-growing districts, his Excellency saw a good deal of the Polynesians. In the course of a speech to those who entertained him there, the Marquis said:—'I have been told that the means by which Polynesians were obtained were not legitimate, but I have failed to perceive this, in so far at least as Queensland is concerned; and, if one can judge by the countenances and manners of the Polynesians, they experience no regret at their position.' But his Excellency pointed out the advantage of giving them religious instruction. It would tend to set at rest an uneasy feeling which at present existed in the country to know that they were inclined to retain the Polynesians, and teach them religion."

I feel that comment is unnecessary, and will therefore conclude with one word of thanks to the reader who may have had the patience to follow me through my adventures without losing his temper; but with two, for any who may write at once to the Secretary of the Erewhon Evangelisation Company, Limited (at the address which shall hereafter be advertised), and request to have his name put down as a shareholder.

P.S.—I had just received and corrected the last proof of the foregoing volume, and was walking down the Strand from Temple Bar to Charing Cross, when on passing Exeter Hall I saw a number of devout-looking people crowding into the building with faces full of interested and complacent anticipation. I stopped, and saw an announcement that a missionary meeting was to be held forthwith, and that the native missionary, the Rev. William Habakkuk, from—(the colony from which I had started on my adventures), would be introduced, and make a short address. After some little difficulty I obtained admission, and heard two or three speeches, which were prefatory to the introduction of Mr. Habakkuk. One of these struck me as perhaps the most presumptuous that I had ever heard. The speaker said that the races of whom Mr. Habakkuk was a specimen, were in all probability the lost ten tribes of Israel. I dared not contradict him then, but I felt angry and injured at hearing the speaker jump to so preposterous a conclusion upon such insufficient grounds. The discovery of the ten tribes was mine, and mine only. I was still in the very height of indignation, when there was a murmur of expectation in the hall, and Mr. Habakkuk was brought forward. The reader may judge of my surprise at finding that he was none other than my old friend Chowbok!

My jaw dropped, and my eyes almost started out of my head with astonishment. The poor fellow was dreadfully frightened, and the storm of applause which greeted his introduction seemed only to add to his confusion. I dare not trust myself to report his speech—indeed I could hardly listen to it, for I was nearly choked with trying to suppress my feelings. I am sure that I caught the words "Adelaide, the Queen Dowager," and I thought that I heard "Mary Magdalene" shortly afterwards, but I had then to leave the hall for fear of being turned out. While on the staircase, I heard another burst of prolonged and rapturous applause, so I suppose the audience were satisfied.

The feelings that came uppermost in my mind were hardly of a very solemn character, but I thought of my first acquaintance with Chowbok, of the scene in the woodshed, of the innumerable lies he had told me, of his repeated attempts upon the brandy, and of many an incident which I have not thought it worth while to dwell upon; and I could not but derive some satisfaction from the hope that my own efforts might have contributed to the change which had been doubtless wrought upon him, and that the rite which I had performed, however unprofessionally, on that wild upland river-bed, had not been wholly without effect. I trust that what I have written about him in the earlier part of my book may not be libellous, and that it may do him no harm with his employers. He was then unregenerate. I must certainly find him out and have a talk with him; but before I shall have time to do so these pages will be in the hands of the public.

At the last moment I see a probability of a complication which causes me much uneasiness. Please subscribe quickly. Address to the Mansion-House, care of the Lord Mayor, whom I will instruct to receive names and subscriptions for me until I can organise a committee.

Erewhon Revisited

AUTHOR'S PREFACE
TO THE ORIGINAL EDITION

I FORGET WHEN, but not very long after I had published "Erewhon" in 1872, it occurred to me to ask myself what course events in Erewhon would probably take after Mr. Higgs, as I suppose I may now call him, had made his escape in the balloon with Arowhena. Given a people in the conditions supposed to exist in Erewhon, and given the apparently miraculous ascent of a remarkable stranger into the heavens with an earthly bride—what would be the effect on the people generally?

There was no use in trying to solve this problem before, say, twenty years should have given time for Erewhonian developments to assume something like permanent shape, and in 1892 I was too busy with books now published to be able to attend to Erewhon. It was not till the early winter of 1900, i.e., as nearly as may be thirty years after the date of Higgs's escape, that I found time to deal with the question above stated, and to answer it, according to my lights, in the book which I now lay before the public.

I have concluded, I believe rightly, that the events described in Chapter XXIV. of "Erewhon" would give rise to such a cataclysmic change in the old Erewhonian opinions as would result in the development of a new religion. Now the development of all new religions follows much the same general course. In all cases the times are more or less out of joint—older faiths are losing their hold upon the masses. At such times, let a personality appear, strong in itself, and made to seem still stronger by association with some supposed transcendent miracle, and it will be easy to raise a Lo here! that will attract many followers. If there be a single great, and apparently well-authenticated, miracle, others will accrete round it; then, in all religions that have so originated, there will follow temples, priests, rites, sincere believers, and unscrupulous exploiters of public credulity. To chronicle the events that followed Higgs's balloon ascent without showing that they were much as they *have been under like conditions in other places, would be to hold the mirror up to something very wide of nature.*

Analogy, however, between courses of events is one thing—historic parallelisms abound; analogy between the main actors in events is a very different one, and one, moreover, of which few examples can be found. The development of the new ideas in Erewhon is a familiar one, but there is no more likeness between Higgs and the founder of any other religion, than there is between Jesus Christ and Mahomet. He is a typical middle-class Englishman, deeply tainted with priggishness in his earlier years, but in great part freed from it by the sweet uses of adversity.

If I may be allowed for a moment to speak about myself, I would say that I have never ceased to profess myself a member of the more advanced wing of the English Broad Church. What those who belong to this wing believe, I believe. What they reject, I reject. No two people think absolutely alike on any subject, but when I converse with advanced Broad Churchmen I find myself in substantial harmony with them. I believe—and should be very sorry if I did not believe—that, mutatis mutandis, such men will find the advice given on pp. 277–281 and 287–291 [Ed.: 348–350 and 354–356 of the present edition] of this book much what, under the supposed circumstances, they would themselves give.

Lastly, I should express my great obligations to Mr. R. A. Streatfeild of the British Museum, who, in the absence from England of my friend Mr. H. Festing Jones, has kindly supervised the corrections of my book as it passed through the press.

SAMUEL BUTLER.

May 1, 1901

CHAPTER I

UPS AND DOWNS OF FORTUNE—MY FATHER STARTS FOR EREWHON

BEFORE TELLING THE story of my father's second visit to the remarkable country which he discovered now some thirty years since, I should perhaps say a few words about his career between the publication of his book in 1872, and his death in the early summer of 1891. I shall thus touch briefly on the causes that occasioned his failure to maintain that hold on the public which he had apparently secured at first.

His book, as the reader may perhaps know, was published anonymously, and my poor father used to ascribe the acclamation with which it was received, to the fact that no one knew who it might not have been written by. *Omne ignotum pro magnifico*, and during its month of anonymity the book was a frequent topic of appreciative comment in good literary circles. Almost coincidently with the discovery that he was a mere nobody, people began to feel that their admiration had been too hastily bestowed, and before long opinion turned all the more seriously against him for this very reason. The subscription, to which the Lord Mayor had at first given his cordial support, was curtly announced as closed before it had been opened a week; it had met with so little success that I will not specify the amount eventually handed over, not without protest, to my father; small, however, as it was, he narrowly escaped being prosecuted for trying to obtain money under false pretences.

The Geographical Society, which had for a few days received him with open arms, was among the first to turn upon him—not, so far as I can ascertain, on account of the mystery in which he had enshrouded the exact whereabouts of Erewhon, nor yet by reason of its being persistently alleged that he was subject to frequent attacks of alcoholic poisoning—but through his own want of tact, and a highly-strung nervous state, which led him to attach too much importance to his own discoveries, and not enough to those of other people. This, at least, was my father's version of the matter, as I heard it from his own lips in the later years of his life.

"I was still very young," he said to me, "and my mind was more or less unhinged by the strangeness and peril of my adventures." Be this as it may I fear there is no doubt that he was injudicious; and an ounce of judgment is worth a pound of discovery.

Hence, in a surprisingly short time, he found himself dropped even by those who had taken him up most warmly, and had done most to find him that employment as a writer of religious tracts on which his livelihood was then dependent. The discredit, however, into which my father fell, had the effect of deterring any considerable number of people from trying to rediscover Erewhon, and thus caused it to remain as unknown to geographers in general as though it had never been found. A few shepherds and cadets at up-country stations had, indeed, tried to follow in my father's footsteps, during the time when his book was still being taken seriously; but they had most of them returned, unable to face the difficulties that had opposed them. Some few, however, had not returned, and though search was made for them, their bodies had not been found. When he reached Erewhon on his second visit, my father learned that others had attempted to visit the country more recently—probably quite independently of his own book; and before he had himself been in it many hours he gathered what the fate of these poor fellows doubtless was.

Another reason that made it more easy for Erewhon to remain unknown, was the fact that the more mountainous districts, though repeatedly prospected for gold, had been pronounced non-auriferous, and as there was no sheep or cattle country, save a few river-bed flats above the upper gorges of any of the rivers, and no game to tempt the sportsman, there was nothing to induce people to penetrate into the fastnesses of the great snowy range. No more, therefore, being heard of Erewhon, my father's book came to be regarded as a mere work of fiction, and I have heard quite recently of its having been seen on a second-hand bookstall, marked "6d., very readable."

Though there was no truth in the stories about my father's being subject to attacks of alcoholic poisoning, yet, during the first few years after his return to England, his occasional fits of ungovernable excitement gave some colour to the opinion that much of what he said he had seen and done might be only subjectively true. I refer more particularly to his interview with Chowbok in the wool-shed, and his highly coloured description of the statues on the top of the pass leading into Erewhon. These were soon set down as forgeries of delirium, and it was maliciously urged, that though in his book he had only admitted having taken "two or three bottles of brandy" with him, he had probably taken at least a dozen; and that if on the night before he reached the statues he had "only four ounces of brandy" left, he must have been drinking heavily for the preceding fortnight or three weeks. Those who read the following pages will, I think, reject all idea that my father was in a state of delirium, not without surprise that any one should have ever entertained it.

It was Chowbok who, if he did not originate these calumnies, did much to disseminate and gain credence for them. He remained in England for some years, and never tired of doing what he could to disparage my father. The cunning creature had ingratiated himself with our leading religious societies, especially with the more evangelical among them. Whatever doubt there might be about his sincerity, there was none about his colour, and a coloured convert in those days was more than Exeter Hall could resist. Chowbok saw that there was no room for him and for my father, and declared my poor father's story to be almost wholly false. It was true, he said, that he and my father had explored the head-waters of the river described in his book, but he denied that my father had gone on without him, and he named the river as one distant by many thousands of miles from the one it really was. He said that after about a fortnight he had returned in company with my father, who by that time had become incapacitated for further travel. At this point he would shrug his shoulders, look mysterious, and thus say "alcoholic poisoning" even more effectively than if he had uttered the words themselves. For a man's tongue lies often in his shoulders.

Readers of my father's book will remember that Chowbok had given a very different version when he had returned to his employer's station; but Time and Distance afford cover under which falsehood can often do truth to death securely.

I never understood why my father did not bring my mother forward to confirm his story. He may have done so while I was too young to know anything about it. But when people have made up their minds, they are impatient of further evidence; my mother, moreover, was of a very retiring disposition. The Italians say:—

"Chi lontano va ammogliare
Sarà ingannato, o vorrà ingannare."

"If a man goes far afield for a wife, he will be deceived—or means deceiving." The proverb is as true for women as for men, and my mother was never quite happy in her new surroundings. Wilfully deceived she assuredly was not, but she could not accustom herself to English modes of thought; indeed she never even nearly mastered our language; my father always talked with her in Erewhonian, and so did I, for as a child she had taught me to do so, and I was as fluent with her language as with my father's. In this respect she often told me I could pass myself off anywhere in Erewhon as a native; I shared also her personal appearance, for though not wholly unlike my father, I had taken more closely after my mother. In mind, if I may venture to say so, I believe I was more like my father.

I may as well here inform the reader that I was born at the end of September, 1871, and was christened John, after my grandfather. From what I have said above he will readily believe that my earliest experiences were somewhat squalid. Memories of childhood rush vividly upon me when I pass through a low London alley and catch the faint sickly smell that pervades it—half paraffin, half black-currants, but wholly something very different. I have a fancy that we lived in Blackmoor Street, off Drury Lane. My father, when first I knew of his doing anything at all, supported my mother and myself by drawing pictures with coloured chalks upon the pavement; I used sometimes to watch him, and marvel at the skill with which he represented fogs, floods, and fires. These three "f's," he would say, were his three best friends, for they were easy to do and brought in halfpence freely. The return of the dove to the ark was his favourite subject. Such a little ark, on such a hazy morning, and such a little pigeon—the rest of the picture being cheap sky, and still cheaper sea; nothing, I have often heard him say, was more popular than this with his clients. He held it to be his masterpiece, but would add with some naïveté that he considered himself a public benefactor for carrying it out in such perishable fashion. "At any rate," he would say, "no one can bequeath one of my many replicas to the nation."

I never learned how much my father earned by his profession, but it must have been something considerable, for we always had enough to eat and drink; I imagine that he did better than many a struggling artist with more ambitious aims. He was strictly temperate during all the time that I knew anything about him, but he was not a teetotaler;

I never saw any of the fits of nervous excitement which in his earlier years had done so much to wreck him. In the evenings, and on days when the state of the pavement did not permit him to work, he took great pains with my education, which he could very well do, for as a boy he had been in the sixth form of one of our foremost public schools. I found him a patient, kindly instructor, while to my mother he was a model husband. Whatever others may have said about him, I can never think of him without very affectionate respect.

Things went on quietly enough, as above indicated, till I was about fourteen, when by a streak of fortune my father became suddenly affluent. A brother of his father's had emigrated to Australia in 1851, and had amassed great wealth. We knew of his existence, but there had been no intercourse between him and my father, and we did not even know that he was rich and unmarried. He died intestate towards the end of 1885, and my father was the only relative he had, except, of course, myself, for both my father's sisters had died young, and without leaving children.

The solicitor through whom the news reached us was, happily, a man of the highest integrity, and also very sensible and kind. He was a Mr. Alfred Emery Cathie, of 15 Clifford's Inn, E.C., and my father placed himself unreservedly in his hands. I was at once sent to a first-rate school, and such pains had my father taken with me that I was placed in a higher form than might have been expected considering my age. The way in which he had taught me had prevented my feeling any dislike for study; I therefore stuck fairly well to my books, while not neglecting the games which are so important a part of healthy education. Everything went well with me, both as regards masters and school-fellows; nevertheless, I was declared to be of a highly nervous and imaginative temperament, and the school doctor more than once urged our headmaster not to push me forward too rapidly—for which I have ever since held myself his debtor.

Early in 1890, I being then home from Oxford (where I had been entered in the preceding year), my mother died; not so much from active illness, as from what was in reality a kind of *maladie du pays*. All along she had felt herself an exile, and though she had borne up wonderfully during my father's long struggle with adversity, she began to break as soon as prosperity had removed the necessity for exertion on her own part.

My father could never divest himself of the feeling that he had wrecked her life by inducing her to share her lot with his own; to say that he was stricken with remorse on losing her is not enough;

he had been so stricken almost from the first year of his marriage; on her death he was haunted by the wrong he accused himself—as it seems to me very unjustly—of having done her, for it was neither his fault nor hers—it was Atè.

His unrest soon assumed the form of a burning desire to revisit the country in which he and my mother had been happier together than perhaps they ever again were. I had often heard him betray a hankering after a return to Erewhon, disguised so that no one should recognise him; but as long as my mother lived he would not leave her. When death had taken her from him, he so evidently stood in need of a complete change of scene, that even those friends who had most strongly dissuaded him from what they deemed a madcap enterprise, thought it better to leave him to himself. It would have mattered little how much they tried to dissuade him, for before long his passionate longing for the journey became so overmastering that nothing short of restraint in prison or a madhouse could have stayed his going; but we were not easy about him.

"He had better go," said Mr. Cathie to me, when I was at home for the Easter vacation, "and get it over. He is not well, but he is still in the prime of life; doubtless he will come back with renewed health and will settle down to a quiet home life again."

This, however, was not said till it had become plain that in a few days my father would be on his way. He had made a new will, and left an ample power of attorney with Mr. Cathie—or, as we always called him, Alfred—who was to supply me with whatever money I wanted: he had put all other matters in order in case anything should happen to prevent his ever returning, and he set out on October 1, 1890, more composed and cheerful than I had seen him for some time past.

I had not realised how serious the danger to my father would be if he were recognised while he was in Erewhon, for I am ashamed to say that I had not yet read his book. I had heard over and over again of his flight with my mother in the balloon, and had long since read his few opening chapters, but I had found, as a boy naturally would, that the succeeding pages were a little dull, and soon put the book aside. My father, indeed, repeatedly urged me not to read it, for he said there was much in it—more especially in the earlier chapters, which I had alone found interesting—that he would gladly cancel if he could. "But there!" he had said with a laugh, "what does it matter?"

He had hardly left, before I read his book from end to end, and, on having done so, not only appreciated the risks that he would have to run, but was struck with the wide difference between his character as he had himself portrayed it, and the estimate I had formed of it from personal knowledge. When, on his return, he detailed to me his adventures, the account he gave of what he had said and done corresponded with my own ideas concerning him; but I doubt not the reader will see that the twenty years between his first and second visit had modified him even more than so long an interval might be expected to do.

I heard from him repeatedly during the first two months of his absence, and was surprised to find that he had stayed for a week or ten days at more than one place of call on his outward journey. On November 26 he wrote from the port whence he was to start for Erewhon, seemingly in good health and spirits; and on December 27, 1891, he telegraphed for a hundred pounds to be wired out to him at this same port. This puzzled both Mr. Cathie and myself, for the interval between November 26 and December 27 seemed too short to admit of his having paid his visit to Erewhon and returned; as, moreover, he had added the words, "Coming home," we rather hoped that he had abandoned his intention of going there.

We were also surprised at his wanting so much money, for he had taken a hundred pounds in gold, which, from some fancy, he had stowed in a small silver jewel-box that he had given my mother not long before she died. He had also taken a hundred pounds' worth of gold nuggets, which he had intended to sell in Erewhon so as to provide himself with money when he got there.

I should explain that these nuggets would be worth in Erewhon fully ten times as much as they would in Europe, owing to the great scarcity of gold in that country. The Erewhonian coinage is entirely silver—which is abundant, and worth much what it is in England—or copper, which is also plentiful; but what we should call five pounds' worth of silver money would not buy more than one of our half-sovereigns in gold.

He had put his nuggets into ten brown holland bags, and he had had secret pockets made for the old Erewhonian dress which he had worn when he had escaped, so that he need never have more than one bag of nuggets accessible at a time. He was not likely, therefore to have been robbed. His passage to the port above referred to had been paid before he started, and it seemed impossible that a man of his very inexpensive habits should have spent two hundred pounds in a single month—for the nuggets would be immediately convertible in an English colony. There was nothing, however, to be done but to cable out the money and wait my father's arrival.

Returning for a moment to my father's old Erewhonian dress, I should say that he had preserved it simply as a memento and without any idea that he should again want it. It was not the court dress that had been provided for him on the occasion of his visit to the king and queen, but the everyday clothing that he had been ordered to wear when he was put in prison, though his English coat, waistcoat, and trousers had been allowed to remain in his own possession. These, I had seen from his book, had been presented by him to the queen (with the exception of two buttons, which he had given to Yram as a keepsake), and had been preserved by her displayed upon a wooden dummy. The dress in which he had escaped had been soiled during the hours that he and my mother had been in the sea, and had also suffered from neglect during the years of his poverty; but he wished to pass himself off as a common peasant or working-man, so he preferred to have it set in order as might best be done, rather than copied.

So cautious was he in the matter of dress that he took with him the boots he had worn on leaving Erewhon, lest the foreign make of his English boots should arouse suspicion. They were nearly new, and when he had had them softened and well greased, he found he could still wear them quite comfortably.

But to return. He reached home late at night one day at the beginning of February, and a glance was enough to show that he was an altered man.

"What is the matter?" said I, shocked at his appearance. "Did you go to Erewhon, and were you ill-treated there?"

"I went to Erewhon," he said, "and I was not ill-treated there, but I have been so shaken that I fear I shall quite lose my reason. Do not ask me more now. I will tell you about it all to-morrow. Let me have something to eat, and go to bed."

When we met at breakfast next morning, he greeted me with all his usual warmth of affection, but he was still taciturn. "I will begin to tell you about it," he said, "after breakfast. Where is your dear mother? How was it that I have . . ."

Then of a sudden his memory returned, and he burst into tears.

I now saw, to my horror, that his mind was gone. When he recovered, he said: "It has all come back again, but at times now I am a blank, and every week am more and more so. I daresay I shall be sensible now for several hours. We will go into the study after breakfast, and I will talk to you as long as I can do so."

Let the reader spare me, and let me spare the reader any description of what we both of us felt.

When we were in the study, my father said, "My dearest boy, get pen and paper and take notes of what I tell you. It will all be disjointed; one day I shall remember this, and another that, but there will not be many more days on which I shall remember anything at all. I cannot write a coherent page. You, when I am gone, can piece what I tell you together, and tell it as I should have told it if I had been still sound. But do not publish it yet; it might do harm to those dear good people. Take the notes now, and arrange them the sooner the better, for you may want to ask me questions, and I shall not be here much longer. Let publishing wait till you are confident that publication can do no harm; and above all, say nothing to betray the whereabouts of Erewhon, beyond admitting (which I fear I have already done) that it is in the Southern hemisphere."

These instructions I have religiously obeyed. For the first days after his return, my father had few attacks of loss of memory, and I was in hopes that his former health of mind would return when he found himself in his old surroundings. During these days he poured forth the story of his adventures so fast, that if I had not had a fancy for acquiring shorthand, I should not have been able to keep pace with him. I repeatedly urged him not to overtax his strength, but he was oppressed by the fear that if he did not speak at once, he might never be able to tell me all he had to say; I had, therefore, to submit, though seeing plainly enough that he was only hastening the complete paralysis which he so greatly feared.

Sometimes his narrative would be coherent for pages together, and he could answer any questions without hesitation; at others, he was now here and now there, and if I tried to keep him to the order of events he would say that he had forgotten intermediate incidents, but that they would probably come back to him, and I should perhaps be able to put them in their proper places.

After about ten days he seemed satisfied that I had got all the facts, and that with the help of the pamphlets which he had brought with him I should be able to make out a connected story. "Remember," he said, "that I thought I was quite well so long as I was in Erewhon, and do not let me appear as anything else."

When he had fully delivered himself, he seemed easier in his mind, but before a month had passed he became completely paralysed, and though he lingered till the beginning of June, he was seldom more than dimly conscious of what was going on around him.

His death robbed me of one who had been a very kind and upright elder brother rather than a father; and so strongly have I felt his influence still present, living and working, as I believe for better within me, that I did not hesitate to copy the epitaph which he saw in the Musical Bank at Fairmead, and to have it inscribed on the very simple monument which he desired should alone mark his grave.

The foregoing was written in the summer of 1891; what I now add should be dated December 3, 1900. If, in the course of my work, I have misrepresented my father, as I fear I may have sometimes done, I would ask my readers to remember that no man can tell another's story without some involuntary misrepresentation both of facts and characters. They will, of course, see that "Erewhon Revisited" is written by one who has far less literary skill than the author of "Erewhon"; but again I would ask indulgence on the score of youth, and the fact that this is my first book. It was written nearly ten years ago, *i.e.*, in the months from March to August, 1891, but for reasons already given it could not then be made public. I have now received permission, and therefore publish the following chapters, exactly, or very nearly exactly, as they were left when I had finished editing my father's diaries, and the notes I took down from his own mouth—with the exception, of course, of these last few lines, hurriedly written as I am on the point of leaving England, of the additions I made in 1892, on returning from my own three hours' stay in Erewhon, and of the Postscript.

CHAPTER II

TO THE FOOT OF THE PASS INTO EREWHON

WHEN MY FATHER reached the colony for which he had left England some twenty-two years previously, he bought a horse, and started up country on the evening of the day after his arrival, which was, as I have said, on one of the last days of November, 1890. He had taken an English saddle with him, and a couple of roomy and strongly made saddle-bags. In these he packed his money, his nuggets, some tea, sugar, tobacco, salt, a flask of brandy, matches, and as many ship's biscuits as he thought he was likely to want; he took no meat, for he could supply himself from some accommodation-house or sheep-station, when nearing the point after which he would have to begin camping out. He rolled his Erewhonian dress and small toilette necessaries inside a warm red blanket, and strapped the roll on to the front part of his saddle. On to other D's, with which his saddle was amply provided, he strapped his Erewhonian boots, a tin pannikin, and a billy that would hold about a quart. I should, perhaps, explain to English readers that a billy is a tin can, the name for which (doubt-less of French Canadian origin) is derived from the words "*faire bouillir*." He also took with him a pair of hobbles and a small hatchet.

He spent three whole days in riding across the plains, and was struck with the very small signs of change that he could detect, but the fall in wool, and the failure, so far, to establish a frozen meat trade, had prevented any material development of the resources of the country. When he had got to the front ranges, he followed up the river next to the north of the one that he had explored years ago, and from the head waters of which he had been led to discover the only practicable pass into Erewhon. He did this, partly to avoid the terribly dangerous descent on to the bed of the more northern river, and partly to escape being seen by shepherds or bullock-drivers who might remember him.

If he had attempted to get through the gorge of this river in 1870, he would have found it impassable; but a few river-bed flats had been discovered above the gorge, on which there was now a shepherd's hut, and on the discovery of these flats a narrow horse track had been made from one end of the gorge to the other.

He was hospitably entertained at the shepherd's hut just mentioned, which he reached on Monday, December 1. He told the shepherd in charge of it that he had come to see if he could find traces of a large wingless bird, whose existence had been reported as having been discovered among the extreme head waters of the river.

"Be careful, sir," said the shepherd; "the river is very dangerous; several people—one only about a year ago—have left this hut, and though their horses and their camps have been found, their bodies have not. When a great fresh comes down, it would carry a body out to sea in twenty-four hours."

He evidently had no idea that there was a pass through the ranges up the river, which might explain the disappearance of an explorer.

Next day my father began to ascend the river. There was so much tangled growth still unburnt wherever there was room for it to grow, and so much swamp, that my father had to keep almost entirely to the river-bed—and here there was a good deal of quicksand. The stones also were often large for some distance together, and he had to cross and recross streams of the river more than once, so that though he travelled all day with the exception of a couple of hours for dinner, he had not made more than some five and twenty miles when he reached a suitable camping ground, where he unsaddled his horse, hobbled him, and turned him out to feed. The grass was beginning to seed, so that though it was none too plentiful, what there was of it made excellent feed.

He lit his fire, made himself some tea, ate his cold mutton and biscuits, and lit his pipe, exactly as he had done twenty years before. There was the clear starlit sky, the rushing river, and the stunted trees on the mountain-side; the woodhens cried, and the "more-pork" hooted out her two monotonous notes exactly as they had done years since; one moment, and time had so flown backwards that youth came bounding back to him with the return of his youth's surroundings; the next, and the intervening twenty years—most of them grim ones—rose up mockingly before him, and the buoyancy of hope yielded to the despondency of admitted failure. By and by buoyancy reasserted itself, and, soothed by the peace and beauty of the night, he wrapped himself up in his blanket and dropped off into a dreamless slumber.

Next morning, *i.e.,* December 3, he rose soon after dawn, bathed in a backwater of the river, got his breakfast, found his horse on the river-bed, and started as soon as he had duly packed and loaded. He had now to cross streams of the river and recross them more often than on the preceding day, and this, though his horse took well to the water, required care; for he was anxious not to wet his saddle-bags, and it was only by crossing at the wide, smooth, water above a rapid, and by picking places where the river ran in two or three streams, that he could find fords where his practised eye told him that the water would not be above his horse's belly—for the river was of great volume. Fortunately, there had been a late fall of snow on the higher ranges, and the river was, for the summer season, low.

Towards evening, having travelled, so far as he could guess, some twenty or five and twenty miles (for he had made another mid-day halt), he reached the place, which he easily recognised, as that where he had camped before crossing to the pass that led into Erewhon. It was the last piece of ground that could be called a flat (though it was in reality only the sloping delta of a stream that descended from the pass) before reaching a large glacier that had encroached on the river-bed, which it traversed at right angles for a considerable distance.

Here he again camped, hobbled his horse, and turned him adrift, hoping that he might again find him some two or three months hence, for there was a good deal of sweet grass here and there, with sow-thistle and anise; and the coarse tussock grass would be in full seed shortly, which alone would keep him going for as long a time as my father expected to be away. Little did he think that he should want him again so shortly.

Having attended to his horse, he got his supper, and while smoking his pipe congratulated himself on the way in which something had smoothed away all the obstacles that had so nearly baffled him on his earlier journey. Was he being lured on to his destruction by some malicious fiend, or befriended by one who had compassion on him and wished him well? His naturally sanguine temperament inclined him to adopt the friendly spirit theory, in the peace of which he again laid himself down to rest, and slept soundly from dark till dawn.

In the morning, though the water was somewhat icy, he again bathed, and then put on his Erewhonian boots and dress. He stowed his European clothes, with some difficulty, into his saddle-bags. Herein also he left his case full of English sovereigns, his spare pipes, his purse, which contained two pounds in gold and seven or eight shillings, part of his stock of tobacco, and whatever provision was left him, except the meat—which he left for sundry hawks and parrots that were eyeing his proceedings apparently without fear of man. His nuggets he concealed in the secret pockets of which I have already spoken, keeping one bag alone accessible.

He had had his hair and beard cut short on shipboard the day before he landed. These he now dyed with a dye that he had brought from England, and which in a few minutes turned them very nearly black. He also stained his face and hands deep brown. He hung his saddle and bridle, his English boots, and his saddle-bags on the highest bough that he could reach, and made them fairly fast with strips of flax leaf, for there was some stunted flax growing on the ground where he had camped. He feared that, do what he might, they would not escape the inquisitive thievishness of the parrots, whose strong beaks could easily cut leather; but he could do nothing more. It occurs to me, though my father never told me so, that it was perhaps with a view to these birds that he had chosen to put his English sovereigns into a metal box, with a clasp to it which would defy them.

He made a roll of his blanket, and slung it over his shoulder; he also took his pipe, tobacco, a little tea, a few ship's biscuits, and his billy and pannikin; matches and salt go without saying. When he had thus ordered everything as nearly to his satisfaction as he could, he looked at his watch for the last time, as he believed, till many weeks should have gone by, and found it to be about seven o'clock. Remembering what trouble it had got him into years before, he took down his saddle-bags, reopened them, and put the watch inside. He then set himself to climb the mountain side, towards the saddle on which he had seen the statues.

CHAPTER III

MY FATHER WHILE CAMPING IS ACCOSTED BY PROFESSORS HANKY AND PANKY

MY FATHER FOUND the ascent more fatiguing than he remembered it to have been. The climb, he said, was steady, and took him between four and five hours, as near as he could guess, now that he had no watch; but it offered nothing that could be called a difficulty, and the watercourse that came down from the saddle was a sufficient guide; once or twice there were waterfalls, but they did not seriously delay him.

After he had climbed some three thousand feet, he began to be on the alert for some sound of ghostly chanting from the statues; but he heard nothing, and toiled on till he came to a sprinkling of fresh snow—part of the fall which he had observed on the preceding day as having whitened the higher mountains; he knew, therefore, that he must now be nearing the saddle. The snow grew rapidly deeper, and by the time he reached the statues the ground was covered to a depth of two or three inches.

He found the statues smaller than he had expected. He had said in his book—written many months after he had seen them—that they were about six times the size of life, but he now thought that four or five times would have been enough to say. Their mouths were much clogged with snow, so that even though there had been a strong wind (which there was not) they would not have chanted. In other respects he found them not less mysteriously impressive than at first. He walked two or three times all around them, and then went on.

The snow did not continue far down, but before long my father entered a thick bank of cloud, and had to feel his way cautiously along the stream that descended from the pass. It was some two hours before he emerged into clear air, and found himself on the level bed of an old lake now grassed over. He had quite forgotten this feature of the descent—perhaps the clouds had hung over it; he was over-joyed, however, to find that the flat ground abounded with a kind of quail, larger than ours, and hardly, if at all, smaller than a partridge. The abundance of these quails surprised him, for he did not remember them as plentiful anywhere on the Erewhonian side of the mountains.

The Erewhonian quail, like its now nearly, if not quite, extinct New Zealand congener, can take three successive flights of a few yards each, but then becomes exhausted; hence quails are only found on ground that is never burned, and where there are no wild animals to molest them; the cats and dogs that accompany European civilisa-tion soon exterminate them; my father, therefore, felt safe in con-cluding that he was still far from any village. Moreover, he could see no sheep or goat's dung; and this surprised him, for he thought he had found signs of pasturage much higher than this. Doubtless, he said to himself, when he wrote his book he had forgotten how long the descent had been. But it was odd, for the grass was good feed enough, and ought, he considered, to have been well stocked.

Tired with his climb, during which he had not rested to take food, but had eaten biscuits, as he walked, he gave himself a good long rest, and when refreshed, he ran down a couple of dozen quails, some of which he meant to eat when he camped for the night, while the others would help him out of a difficulty which had been troubling him for some time.

What was he to say when people asked him, as they were sure to do, how he was living? And how was he to get enough Erewhonian money to keep him going till he could find some safe means of sell-ing a few of his nuggets? He had had a little Erewhonian money when he went up in the balloon, but had thrown it over, with everything else except the clothes he wore and his MSS., when the balloon was nearing the water. He had nothing with him that he dared offer for sale, and though he had plenty of gold, was in reality penniless.

When, therefore, he saw the quails, he again felt as though some friendly spirit was smoothing his way before him. What more easy than to sell them at Coldharbour (for so the name of the town in which he had been imprisoned should be translated), where he knew they were a delicacy, and would fetch him the value of an English shilling a piece?

It took him between two and three hours to catch two dozen. When he had thus got what he considered a sufficient stock, he tied their legs together with rushes, and ran a stout stick through the whole lot. Soon afterwards he came upon a wood of stunted pines, which, though there was not much undergrowth, nevertheless afforded considerable shelter and enabled him to gather wood enough to make himself a good fire. This was acceptable, for though the days were long, it was now evening, and as soon as the sun had gone the air became crisp and frosty.

Here he resolved to pass the night. He chose a part where the trees were thickest, lit his fire, plucked and cleaned four quails, filled his billy with water from the stream hard by, made tea in his pannikin, grilled two of his birds on the embers, ate them, and when he had done all this, he lit his pipe and began to think things over.

"So far so good," said he to himself; but hardly had the words passed through his mind before he was startled by the sound of voices, still at some distance, but evidently drawing towards him.

He instantly gathered up his billy, pannikin, tea, biscuits, and blanket, all of which he had determined to discard and hide on the following morning; everything that could betray him he carried full haste into the wood some few yards off, in the direction opposite to that from which the voices were coming, but he let his quails lie where they were, and put his pipe and tobacco in his pocket.

The voices drew nearer and nearer, and it was all my father could do to get back and sit down innocently by his fire, before he could hear what was being said.

"Thank goodness," said one of the speakers (of course in the Erewhonian language), "we seem to be finding somebody at last. I hope it is not some poacher; we had better be careful."

"Nonsense!" said the other. "It must be one of the rangers. No one would dare to light a fire while poaching on the King's preserves. What o'clock do you make it?"

"Half after nine." And the watch was still in the speaker's hand as he emerged from darkness into the glowing light of the fire. My father glanced at it, and saw that it was exactly like the one he had worn on entering Erewhon nearly twenty years previously.

The watch, however, was a very small matter; the dress of these two men (for there were only two) was far more disconcerting. They were not in the Erewhonian costume. The one was dressed like an Englishman or would-be Englishman, while the other was wearing the same kind of clothes but turned the wrong way round, so that when his face was towards my father his body seemed to have its back towards him, and *vice versâ*. The man's head, in fact, appeared to have been screwed right round; and yet it was plain that if he were stripped he would be found built like other people.

What could it all mean? The men were about fifty years old. They were well-to-do people, well clad, well fed, and were felt instinctively by my father to belong to the academic classes. That one of them should be dressed like a sensible Englishman dismayed my father as much as that the other should have a watch, and look as if he had just broken out of Bedlam, or as King Dagobert must have looked if he had worn all his clothes as he is said to have worn his breeches. Both wore their clothes so easily—for he who wore them reversed had evidently been measured with a view to this absurd fashion—that it was plain their dress was habitual.

My father was alarmed as well as astounded, for he saw that what little plan of campaign he had formed must be reconstructed, and he had no idea in what direction his next move should be taken; but he was a ready man, and knew that when people have taken any idea into their heads, a little confirmation will fix it. A first idea is like a strong seedling; it will grow if it can.

In less time than it will have taken the reader to get through the last foregoing paragraphs, my father took up the cue furnished him by the second speaker.

"Yes," said he, going boldly up to this gentleman, "I am one of the rangers, and it is my duty to ask you what you are doing here upon the King's preserves."

"Quite so, my man," was the rejoinder. "We have been to see the statues at the head of the pass, and have a permit from the Mayor of Sunch'ston to enter upon the preserves. We lost ourselves in the thick fog, both going and coming back."

My father inwardly blessed the fog. He did not catch the name of the town, but presently found that it was commonly pronounced as I have written it.

"Be pleased to show it me," said my father in his politest manner. On this a document was handed to him.

I will here explain that I shall translate the names of men and places, as well as the substance of the document; and I shall translate all names in future. Indeed I have just done so in the case of Sunch'ston. As an example, let me explain that the true Erewhonian names for Hanky and Panky, to whom the reader will be immediately introduced, are Sukoh and Sukop—names too cacophonous to be read with pleasure by the English public. I must ask the reader to believe that in all cases I am doing my best to give the spirit of the original name.

I would also express my regret that my father did not either uniformly keep to the true Erewhonian names, as in the cases of Senoj, Nosnibor, Ydgrun, Thims, &c—names which occur constantly in Erewhon—or else invariably invent a name, as he did whenever he considered the true name impossible. My poor mother's name, for example, was really Nna Haras, and Mahaina's Enaj Ysteb, which he dared not face. He, therefore, gave these characters the first names that euphony suggested, without any attempt at translation. Rightly or wrongly, I have determined to keep consistently to translation for all names not used in my father's book; and throughout, whether as regards names or conversations, I shall translate with the freedom without which no translation rises above construe level.

Let us now return to the permit. The earlier part of the document was printed, and ran as follows:

"Extracts from the Act for the afforesting of certain lands lying between the town of Sunchildston, formerly called Coldharbour, and the mountains which bound the kingdom of Erewhon, passed in the year Three, being the eighth year of the reign of his Most Gracious Majesty King Well-beloved the Twenty-Second.

"Whereas it is expedient to prevent any of his Majesty's subjects from trying to cross over into unknown lands beyond the mountains, and in the manner to protect his Majesty's kingdom from intrusion on the part of foreign devils, it is hereby enacted that certain lands, more particularly described hereafter, shall be afforested and set apart as a hunting-ground for his Majesty's private use.

"It is also enacted that the Rangers and Under-rangers shall be required to immediately kill without parley any foreign devil whom they may encounter coming from the other side of the mountains. They are to weight the body, and throw it into the Blue Pool under the waterfall shown on the plan hereto annexed; but on pain of imprisonment for life they shall not reserve to their own use any article belonging to the deceased. Neither shall they divulge what they have done to any one save the Head Ranger, who shall report the circumstances of the case fully and minutely to his Majesty.

"As regards any of his Majesty's subjects who may be taken while trespassing on his Majesty's preserves without a special permit signed by the Mayor of Sunchildston, or any who may be convicted of poaching on the said preserves, the Rangers shall forthwith arrest them and bring them before the Mayor of Sunchildston, who shall enquire into their antecedents, and punish them with such term of imprisonment, with hard labour, as he may think fit, provided that no such term be of less duration than twelve calendar months.

"For the further provisions of the said Act, those whom it may concern are referred to the Act in full, a copy of which may be seen at the official residence of the Mayor of Sunchildston."

Then followed in MS. "XIX. xii. 29. Permit Professor Hanky, Royal Professor of Worldly Wisdom, at Bridgeford, seat of learning, city of the people who are above suspicion, and Professor Panky, Royal Professor of Unworldly Wisdom in the said city, or either of them" [here the MS. ended, the rest of the permit being in print] "to pass freely during the space of forty-eight hours from the date hereof, over the King's preserves, provided, under pain of imprisonment with hard labour for twelve months, that they do not kill, nor cause to be killed, nor eat, if another have killed, any one or more of his Majesty's quails."

The signature was such a scrawl that my father could not read it, but underneath was printed, "Mayor of Sunchildston, formerly called Coldharbour."

What a mass of information did not my father gather as he read, but what a far greater mass did he not see that he must get hold of ere he could reconstruct his plans intelligently.

"The year three," indeed; and XIX. xii. 29, in Roman and Arabic characters! There were no such characters when he was in Erewhon before. It flashed upon him that he had repeatedly shown them to the Nosnibors, and had once even written them down. It could not be that . . . No, it was impossible; and yet there was the European dress, aimed at by the one Professor, and attained by the other. Again "XIX." what was that? "xii." might do for December, but it was now the 4th of December not the 29th. "Afforested," too? Then that was why he had seen no sheep tracks. And how about the quails he had so innocently killed? What would have happened if he had tried to sell them in Coldharbour? What other like fatal error might he not ignorantly commit? And why had Coldharbour become Sunchildston?

These thoughts raced through my poor father's brain as he slowly perused the paper handed to him by the Professors. To give himself time he feigned to be a poor scholar, but when he had delayed as long as he dared, he returned it to the one who had given it him. Without changing a muscle he said—

"Your permit, sir, is quite regular. You can either stay here the night or go on to Sunchildston as you think fit. May I ask which of you two gentlemen is Professor Hanky, and which Professor Panky?"

"My name is Panky," said the one who had the watch, who wore his clothes reversed, and who had thought my father might be a poacher.

"And mine Hanky," said the other.

"What do you think, Panky," he added, turning to his brother Professor, "had we not better stay here till sunrise? We are both of us tired, and this fellow can make us a good fire. It is very dark, and there will be no moon this two hours. We are hungry, but we can hold out till we get to Sunchildston; it cannot be more than eight or nine miles further down."

Panky assented, but then, turning sharply to my father, he said, "My man, what are you doing in the forbidden dress? Why are you not in ranger's uniform, and what is the meaning of all those quails?" For his seedling idea that my father was in reality a poacher was doing its best to grow.

Quick as thought my father answered, "The Head Ranger sent me a message this morning to deliver him three dozen quails at Sunchildston by to-morrow afternoon. As for the dress, we can run the quails down quicker in it, and he says nothing to us so long as we only wear out old clothes and put on our uniforms before we near the town. My uniform is in the ranger's shelter an hour and a half higher up the valley."

"See what comes," said Panky, "of having a whippersnapper not yet twenty years old in the responsible post of Head Ranger. As for this fellow, he may be speaking the truth, but I distrust him."

"The man is all right, Panky," said Hanky, "and seems to be a decent fellow enough." Then to my father, "How many brace have you got?" And he looked at them a little wistfully.

"I have been at it all day, sir, and I have only got eight brace. I must run down ten more brace to-morrow."

"I see, I see." Then, turning to Panky he said, "Of course, they are wanted for the Mayor's banquet on Sunday. By the way, we have not yet received our invitation; I suppose we shall find it when we get back to Sunchildston."

"Sunday, Sunday, Sunday!" groaned my father inwardly; but he changed not a muscle of his face, and said stolidly to Professor Hanky, "I think you must be right, sir; but there was nothing said about it to me. I was only told to bring the birds."

Thus tenderly did he water the Professor's second seedling. But Panky had his seedling too, and Cain-like, was jealous that Hanky's should flourish while his own was withering.

"And what, pray, my man," he said somewhat peremptorily to my father, "are those two plucked quails doing? Were you to deliver them plucked? And what bird did those bones belong to which I see lying by the fire with the flesh all eaten off them? Are the under-rangers allowed not only to wear the forbidden dress but to eat the King's quails as well?"

The form in which the question was asked gave my father his cue. He laughed heartily, and said, "Why, sir, those plucked birds are landrails, not quails, and those bones are landrail bones. Look at this thigh-bone; was there ever a quail with such a bone as that?"

I cannot say whether or no Professor Panky was really deceived by the sweet effrontery with which my father proffered him the bone. If he was taken in, his answer was dictated simply by a donnish unwillingness to allow any one to be better informed on any subject than he was himself.

My father, when I suggested this to him, would not hear of it. "Oh, no," he said; "the man knew well enough that I was lying." However this may be, the Professor's manner changed.

"You are right," he said, "I thought they were landrail bones, but was not sure till I had one in my hand. I see, too, that the plucked birds are landrails, but there is little light, and I have not often seen them without their feathers."

"I think," said my father to me, "that Hanky knew what his friend meant, for he said, 'Panky, I am very hungry.'"

"Oh, Hanky, Hanky," said the other, modulating his harsh voice till it was quite pleasant. "Don't corrupt the poor man."

"Panky, drop that; we are not at Bridgeford now; I am very hungry, and I believe half those birds are not quails but landrails."

My father saw he was safe. He said, "Perhaps some of them might prove to be so, sir, under certain circumstances. I am a poor man, sir."

"Come, come," said Hanky; and he slipped a sum equal to about half-a-crown into my father's hand.

"I do not know what you mean, sir," said my father, "and if I did, half-a-crown would not be nearly enough."

"Hanky," said Panky, "you must get this fellow to give you lessons."

CHAPTER IV

MY FATHER OVERHEARS MORE OF HANKY AND PANKY'S CONVERSATION

MY FATHER, SCHOOLED under adversity, knew that it was never well to press advantage too far. He took the equivalent of five shillings for three brace, which was somewhat less than the birds would have been worth when things were as he had known them. Moreover, he consented to take a shilling's worth of Musical Bank money, which (as he has explained in his book) has no appreciable value outside these banks. He did this because he knew that it would be respectable to be seen carrying a little Musical Bank money, and also because he wished to give some of it to the British Museum, where he knew that this curious coinage was unrepresented. But the coins struck him as being much thinner and smaller than he had remembered them.

It was Panky, not Hanky, who had given him the Musical Bank money. Panky was the greater humbug of the two, for he would humbug even himself—a thing, by the way, not very hard to do; and yet he was the less successful humbug, for he could humbug no one who was worth humbugging—not for long. Hanky's occasional frankness put people off their guard. He was the mere common, superficial, perfunctory Professor, who, being a Professor, would of course profess, but would not lie more than was in the bond; he was log-rolled and log-rolling, but still, in a robust wolfish fashion, human.

Panky, on the other hand, was hardly human; he had thrown himself so earnestly into his work, that he had become a living lie. If he had had to play the part of Othello he would have blacked himself all over and very likely smothered his Desdemona in good earnest. Hanky would hardly have blacked himself behind the ears and his Desdemona would have been quite safe.

Philosophers are like quails in the respect that they can take two or three flights of imagination but rarely more without an interval of repose. The Professors had imagined my father to be a poacher and a ranger; they had imagined the quails to be wanted for Sunday's banquet; they had imagined that they imagined (at least Panky had) that they were about to eat landrails; they were now exhausted and cowered down into the grass of their ordinary conversation paying no more attention to my father than if he had been a dog. He, poor man, drank in every word they said, while seemingly intent on nothing but his quails, each one of which he cut up with a knife borrowed from Hanky. Two had been plucked already, so he laid these at once upon the clear embers.

"I do not know what we are to do with ourselves," said Hanky, "till Sunday. To-day is Thursday—it is the twenty-ninth, is it not? Yes, of course it is—Sunday is the first. Besides, it is on our permit. To-morrow we can rest; what, I wonder, can we do on Saturday? But the others will be here then, and we can tell them about the statues."

"Yes, but mind you do not blurt out anything about the landrails."

"I think we may tell Dr. Downie."

"Tell nobody," said Panky.

Then they talked about the statues, concerning which it was plain that nothing was known. But my father soon broke in upon their conversation with the first instalment of quails, which a few minutes had sufficed to cook.

"What a delicious bird a quail is," said Hanky.

"Landrail, Hanky, landrail," said the other reproachfully.

Having finished the first birds in a very few minutes they returned to the statues.

"Old Mrs. Nosnibor," said Panky, "says the Sunchild told her they were symbolic of ten tribes who had incurred the displeasure of the sun, his father."

I make no comment on my father's feelings.

"Of the sun! his fiddlesticks' ends," retorted Hanky. "He never called the sun his father. Besides, from all I have heard about him, I take it he was a precious idiot."

"O Hanky, Hanky! you will wreck the whole thing if you ever allow yourself to talk in that way."

"You are more likely to wreck it yourself, Panky, by never doing so. People like being deceived, but they like also to have an inkling of their own deception, and you never inkle them."

"The Queen," said Panky, returning to the statues, "sticks to it that . . ."

"Here comes another bird," interrupted Hanky; "never mind about the Queen."

The bird was soon eaten, whereon Panky again took up his parable about the Queen.

"The Queen says they are connected with the cult of the ancient Goddess Kiss-me-quick."

"What if they are? But the Queen sees Kiss-me-quick in everything. Another quail, if you please, Mr. Ranger."

My father brought up another bird almost directly. Silence while it was being eaten.

"Talking of the Sunchild," said Panky; "did you ever see him?"

"Never set eyes on him, and hope I never shall."

And so on till the last bird was eaten.

"Fellow," said Panky, "fetch some more wood; the fire is nearly dead."

"I can find no more, sir," said my father, who was afraid lest some genuine ranger might be attracted by the light, and was determined to let it go out as soon as he had done cooking.

"Never mind," said Hanky, "the moon will be up soon."

"And now, Hanky," said Panky, "tell me what you propose to say on Sunday. I suppose you have pretty well made up your mind about it by this time."

"Pretty nearly. I shall keep it much on the usual lines. I shall dwell upon the benighted state from which the Sunchild rescued us, and shall show how the Musical Banks, by at once taking up the movement, have been the blessed means of its now almost universal success. I shall talk about the immortal glory shed upon Sunch'ston by the Sunchild's residence in the prison, and wind up with the Sunchild Evidence Society, and an earnest appeal for funds to endow the canonries required for the due service of the temple."

"Temple! What temple?" groaned my father inwardly.

"And what are you going to do about the four black and white horses?"

"Stick to them, of course—unless I make them six."

"I really do not see why they might not have been horses."

"I dare say you do not," returned the other drily, "but they were black and white storks, and you know that as well as I do. Still, they have caught on, and they are in the altar-piece, prancing and curvetting magnificently, so I shall trot them out."

"Altar-piece! Altar-piece!" again groaned my father inwardly.

He need not have groaned, for when he came to see the so-called altar-piece he found that the table above which it was placed had nothing in common with the altar in a Christian church. It was a mere table, on which were placed two bowls full of Musical Bank coins; two cashiers, who sat on either side of it, dispensed a few of these to all comers, while there was a box in front of it wherein people deposited coin of the realm according to their will or ability. The idea of sacrifice was not contemplated, and the position of the table, as well as the name given to it, was an instance of the way in which the Erewhonians had caught names and practices from my father, without understanding what they either were or meant. So, again, when Professor Hanky had spoken of canonries, he had none but the vaguest idea of what a canonry is.

I may add further that as a boy my father had had his Bible well drilled into him, and never forgot it. Hence biblical passages and expressions had been often in his mouth, as the effect of mere unconscious cerebration. The Erewhonians had caught many of these, sometimes corrupting them so that they were hardly recognisable. Things that he remembered having said were continually meeting him during the few days of his second visit, and it shocked him deeply to meet some gross travesty of his own words, or of words more sacred than his own, and yet to be unable to correct it. "I wonder," he said to me, "that no one has ever hit on this as a punishment for the damned in Hades."

Let me now return to Professor Hanky, whom I fear that I have left too long.

"And of course," he continued, "I shall say all sorts of pretty things about the Mayoress—for I suppose we must not even think of her as Yram now."

"The Mayoress," replied Panky, "is a very dangerous woman; see how she stood out about the way in which the Sunchild had worn his clothes before they gave him the then Erewhonian dress. Besides, she is a sceptic at heart, and so is that precious son of hers."

"She was quite right," said Hanky, with something of a snort. "She brought him his dinner while he was still wearing the clothes he came in, and if men do not notice how a man wears his clothes, women do. Besides, there are many living who saw him wear them."

"Perhaps," said Panky, "but we should never have talked the King over if we had not humoured him on this point. Yram nearly wrecked us by her obstinacy. If we had not frightened her, and if your study, Hanky, had not happened to have been burned . . ."

"Come, come, Panky, no more of that."

"Of course I do not doubt that it was an accident; nevertheless, if your study had not been accidentally burned, on the very night the clothes were entrusted to you for earnest, patient, careful, scientific investigation—and Yram very nearly burned too—we should never have carried it through. See what work we had to get the King to allow the way in which the clothes were worn to be a matter of opinion, not dogma. What a pity is it that the clothes were not burned before the King's tailor had copied them."

Hanky laughed heartily enough. "Yes," he said, "it was touch and go. Why, I wonder, could not the Queen have put the clothes on a dummy that would show back from front? As soon as it was brought into the council chamber the King jumped to a conclusion, and we had to bundle both dummy and Yram out of the royal presence, for neither she nor the King would budge an inch."

Even Panky smiled. "What could we do? The common people almost worship Yram; and so does her husband, though her fair-haired eldest son was born barely seven months after marriage. The people in these parts like to think that the Sunchild's blood is in the country, and yet they swear through thick and thin that he is the Mayor's duly begotten offspring—Faugh! Do you think they would have stood his being jobbed into the rangership by any one else but Yram?"

My father's feelings may be imagined, but I will not here interrupt the Professors.

"Well, well," said Hanky; "for men must rob and women must job so long as the world goes on. I did the best I could. The King would never have embraced Sunchildism if I had not told him he was right; then, when satisfied that we agreed with him, he yielded to popular prejudice and allowed the question to remain open. One of his Royal Professors was to wear the clothes one way, and the other the other."

"My way of wearing them," said Panky, "is much the most convenient."

"Not a bit of it," said Hanky warmly. On this the two Professors fell out, and the discussion grew so hot that my father interfered by advising them not to talk so loud lest another ranger should hear them. "You know," he said, "there are a good many landrail bones lying about, and it might be awkward."

The Professors hushed at once. "By the way," said Panky, after a pause, "it is very strange about those footprints in the snow. The man had evidently walked round the statues two or three times as though they were strange to him, and he had certainly come from the other side."

"It was one of the rangers," said Hanky impatiently, "who had gone a little beyond the statues, and come back again."

"Then we should have seen his footprints as he went. I am glad I measured them."

"There is nothing in it; but what were your measurements?"

"Eleven inches by four and a half; nails on the soles; one nail missing on the right foot and two on the left." Then, turning to my father quickly, he said, "My man, allow me to have a look at your boots."

"Nonsense, Panky, nonsense!"

Now my father by this time was wondering whether he should not set upon these two men, kill them if he could, and make the best of his way back, but he had still a card to play.

"Certainly, sir," said he, "but I should tell you that they are not my boots."

He took off his right boot and handed it to Panky.

"Exactly so! Eleven inches by four and a half and one nail missing. And now, Mr. Ranger, will you be good enough to explain how you became possessed of that boot. You need not show me the other." And he spoke like an examiner who was confident that he could floor his examinee in *vivâ voce*.

"You know our orders," answered my father, "you have seen them on your permit. I met one of those foreign devils from the other side, of whom we have had more than one lately; he came from out of the clouds that hang higher up, and as he had no permit and could not speak a word of our language, I gripped him, flung him, and strangled him. Thus far I was only obeying orders, but seeing how much better his boots were than mine, and finding that they would fit me, I resolved to keep them. You may be sure I should not have done so if I had known there was snow on the top of the pass."

"He could not invent that," said Hanky; "it is plain that he has not been up to the statues."

Panky was staggered. "And of course," said he ironically, "you took nothing from this poor wretch except his boots."

"Sir," said my father, "I will make a clean breast of everything. I flung his body, his clothes, and my old boots into the pool; but I kept his blankets, some things he used for cooking and some strange stuff that looks like dried leaves, as well as a small bag of something which I believe is gold. I thought I could sell the lot to some dealer in curiosities who would ask no questions."

"And what, pray, have you done with all these things?"

"They are here, sir." And as he spoke he dived into the wood, returning with the blanket, billy, pannikin, tea and the little bag of nuggets which he had kept accessible.

"This is very strange," said Hanky, who was beginning to be afraid of my father when he learned that he sometimes killed people.

Here the Professors talked hurriedly to one another in a tongue which my father could not understand, but which he felt sure was the hypothetical language of which he has spoken in his book.

Presently Hanky said to my father quite civilly, "And what, my good man, do you propose to do with all these things? I should tell you at once that what you take to be gold is nothing of the kind; it is a base metal, hardly, if at all, worth more than copper."

"I have had enough of them; to-morrow morning I shall take them with me to the Blue Pool, and drop them into it."

"It is a pity you should do that," said Hanky musingly: "the things are interesting as curiosities, and—and—and—what will you take for them?"

"I could not do it, sir," answered my father. "I would not do it, no, not for——" and he named a sum equivalent to about five pounds of our money. For he wanted Erewhonian money, and thought it worth his while to sacrifice his ten pounds' worth of nuggets in order to get a supply of current coin.

Hanky tried to beat him down, assuring him that no curiosity dealer would give half as much, and my father so far yielded as to take £4, 10s. in silver, which, as I have already explained, would not be worth more than half a sovereign in gold. At this figure a bargain was struck, and the Professors paid up without offering him a single Musical Bank coin. They wanted to include the boots in the purchase, but here my father stood out.

But he could not stand out as regards another matter, which caused him some anxiety. Panky insisted that my father should give them a receipt for the money, and there was an altercation between the Professors on this point, much longer than I can here find space to give. Hanky argued that a receipt was useless, inasmuch as it would be ruin to my father ever to refer to the subject again. Panky, however, was anxious, not lest my father should again claim the money, but (though he did not say so outright) lest Hanky should claim the whole purchase as his own. In the end Panky, for a wonder, carried the day, and a receipt was drawn up to the effect that the undersigned acknowledged to have received from Professors Hanky and Panky the sum of £4, 10s. (I translate the amount), as joint purchasers of certain pieces of yellow ore, a blanket, and sundry articles found without an owner in the King's preserves. This paper was dated, as the permit had been, XIX. xii. 29.

My father, generally so ready, was at his wits' end for a name, and could think of none but Mr. Nosnibor's. Happily, remembering that this gentleman had also been called Senoj—a name common enough in Erewhon—he signed himself, "Senoj, Under-ranger."

Panky was now satisfied. "We will put it in the bag," he said, "with the pieces of yellow ore."

"Put it where you like," said Hanky contemptuously; and into the bag it was put.

When all was now concluded, my father laughingly said, "If you have dealt unfairly by me, I forgive you. My motto is, 'Forgive us our trespasses, as we forgive them that trespass against us.'"

"Repeat those last words," said Panky eagerly. My father was alarmed at his manner, but thought it safer to repeat them.

"You hear that, Hanky? I am convinced; I have not another word to say. The man is a true Erewhonian; he has our corrupt reading of the Sunchild's prayer."

"Please explain."

"Why, can you not see?" said Panky, who was by way of being great at conjectural emendations. "Can you not see how impossible it is that the Sunchild, or any of the people to whom he declared (as we now know provisionally) that he belonged, could have made the forgiveness of his own sins depend on the readiness with which he forgave other people? No man in his senses would dream of such a thing. It would be asking a supposed all-powerful being not to forgive his sins at all, or at best to forgive them imperfectly. No; Yram got it wrong. She mistook 'but do not' for 'as we.' The sound of the words is very much alike; the correct reading should obviously be, 'Forgive us our trespasses, but do not forgive them that trespass against us.' This makes sense, and turns an impossible prayer into one that goes straight to the heart of every one of us." Then, turning to my father, he said, "You can see this, my man, can you not, as soon as it is pointed out to you?"

My father said that he saw it now, but had always heard the words as he had himself spoken them.

"Of course you have, my good fellow, and it is because of this that I know they never can have reached you except from an Erewhonian source."

Hanky smiled, snorted, and muttered in an undertone, "I shall begin to think that this fellow is a foreign devil after all."

"And now, gentlemen," said my father, "the moon is risen. I must be after the quails at daybreak; I will therefore go to the rangers' shelter" (a shelter, by the way, which existed only in my father's invention), "and get a couple of hours' sleep so as to be both close to the quail-ground and fresh for running. You are so near the boundary of the preserves that you will not want your permit further; no one will meet you and should any one do so you need only give your names and say that you have made a mistake. You will have to give it up to-morrow at the Ranger's office; it will save you trouble if I collect it now and give it up when I deliver my quails.

"As regards the curiosities, hide them as you best can outside the limits. I recommend you to carry them at once out of the forest and rest beyond the limits rather than here. You can then recover them whenever and in whatever way you may find convenient. But I hope you will say nothing about any foreign devil's having come over on to this side. Any whisper to this effect unsettles people's minds, and they are too much unsettled already; hence our orders to kill any one from over there at once and to tell no one but the Head Ranger. I was forced by you, gentlemen, to disobey these orders in self-defence; I must trust your generosity to keep what I have told you secret. I shall of course report it to the Head Ranger. And now if you think proper you can give me up your permit."

All this was so plausible that the Professors gave up their permit without a word but thanks. They bundled their curiosities hurriedly into "the poor foreign devil's" blanket, reserving a more careful packing till they were out of the preserves. They wished my father a very good night, and all success with his quails in the morning; they thanked him again for the care he had taken of them in the matter of the landrails, and Panky even went so far as to give him a few Musical Bank coins, which he gratefully accepted. They then started off in the direction of Sunch'ston.

My father gathered up the remaining quails, some of which he meant to eat in the morning, while the others he would throw away as soon as he could find a safe place. He turned towards the mountains, but before he had gone a dozen yards he heard a voice, which he recognised as Panky's, shouting after him, and saying—

"Mind you do not forget the true reading of the Sunchild's prayer."

"You are an old fool," shouted my father in English, knowing that he could hardly be heard, still less understood, and thankful to relieve his feelings.

CHAPTER V

MY FATHER MEETS A SON, OF WHOSE EXISTENCE HE WAS IGNORANT, AND STRIKES A BARGAIN WITH HIM.

THE INCIDENTS RECORDED in the last two chapters had occupied about two hours, so that it was nearly midnight before my father could begin to retrace his steps and make towards the camp that he had left that morning. This was necessary, for he could not go any further in a costume that he now knew to be forbidden. At this hour no ranger was likely to meet him before he reached the statues, and by making a push for it he could return in time to cross the limits of the preserves before the Professors' permit had expired. If challenged, he must brazen it out that he was one or other of the persons therein named.

Fatigued though he was, he reached the statues, as near as he could guess, at about three in the morning. What little wind there had been was warm, so that the tracks, which the Professors must have seen shortly after he had made them, had disappeared. The statues looked very weird in the moonlight, but they were not chanting.

While ascending he pieced together the information he had picked up from the Professors. Plainly, the Sunchild, or child of the sun, was none other than himself, and the new name of Coldharbour was doubtless intended to commemorate the fact that this was the first town he had reached in Erewhon. Plainly, also, he was supposed to be of superhuman origin—his flight in the balloon having been not unnaturally believed to be miraculous. The

Erewhonians had for centuries been effacing all knowledge of their former culture; archæologists, indeed, could still glean a little from museums, and from volumes hard to come by, and still harder to understand; but archæologists were few, and even though they had made researches (which they may or may not have done), their labours had never reached the masses. What wonder, then, that the mushroom spawn of myth, ever present in an atmosphere highly charged with ignorance, had germinated in a soil so favourably prepared for its reception?

He saw it all now. It was twenty years next Sunday since he and my mother had eloped. That was the meaning of XIX. xii. 29. They had made a new era, dating from the day of his return to the palace of the sun with a bride who was doubtless to unite the Erewhonian nature with that of the sun. The New Year, then, would date from Sunday, December 7 which would therefore become XX. i. i. The Thursday, now nearly if not quite over, being only two days distant from the end of a month of thirty-one days, which was also the last of the year, would be XIX. xii. 29, as on the Professors' permit.

I should like to explain here what will appear more clearly on a later page—I mean, that the Erewhonians, according to their new system, do not believe the sun to be a god except as regards this world and his other planets. My father had told them a little about astronomy, and had assured them that all the fixed stars were suns like our own, with planets revolving round them, which were probably tenanted by intelligent living beings, however unlike they might be to ourselves. From this they evolved the theory that the sun was the ruler of this planetary system, and that he must be personified, as they personified the air-god, the gods of time and space, hope, justice, and the other deities mentioned in my father's book. They retain their old belief in the actual existence of these gods but they now make them all subordinate to the sun. The nearest approach they make to our own conception of God is to say that He is the ruler over all the suns throughout the universe—the suns being to Him much as our planets and their denizens are to our own sun. They deny that He takes more interest in one sun and its system than in another. All the suns with their attendant planets are supposed to be equally His children, and He deputes to each sun the supervision and protection of its own system. Hence they say that though we may pray to the air-god, &c., and even to the sun, we must not pray to God. We may be thankful to Him for watching over the suns, but we must not go further.

Going back to my father's reflections, he perceived that the Erewhonians had not only adopted our calendar, as he had repeatedly explained it to the Nosnibors, but had taken our week as well, and were making Sunday a high day, just as we do. Next Sunday, in commemoration of the twentieth year after his ascent, they were about to dedicate a temple to him; in this there was to be a picture showing himself and his earthly bride on their heavenward journey, in a chariot drawn by four black and white horses—which, however, Professor Hanky had positively affirmed to have been only storks.

Here I interrupted my father. "But were there," I said, "any storks?"

"Yes," he answered. "As soon as I heard Hanky's words I remembered that a flight of some four or five of the large storks so common in Erewhon during the summer months had been wheeling high aloft in one of those aerial dances that so much delight them. I had quite forgotten it, but it came back to me at once that these creatures, attracted doubtless by what they took to be an unknown kind of bird, swooped down towards the balloon and circled round it like so many satellites to a heavenly body. I was fearful lest they should strike at it with their long and formidable beaks, in which case all would have been soon over; either they were afraid, or they had satisfied their curiosity—at any rate, they let us alone; but they kept with us till we were well away from the capital. Strange, how completely this incident had escaped me."

I return to my father's thoughts as he made his way back to his old camp.

As for the reversed position of Professor Panky's clothes, he remembered having given his own old ones to the Queen, and having thought that she might have got a better dummy on which to display them than the headless scarecrow, which, however, he supposed was all her ladies-in-waiting could lay their hands on at the moment. If that dummy had never been replaced, it was perhaps not very strange that the King could not at the first glance tell back from front, and if he did not guess right at first, there was little chance of his changing, for his first ideas were apt to be his last. But he must find out more about this.

Then how about the watch? Had their views about machinery also changed? Or was there an exception made about any machine that he had himself carried?

Yram too. She must have been married not long after she and he had parted. So she was now wife to the Mayor, and was evidently able to have things pretty much her own way in Sunch'ston, as he supposed he must now call it. Thank heaven she was prosperous! It was interesting to know that she was at heart a sceptic, as was also her light-haired son, now Head Ranger. And that son? Just twenty years of age! Born seven months after marriage! Then the Mayor doubtless had light hair too; but why did not those wretches say in which month Yram was married? If she had married soon after he had left, this was why he had not been sent for or written to. Pray heaven it was so. As for current gossip, people would talk, and if the lad was well begotten, what could it matter to them whose son he was? "But," thought my father, "I am glad I did not meet him on my way down. I had rather have been killed by some one else."

Hanky and Panky again. He remembered Bridgeford as the town where the Colleges of Unreason had been most rife; he had visited it, but he had forgotten that it was called "The city of the people who are above suspicion." Its Professors were evidently going to muster in great force on Sunday; if two of them had robbed him, he could forgive them, for the information he had gleaned from them had furnished him with a *pied à terre*. Moreover, he had got as much Erewhonian money as he should want, for he had resolved to retrace his steps immediately after seeing the temple dedicated to himself. He knew the danger he should run in returning over the preserves without a permit, but his curiosity was so great that he resolved to risk it.

Soon after he had passed the statues he began to descend, and it being now broad day, he did so by leaps and bounds, for the ground was not precipitous. He reached his old camp soon after five—this, at any rate, was the hour at which he set his watch on finding that it had run down during his absence. There was now no reason why he should not take it with him, so he put it in his pocket. The parrots had attacked his saddle-bags, saddle, and bridle, as they were sure to do, but they had not got inside the bags. He took out his English clothes and put them on—stowing his bags of gold in various pockets, but keeping his Erewhonian money in the one that was most accessible. He put his Erewhonian dress back into the saddle-bags, intending to keep it as a curiosity; he also refreshed the dye upon his hands, face, and hair; he lit himself a fire, made tea, cooked and ate two brace of quails, which he had plucked while walking so as to save time, and then flung himself on to the ground to snatch an hour's very necessary rest. When he awoke he found he had slept two hours, not one, which was perhaps as well, and by eight he began to reascend the pass.

He reached the statues about noon, for he allowed himself not a moment's rest. This time there was a stiffish wind, and they were chanting lustily. He passed them with all speed, and had nearly reached the place where he had caught the quails, when he saw a man in a dress which he guessed at once to be a ranger's, but which, strangely enough, seeing that he was in the King's employ, was not reversed. My father's heart beat fast; he got out his permit and held it open in his hand, then with a smiling face he went towards the Ranger, who was standing his ground.

"I believe you are the Head Ranger," said my father, who saw that he was still smooth-faced and had light hair. "I am Professor Panky, and here is my permit. My brother Professor has been prevented from coming with me, and, as you see, I am alone."

My father had professed to pass himself off as Panky, for he had rather gathered that Hanky was the better known man of the two.

While the youth was scrutinising the permit, evidently with suspicion, my father took stock of him, and saw his own past self in him too plainly—knowing all he knew—to doubt whose son he was. He had the greatest difficulty in hiding his emotion, for the lad was indeed one of whom any father might be proud. He longed to be able to embrace him and claim him for what he was, but this, as he well knew, might not be. The tears again welled into his eyes when he told me of the struggle with himself that he had then had.

"Don't be jealous, my dearest boy," he said to me. "I love you quite as dearly as I love him, or better, but he was sprung upon me so suddenly, and dazzled me with his comely debonair face, so full of youth, and health, and frankness. Did you see him, he would go straight to your heart, for he is wonderfully like you in spite of your taking so much after your poor mother."

I was not jealous; on the contrary, I longed to see this youth, and find in him such a brother as I had often wished to have. But let me return to my father's story.

The young man, after examining the permit, declared it to be in form, and returned it to my father, but he eyed him with polite disfavour.

"I suppose," he said, "you have come up, as so many are doing, from Bridgeford and all over the country, to the dedication on Sunday."

"Yes," said my father. "Bless me!" he added, "what a wind you have up here! How it makes one's eyes water, to be sure"; but he spoke with a cluck in his throat which no wind that blows can cause.

"Have you met any suspicious characters between here and the statues?" asked the youth. "I came across the ashes of a fire lower down; there had been three men sitting for some time round it, and they had all been eating quails. Here are some of the bones and feathers, which I shall keep. They had not been gone more than a couple of hours, for the ashes were still warm; they are getting bolder and bolder—who would have thought they would dare to light a fire? I suppose you have not met any one; but if you have seen a single person, let me know."

My father said quite truly that he had met no one. He then laughingly asked how the youth had been able to discover as much as he had.

"There were three well-marked forms, and three separate lots of quail bones hidden in the ashes. One man had done all the plucking. This is strange, but I dare say I shall get at it later."

After a little further conversation the Ranger said he was now going down to Sunch'ston, and, though somewhat curtly, proposed that he and my father should walk together.

"By all means," answered my father.

Before they had gone more than a few hundred yards his companion said, "If you will come with me a little to the left, I can show you the Blue Pool."

To avoid the precipitous ground over which the stream here fell, they had diverged to the right, where they had found a smoother descent; returning now to the stream, which was about to enter on a level stretch for some distance, they found themselves on the brink of a rocky basin, of no great size, but very blue, and evidently deep.

"This," said the Ranger, "is where our orders tell us to fling any foreign devil who comes over from the other side. I have only been Head Ranger about nine months, and have not yet had to face this horrid duty; but," and here he smiled, "when I first caught sight of you I thought I should have to make a beginning. I was very glad when I saw you had a permit."

"And how many skeletons do you suppose are lying at the bottom of this pool?"

"I believe not more than seven or eight in all. There were three or four about eighteen years ago, and about the same number of late years; one man was flung here only about three months before I was appointed. I have the full list, with dates, down in my office, but the rangers never let people in Sunch'ston know when they have Blue-Pooled any one; it would unsettle men's minds, and some of them would be coming up here in the dark to drag the pool, and see whether they could find anything on the body."

My father was glad to turn away from this most repulsive place. After a time he said, "And what do you good people hereabouts think of next Sunday's grand doings?"

Bearing in mind what he had gleaned from the Professors about the Ranger's opinions, my father gave a slightly ironical turn to his pronunciation of the words "grand doings." The youth glanced at him with a quick penetrative look, and laughed as he said, "The doings will be grand enough."

"What a fine temple they have built," said my father. "I have not yet seen the picture, but they say the four black and white horses are magnificently painted. I saw the Sunchild ascend, but I saw no horses in the sky, nor anything like horses."

The youth was much interested. "Did you really see him ascend?" he asked; "and what, pray, do you think it all was?"

"Whatever it was, there were no horses."

"But there must have been, for, as you of course know, they have lately found some droppings from one of them, which have been miraculously preserved, and they are going to show them next Sunday in a gold reliquary."

"I know," said my father, who, however, was learning the fact for the first time. "I have not yet seen this precious relic, but I think they might have found something less unpleasant."

"Perhaps they would if they could," replied the youth, laughing, "but there was nothing else that the horses could leave. It is only a number of curiously rounded stones, and not at all like what they say it is."

"Well, well," continued my father, "but relic or no relic, there are many who, while they fully recognise the value of the Sunchild's teaching, dislike these cock and bull stories as blasphemy against God's most blessed gift of reason. There are many in Bridgeford who hate this story of the horses."

The youth was now quite reassured. "So there are here, sir," he said warmly, "and who hate the Sunchild too. If there is such a hell as he used to talk about to my mother, we doubt not but that he will be cast into its deepest fires. See how he has turned us all upside down. But we dare not say what we think. There is no courage left in Erewhon."

Then waxing calmer he said, "It is you Bridgeford people and your Musical Banks that have done it all. The Musical Bank Managers saw that the people were falling away from them. Finding that the vulgar believed this foreign devil Higgs—for he gave this name to my mother when he was in prison—finding that—— But you know all this as well as I do. How can you Bridgeford Professors pretend to believe about these horses, and about the Sunchild's being son to the sun, when all the time you know there is no truth in it?"

"My son—for considering the difference in our ages I may be allowed to call you so—we at Bridgeford are much like you at Sunch'ston; we dare not always say what we think. Nor would it be wise to do so, when we should not be listened to. This fire must burn itself out, for it has got such hold that nothing can either stay or turn it. Even though Higgs himself were to return and tell it from the house-tops that he was a mortal—ay, and a very common one— he would be killed, but not believed."

"Let him come; let him show himself, speak out and die, if the people choose to kill him. In that case I would forgive him, accept him for my father, as silly people sometimes say he is, and honour him to my dying day."

"Would that be a bargain?" said my father, smiling in spite of emotion so strong that he could hardly bring the words out of his mouth.

"Yes, it would," said the youth doggedly.

"Then let me shake hands with you on his behalf, and let us change the conversation."

He took my father's hand, doubtfully and somewhat disdainfully, but he did not refuse it.

CHAPTER VI

FURTHER CONVERSATION BETWEEN FATHER AND SON—THE PROFESSORS' HOARD

IT IS ONE thing to desire a conversation to be changed, and another to change it. After some little silence my father said, "And may I ask what name your mother gave you?"

"My name," he answered, laughing, "is George and I wish it were some other, for it is the first name of that arch-impostor Higgs. I hate it as I hate the man who owned it."

My father said nothing but he hid his face in his hands.

"Sir," said the other, "I fear you are in some distress."

"You remind me," replied my father, "of a son who was stolen from me when he was a child. I searched for him during many years, and at last fell in with him by accident, to find him all the heart of father could wish. But alas! he did not take kindly to me as I to him, and after two days he left me; nor shall I ever again see him."

"Then, sir, had I not better leave you?"

"No, stay with me till your road takes you elsewhere; for though I cannot see my son, you are so like him that I could almost fancy he is with me. And now—for I shall show no more weakness—you say your mother knew the Sunchild, as I am used to call him. Tell me what kind of a man she found him."

"She liked him well enough in spite of his being a little silly. She does not believe he ever called himself child of the sun. He used to say he had a father in heaven to whom he prayed, and who could hear him; but he said that all of us, my mother as much as he, have this unseen father. My mother does not believe he meant doing us any harm, but only that he wanted to get himself and Mrs. Nosnibor's younger daughter out of the country. As for there having been anything supernatural about the balloon, she will have none of it; she says that it was some machine which he knew how to make, but which we have lost the art of making, as we have of many another.

"This is what she says amongst ourselves, but in public she confirms all that the Musical Bank Managers say about him. She is afraid of them. You know, perhaps, that Professor Hanky, whose name I see on your permit, tried to burn her alive?"

"Thank heaven!" thought my father, "that I am Panky;" but aloud he said, "Oh, horrible! horrible! I cannot believe this even of Hanky."

"He denies it, and we say we believe him; he was most kind and attentive to my mother during all the rest of her stay in Bridgeford. He and she parted excellent friends, but I know what she thinks. I shall be sure to see him while he is in Sunch'ston, I shall have to be civil to him but it makes me sick to think of it."

"When shall you see him?" said my father, who was alarmed at learning that Hanky and the Ranger were likely to meet. Who could tell but that he might see Panky too?

"I have been away from home a fortnight, and shall not be back till late on Saturday night. I do not suppose I shall see him before Sunday."

"That will do," thought my father, who at that moment deemed that nothing would matter to him much when Sunday was over. Then, turning to the Ranger, he said, "I gather, then, that your mother does not think so badly of the Sunchild after all?"

"She laughs at him sometimes, but if any of us boys and girls say a word against him we get snapped up directly. My mother turns every one round her finger. Her word is law in Sunch'ston; every one obeys her; she has faced more than one mob, and quelled them when my father could not do so."

"I can believe all you say of her. What other children has she besides yourself?"

"We are four sons, of whom the youngest is now fourteen, and three daughters."

"May all health and happiness attend her and you, and all of you, henceforth and forever," and my father involuntarily bared his head as he spoke.

"Sir," said the youth, impressed by the fervency of my father's manner, "I thank you, but you do not talk as Bridgeford Professors generally do, so far as I have seen or heard them. Why do you wish us all well so very heartily? Is it because you think I am like your son, or is there some other reason?"

"It is not my son alone that you resemble," said my father tremulously, for he knew he was going too far. He carried it by adding, "You resemble all who love truth and hate lies, as I do."

"Then, sir," said the youth gravely, "you much belie your reputation. And now I must leave you for another part of the preserves, where I think it likely that last night's poachers may now be, and where I shall pass the night in watching for them. You may want your permit for a few miles further, so I will not take it. Neither need you give it up at Sunch'ston. It is dated, and will be useless after this evening."

With this he strode off into the forest, bowing politely but somewhat coldly, and without encouraging my father's half proffered hand.

My father turned sad and unsatisfied away.

"It serves me right," he said to himself; "he ought never to have been my son; and yet, if such men can be brought by hook or by crook into the world, surely the world should not ask questions about the bringing. How cheerless everything looks now that he has left me."

———

By this time it was three o'clock, and in another few minutes my father came upon the ashes of the fire beside which he and the Professors had supped on the preceding evening. It was only some eighteen hours since they had come upon him, and yet what an age it seemed! It was well the Ranger had left him, for though my father, of course, would have known nothing about either fire or poachers, it might have led to further falsehood, and by this time he had become exhausted—not to say, for the time being, sick of lies altogether.

He trudged slowly on, without meeting a soul, until he came upon some stones that evidently marked the limits of the preserves. When he had got a mile or so beyond these, he struck a narrow and not much frequented path, which he was sure would lead him towards Sunch'ston, and soon afterwards, seeing a huge old chestnut tree some thirty or forty yards from the path itself, he made towards it and flung himself on the ground beneath its branches. There were abundant signs that he was nearing farm lands and homesteads, but there was no one about, and if any one saw him there was nothing in his appearance to arouse suspicion.

He determined, therefore, to rest here till hunger should wake him, and drive him into Sunch'ston, which, however, he did not wish to reach till dusk if he could help it. He meant to buy a valise and a few toilette necessaries before the shops should close, and then engage a bedroom at the least frequented inn he could find that looked fairly clean and comfortable.

He slept till nearly six, and on waking gathered his thoughts together. He could not shake his newly found son from out of them, but there was no good in dwelling upon him now, and he turned his thoughts to the Professors. How, he wondered, were they getting on, and what had they done with the things they had bought from him?

"How delightful it would be," he said to himself, "if I could find where they have hidden their hoard, and hide it somewhere else."

He tried to project his mind into those of the Professors, as though they were a team of straying bullocks whose probable action he must determine before he set out to look for them.

On reflection, he concluded that the hidden property was not likely to be far from the spot on which he now was. The Professors would wait till they had got some way down towards Sunch'ston, so as to have readier access to their property when they wanted to remove it; but when they came upon a path and other signs that inhabited dwellings could not be far distant, they would begin to look out for a hiding-place. And they would take pretty well the first that came. "Why, bless my heart," he exclaimed, "this tree is hollow; I wonder whether——" and on looking up he saw an innocent little strip of the very tough fibrous leaf commonly used while green as string, or even rope, by the Erewhonians. The plant that makes this leaf is so like the ubiquitous New Zealand *Phormium tenax*, or flax, as it is there called, that I shall speak of it as flax in future, as indeed I have already done without explanation on an earlier page; for this plant grows on both sides of the great range. The piece of flax, then, which my father caught sight of was fastened, at no great height from the ground, round the branch of a strong sucker that had grown from the roots of the chestnut tree, and going thence for a couple of feet or so towards the place where the parent tree became hollow, it disappeared into the cavity below. My father had little difficulty in swarming the sucker till he reached the bough on to which the flax was tied, and soon found himself hauling up something from the bottom of the tree. In less time than it takes to tell the tale he saw his own familiar red blanket begin to show above the broken edge of the hollow, and in another second there was a clinkum-clankum as the bundle fell upon the ground. This was caused by the billy and the pannikin, which were wrapped inside the blanket. As for the blanket, it had been tied tightly at both ends, as well as at several points between, and my father inwardly complimented the Professors on·the neatness with which they had packed and hidden their purchase. "But," he said to himself with a laugh, "I think one of them must have got on the other's back to reach that bough."

"Of course," thought he, "they will have taken the nuggets with them." And yet he had seemed to hear a dumping as well as a clinkum-clankum. He undid the blanket, carefully untying every knot and keeping the flax. When he had unrolled it, he found to his very pleasurable surprise that the pannikin was inside the billy, and the nuggets with the receipt inside the pannikin. The paper containing the tea having been torn, was wrapped up in a handkerchief marked with Hanky's name.

"Down, conscience, down!" he exclaimed as he transferred the nuggets, receipt, and handkerchief to his own pocket. "Eye of my soul that you are! if you offend me I must pluck you out." His conscience feared him and said nothing. As for the tea he left it in its torn paper.

He then put the billy, pannikin, and tea back again inside the blanket, which he tied neatly up, tie for tie with the Professor's own flax, leaving no sign of any disturbance. He again swarmed the sucker, till he reached the bough to which the blanket and its contents had been made fast, and having attached the bundle, he dropped it back into the hollow of the tree. He did everything quite leisurely, for the Professors would be sure to wait till nightfall before coming to fetch their property away.

"If I take nothing but the nuggets," he argued, "each of the Professors will suspect the other of having conjured them into his own pocket while the bundle was being made up. As for the handkerchief, they must think what they like; but it will puzzle Hanky to know why Panky should have been so anxious for a receipt, if he meant stealing the nuggets. Let them muddle it out their own way."

Reflecting further, he concluded, perhaps rightly, that they had left the nuggets where he had found them, because neither could trust the other not to filch a few, if he had them in his own possession, and they could not make a nice division without a pair of scales. "At any rate," he said to himself, "there will be a pretty quarrel when they find them gone."

Thus charitably did he brood over things that were not to happen. The discovery of the Professors' hoard had refreshed him almost as much as his sleep had done, and it being now past seven, he lit his pipe—which, however, he smoked as furtively as he had done when he was a boy at school, for he knew not whether smoking had yet become an Erewhonian virtue or no—and walked briskly on towards Sunch'ston.

CHAPTER VII

SIGNS OF THE NEW ORDER OF THINGS CATCH MY FATHER'S EYE ON EVERY SIDE

HE HAD NOT gone far before a turn in the path—now rapidly widening—showed him two high towers, seemingly some two miles off; these he felt sure must be at Sunch'ston; he therefore stepped out, lest he should find the shops shut before he got there.

On his former visit he had seen little of the town, for he was in prison during his whole stay. He had had a glimpse of it on being brought there by the people of the village where he had spent his first night in Erewhon—a village which he had seen at some little distance on his right hand, but which it would have been out of his way to visit, even if he had wished to do so; and he had seen the Museum of old machines, but on leaving the prison he had been blindfolded. Nevertheless he felt sure that if the towers had been there he should have seen them, and rightly guessed that they must belong to the temple which was to be dedicated to himself on Sunday.

When he had passed through the suburbs he found himself in the main street. Space will not allow me to dwell on more than a few of the things which caught his eye, and assured him that the change in Erewhonian habits and opinions had been even more cataclysmic than he had already divined. The first important building that he came to proclaimed itself as the College of Spiritual Athletics, and in the window of a shop that was evidently affiliated to the college he saw an announcement that moral try-your-strengths, suitable for every kind of ordinary temptation, would be provided on the shortest notice. Some of those that aimed at the more common kinds of temptation were kept in stock, but these consisted chiefly of trials to the temper. On dropping, for example, a penny into a slot, you could have a jet of fine pepper, flour, or brick-dust, whichever you might prefer, thrown on to your face, and thus discover whether your composure stood in need of further development or no. My father gathered this from the writing that was pasted on to the try-your-strength, but he had no time to go inside the shop and test either the machine or his own temper. Other temptations to irritability required the agency of living people, or at any rate living beings. Crying children, screaming parrots, a spiteful monkey, might be hired on ridiculously easy terms. He saw one advertisement, nicely framed, which ran as follows:

"Mrs. Tantrums, Nagger, certificated by the College of Spiritual Athletics. Terms for ordinary nagging, two shillings and sixpence per hour. Hysterics extra."

Then followed a series of testimonials—for example:—

"Dear Mrs. Tantrums,—I have for years been tortured with a husband of unusually peevish, irritable temper, who made my life so intolerable that

I sometimes answered him in a way that led to his using personal violence towards me. After taking a course of twelve sittings from you, I found my husband's temper comparatively angelic, and we have ever since lived together in complete harmony."

Another was from a husband:—

"Mr.—— presents his compliments to Mrs. Tantrums, and begs to assure her that her extra special hysterics have so far surpassed anything his wife can do, as to render him callous to those attacks which he had formerly found so distressing."

There were many others of a like purport, but time did not permit my father to do more than glance at them. He contented himself with the two following, of which the first ran:—

"He did try it at last. A little correction of the right kind taken at the right moment is invaluable. No more swearing. No more bad language of any kind. A lamb-like temper ensured in about twenty minutes, by a single dose of one of our spiritual indigestion tabloids. In cases of all the more ordinary moral ailments, from simple lying, to homicidal mania, in cases again of tendency to hatred, malice, and uncharitableness; of atrophy or hypertrophy of the conscience, of costiveness or diarrhœa of the sympathetic instincts, &c., &c., our spiritual indigestion tabloids will afford unfailing and immediate relief.

"N. B.—A bottle or two of our Sunchild Cordial will assist the operation of the tabloids."

The second and last that I can give was as follows:—

"All else is useless. If you wish to be a social success, make yourself a good listener. There is no short cut to this. A would-be listener must learn the rudiments of his art and go through the mill like other people. If he would develop a power of suffering fools gladly, he must begin by suffering them without the gladness. Professor Proser, ex-straightener, certificated bore, pragmatic or coruscating, with or without anecdotes, attends pupils at their own houses. Terms moderate.

"Mrs. Proser, whose success as a professional mind-dresser is so well known that lengthened advertisement is unnecessary, prepares ladies or gentlemen with appropriate remarks to be made at dinner-parties or at-homes. Mrs. P. keeps herself well up to date with all the latest scandals."

"Poor, poor, straighteners!" said my father to himself. "Alas! that it should have been my fate to ruin you—for I suppose your occupation is gone."

Tearing himself away from the College of Spiritual Athletics and its affiliated shop, he passed on a few doors, only to find himself looking in at what was neither more nor less than a chemist's shop. In the window there were advertisements which showed that the practice of medicine was now legal, but my father could not stay to copy a single one of the fantastic announcements that a hurried glance revealed to him.

It was also plain here, as from the shop already more fully described, that the edicts against machines had been repealed, for there were physical try-your-strengths, as in the other shop there had been moral ones, and such machines under the old law would not have been tolerated for a moment.

My father made his purchases just as the last shops were closing. He noticed that almost all of them were full of articles labelled "Dedication." There was Dedication gingerbread, stamped with a moulded representation of the new temple; there were Dedication syrups, Dedication pocket-handkerchiefs, also showing the temple, and in one corner giving a highly idealised portrait of my father himself. The chariot and the horses figured largely, and in the confectioners' shops there were models of the newly discovered relic—made, so my father thought, with a little heap of cherries or strawberries, smothered in chocolate. Outside one tailor's shop he saw a flaring advertisement which can only be translated, "Try our Dedication trousers, price ten shillings and sixpence."

Presently he passed the new temple, but it was too dark for him to do more than see that it was a vast fane, and must have cost an untold amount of money. At every turn he found himself more and more shocked, as he realised more and more fully the mischief he had already occasioned, and the certainty that this was small as compared with that which would grow up hereafter.

"What," he said to me, very coherently and quietly, "was I to do? I had struck a bargain with that dear fellow, though he knew not what I meant, to the effect that I should try to undo the harm I had done, by standing up before the people on Sunday and saying who I was. True, they would not believe me. They would look at my hair and see it black, whereas it should be very light. On this they would look no further, but very likely tear me to pieces then and there. Suppose that the authorities held a *post-mortem* examination, and that many who knew me (let alone that all my measurements and marks were recorded twenty years ago) identified the body as mine: would those in power admit that I was the Sunchild? Not they. The interests vested in my being now in the palace of the sun are too great to allow of my having been torn to pieces in Sunch'ston, no matter how truly I had been torn; the whole thing would be hushed up, and the utmost that could come of it would be a heresy which would in time be crushed.

"On the other hand, what business have I with 'would be' or 'would not be?' Should I not speak out, come what may, when I see a whole people being led astray by those who are merely exploiting them for their own ends? Though I could do but little, ought I not to do that little? What did that good fellow's instinct—so straight from heaven, so true, so healthy—tell him? What did my own instinct answer? What would the conscience of any honourable man answer? Who can doubt?

"And yet, is there not reason? and is it not God-given as much as instinct? I remember having heard an anthem in my young days, 'O where shall wisdom be found? the deep saith it is not in me.' As the singers kept on repeating the question, I kept on saying sorrowfully to myself—'Ah, where, where, where?' and when the triumphant answer came, 'The fear of the Lord, that is wisdom, and to depart from evil is understanding,' I shrunk ashamed into myself for not having foreseen it. In later life, when I have tried to use this answer as a light by which I could walk, I found it served but to the raising of another question, 'What is the fear of the Lord, and what is evil in this, particular case?' And my easy method with spiritual dilemmas proved to be but a case of *ignotum per ignotius.*

"If Satan himself is at times transformed into an angel of light, are not angels of light sometimes transformed into the likeness of Satan? If the devil is not so black as he is painted, is God always so white? And is there not another place in which it is said, 'The fear of the Lord is the beginning of wisdom,' as though it were not the last word upon the subject? If a man should not do evil that good may come, so neither should he do good that evil may come; and though it were good for me to speak out, should I not do better by refraining?

"Such were the lawless and uncertain thoughts that tortured me very cruelly, so that I did what I had not done for many a long year—I prayed for guidance. 'Shew me Thy will, O Lord,' I cried in great distress, 'and strengthen me to do it when Thou hast shewn it me.' But there was no answer. Instinct tore me one way and reason another. Whereon I settled that I would obey the reason with which God had endowed me, unless the instinct He had also given me should thrash it out of me. I could get no further than this, that the Lord hath mercy on whom He will have mercy, and whom He willeth He hardeneth; and again I prayed that I might be among those on whom He would show His mercy.

"This was the strongest internal conflict that I ever remember to have felt, and it was at the end of it that I perceived the first, but as yet very faint, symptoms of that sickness from which I shall not recover. Whether this be a token of mercy or no, my Father which is in heaven knows, but I know not."

From what my father afterwards told me, I do not think the above reflections had engrossed him for more than three or four minutes; the giddiness which had for some seconds compelled him to lay hold of the first thing he could catch at in order to avoid falling, passed away without leaving a trace behind it, and his path seemed to become comfortably clear before him. He settled it that the proper thing to do would be to buy some food, start back at once while his permit was still valid, help himself to the property which he had sold to the Professors, leaving the Erewhonians to wrestle as they best might with the lot that it had pleased Heaven to send them.

This, however, was too heroic a course. He was tired, and wanted a night's rest in a bed; he was hungry, and wanted a substantial meal; he was curious, moreover, to see the temple dedicated to himself, and hear Hanky's sermon; there was also his further difficulty, he would have to take what he had sold the Professors without returning them their £4, 10s., for he could not do without his blanket, &c.; and even if he left a bag of nuggets made fast to the sucker, he must either place it where it could be seen so easily that it would very likely get stolen, or hide it so cleverly that the Professors would never find it. He therefore compromised by concluding that he would sup and sleep in Sunch'ston, get through the morrow as he best could without attracting attention, deepen the stain on his face and hair, and rely on the change so made in his appearance to prevent his being recognised at the dedication of the temple. He would do nothing to disillusion the people—to do this would only be making bad worse. As soon as the service was over, he would set out towards the preserves, and, when it was well dark, make for the statues. He hoped that on such a great day the rangers might be many of them in Sunch'ston; if there were any about, he must trust to the moonless night and his own quick eyes and ears to get him through the preserves safely.

The shops were by this time closed, but the keepers of a few stalls were trying by lamplight to sell the wares they had not yet got rid of. One of these was a bookstall, and, running his eye over some of the volumes, my father saw one entitled—

> "The Sayings of the Sunchild during his stay in Erewhon, to which is added a true account of his return to the palace of the sun with his Erewhonian bride. This is the only version authorised by the Presidents and Vice-Presidents of the Musical Banks; all other versions being imperfect and inaccurate."—Bridgeford, XVIII, 150 pp. 8vo, Price 3s.

The reader will understand that I am giving the prices as nearly as I can in their English equivalents. Another title was—

> "The Sacrament of Divorce: an Occasional Sermon preached by Dr. Gurgoyle, President of the Musical Banks for the Province of Sunch'ston." 8vo, 16 pp. 6d.

Other titles ran—
> "Counsels of Imperfection." 8vo, 20 pp. 6d.
> "Hygiene; or, How to Diagnose your Doctor." 8vo, 10 pp. 3d.
> "The Physics of Vicarious Existence," by Dr. Gurgoyle, President of the Musical Banks for the Province of Sunch'ston. 8vo, 20 pp. 6d.

There were many other books whose titles would probably have attracted my father as much as those that I have given, but he was too tired and hungry to look at more. Finding that he could buy all the foregoing for 4s 9d., he bought them and stuffed them into the valise that he had just bought. His purchases in all had now amounted to a little over £1, 10s. (silver), leaving him about £3 (silver), including the money for which he had sold the quails, to carry him on till Sunday afternoon. He intended to spend say £2 (silver), and keep the rest of the money in order to give it to the British Museum.

He now began to search for an inn, and walked about the less fashionable parts of the town till he found an unpretending tavern, which he thought would suit him. Here, on importunity, he was given a servant's room at the top of the house, all others being engaged by visitors who had come for the dedication. He ordered a meal, of which he stood in great need, and having eaten it, he retired early for the night. But he smoked a pipe surreptitiously up the chimney before he got into bed.

Meanwhile other things were happening, of which, happily for his repose, he was still ignorant, and which he did not learn till a few days later. Not to depart from chronological order I will deal with them in my next chapter.

CHAPTER VIII

YRAM, NOW MAYORESS, GIVES A DINNER-PARTY, IN THE COURSE OF WHICH SHE IS DISQUIETED BY WHAT SHE LEARNS FROM PROFESSOR HANKY: SHE SENDS FOR HER SON GEORGE AND QUESTIONS HIM

THE PROFESSORS, RETURNING to their hotel early on the Friday morning, found a note from the Mayoress urging them to be her guests during the remainder of their visit, and to meet other friends at dinner on the same evening. They accepted, and then went to bed; for they had passed the night under the tree in which they had hidden their purchase, and, as may be imagined, had slept but little. They rested all day, and transferred themselves and their belongings to the Mayor's house in time to dress for dinner.

When they came down into the drawing-room they found a brilliant company assembled, chiefly Musical-Bankical like themselves. There was Dr. Downie, Professor of Logomachy, and perhaps the most subtle dialectician in Erewhon. He could say nothing in more words than any man of his generation. His text-book on the "Art of Obscuring Issues" had passed through ten or twelve editions, and was in the hands of all aspirants for academic distinction. He had earned a high reputation for sobriety of judgment by resolutely refusing to have definite views on any subjects; so safe a man was he considered, that while still quite young he had been appointed to the lucrative post of Thinker in Ordinary to the Royal Family. There was Mr. Principal Crank, with his sister Mrs. Quack; Professors Gabb and Bawl, with their wives and two or three erudite daughters.

Old Mrs. Humdrum (of which more anon) was there of course, with her venerable white hair and rich black satin dress, looking the very ideal of all that a stately old dowager ought to be. In society she was commonly known as Ydgrun, so perfectly did she correspond with the conception of this strange goddess formed by the Erewhonians. She was one of those who had visited my father when he was in prison twenty years earlier. When he told me that she was now called Ydgrun, he said, "I am sure that the Erinyes were only Mrs. Humdrums, and that they were delightful people when you came to know them. I do not believe they did the awful things we say they did. I think, but am not quite sure, that they let Orestes off; but even though they had not pardoned him, I doubt whether they would have done anything more dreadful to him than issue a *mot d'ordre* that he was not to be asked to any more afternoon teas. This, however, would be down-right torture to some people. At any rate," he continued, "be it the Erinyes, or Mrs. Grundy, or Ydgrun, in all times and places it is woman who decides whether society is to condone an offence or no."

Among the most attractive ladies present was one for whose Erewhonian name I can find no English equivalent, and whom I must therefore call Miss La Frime. She was Lady President of the principal establishment for the higher education of young ladies, and so celebrated was she, that pupils flocked to her from all parts of the surrounding country. Her primer (written for the Erewhonian Arts and Science Series) on the Art of Man-killing, was the most complete thing of the kind that had yet been done; but ill-natured people had been heard to say that she had killed all her own admirers so effectually that not one of them had ever lived to marry her. According to Erewhonian custom the successful marriages of the pupils are inscribed yearly on the oak panelling of the college refectory, and a reprint from these in pamphlet form accompanies all the prospectuses that are sent out to parents. It was alleged that no other ladies' seminary in Erewhon could show such a brilliant record during all the years of Miss La Frime's presidency. Many other guests of less note were there, but the lions of the evening were the two Professors whom we have already met with, and more particularly Hanky, who took the Mayoress in to dinner. Panky, of course, wore his clothes reversed, as did Principal Crank and Professor Gabb; the others were dressed English fashion.

Everything hung upon the hostess, for the host was little more than a still handsome figure-head. He had been remarkable for his good looks as a young man, and Strong is the nearest approach I can get to a translation of his Erewhonian name. His face inspired confidence at once, but he was a man of few words, and had little of that grace which in his wife set every one instantly at his or her ease. He knew that all would go well so long as he left everything to her, and kept himself as far as might be in the background.

Before dinner was announced there was the usual buzz of conversation, chiefly occupied with salutations, good wishes for Sunday's weather, and admiration for the extreme beauty of the Mayoress's three daughters, the two elder of whom were already out; while the third, though only thirteen, might have passed for a year or two older. Their mother was so much engrossed with receiving her guests that it was not till they were all at table that she was able to ask Hanky what he thought of the statues, which she had heard that he and Professor Panky had been to see. She was told how much interested he had been with them, and how unable he had been to form any theory as to their date or object. He then added, appealingly to Panky, who was on the Mayoress's left hand, "but we had rather a strange adventure on our way down, had we not, Panky? We got lost, and were benighted in the forest. Happily we fell in with one of the rangers who had lit a fire."

"Do I understand, then," said Yram, as I suppose we may as well call her, "that you were out all last night? How tired you must be! But I hope you had enough provisions with you?"

"Indeed we were out all night. We staid by the ranger's fire till midnight, and then tried to find our way down, but we gave it up soon after we had got out of the forest, and then waited under a large chestnut tree till four or five this morning. As for food, we had not so much as a mouthful from about three in the afternoon till we got to our inn early this morning."

"Oh, you poor, poor people! how tired you must be."

"No; we made a good breakfast as soon as we got in, and then went to bed, where we staid till it was time for us to come to your house."

Here Panky gave his friend a significant look, as much as to say that he had said enough.

This set Hanky on at once. "Strange to say, the ranger was wearing the old Erewhonian dress. It did me good to see it again after all these years. It seems your son lets his men wear what few of the old clothes they may still have, so long as they keep well away from the town. But fancy how carefully these poor fellows husband them; why, it must be seventeen years since the dress was forbidden!"

We all of us have skeletons, large or small, in some cupboard of our lives, but a well regulated skeleton that will stay in its cupboard quietly does not much matter. There are skeletons, however, which can never be quite trusted not to open the cupboard door at some awkward moment, go down stairs, ring the hall-door bell, with grinning face announce themselves as the skeleton, and ask whether the master or mistress is at home. This kind of skeleton, though no bigger than a rabbit, will sometimes loom large as that of a dinotherium. My father was Yram's skeleton. True, he was a mere skeleton of a skeleton, for the chances were thousands to one that he and my mother had perished long years ago; and even though he rang at the bell, there was no harm that he either could or would now do to her or hers; still, so long as she did not certainly know that he was dead, or otherwise precluded from returning, she could not be sure that he would not one day come back by the way that he would alone know, and she had rather he should not do so.

Hence, on hearing from Professor Hanky that a man had been seen between the statues and Sunch'ston wearing the old Erewhonian dress, she was disquieted and perplexed. The excuse he had evidently made to the Professors aggravated her uneasiness, for it was an obvious attempt to escape from an unexpected difficulty. There could be no truth in it. Her son would as soon think of wearing the old dress himself as of letting his men do so; and as for having old clothes still to wear out after seventeen years, no one but a Bridgeford Professor would accept this. She saw, therefore, that she must keep her wits about her, and lead her guests on to tell her as much as they could be induced to do.

"My son," she said innocently, "is always considerate to his men, and that is why they are so devoted to him. I wonder which of them it was? In what part of the preserves did you fall in with him?"

Hanky described the place, and gave the best idea he could of my father's appearance.

"Of course he was swarthy like the rest of us?"

"I saw nothing remarkable about him, except that his eyes were blue and his eyelashes nearly white, which, as you know, is rare in Erewhon. Indeed, I do not remember ever before to have seen a man with dark hair and complexion but light eyelashes. Nature is always doing something unusual."

"I have no doubt," said Yram, "that he was the man they call Blacksheep, but I never noticed this peculiarity in him. If he was Blacksheep, I am afraid you must have found him none too civil; he is a rough diamond, and you would hardly be able to understand his uncouth Sunch'ston dialect."

"On the contrary, he was most kind and thoughtful—even so far as to take our permit from us, and thus save us the trouble of giving it up at your son's office. As for his dialect, his grammar was often at fault, but we could quite understand him."

"I am glad to hear he behaved better than I could have expected. Did he say in what part of the preserves he had been?"

"He had been catching quails between the place where we saw him and the statues; he was to deliver three dozen to your son this afternoon for the Mayor's banquet on Sunday."

This was worse and worse. She had urged her son to provide her with a supply of quails for Sunday's banquet, but he had begged her not to insist on having them. There was no close time for them in Erewhon, but he set his face against their being seen at table in spring and summer. During the winter, when any great occasion arose, he had allowed a few brace to be provided.

"I asked my son to let me have some," said Yram, who was now on full scent. She laughed genially as she added, "Can you throw any light upon the question whether I am likely to get my three dozen? I have had no news as yet."

"The man had taken a good many; we saw them but did not count them. He started about midnight for the ranger's shelter, where he said he should sleep till daybreak, so as to make up his full tale betimes."

Yram had heard her son complain that there were no shelters on the preserves, and state his intention of having some built before the winter. Here too, then, the man's story must be false. She changed the conversation for the moment, but quietly told a servant to send high and low in search of her son, and if he could be found, to bid him come to her at once. She then returned to her previous subject.

"And did not this heartless wretch, knowing how hungry you must both be, let you have a quail or two as an act of pardonable charity?"

"My dear Mayoress, how can you ask such a question? We knew you would want all you could get; moreover, our permit threatened us with all sorts of horrors if we so much as ate a single quail. I assure you we never even allowed a thought of eating one of them to cross our minds."

"Then," said Yram to herself, "they gorged upon them." What could she think? A man who wore the old dress, and therefore who had almost certainly been in Erewhon, but had been many years away from it; who spoke the language well, but whose grammar was defective—hence, again, one who had spent some time in Erewhon; who knew nothing of the afforesting law now long since enacted, for how else would he have dared to light a fire and be seen with quails in his possession; an adroit liar, who on gleaning information from the Professors had hazarded an excuse for immediately retracing his steps; a man, too, with blue eyes and light eyelashes. What did it matter about his hair being dark and his complexion swarthy— Higgs was far too clever to attempt a second visit to Erewhon without dying his hair and staining his face and hands. And he had got their permit out of the Professors before he left them; clearly, then, he meant coming back, and coming back at once before the permit had expired. How could she doubt? My father, she felt sure, must by this time be in Sunch'ston. He would go back to change his clothes, which would not be very far down on the other side the pass, for he would not put on his old Erewhonian dress till he was on the point of entering Erewhon; and he would hide his English dress rather than throw it away, for he would want it when he went back again. It would be quite possible, then, for him to get through the forest before the permit was void, and he would be sure to go on to Sunch'ston for the night.

She chatted unconcernedly, now with one guest now with another, while they in their turn chatted unconcernedly with one another.

Miss La Frime to Mrs. Humdrum: "You know how he got his professorship? No? I thought every one knew that. The question the candidates had to answer was, whether it was wiser during a long stay at a hotel to tip the servants pretty early, or to wait till the stay was ended. All the other candidates took one side or the other, and argued their case in full. Hanky sent in three lines to the effect that the proper thing to do would be to promise at the beginning, and go away without giving. The King, with whom the appointment rested, was so much pleased with this answer that he gave Hanky the professorship without so much as looking . . ."

Professor Gabb to Mrs. Humdrum: "Oh, no, I can assure you there is no truth in it. What happened was this. There was the usual crowd, and the people cheered Professor after Professor, as he stood before them in the great Bridgeford theatre and satisfied them that a lump of butter which had been put into his mouth would not melt in it. When Hanky's turn came he was taken suddenly unwell, and had to leave the theatre, on which there was a report in the house that the butter had melted; this was at once stopped by the return of the Professor. Another piece of butter was put into his mouth, and on being taken out after the usual time, was found to show no signs of having . . ."

Miss Bawl to Mr. Principal Crank: . . . "The Manager was so tall, you know, and then there was that little mite of an assistant manager—it *was* so funny. For the assistant manager's voice was ever so much louder than the . . ."

Mrs. Bawl to Professor Gabb: . . . "Live for art! If I had to choose whether I would lose either art or science, I have not the smallest hesitation in saying that I would lose . . ."

The Mayor and Dr. Downie: . . . "That you are to be canonised at the close of the year along with Professors Hanky and Panky?"

"I believe it is his Majesty's intention that the Professors and myself are to head the list of the Sunchild's Saints, but we have all of us got to . . ."

And so on, and so on, buzz, buzz, buzz, over the whole table. Presently Yram turned to Hanky and said—

"By the way, Professor, you must have found it very cold up at the statues, did you not? But I suppose the snow is all gone by this time?"

"Yes, it was cold, and though the winter's snow is melted, there had been a recent fall. Strange to say, we saw fresh footprints in it, as of some one who had come up from the other side. But thereon hangs a tale, about which I believe I should say nothing."

"Then say nothing, my dear Professor," said Yram with a frank smile. "Above all," she added quietly and gravely, "say nothing to the Mayor, nor to my son, till after Sunday. Even a whisper of some one coming over from the other side disquiets them, and they have enough on hand for the moment."

Panky, who had been growing more and more restive at his friend's outspokenness, but who had encouraged it more than once by vainly trying to check it, was relieved at hearing his hostess do for him what he could not do for himself. As for Yram, she had got enough out of the Professor to be now fully dissatisfied, and mentally informed them that they might leave the witness-box. During the rest of dinner she let the subject of their adventure severely alone.

It seemed to her as though dinner was never going to end; but in the course of time it did so, and presently the ladies withdrew. As they were entering the drawing-room a servant told her that her son had been found more easily than was expected, and was now in his own room dressing.

"Tell him," she said, "to stay there till I come, which I will do directly."

She remained for a few minutes with her guests, and then, excusing herself quietly to Mrs. Humdrum, she stepped out and hastened to her son's room. She told him that Professors Hanky and Panky were staying in the house, and that during dinner they had told her something he ought to know, but which there was no time to tell him until her guests were gone. "I had rather," she said, "tell you about it before you see the Professors, for if you see them the whole thing will be reopened, and you are sure to let them see how much more there is in it than they suspect. I want everything hushed up for the moment; do not, therefore, join us. Have dinner sent to you in your father's study. I will come to you about midnight."

"But, my dear mother," said George, "I have seen Panky already. I walked down with him a good long way this afternoon."

Yram had not expected this, but she kept her countenance. "How did you know," said she, "that he was Professor Panky? Did he tell you so?"

"Certainly he did. He showed me his permit, which was made out in favour of Professors Hanky and Panky, or either of them. He said Hanky had been unable to come with him, and that he was himself Professor Panky."

Yram again smiled very sweetly. "Then, my dear boy," she said, "I am all the more anxious that you should not see him now. See nobody but the servants and your brothers, and wait till I can enlighten you. I must not stay another moment; but tell me this much, have you seen any signs of poachers lately?"

"Yes; there were three last night."

"In what part of the preserves?"

Her son described the place.

"You are sure they had been killing quails?"

"Yes, and eating them—two on one side of a fire they had lit, and one on the other; this last man had done all the plucking."

"Good!"

She kissed him with more than even her usual tenderness, and returned to the drawing-room.

During the rest of the evening she was engaged in earnest conversation with Mrs. Humdrum, leaving her other guests to her daughters and to themselves. Mrs. Humdrum had been her closest friend for many years, and carried more weight than any one else in Sunch'ston, except, perhaps, Yram herself. "Tell him everything," she said to Yram at the close of their conversation; "we all dote upon him; trust him frankly, as you trusted your husband before you let him marry you. No lies, no reserves, no tears, and all will come right. As for me, command me," and the good old lady rose to take her leave with as kind a look on her face as ever irradiated saint or angel. "I go early," she added, "for the others will go when they see me do so, and the sooner you are alone the better."

By half an hour before midnight her guests had gone. Hanky and Panky were given to understand that they must still be tired, and had better go to bed. So was the Mayor; so were her sons and daughters, except of course George, who was waiting for her with some anxiety, for he had seen that she had something serious to tell him. Then she went down into the study. Her son embraced her as she entered, and moved an easy chair for her, but she would not have it.

"No; I will have an upright one." Then, sitting composedly down on the one her son placed for her, she said—

"And now to business. But let me first tell you that the Mayor was told, twenty years ago, all the more important part of what you will now hear. He does not yet know what has happened within the last few hours, but either you or I will tell him to-morrow."

CHAPTER IX

INTERVIEW BETWEEN YRAM
AND HER SON

"What did you think of Panky?"

"I could not make him out. If he had not been a Bridgeford Professor I might have liked him; but you know how we all of us distrust those people."

"Where did you meet him?"

"About two hours lower down than the statues."

"At what o'clock?"

"It might be between two and half-past."

"I suppose he did not say that at that hour he was in bed at his hotel in Sunch'ston. Hardly! Tell me what passed between you."

"He had his permit open before we were within speaking distance. I think he feared I should attack him without making sure whether he was a foreign devil or no. I have told you he said he was Professor Panky."

"I suppose he had a dark complexion and black hair like the rest of us?"

"Dark complexion and hair purplish rather than black. I was surprised to see that his eyelashes were as light as my own, and his eyes were blue like mine—but you will have noticed this at dinner."

"No, my dear, I did not, and I think I should have done so if it had been there to notice."

"Oh, but it was so indeed."

"Perhaps. Was there anything strange about his way of talking?"

"A little about his grammar, but these Bridgeford Professors have often risen from the ranks. His pronunciation was nearly like yours and mine."

"Was his manner friendly?"

"Very; more so than I could understand at first, I had not, however, been with him long before I saw tears in his eyes, and when I asked him whether he was in distress, he said I reminded him of a son whom he had lost and had found after many years, only to lose him almost immediately for ever. Hence his cordiality towards me."

"Then," said Yram half hysterically to herself, "he knew who you were. Now, how, I wonder, did he find that out?" All vestige of doubt as to who the man might be had now left her.

"Certainly he knew who I was. He spoke about you more than once, and wished us every kind of prosperity, baring his head reverently as he spoke."

"Poor fellow! Did he say anything about Higgs?"

"A good deal, and I was surprised to find he thought about it all much as we do. But when I said that if I could go down into the hell of which Higgs used to talk to you while he was in prison, I should expect to find him in its hottest fire, he did not like it."

"Possibly not, my dear. Did you tell him how the other boys, when you were at school, used sometimes to say you were son to this man Higgs, and that the people of Sunch'ston used to say so also, till the Mayor trounced two or three people so roundly that they held their tongues for the future?"

"Not all that, but I said that silly people had believed me to be the Sunchild's son, and what a disgrace I should hold it to be son to such an impostor."

"What did he say to this?"

"He asked whether I should feel the disgrace less if Higgs were to undo the mischief he had caused by coming back and shewing himself to the people for what he was. But he said it would be no use for him to do so, inasmuch as people would kill him but would not believe him."

"And you said?"

"Let him come back, speak out, and chance what might befall him. In that case, I should honour him, father or no father."

"And he?"

"He asked if that would be a bargain; and when I said it would, he grasped me warmly by the hand on Higgs's behalf—though what it could matter to him passes my comprehension."

"But he saw that even though Higgs were to show himself and say who he was, it would mean death to himself and no good to any one else?"

"Perfectly."

"Then he can have meant nothing by shaking hands with you. It was an idle jest. And now for your poachers. You do not know who they were? I will tell you. The two who sat on the one side the fire were Professors Hanky and Panky from the City of the People who are above Suspicion."

"No," said George vehemently. "Impossible."

"Yes, my dear boy, quite possible, and whether possibly or impossibly, assuredly true."

"And the third man?"

"The third man was dressed in the old costume. He was in possession of several brace of birds. The Professors vowed they had not eaten any——"

"Oh yes, but they had," blurted out George.

"Of course they had, my dear; and a good thing too. Let us return to the man in the old costume."

"That is puzzling. Who did he say he was?"

"He said he was one of your men; that you had instructed him to provide you with three dozen quails for Sunday; and that you let your men wear the old costume if they had any of it left, provided——"

This was too much for George; he started to his feet. "What, my dearest mother, does all this mean? You have been playing with me all through. What is coming?"

"A very little more, and you shall hear. This man staid with the Professors till nearly midnight, and then left them on the plea that he would finish the night in the Ranger's shelter——"

"Ranger's shelter, indeed! Why——"

"Hush, my darling boy, be patient with me. He said he must be up betimes, to run down the rest of the quails you had ordered him to bring you. But before leaving the Professors he beguiled them into giving him up their permit."

"Then," said George, striding about the room with his face flushed and his eyes flashing, "he was the man with whom I walked down this afternoon."

"Exactly so."

"And he must have changed his dress?"

"Exactly so."

"But where and how?"

"At some place not very far down on the other side the range, where he had hidden his old clothes."

"And who, in the name of all that we hold most sacred, do you take him to have been—for I see you know more than you have yet told me?"

"My son, he was Higgs the Sunchild, father to that boy whom I love next to my husband more dearly than any one in the whole world."

She folded her arms about him for a second, without kissing him, and left him. "And now," she said, the moment she had closed the door—"and now I may cry."

———————

She did not cry for long, and having removed all trace of tears as far as might be, she returned to her son outwardly composed and cheerful. "Shall I say more now," she said, seeing how grave he looked, "or shall I leave you, and talk further with you to-morrow?"

"Now—now—now!"

"Good! A little before Higgs came here, the Mayor, as he now is, poor, handsome, generous to a fault so far as he had the wherewithal, was adored by all the women of his own rank in Sunch'ston. Report said that he had adored many of them in return, but after having known me for a very few days, he asked me to marry him, protesting that he was a changed man. I liked him, as every one else did, but I was not in love with him, and said so; he said he would give me as much time as I chose, if I would not point-blank refuse him; and so the matter was left.

"Within a week or so Higgs was brought to the prison, and he had not been there long before I found or thought I found, that I liked him better than I liked Strong. I was a fool—but there! As for Higgs, he liked, but did not love me. If I had let him alone he would have done the like by me; and let each other alone we did, till the day before he was taken down to the capital. On that day, whether through his fault or mine I know not—we neither of us meant it—it was as though Nature, my dear, was determined that you should not slip through her fingers—well, on that day we took it into our heads that we were broken-hearted lovers—the rest followed. And how, my dearest boy, as I look upon you, can I feign repentance?

"My husband, who never saw Higgs, and knew nothing about him except the too little that I told him, pressed his suit, and about a month after Higgs had gone, having recovered my passing infatuation for him, I took kindly to the Mayor and accepted him, without telling him what I ought to have told him—but the words stuck in my throat. I had not been engaged to him many days before I found that there was something which I should not be able to hide much longer.

"You know, my dear, that my mother had been long dead, and I never had a sister or any near kinswoman. At my wits' end who I should consult, instinct drew me to Mrs. Humdrum, then a woman of about five-and-forty. She was a grand lady, while I was about the rank of one of my own housemaids. I had no claim on her; I went to her as a lost dog looks into the faces of people on a road, and singles out the one who will most surely help him. I had had a good look at her once as she was putting on her gloves, and I liked the way she did it. I marvel at my own boldness. At any rate, I asked to see her, and told her my story exactly as I have now told it to you.

"'You have no mother?' she said, when she had heard all.

"'No.'

"'Then, my dear, I will mother you myself. Higgs is out of the question, so Strong must marry you at once. We will tell him everything, and I, on your behalf, will insist upon it that the engagement is at an end. I hear good reports of him, and if we are fair towards him he will be generous towards us. Besides, I believe he is so much in love with you that he would sell his soul to get you. Send him to me. I can deal with him better than you can.'"

"And what," said George, "did my father, as I shall always call him, say to all this?"

"Truth bred chivalry in him at once. 'I will marry her,' he said, with hardly a moment's hesitation, 'but it will be better that I should not be put on any lower footing than Higgs was. I ought not to be denied anything that has been allowed to him. If I am trusted, I can trust myself to trust and think no evil either of Higgs or her. They were pestered beyond endurance, as I have been ere now. If I am held at arm's length till I am fast bound, I shall marry Yram just the same, but I doubt whether she and I shall ever be quite happy.'

"'Come to my house this evening,' said Mrs. Humdrum, 'and you will find Yram there.' He came, he found me, and within a fortnight we were man and wife."

"How much does not all this explain," said George, smiling but very gravely. "And you are going to ask me to forgive you for robbing me of such a father."

"He has forgiven me, my dear, for robbing him of such a son. He never reproached me. From that day to this he has never given me a harsh word or even syllable. When you were born he took to you at once, as, indeed, who could help doing? for you were the sweetest child both in looks and temper that it is possible to conceive. Your having light hair and eyes made things more difficult; for this, and your being born, almost to the day, nine months after Higgs had left us, made people talk—but your father kept their tongues within bounds. They talk still, but they liked what little they saw of Higgs, they like the Mayor and me, and they like you the best of all; so they please themselves by having the thing both ways. Though, therefore, you are son to the Mayor, Higgs cast some miraculous spell upon me before he left, whereby my son should be in some measure his as well as the Mayor's. It was this miraculous spell that caused you to be born two months too soon, and we called you by Higgs's first name as though to show that we took that view of the matter ourselves.

"Mrs. Humdrum, however, was very positive that there was no spell at all. She had repeatedly heard her father say that the Mayor's grandfather was light-haired and blue-eyed, and that every third generation in that family a light-haired son was born. The people believe this too. Nobody disbelieves Mrs. Humdrum, but they like the miracle best, so that is how it has been settled.

"I never knew whether Mrs. Humdrum told her husband, but I think she must; for a place was found almost immediately for my husband in Mr. Humdrum's business. He made himself useful; after a few years he was taken into partnership, and on Mr. Humdrum's death became head of the firm. Between ourselves, he says laughingly that all his success in life was due to Higgs and me."

"I shall give Mrs. Humdrum a double dose of kissing," said George thoughtfully, "next time I see her."

"Oh, do, do; she will so like it. And now, my darling boy, tell your poor mother whether or no you can forgive her."

He clasped her in his arms and kissed her again and again, but for a time he could find no utterance. Presently he smiled, and said, "Of course I do, but it is you who should forgive me, for was it not all my fault?"

When Yram, too, had become more calm, she said, "It is late, and we have no time to lose. Higgs's coming at this time is mere accident; if he had had news from Erewhon he would have known much that he did not know. I cannot guess why he has come—probably through mere curiosity, but he will hear or have heard—yes, you and he talked about it—of the temple; being here, he will want to see the dedication. From what you have told me I feel sure that he will not make a fool of himself by saying who he is, but in spite of his disguise he may be recognised. I do not doubt that he is now in Sunch'ston; therefore, to-morrow morning scour the town to find him. Tell him he is discovered, tell him you know from me that he is your father, and that I wish to see him with all good-will towards him. He will come. We will then talk to him, and show him that he must go back at once. You can escort him to the statues; after passing them he will be safe. He will give you no trouble, but if he does, arrest him on a charge of poaching, and take him to the gaol, where we must do the best we can with him—but he will give you none. We need say nothing to the Professors. No one but ourselves will know of his having been here."

On this she again embraced her son and left him. If two photographs could have been taken of her, one as she opened the door and looked fondly back on George, and the other as she closed it behind her, the second portrait would have seemed taken ten years later than the first.

As for George, he went gravely but not unhappily to his own room. "So that ready, plausible fellow," he muttered to himself, "was my own father. At any rate, I am not son to a fool—and he liked me."

CHAPTER X

MY FATHER, FEARING RECOGNITION AT SUNCH'STON, BETAKES HIMSELF TO THE NEIGHBOURING TOWN OF FAIRMEAD

I WILL NOW return to my father. Whether from fatigue or over-excitement, he slept only by fits and starts, and when awake he could not rid himself of the idea that, in spite of his disguise, he might be recognised, either at his inn or in the town, by some one of the many who had seen him when he was in prison. In this case there was no knowing what might happen, but at best discovery would probably prevent his seeing the temple dedicated to himself, and hearing Professor Hanky's sermon, which he was particularly anxious to do.

So strongly did he feel the real or fancied danger he should incur by spending Saturday in Sunch'ston, that he rose as soon as he heard any one stirring, and having paid his bill, walked quietly out of the house, without saying where he was going.

There was a town about ten miles off, not so important as Sunch'ston, but having some 10,000 inhabitants; he resolved to find accommodation there for the day and night, and to walk over to Sunch'ston in time for the dedication ceremony, which he had found, on inquiry, would begin at eleven o'clock.

The country between Sunch'ston and Fairmead, as the town just referred to was named, was still mountainous, and being well wooded as well as well watered, abounded in views of singular beauty; but I have no time to dwell on the enthusiasm with which my father described them to me. The road took him at right angles to the main road down the valley from Sunch'ston to the capital, and this was one reason why he had chosen Fairmead rather than Clearwater, which was the next town lower down on the main road. He did not, indeed, anticipate that any one would want to find him, but whoever might so want would be more likely to go straight down the valley than to turn aside towards Fairmead.

On reaching this place, he found it pretty full of people, for Saturday was market-day. There was a considerable open space in the middle of the town, with an arcade running round three sides of it, while the fourth was completely taken up by the venerable Musical Bank of the city, a building which had weathered the storms of more than five centuries. On the outside of the wall, abutting on the market-place, were three wooden *sedilia*, in which the Mayor and two coad-jutors sate weekly on market-days to give advice, redress grievances, and, if necessary (which it very seldom was) to administer correction.

My father was much interested in watching the proceedings in a case which he found on inquiry to be not infrequent. A man was complaining to the Mayor that his daughter, a lovely child of eight years old, had none of the faults common to children of her age, and, in fact, seemed absolutely deficient in immoral sense. She never told lies, had never stolen so much as a lollipop, never showed any recalcitrancy about saying her prayers, and by her incessant obedience had filled her poor father and mother with the gravest anxiety as regards her future well-being. He feared it would be necessary to send her to a deformatory.

"I have generally found," said the Mayor, gravely but kindly, "that the fault in these distressing cases lies rather with the parent than the children. Does the child never break anything by accident?"

"Yes," said the father.

"And you have duly punished her for it?"

"Alas! sir, I fear I only told her she was a naughty girl, and must not do it again."

"Then how can you expect your child to learn those petty arts of deception without which she must fall an easy prey to any one who wishes to deceive her? How can she detect lying in other people unless she had had some experience of it in her own practice? How, again, can she learn when it will be well for her to lie, and when to refrain from doing so, unless she has made many a mistake on a small scale while at an age when mistakes do not greatly matter? The Sunchild (and here he reverently raised his hat), as you may read in chapter thirty-one of his Sayings, has left us a touching tale of a little boy, who, having cut down an apple tree in his father's garden, lamented his inability to tell a lie. Some commentators, indeed, have held that the evidence was so strongly against the boy that no lie would have been of any use to him, and that his perception of this fact was all that he intended to convey; but the best authorities take his simple words, 'I cannot tell a lie,' in their most natural sense, as being his expression of regret at the way in which his education had been neglected. If that case had come before me, I should have punished the boy's father, unless he could show that the best authorities are mistaken (as indeed they too generally are), and that under more favourable circumstances the boy would have been able to lie, and would have lied accordingly.

"There is no occasion for you to send your child to a deformatory. I am always averse to extreme measures when I can avoid them. Moreover, in a deformatory she would be almost certain to fall in with characters as intractable as her own. Take her home and whip her next time she so much as pulls about the salt. If you will do this whenever you get a chance, I have every hope that you will have no occasion to come to me again."

"Very well, sir," said the father, "I will do my best, but the child is so instinctively truthful that I am afraid whipping will be of little use."

There were other cases, none of them serious, which in the old days would have been treated by a straightener. My father had already surmised that the straightener had become extinct as a class, having been superseded by the Managers and Cashiers of the Musical Banks, but this became more apparent as he listened to the cases that next came on. These were dealt with quite reasonably, except that the magistrate always ordered an emetic and a strong purge in addition to the rest of his sentence, as holding that all diseases of the moral sense spring from impurities within the body, which must be cleansed before there could be any hope of spiritual improvement. If any devils were found in what passed from the prisoner's body, he was to be brought up again; for in this case the rest of the sentence might very possibly be remitted.

When the Mayor and his coadjutors had done sitting, my father strolled round the Musical Bank and entered it by the main entrance, which was on the top of a flight of steps that went down on to the principal street of the town. How strange it is that, no matter how gross a superstition may have polluted it, a holy place, if hallowed by long veneration, remains always holy. Look at Delphi. What a fraud it was, and yet how hallowed it must ever remain. But letting this pass, Musical Banks, especially when of great age, always fascinated my father, and being now tired with his walk, he sat down on one of the many rush-bottomed seats, and (for there was no service at this hour) gave free rein to meditation.

How peaceful it all was with its droning old-world smell of ancestor, dry rot, and stale incense. As the clouds came and went, the grey-green, cobweb-chastened, light ebbed and flowed over the walls and ceiling; to watch the fitfulness of its streams was a sufficient occupation. A hen laid an egg outside and began to cackle—it was an event of magnitude; a peasant sharpening his scythe, a blacksmith hammering at his anvil, the clack of a wooden shoe upon the pavement, the boom of a bumble-bee, the dripping of the fountain, all these things, with such concert as they kept, invited the dewy-feathered sleep that visited him, and held him for the best part of an hour.

My father has said that the Erewhonians never put up monuments or write epitaphs for their dead, and this he believed to be still true; but it was not so always, and on waking his eye was caught by a monument of great beauty, which bore a date of about 1550 of our era. It was to an old lady, who must have been very loveable if the sweet smiling face of her recumbent figure was as faithful to the original as its strongly marked individuality suggested. I need not give the earlier part of her epitaph, which was conventional enough, but my father was so struck with the concluding lines, that he copied them into the note-book which he always carried in his pocket. They ran:—

> I fall asleep in the full and certain hope
> That my slumber shall not be broken;
> And that though I be all-forgetting,
> Yet shall I not be all-forgotten,
> But continue that life in the thoughts and deeds
> Of those I loved,
> Into which, while the power to strive was yet vouchsafed me,
> I fondly strove to enter.

My father deplored his inability to do justice to the subtle tenderness of the original, but the above was the nearest he could get to it.

How different this from the opinions concerning a future state which he had tried to set before the Erewhonians some twenty years earlier. It all came back to him, as the storks had done, now that he was again in an Erewhonian environment, and he particularly remembered how one youth had inveighed against our European notions of heaven and hell with a contemptuous flippancy that nothing but youth and ignorance could even palliate.

"Sir," he had said to my father, "your heaven will not attract me unless I can take my clothes and my luggage. Yes; and I must lose my luggage and find it again. On arriving, I must be told that it has unfortunately been taken to a wrong circle, and that there may be some difficulty in recovering it—or it shall have been sent up to a mansion number five hundred thousand millions nine hundred thousand forty six thousand eight hundred and eleven, whereas it should have gone to four hundred thousand millions, &c., &c.; and am I sure that I addressed it rightly? Then, when I am just getting cross enough to run some risk of being turned out, the luggage shall make its appearance, hat-box, umbrella, rug, golf-sticks, bicycle and everything else all quite correct and in my delight I shall tip the angel double and realise that I am enjoying myself.

"Or I must have asked what I could have for breakfast, and be told I could have boiled eggs, or eggs and bacon, or filleted plaice. 'Filleted plaice,' I shall exclaim, 'no! not that. Have you any red mullets?' And the angel will say, 'Why no, sir, the gulf has been so rough that there has hardly any fish come in this three days, and there has been such a run on it that we have nothing left but plaice.'

" 'Well, well,' I shall say, 'have you any kidneys?'

" 'You can have one kidney, sir,' will be the answer.

" 'One kidney, indeed, and you call this heaven! At any rate you will have sausages?'

"Then the angel will say, 'We shall have some after Sunday, sir, but we are quite out of them at present.'

"And I shall say, somewhat sulkily, 'Then I suppose I must have eggs and bacon.'

"But in the morning there will come up a red mullet, beautifully cooked, a couple of kidneys and three sausages browned to a turn, and seasoned with just so much sage and thyme as will savour without overwhelming them; and I shall eat everything. It shall then transpire that the angel knew about the luggage, and what I was to have for breakfast, all the time, but wanted to give me the pleasure of finding things turn out better than I had expected. Heaven would be a dull place without such occasional petty false alarms as these."

I have no business to leave my father's story, but the mouth of the ox that treadeth out the corn should not be so closely muzzled that he cannot sometimes filch a mouthful for himself; and when I had copied out the foregoing somewhat irreverent paragraphs, which I took down (with no important addition or alteration) from my father's lips, I could not refrain from making a few reflections of my own, which I will ask the reader's forbearance if I lay before him.

Let heaven and hell alone, but think of Hades, with Tantalus, Sisyphus, Tityus, and all the rest of them. How futile were the attempts of the old Greeks and Romans to lay before us any plausible conception of eternal torture. What were the Danaids doing but that which each one of us has to do during his or her whole life? What are our bodies if not sieves that we are for ever trying to fill, but which we must refill continually without hope of being able to keep them full for long together? Do we mind this? Not so long as we can get the wherewithal to fill them; and the Danaids never seem to have run short of water. They would probably ere long take to clearing out any obstruction in their sieves if they found them getting choked. What could it matter to them whether the sieves got full or no? They were not paid for filling them.

Sisyphus, again! Can any one believe that he would go on rolling that stone year after year and seeing it roll down again unless he liked seeing it? We are not told that there was a dragon which attacked him whenever he tried to shirk. If he had greatly cared about getting his load over the last pinch, experience would have shown him some way of doing so. The probability is that he got to enjoy the downward rush of his stone, and very likely amused himself by so timing it as to cause the greatest scare to the greatest number of the shades that were below.

What though Tantalus found the water shun him and the fruits fly from him when he tried to seize them? The writer of the "Odyssey" gives us no hint that he was dying of thirst or hunger. The pores of his skin would absorb enough water to prevent the first, and we may be sure that he got fruit enough, one way or another, to keep him going.

Tityus, as an effort after the conception of an eternity of torture, is not successful. What could an eagle matter on the liver of a man whose body covered nine acres? Before long he would find it an agreeable stimulant. If, then, the greatest minds of antiquity could invent nothing that should carry better conviction of eternal torture, is it likely that the conviction can be carried at all?

Methought I saw Jove sitting on the topmost ridges of Olympus and confessing failure to Minerva. "I see, my dear," he said, "that there is no use in trying to make people very happy or very miserable for long together. Pain, if it does not soon kill, consists not so much in present suffering as in the still recent memory of a time when there was less, and in the fear that there will soon be more; and so happiness lies less in immediate pleasure than in lively recollection of a worse time and lively hope of better."

As for the young gentleman above referred to, my father met him with the assurance that there had been several cases in which living people had been caught up into heaven or carried down into hell, and been allowed to return to earth and report what they had seen; while to others visions had been vouchsafed so clearly that thousands of authentic pictures had been painted of both states. All incentive to good conduct, he had then alleged, was found to be at once removed from those who doubted the fidelity of these pictures.

This at least was what he had then said, but I hardly think he would have said it at the time of which I am now writing. As he continued to sit in the Musical Bank, he took from his valise the pamphlet on "The Physics of Vicarious Existence," by Dr. Gurgoyle, which he had bought on the preceding evening, doubtless being led to choose this particular work by the tenor of the old lady's epitaph.

The second title he found to run, "Being Strictures on Certain Heresies concerning a Future State that have been Engrafted on the Sunchild's Teaching."

My father shuddered as he read this title. "How long," he said to himself, "will it be before they are at one another's throats?"

On reading the pamphlet, he found it added little to what the epitaph had already conveyed; but it interested him, as showing that, however cataclysmic a change of national opinions may appear to be, people will find means of bringing the new into more or less conformity with the old.

Here it is a mere truism to say that many continue to live a vicarious life long after they have ceased to be aware of living. This view is as old as the *non omnis moriar* of Horace, and we may be sure some thousands of years older. It is only, therefore, with much diffidence that I have decided to give a *résumé* of opinions many of which those whom I alone wish to please will have laid to heart from their youth upwards. In brief, Dr. Gurgoyle's contention comes to little more than saying that the quick are more dead, and the dead more quick, than we commonly think. To be alive, according to him, is only to be unable to understand how dead one is, and to be dead is only to be invincibly ignorant concerning our own livingness—for the dead would be as living as the living if we could only get them to believe it.

CHAPTER XI

PRESIDENT GURGOYLE'S PAMPHLET "ON THE PHYSICS OF VICARIOUS EXISTENCE"

BELIEF, LIKE ANY other moving body, follows the path of least resistance, and this path had led Dr. Gurgoyle to the conviction, real or feigned, that my father was son to the sun, probably by the moon, and that his ascent into the sky with an earthly bride was due to the sun's interference with the laws of nature. Nevertheless he was looked upon as more or less of a survival, and was deemed lukewarm, if not heretical, by those who seemed to be the pillars of the new system.

My father soon found that not even Panky could manipulate his teaching more freely than the Doctor had done. My father had taught that when a man was dead there was an end of him, until he should rise again in the flesh at the last day, to enter into eternity either of happiness or misery. He had, indeed, often talked of the immortality which some achieve even in this world; but he had cheapened this, declaring it to be an unsubstantial mockery, that could give no such comfort in the hour of death as was unquestionably given by belief in heaven and hell.

Dr. Gurgoyle, however, had an equal horror, on the one hand, of anything involving resumption of life by the body when it was once dead and on the other of the view that life ended with the change which we call death. He did not, indeed, pretend that he could do much to take away the sting from death, nor would he do this if he could, for if men did not fear death unduly, they would often court it unduly. Death can only be belauded at the cost of belittling life; but he held that a reasonable assurance of fair fame after death is a truer consolation to the dying, a truer comfort to surviving friends, and a more real incentive to good conduct in this life, than any of the consolations or incentives falsely fathered upon the Sunchild.

He began by setting aside every saying ascribed, however truly, to my father, if it made against his views, and by putting his own glosses on all that he could gloze into an appearance of being in his favour. I will pass over his attempt to combat the rapidly spreading belief in a heaven and hell such as we accept and will only summarise his contention that, of our two lives—namely, the one we live in our own persons, and that other life which we live in other people both before our reputed death and after it—the second is as essential a factor of our complete life as the first is, and sometimes more so.

Life, he urged, lies not in bodily organs, but in the power to use them, and in the use that is made of them—that is to say, in the work they do. As the essence of a factory is not in the building wherein the work is done nor yet in the implements used in turning it out, but in the will-power of the master and in the goods he makes; so the true life of a man is in his will and work, not in his body. "Those," he argued, "who make the life of a man reside within his body, are like one who should mistake the carpenter's tool-box for the carpenter."

He maintained that this had been my father's teaching, for which my father heartily trusts that he may be forgiven.

He went on to say that our will-power is not wholly limited to the working of its own special system of organs, but under certain conditions can work and be worked upon by other will-powers like itself: so that if, for example, A's will-power has got such hold on B's as to be able, through B, to work B's mechanism, what seems to have been B's action will in reality have been more A's than B's and this in the same real sense as though the physical action had been effected through A's own mechanical system—A, in fact, will have been living in B. The universally admitted maxim that he who does this or that by the hand of an agent does it himself, shows that the foregoing view is only a roundabout way of stating what common sense treats as a matter of course.

Hence, though A's individual will-power must be held to cease when the tools it works with are destroyed or out of gear, yet, so long as any survivors were so possessed by it while it was still efficient, or, again, become so impressed by its operation on them through work that he has left as to act in obedience to his will-power rather than their own, A has a certain amount of *bonâ fide* life still remaining. His vicarious life is not affected by the dissolution of his body; and in many cases the sum total of a man's vicarious action and of its outcome exceeds to an almost infinite extent the sum total of those actions and works that were effected through the mechanism of his own physical organs. In these cases his vicarious life is more truly his life than any that he lived in his own person.

"True," continued the Doctor, "while living in his own person, a man knows, or thinks he knows, what he is doing, whereas we have no reason to suppose such knowledge on the part of one whose body is already dust; but the consciousness of the doer has less to do with the livingness of the deed than people generally admit. We know nothing of the power that sets our heart beating, nor yet of the beating itself so long as it is normal. We know nothing of our breathing or of our digestion, of the all-important work we achieved as embryos, nor of our growth from infancy to manhood. No one will say that these were not actions of a living agent, but the more normal, the healthier, and thus the more truly living, the agent is, the less he will know or have known of his own action. The part of our bodily life that enters into our consciousness is very small as compared with that of which we have no consciousness. What completer proof can we have that livingness consists in deed rather than in consciousness of deed?

"The foregoing remarks are not intended to apply so much to vicarious action in virtue, we will say, of a settlement, or testamentary disposition that cannot be set aside. Such action is apt to be too unintelligent, too far from variation and quick change to rank as true vicarious action; indeed it is not rarely found to effect the very opposite of what the person who made the settlement or will desired. They are meant to apply to that more intelligent and versatile action engendered by affectionate remembrance. Nevertheless, even the compulsory vicarious action taken in consequence of a will, and indeed the very name "will" itself, shows that though we cannot take either flesh or money with us, we can leave our will-power behind us in very efficient operation.

"This vicarious life (on which I have insisted, I fear at unnecessary length, for it is so obvious that none can have failed to realise it) is lived by every one of us before death as well as after it, and is little less important to us than that of which we are to some extent conscious in our own persons. A man, we will say, has written a book which delights or displeases thousands of whom he knows nothing, and who know nothing of him. The book, we will suppose, has considerable, or at any rate some influence on the action of these people. Let us suppose the writer fast asleep while others are enjoying his work, and acting in consequence of it, perhaps at long distances from him. Which is his truest life—the one he is leading in them, or that equally unconscious life residing in his own sleeping body? Can there be a doubt that the vicarious life is the more efficient?

"Or when we are waking, how powerfully does not the life we are living in others pain or delight us, according as others think ill or well of us? How truly do we not recognise it as part of our own existence, and how great an influence does not the fear of the present hell in men's bad thoughts, and the hope of a present heaven in their good ones, influence our own conduct? Have we not here a true heaven and a true hell, as compared with the efficiency of which these gross material ones so falsely engrafted on to the Sunchild's teaching are but as the flint implements of a prehistoric race? 'If a man,' said the Sunchild, 'fear not man, whom he hath seen, neither will he fear God, whom he hath not seen.'"

My father again assures me that he never said this. Returning to Dr. Gurgoyle, he continued:—

"It may be urged that on a man's death one of the great factors of his life is so annihilated that no kind of true life can be any further conceded to him. For to live is to be influenced, as well as to influence; and when a man is dead how can he be influenced? He can haunt, but he cannot any more be haunted. He can come to us, but we cannot go to him. On ceasing, therefore, to be impressionable, so great a part of that wherein his life consisted is removed, that no true life can be conceded to him.

"I do not pretend that a man is as fully alive after his so-called death as before it. He is not. All I contend for is that a considerable amount of efficient life still remains to some of us, and that a little life remains to all of us, after what we commonly regard as the complete cessation of life. In answer, then, to those who have just urged that the destruction of one of the two great factors of life destroys life altogether, I reply that the same must hold good as regards death.

"If to live is to be influenced and to influence, and if a man cannot be held as living when he can no longer be influenced, surely to die is to be no longer able either to influence or be influenced, and a man cannot be held dead until both these two factors of death are present. If failure of the power to be influenced vitiates life, presence of the power to influence vitiates death. And no one will deny that a man can influence for many a long year after he is vulgarly reputed as dead.

"It seems, then, that there is no such thing as either absolute life without any alloy of death, nor absolute death without any alloy of life, until, that is to say, all posthumous power to influence has faded away, and this, perhaps, is what the Sunchild meant by saying that in the midst of life we are in death, and so also that in the midst of death we are in life.

"And there is this, too. No man can influence fully until he can no more be influenced—that is to say, till after his so-called death. Till then, his 'he' is still unsettled. We know not what other influences may not be brought to bear upon him that may change the character of the influence he will exert on ourselves. Therefore, he is not fully living till he is no longer living. He is an incomplete work, which cannot have full effect till finished. And as for his vicarious life—which we have seen to be very real—this can be, and is, influenced by just appreciation, undue praise or calumny, and is subject, it may be, to secular vicissitudes of good and evil fortune.

"If this is not true, let us have no more talk about the immortality of great men and women. The Sunchild was never weary of talking to us (as we then sometimes thought, a little tediously) about a great poet of that nation to which it pleased him to feign that he belonged. How plainly can we not now see that his words were spoken for our learning—for the enforcement of that true view of heaven and hell on which I am feebly trying to insist? The poet's name, he said, was Shakespeare. Whilst he was alive, very few people understood his greatness; whereas now, after some three hundred years, he is deemed the greatest poet that the world has ever known. 'Can this man,' he asked, 'be said to have been truly born till many a long year after he had been reputed as truly dead? While he was in the flesh, was he more than a mere embryo growing towards birth into that life of the world to come in which he now shines so gloriously? What a small thing was that flesh and blood life, of which he was alone conscious, as compared with that fleshless life which he lives but knows not in the lives of millions, and which, had it ever been fully revealed even to his imagination, we may be sure that he could not have reached?'

"These were the Sunchild's words, as repeated to me by one of his chosen friends while he was yet amongst us. Which, then, of this man's two lives should we deem best worth having, if we could choose one or the other, but not both? The felt or the unfelt? Who would not go cheerfully to block or stake if he knew that by doing so he could win such life as this poet lives, though he also knew that on having won it he could know no more about it? Does not this prove that in our heart of hearts we deem an unfelt life, in the heaven of men's loving thoughts, to be better worth having than any we can reasonably hope for and still feel?

"And the converse of this is true; many a man has unhesitatingly laid down his felt life to escape unfelt infamy in the hell of men's hatred and contempt. As body is the sacrament, or outward and visible sign, of mind, so is posterity the sacrament of those who live after death. Each is the mechanism through which the other becomes effective.

"I grant that many live but a short time when the breath is out of them. Few seeds germinate as compared with those that rot or are eaten, and most of this world's denizens are little more than still-born as regards the larger life, while none are immortal to the end of time. But the end of time is not worth considering; not a few live as many centuries as either they or we need think about, and surely the world, so far as we can guess its object, was made rather to be enjoyed than to last. 'Come and go' pervades all things of which we have knowledge, and if there was any provision made, it seems to have been for a short life and a merry one, with enough chance of extension beyond the grave to be worth trying for, rather than for the perpetuity even of the best and noblest.

"Granted, again, that few live after death as long or as fully as they had hoped to do, while many, when quick, can have had none but the faintest idea of the immortality that awaited them; it is nevertheless true that none are so still-born on death as not to enter into a life of some sort, however short and humble. A short life or a long one can no more be bargained for in the unseen world than in the seen; as, however, care on the part of parents can do much for the longer life and greater well-being of their offspring in this world, so the conduct of that offspring in this world does much both to secure for itself longer tenure of life in the next, and to determine whether that life shall be one of reward or punishment.

"'Reward or punishment,' some reader will perhaps exclaim; 'what mockery, when the essence of reward and punishment lies in their being felt by those who have earned them.' I can do nothing with those who either cry for the moon, or deny that it has two sides, on the ground that we can see but one. Here comes in faith, of which the Sunchild said, that though we can do little with it we can do nothing without it. Faith does not consist, as some have falsely urged, in believing things on insufficient evidence; this is not faith, but faithlessness to all that we should hold most faithfully. Faith consists in holding that the instincts of the best men and women are in themselves an evidence which may not be set aside lightly; and the best men and women have ever held that death is better than dishonour, and desirable if honour is to be won thereby.

"It follows, then, that though our conscious flesh and blood life is the only one that we can fully apprehend, yet we do also indeed move, even here, in an unseen world, wherein, when our palpable life is ended, we shall continue to live for a shorter or longer time—reaping roughly though not infallibly, much as we have sown. Of this unseen world the best men and women will be almost as heedless while in the flesh as they will be when their life in flesh is over; for, as the Sunchild often said, 'The Kingdom of Heaven cometh not by observation.' It will be all in all to them, and at the same time nothing, for the better people they are, the less they will think of anything but this present life.

"What an ineffable contradiction in terms have we not here. What a reversal, is it not, of all this world's canons, that we should hold even the best of all that we can know or feel in this life to be a poor thing as compared with hopes the fulfilment of which we can never either feel or know. Yet we all hold this, however little we may admit it to ourselves. For the world at heart despises its own canons."

I cannot quote further from Dr. Gurgoyle's pamphlet; suffice it that he presently dealt with those who say that it is not right of any man to aim at thrusting himself in among the living when he has had his day. "Let him die," say they, "and let die as his fathers before him." He argued that as we had a right to pester people till we got ourselves born, so also we have a right to pester them for extension of life beyond the grave. Life, whether before the grave or afterwards, is like love—all reason is against it, and all healthy instinct for it. Instinct on such matters is the older and safer guide; no one, therefore, should seek to efface himself as regards the next world more than as regards this. If he is to be effaced, let others efface him; do not let him commit suicide. Freely we have received; freely, therefore, let us take as much more as we can get, and let it be a stand-up fight between ourselves and posterity to see whether it can get rid of us or no. If it can, let it; if it cannot, it must put up with us. It can better care for itself than we can for ourselves when the breath is out of us.

Not the least important duty, he continued, of posterity towards itself lies in passing righteous judgment on the forbears who stand up before it. They should be allowed the benefit of a doubt, and peccadilloes should be ignored; but when no doubt exists that a man was engrainedly mean and cowardly, his reputation must remain in the Purgatory of Time for a term varying from, say, a hundred to two thousand years. After a hundred years it may generally come down, though it will still be under a cloud. After two thousand years it may be mentioned in any society without holding up of hands in horror. Our sense of moral guilt varies inversely as the square of its distance in time and space from ourselves.

Not so with heroism; this loses no lustre through time and distance. Good is gold; it is rare, but it will not tarnish. Evil is like dirty water—plentiful and foul, but it will run itself clear of taint.

The Doctor having thus expatiated on his own opinions concerning heaven and hell, concluded by tilting at those which all right-minded people hold among ourselves. I shall adhere to my determination not to reproduce his arguments; suffice it that though less flippant than those of the young student whom I have already referred to, they were more plausible; and though I could easily demolish them, the reader will probably prefer that I should not set them up for the mere pleasure of knocking them down. Here, then, I take my leave of good Dr. Gurgoyle and his pamphlet; neither can I interrupt my story further by saying anything about the other two pamphlets purchased by my father.

CHAPTER XII

GEORGE FAILS TO FIND MY FATHER, WHEREON YRAM CAUTIONS THE PROFESSORS

ON THE MORNING after the interview with her son described in a foregoing chapter, Yram told her husband what she had gathered from the Professors, and said that she was expecting Higgs every moment, inasmuch as she was confident that George would soon find him.

"Do you what you like, my dear," said the Mayor. "I shall keep out of the way, for you will manage him better without me. You know what I think of you."

He then went unconcernedly to his breakfast at which the Professors found him somewhat taciturn. Indeed they set him down as one of the dullest and most uninteresting people they had ever met.

When George returned and told his mother that though he had at last found the inn at which my father had slept, my father had left and could not be traced, she was disconcerted, but after a few minutes she said—

"He will come back here for the dedication, but there will be such crowds that we may not see him till he is inside the temple, and it will save trouble if we can lay hold on him sooner. Therefore, ride either to Clearwater or Fairmead, and see if you can find him. Try Fairmead first; it is more out of the way. If you cannot hear of him there, come back, get another horse, and try Clearwater. If you fail here too, we must give him up, and look out for him in the temple to-morrow morning."

"Are you going to say anything to the Professors?"

"Not if you bring Higgs here before nightfall. If you cannot do this I must talk it over with my husband; I shall have some hours in which to make up my mind. Now go—the sooner the better."

It was nearly eleven, and in a few minutes George was on his way. By noon he was at Fairmead, where he tried all the inns in vain for news of a person answering the description of my father—for, not knowing what name my father might choose to give, he could trust only to description. He concluded that since my father could not be heard of in Fairmead by one o'clock (as it nearly was by the time he had been round all the inns) he must have gone somewhere else; he therefore rode back to Sunch'ston, made a hasty lunch, got a fresh horse, and rode to Clearwater, where he met with no better success. At all the inns both at Fairmead and Clearwater he left word that if the person he had described came later in the day, he was to be told that the Mayoress particularly begged him to return at once to Sunch'ston, and come to the Mayor's house.

Now all the time that George was at Fairmead my father was inside the Musical Bank, which he had entered before going to any inn. Here he had been sitting for nearly a couple of hours, resting, dreaming, and reading Bishop Gurgoyle's pamphlet. If he had left the Bank five minutes earlier, he would probably have been seen by George in the main street of Fairmead—as he found out on reaching the inn which he selected and ordered dinner.

He had hardly got inside the house before the waiter told him that young Mr. Strong, the Ranger from Sunch'ston, had been enquiring for him and had left a message for him, which was duly delivered.

My father, though in reality somewhat disquieted, showed no uneasiness, and said how sorry he was to have missed seeing Mr. Strong. "But," he added, "it does not much matter; I need not go back this afternoon, for I shall be at Sunch'ston to-morrow morning and will go straight to the Mayor's."

He had no suspicion that he was discovered, but he was a good deal puzzled. Presently he inclined to the opinion that George, still believing him to be Professor Panky, had wanted to invite him to the banquet on the following day—for he had no idea that Hanky and Panky were staying with the Mayor and Mayoress. Or perhaps the Mayor and his wife did not like so distinguished a man's having been unable to find a lodging in Sunch'ston, and wanted him to stay with them. Ill satisfied as he was with any theory he could form, he nevertheless reflected that he could not do better than stay where he was for the night, inasmuch as no one would be likely to look for him a second time at Fairmead. He therefore ordered his room at once.

It was nearly seven before George got back to Sunch'ston. In the meantime Yram and the Mayor had considered the question whether anything was to be said to the Professors or no. They were confident that my father would not commit himself—why, indeed, should he have dyed his hair and otherwise disguised himself, if he had not intended to remain undiscovered? Oh no; the probability was that if nothing was said to the Professors now, nothing need ever be said, for my father might be escorted back to the statues by George on the Sunday evening and be told that he was not to return. Moreover, even though something untoward were to happen after all, the Professors would have no reason for thinking that their hostess had known of the Sunchild's being in Sunch'ston.

On the other hand, they were her guests, and it would not be handsome to keep Hanky, at any rate, in the dark, when the knowledge that the Sunchild was listening to every word he said might make him modify his sermon not a little. It might or it might not, but that was a matter for him, not her. The only question for her was whether or no it would be sharp practice to know what she knew and say nothing about it. Her husband hated *finesse* as much as she did, and they settled it that though the question was a nice one, the more proper thing to do would be to tell the Professors what it might so possibly concern one or both of them to know.

On George's return without news of my father, they found he thought just as they did; so it was arranged that they should let the Professors dine in peace, but tell them about the Sunchild's being again in Erewhon as soon as dinner was over.

"Happily," said George, "they will do no harm. They will wish Higgs's presence to remain unknown, as much as we do, and they will be glad that he should be got out of the country immediately."

"Not so, my dear," said Yram. "'Out of the country' will not do for those people. Nothing short of 'out of the world' will satisfy them."

"That," said George promptly, "must not be."

"Certainly not, my dear, but that is what they will want. I do not like having to tell them, but I am afraid we must."

"Never mind," said the Mayor, laughing. "Tell them, and let us see what happens."

They then dressed for dinner, where Hanky and Panky were the only guests. When dinner was over Yram sent away her other children, George alone remaining. He sat opposite the Professors, while the Mayor and Yram were at the two ends of the table.

"I am afraid, dear Professor Hanky," said Yram, "that I was not quite open with you last night, but I wanted time to think things over, and I know you will forgive me when you remember what a number of guests I had to attend to." She then referred to what Hanky had told her about the supposed ranger, and showed him how obvious it was that this man was a foreigner, who had been for some time in Erewhon more than seventeen years ago, but had had no communication with it since then. Having pointed sufficiently, as she thought, to the Sunchild, she said, "You see who I believe this man to have been. Have I said enough, or shall I say more?"

"I understand you," said Hanky, "and I agree with you that the Sunchild will be in the temple to-morrow. It is a serious business, but I shall not alter my sermon. He must listen to what I may choose to say, and I wish I could tell him what a fool he was for coming here. If he behaves himself, well and good: your son will arrest him quietly after service, and by night he will be in the Blue Pool. Your son is bound to throw him there as a foreign devil, without the formality of a trial. It would be a most painful duty to me, but unless I am satisfied that that man has been thrown into the Blue Pool, I shall have no option but to report the matter at headquarters. If, on the other hand, the poor wretch makes a disturbance, I can set the crowd on to tear him to pieces."

George was furious, but he remained quite calm, and left everything to his mother.

"I have nothing to do with the Blue Pool," said Yram drily. "My son, I doubt not, will know how to do his duty; but if you let the people kill this man, his body will remain, and an inquest must be held, for the matter will have been too notorious to be hushed up. All Higgs's measurements and all marks on his body were recorded, and these alone would identify him. My father, too, who is still master of the gaol, and many another, could swear to him. Should the body prove, as no doubt it would, to be that of the Sunchild, what is to become of Sunchildism?"

Hanky smiled. "It would not be proved. The measurements of a man of twenty or thereabouts would not correspond with this man's. All we Professors should attend the inquest, and half Bridgeford is now in Sunch'ston. No matter though nine-tenths of the marks and measurements corresponded, so long as there is a tenth that does not do so, we should not be flesh and blood if we did not ignore the nine points and insist only on the tenth. After twenty years we shall find enough to serve our turn. Think of what all the learning of the country is committed to; think of the change in all our ideas and institutions; think of the King and of Court influence. I need not enlarge. We shall not permit the body to be the Sunchild's. No matter what evidence you may produce, we shall sneer it down, and say we must have more before you can expect us to take you seriously; if you bring more, we shall pay no attention; and the more you bring the more we shall laugh at you. No doubt those among us who are by way of being candid will admit that your arguments ought to be considered, but you must not expect that it will be any part of their duty to consider them.

"And even though we admitted that the body had been proved up to the hilt to be the Sunchild's, do you think that such a trifle as that could affect Sunchildism? Hardly. Sunch'ston is no match for Bridgeford and the King; our only difficulty would lie in settling which was the most plausible way of the many plausible ways in which the death could be explained. We should hatch up twenty theories in less than twenty hours, and the last state of Sunchildism would be stronger than the first. For the people want it, and so long as they want it they will have it. At the same time the supposed identification of the body, even by some few ignorant people here, might lead to a local heresy that is as well avoided, and it will be better that your son should arrest the man before the dedication, if he can be found, and throw him into the Blue Pool without any one but ourselves knowing that he has been here at all."

I need not dwell on the deep disgust with which this speech was listened to, but the Mayor, and Yram, and George said not a word.

"But, Mayoress," said Panky, who had not opened his lips so far, "are you sure that you are not too hasty in believing this stranger to be the Sunchild? People are continually thinking that such and such another is the Sunchild come down again from the sun's palace and going to and fro among us. How many such stories, sometimes very plausibly told, have we not had during the last twenty years? They never take root, and die out of themselves as suddenly as they spring up. That the man is a poacher can hardly be doubted; I thought so the moment I saw him; but I think I can also prove to you that he is not a foreigner, and, therefore, that he is not the Sunchild. He quoted the Sunchild's prayer with a corruption that can have only reached him from an Erewhonian source—"

Here Hanky interrupted him somewhat brusquely.

"The man, Panky," said he, "was the Sunchild; and he was not a poacher, for he had no idea that he was breaking the law; nevertheless, as you say, Sunchildism on the brain has been a common form of mania for several years. Several persons have even believed themselves to be the Sunchild. We must not forget this, if it should get about that Higgs has been here."

Then, turning to Yram, he said sternly, "But come what may, your son must take him to the Blue Pool at nightfall."

"Sir," said George, with perfect suavity, "you have spoken as though you doubted my readiness to do my duty. Let me assure you very solemnly that when the time comes for me to act, I shall act as duty may direct."

"I will answer for him," said Yram, with even more than her usual quick, frank smile, "that he will fulfil his instructions to the letter, unless," she added, "some black and white horses come down from heaven and snatch poor Higgs out of his grasp. Such things have happened before now."

"I should advise your son to shoot them if they do," said Hanky drily and sub-defiantly.

Here the conversation closed; but it was useless trying to talk of anything else, so the Professors asked Yram to excuse them if they retired early, in view of the fact that they had a fatiguing day before them. This excuse their hostess readily accepted.

"Do not let us talk any more now," said Yram as soon as they had left the room. "It will be quite time enough when the dedication is over. But I rather think the black and white horses will come."

"I think so too, my dear," said the Mayor laughing.

"They shall come," said George gravely; "but we have not yet got enough to make sure of bringing them. Higgs will perhaps be able to help me to-morrow."

———

"Now what," said Panky as they went upstairs, "does that woman mean—for she means something? Black and white horses indeed!"

"I do not know what she means to do," said the other, "but I know that she thinks she can best us."

"I wish we had not eaten those quails."

"Nonsense, Panky; no one saw us but Higgs, and the evidence of a foreign devil, in such straits as his, could not stand for a moment. We did not eat them. No, no; she has something that she thinks better than that. Besides, it is absolutely impossible that she should have heard what happened. What I do not understand is, why she should have told us about the Sunchild's being here at all. Why not have left us to find it out or to know nothing about it? I do not understand it."

So true is it, as Euclid long since observed, that the less cannot comprehend that which is the greater. True, however, as this is, it is also sometimes true that the greater cannot comprehend the less. Hanky went musing to his own room and threw himself into an easy chair to think the position over. After a few minutes he went to a table on which he saw pen, ink, and paper, and wrote a short letter; then he rang the bell.

When the servant came he said, "I want to send this note to the manager of the new temple, and it is important that he should have it to-night. Be pleased, therefore, to take it to him and deliver it into his own hands; but I had rather you said nothing about it to the Mayor or Mayoress, nor to any of your fellow-servants. Slip out unperceived if you can. When you have delivered the note, ask for an answer at once, and bring it to me."

So saying, he slipped a sum equal to about five shillings into the man's hand.

The servant returned in about twenty minutes, for the temple was quite near, and gave a note to Hanky, which ran, "Your wishes shall be attended to without fail."

"Good!" said Hanky to the man. "No one in the house knows of your having run this errand for me?"

"No one, sir."

"Thank you! I wish you a very good night."

CHAPTER XIII

A VISIT TO THE PROVINCIAL DEFORMATORY AT FAIRMEAD

HAVING FINISHED HIS early dinner, and not fearing that he should be either recognised at Fairmead or again enquired after from Sunch'ston, my father went out for a stroll round the town, to see what else he could find that should be new and strange to him. He had not gone far before he saw a large building with an inscription saying that it was the Provincial Deformatory for Boys. Underneath the larger inscription there was a smaller one—one of those corrupt versions of my father's sayings, which, on dipping into the Sayings of the Sunchild, he had found to be so vexatiously common. The inscription ran:—

"When the righteous man turneth away from the righteousness that he hath committed, and doeth that which is a little naughty and wrong, he will generally be found to have gained in amiability what he has lost in righteousness."—Sunchild Sayings, chap. xxii. v. 15.

The case of the little girl that he had watched earlier in the day had filled him with a great desire to see the working of one of these curious institutions; he therefore resolved to call on the head-master (whose name he found to be Turvey), and enquired about terms, alleging that he had a boy whose incorrigible rectitude was giving him much anxiety. The information he had gained in the forenoon would be enough to save him from appearing to know nothing of the system. On having rung the bell, he announced himself to the servant as a Mr. Senoj, and asked if he could see the Principal.

Almost immediately he was ushered into the presence of a beaming, dapper-looking, little old gentleman, quick of speech and movement, in spite of some little portliness.

"Ts, ts, ts," he said, when my father had enquired about terms and asked whether he might see the system at work. "How unfortunate that you should have called on a Saturday afternoon. We always have a half-holiday. But stay—yes—that will do very nicely; I will send for them into school as a means of stimulating their refractory system."

He called his servant and told him to ring the boys into school. Then, turning to my father he said, "Stand here, sir, by the window; you will see them all come trooping in. H'm, h'm, I am sorry to see them still come back as soon as they hear the bell. I suppose I shall ding some recalcitrancy into them some day, but it is uphill work. Do you see the head-boy—the third of those that are coming up the path? I shall have to get rid of him. Do you see him? he is going back to whip up the laggers—and now he has boxed a boy's ears: that boy is one of the most hopeful under my care. I feel sure he has been using improper language, and my head-boy has checked him instead of encouraging him." And so on till the boys were all in school.

"You see, my dear sir," he said to my father, "we are in an impossible position. We have to obey instructions from the Grand Council of Education at Bridgeford, and they have established these institutions in consequence of the Sunchild's having said that we should aim at promoting the greatest happiness of the greatest number. This, no doubt, is a sound principle, and the greatest number are by nature somewhat dull, conceited, and unscrupulous. They do not like those who are quick, unassuming, and sincere; how, then, consistently with the first principles either of morality or political economy as revealed to us by the Sunchild, can we encourage such people if we can bring sincerity and modesty fairly home to them? We cannot do so. And we must correct the young as far as possible from forming habits which, unless indulged in with the greatest moderation, are sure to ruin them.

"I cannot pretend to consider myself very successful. I do my best, but I can only aim at making my school a reflection of the outside world. In the outside world we have to tolerate much that is prejudicial to the greatest happiness of the greatest number, partly because we cannot always discover in time who may be let alone as being genuinely insincere, and who are in reality masking sincerity under a garb of flippancy, and partly also because we wish to err on the side of letting the guilty escape, rather than of punishing the innocent. Thus many people who are perfectly well known to belong to the straightforward classes are allowed to remain at large, and may be even seen hobnobbing with the guardians of public immorality. Indeed it is not in the public interest that straightforwardness should be extirpated root and branch, for the presence of a small modicum of sincerity acts as a wholesome irritant to the academicism of the greatest number, stimulating it to consciousness of its own happy state, and giving it something to look down upon. Moreover, we hold it useful to have a certain number of melancholy examples, whose notorious failure shall serve as a warning to those who neglect cultivating that power of immoral self-control which shall prevent them from saying, or even thinking, anything that shall not immediately and palpably minister to the happiness, and hence meet the approval, of the greatest number."

By this time the boys were all in school. "There is not one prig in the whole lot," said the head-master sadly. "I wish there was, but only those boys come here who are notoriously too good to become current coin in the world unless they are hardened with an alloy of vice. I should have liked to show you our gambling, book-making, and speculation class, but the assistant-master who attends to this branch of our curriculum is gone to Sunch'ston this afternoon. He has friends who have asked him to see the dedication of the new temple, and he will not be back till Monday. I really do not know what I can do better for you than examine the boys in Counsels of Imperfection."

So saying, he went into the schoolroom, over the fireplace of which my father's eye caught an inscription, "Resist good, and it will fly from you. Sunchild's Sayings, xvii. 2." Then, taking down a copy of the work just named from a shelf above his desk, he ran his eye over a few of its pages.

He called up a class of about twenty boys.

"Now, my boys," he said, "why is it so necessary to avoid extremes of truthfulness?"

"It is not necessary, sir," said one youngster, "and the man who says that it is so is a scoundrel."

"Come here, my boy, and hold out your hand." When he had done so, Mr. Turvey gave him two sharp cuts with a cane. "There now, go down to the bottom of the class and try not to be so extremely truthful in future." Then, turning to my father, he said, "I hate caning them, but it is the only way to teach them. I really do believe that boy will know better than to say what he thinks another time."

He repeated his question to the class, and the head-boy answered, "Because, sir, extremes meet, and extreme truth will be mixed with extreme falsehood."

"Quite right, my boy. Truth is like religion; it has only two enemies—the too much and the too little. Your answer is more satisfactory than some of your recent conduct had led me to expect."

"But, sir, you punished me only three weeks ago for telling you a lie."

"Oh yes; why, so I did; I had forgotten. But then you overdid it. Still it was a step in the right direction."

"And now, my boy," he said to a very frank and ingenious youth about half way up the class, "and how is truth best reached?"

"Through the falling out of thieves, sir."

"Quite so. Then it will be necessary that the more earnest, careful, patient, self-sacrificing enquirers after truth should have a good deal of the thief about them, though they are very honest people at the same time. Now what does the man" (who on enquiry my father found to be none other than Mr. Turvey himself) "say about honesty?"

"He says, sir, that honesty does not consist in never stealing, but in knowing how and where it will be safe to do so."

"Remember," said Mr. Turvey to my father, "how necessary it is that we should have a plentiful supply of thieves, if honest men are ever to come by their own."

He spoke with the utmost gravity, evidently quite easy in his mind that his scheme was the only one by which truth could be successfully attained. "But pray let me have any criticism you may feel inclined to make."

"I have none," said my father. "Your system commends itself to common sense; it is the one adopted in the law courts, and it lies at the very foundation of party government. If your academic bodies can supply the country with a sufficient number of thieves—which I have no doubt they can—there seems no limit to the amount of truth that may be attained. If, however, I may suggest the only difficulty that occurs to me, it is that academic thieves show no great alacrity in falling out, but incline rather to back each other up through thick and thin."

"Ah, yes," said Mr. Turvey, "there is that difficulty; nevertheless circumstances from time to time arise to get them by the ears in spite of themselves. But from whatever point of view you may look at the question, it is obviously better to aim at imperfection than perfection; for if we aim steadily at imperfection, we shall probably get it within a reasonable time, whereas to the end of our days we should never reach perfection. Moreover, from a worldly point of view, there is no mistake so great as that of being always right." He then turned to his class and said—

"And now tell me what did the Sunchild tell us about God and Mammon?"

The head-boy answered: "He said that we must serve both, for no man can serve God well and truly who does not serve Mammon a little also; and no man can serve Mammon effectually unless he serve God largely at the same time."

"What were his words?"

"He said, 'Cursed be they that say, "Thou shalt not serve God and Mammon," for it is the whole duty of man to know how to adjust the conflicting claims of these two deities.' "

Here my father interposed. "I knew the Sunchild; and I more than once heard him speak of God and Mammon. He never varied the form of the words he used, which were to the effect that a man must serve either God or Mammon, but that he could not serve both."

"Ah!" said Mr. Turvey, "that no doubt was his exoteric teaching, but Professors Hanky and Panky have assured me most solemnly that his esoteric teaching was as I have given it. By the way, these gentlemen are both, I understand, at Sunch'ston, and I think it quite likely that I shall have a visit from them this afternoon. If you do not know them I should have great pleasure in introducing you to them; I was at Bridgeford with both of them."

"I have had the pleasure of meeting them already," said my father, "and as you are by no means certain that they will come, I will ask you to let me thank you for all that you have been good enough to shew me, and bid you good-afternoon. I have a rather pressing engagement—"

"My dear sir, you must please give me five minutes more. I shall examine the boys in the Musical Bank Catechism." He pointed to one of them, and said, "Repeat your duty towards your neighbour."

"My duty towards my neighbour," said the boy, "is to be quite sure that he is not likely to borrow money of me before I let him speak to me at all, and then to have as little to do with him as—"

At this point there was a loud ring at the door bell. "Hanky and Panky come to see me, no doubt," said Mr. Turvey. "I do hope it is so. You must stay and see them."

"My dear sir," said my father, putting his handkerchief up to his face. "I am taken suddenly unwell and must positively leave you." He said this in so peremptory a tone that Mr. Turvey had to yield. My father held his handkerchief to his face as he went through the passage and hall, but when the servant opened the door he took it down, for there was no Hanky or Panky—no one, in fact, but a poor, wizened old man who had come, as he did every other Saturday afternoon, to wind up the Deformatory clocks.

Nevertheless, he had been scared, and was in a very wicked-fleeth-when-no-man-pursueth frame of mind. He went to his inn, and shut himself up in his room for some time, taking notes of all that had happened to him in the last three days. But even at his inn he no longer felt safe. How did he know but that Hanky and Panky might have driven over from Sunch'ston to see Mr. Turvey, and might put up at this very house? or they might even be going to spend the night here. He did not venture out of his room till after seven, by which time he had made rough notes of as much of the foregoing chapters as had come to his knowledge so far. Much of what I have told as nearly as I could in the order in which it happened, he did not learn till later. After giving the merest outline of his interview with Mr. Turvey, he wrote a note as follows:—

"I suppose I must have held forth about the greatest happiness of the greatest number, but I had quite forgotten it, though I remember repeatedly quoting my favourite proverb, 'Every man for himself, and the devil take the hindmost.' To this they have paid no attention."

By seven his panic about Hanky and Panky ended, for if they had not come by this time, they were not likely to do so. Not knowing that they were staying at the Mayor's, he had rather settled it that they would now stroll up to the place where they had left their hoard and bring it down as soon as night had fallen. And it is quite possible that they might have found some excuse for doing this, when dinner was over, if their hostess had not undesignedly hindered them by telling them about the Sunchild. When the conversation recorded in the preceding chapter was over, it was too late for them to make any plausible excuse for leaving the house; we may be sure, therefore, that much more had been said than Yram and George were able to remember and report to my father.

After another stroll about Fairmead, during which he saw nothing but what on a larger scale he had already seen at Sunch'ston, he returned to his inn at about half-past eight, and ordered supper in a public room that corresponded with the coffee-room of an English hotel.

CHAPTER XIV

MY FATHER MAKES THE ACQUAINTANCE OF MR. BALMY, AND WALKS WITH HIM NEXT DAY TO SUNCH'STON

UP TO THIS point, though he had seen enough to show him the main drift of the great changes that had taken place in Erewhonian opinions, my father had not been able to glean much about the history of the transformation. He could see that it had all grown out of the supposed miracle of his balloon ascent, and he could understand that the ignorant masses had been so astounded by an event so contrary to all their experience, that their faith in experience was utterly routed and demoralised. If a man and a woman might rise from the earth and disappear into the sky, what else might not happen? If they had been wrong in thinking such a thing impossible, in how much else might they not be mistaken also? The ground was shaken under their very feet.

It was not as though the thing had been done in a corner. Hundreds of people had seen the ascent; and even if only a small number had been present, the disappearance of the balloon, of my mother, and of my father himself, would have confirmed their story. My father, then, could understand that a single incontrovertible miracle of the first magnitude should unroot the hedges of caution in the minds of the common people, but he could not understand how such men as Hanky and Panky, who evidently did not believe that there had been any miracle at all, had been led to throw themselves so energetically into a movement so subversive of all their traditions, when, as it seemed to him, if they had held out they might have pricked the balloon bubble easily enough, and maintained everything *in statu quo*.

How, again, had they converted the King—if they had converted him? The Queen had had full knowledge of all the preparations for the ascent. The King had had everything explained to him. The workmen and workwomen who had made the balloon and the gas could testify that none but natural means had been made use of—means which, if again employed any number of times, would effect a like result. How could it be that when the means of resistance were so ample and so easy, the movement should nevertheless have been irresistible? For had it not been irresistible, was it to be believed that astute men like Hanky and Panky would have let themselves be drawn into it?

What then had been its inner history? My father had so fully determined to make his way back on the following evening, that he saw no chance of getting to know the facts—unless, indeed, he should be able to learn something from Hanky's sermon; he was therefore not sorry to find an elderly gentleman of grave but kindly aspect seated opposite to him when he sat down to supper.

The expression on this man's face was much like that of the early Christians as shown in the S. Giovanni Laterano bas-reliefs at Rome, and again, though less aggressively self-confident, like that on the faces of those who have joined the Salvation Army. If he had been in England, my father would have set him down as a Swedenborgian; this being impossible, he could only note that the stranger bowed his head, evidently saying a short grace before he began to eat, as my father had always done when he was in Erewhon before. I will not say that my father had never omitted to say grace during the whole of the last twenty years, but he said it now, and unfortunately forgetting himself, he said it in the English language, not loud, but nevertheless audibly.

My father was alarmed at what he had done, but there was no need, for the stranger immediately said, "I hear, sir, that you have the gift of tongues. The Sunchild often mentioned it to us, as having been vouchsafed long since to certain of the people, to whom, for our learning, he saw fit to feign that he belonged. He thus foreshadowed prophetically its manifestation also among ourselves. All which, however, you must know as well as I do. Can you interpret?"

My father was much shocked, but he remembered having frequently spoken of the power of speaking in unknown tongues which was possessed by many of the early Christians, and he also remembered that in times of high religious enthusiasm this power had repeatedly been imparted, or supposed to be imparted, to devout believers in the middle ages. It grated upon him to deceive one who was so obviously sincere, but to avoid immediate discomfiture he fell in with what the stranger had said.

"Alas! sir," said he, "that rarer and more precious gift has been withheld from me; nor can I speak in an unknown tongue, unless as it is borne in upon me at the moment. I could not even repeat the words that have just fallen from me."

"That," replied the stranger, "is almost invariably the case. These illuminations of the spirit are beyond human control. You spoke in so low a tone that I cannot interpret what you have just said, but should you receive a second inspiration later, I shall doubtless be able to interpret it for you. I have been singularly gifted in this respect— more so, perhaps, than any other interpreter in Erewhon."

My father mentally vowed that no second inspiration should be vouchsafed to him, but presently remembering how anxious he was for information on the points touched upon at the beginning of this chapter, and seeing that fortune had sent him the kind of man who would be able to enlighten him, he changed his mind; nothing, he reflected, would be more likely to make the stranger talk freely with him, than the affording him an opportunity for showing off his skill as an interpreter.

Something, therefore, he would say, but what? No one could talk more freely when the train of his thoughts, or the conversation of others, gave him his cue, but when told to say an unattached "something," he could not even think of "How do you do this morning? it is a very fine day"; and the more he cudgelled his brains for "something" the more they gave no response. He could not even converse further with the stranger beyond plain "yes" and "no"; so he went on with his supper and in thinking of what he was eating and drinking for the moment forgot to ransack his brain. No sooner had he left off ransacking it, than it suggested something—not, indeed, a very brilliant something, but still something. On having grasped it.

he laid down his knife and fork, and with the air of one distraught he said—

> "My name is Norval, on the Grampian Hills
> My father feeds his flock—a frugal swain."

"I heard you," exclaimed the stranger, "and I can interpret every word of what you have said, but it would not become me to do so, for you have conveyed to me a message more comforting than I can bring myself to repeat even to him who has conveyed it."

Having said this he bowed his head, and remained for some time wrapped in meditation. My father kept a respectful silence, but after a little time he ventured to say in a low tone, how glad he was to have been the medium through whom a comforting assurance had been conveyed. Presently, on finding himself encouraged to renew the conversation, he threw out a deferential feeler as to the causes that might have induced Mr. Balmy to come to Fairmead. "Perhaps," he said, "you, like myself, have come to these parts in order to see the dedication of the new temple; I could not get a lodging in Sunch'ston, so I walked down here this morning."

This, it seemed, had been Mr. Balmy's own case, except that he had not yet been to Sunch'ston. Having heard that it was full to overflowing, he had determined to pass the night at Fairmead, and walk over in the morning—starting soon after seven, so as to arrive in good time for the dedication ceremony. When my father heard this, he proposed that they should walk together, to which Mr. Balmy gladly consented; it was therefore arranged that they should go to bed early, breakfast soon after six, and then walk to Sunch'ston. My father then went to his own room, where he again smoked a surreptitious pipe up the chimney.

Next morning the two men breakfasted together, and set out as the clock was striking seven. The day was lovely beyond the power of words, and still fresh—for Fairmead was some 2500 feet above the sea, and the sun did not get above the mountains that overhung it on the east side, till after eight o'clock. Many persons were also starting for Sunch'ston, and there was a procession got up by the Musical Bank Managers of the town, who walked in it, robed in rich dresses of scarlet and white embroidered with much gold thread. There was a banner displaying an open chariot in which the Sunchild and his bride were seated, beaming with smiles, and in attitudes suggesting that they were bowing to people who were below them.

The chariot was, of course, drawn by the four black and white horses of which the reader has already heard, and the balloon had been ignored. Readers of my father's book will perhaps remember that my mother was not seen at all—she was smuggled into the car of the balloon along with sundry rugs, under which she lay concealed till the balloon had left the earth. All this went for nothing. It has been said that though God cannot alter the past, historians can; it is perhaps because they can be useful to Him in this respect that He tolerates their existence. Painters, my father now realised, can do all that historians can, with even greater effect.

Women headed the procession—the younger ones dressed in white, with veils and chaplets of roses, blue cornflower, and peasant's eye Narcissus, while the older women were more soberly attired. The Bank Managers and the banner headed the men, who were mostly peasants, but among them were a few who seemed to be of higher rank, and these, for the most part, though by no means all of them, wore their clothes reversed—as I have forgotten to say was done also by Mr. Balmy. Both men and women joined in singing a litany the words of which my father could not catch; the tune was one he had been used to play on his apology for a flute when he was in prison, being, in fact, none other than "Home, Sweet Home." There was no harmony; they never got beyond the first four bars, but these they must have repeated, my father thought, at least a hundred times between Fairmead and Sunch'ston. "Well," said he to himself, "however little else I may have taught them, I at any rate gave them the diatonic scale."

He now set himself to exploit his fellow-traveller, for they soon got past the procession.

"The greatest miracle," said he, "in connection with this whole matter, has been—so at least it seems to me—not the ascent of the Sunchild with his bride, but the readiness with which the people generally acknowledge its miraculous character. I was one of those that witnessed the ascent, but I saw no signs that the crowd appreciated its significance. They were astounded, but they did not fall down and worship."

"Ah," said the other, "but you forget the long drought and the rain that the Sunchild immediately prevailed on the air-god to send us. He had announced himself as about to procure it for us; it was on this ground that the King assented to the preparation of those material means that were necessary before the horses of the sun could attach themselves to the chariot into which the balloon was immediately transformed. Those horses might not be defiled by contact with this gross earth. I too witnessed the ascent; at the moment, I grant you, I saw neither chariot nor horses, and almost all those present shared my own temporary blindness; the whole action from the moment when the balloon left the earth, moved so rapidly, that we were flustered, and hardly knew what it was that we were really seeing. It was not till two or three years later that I found the scene presenting itself to my soul's imaginary sight in the full splendour which was no doubt witnessed, but not apprehended, by my bodily vision."

"There," said my father, "you confirm an opinion that I have long held—nothing is so misleading as the testimony of eye-witnesses."

"A spiritual enlightenment from within," returned Mr. Balmy, "is more to be relied on than any merely physical affluence from external objects. Now, when I shut my eyes, I see the balloon ascend a little way, but almost immediately the heavens open, the horses descend, the balloon is transformed, and the glorious pageant careers onward till it vanishes into the heaven of heavens. Hundreds with whom I have conversed assure me that their experience has been the same as mine. Has yours been different?"

"Oh no, not at all; but I always see some storks circling round the balloon before I see any horses."

"How strange! I have heard others also say that they saw the storks you mention; but let me do my utmost I cannot force them into my mental image of the scene. This shows, as you were saying just now, how incomplete the testimony of an eye-witness often is. It is quite possible that the storks were there, but the horses and the chariot have impressed themselves more vividly on my mind than anything else has."

"Quite so; and I am not without hope that even at this late hour some further details may yet be revealed to us."

"It is possible, but we should be as cautious in accepting any fresh details as in rejecting them. Should some heresy obtain wide acceptance, visions will perhaps be granted to us that may be useful in refuting it, but otherwise I expect nothing more."

"Neither do I, but I have heard people say that inasmuch as the Sunchild said he was going to interview the air-god in order to send us rain, he was more probably son to the air-god than to the sun. Now here is a heresy which—"

"But, my dear sir," said Mr. Balmy, interrupting him with great warmth, "he spoke of his father in heaven as endowed with attributes far exceeding any that can be conceivably ascribed to the air-god. The power of the air-god does not extend beyond our own atmosphere."

"Pray believe me," said my father, who saw by the ecstatic gleam in his companion's eye that there was nothing to be done but to agree with him, "that I accept—"

"Hear me to the end," replied Mr. Balmy. "Who ever heard the Sunchild claim relationship with the air-god? He could command the air-god, and evidently did so, halting no doubt for this beneficent purpose on his journey towards his ultimate destination. Can we suppose that the air-god, who had evidently intended withholding the rain from us for an indefinite period, should have so immediately relinquished his designs against us at the intervention of any less exalted personage than the sun's own offspring? Impossible!"

"I quite agree with you," exclaimed my father, "it is out of the—"

"Let me finish what I have to say. When the rain came so copiously for days, even those who had not seen the miraculous ascent found its consequences come so directly home to them, that they had no difficulty in accepting the report of others. There was not a farmer or cottager in the land but heaved a sigh of relief at rescue from impending ruin, and they all knew it was the Sunchild who had promised the King that he would make the air-god send it. So abundantly, you will remember, did it come, that we had to pray to him to stop it, which in his own good time he was pleased to do."

"I remember," said my father, who was at last able to edge in a word, "that it nearly flooded me out of house and home. And yet, in spite of all this, I hear that there are many at Bridgeford who are still hardened unbelievers."

"Alas! you speak too truly. Bridgeford and the Musical Banks for the first three years fought tooth and nail to blind those whom it was their first duty to enlighten. I was a Professor of the hypothetical language, and you may perhaps remember how I was driven from my chair on account of the fearlessness with which I expounded the deeper mysteries of Sunchildism."

"Yes, I remember well how cruelly—" but my father was not allowed to get beyond "cruelly."

"It was I who explained the Sunchild had represented himself as belonging to a people in many respects analogous to our own, when no such people can have existed. It was I who detected that the supposed nation spoken of by the Sunchild was an invention designed in order to give us instruction by the light of which we might more easily remodel our institutions. I have sometimes thought that my gift of interpretation was vouchsafed to me in recognition of the humble services that I was hereby allowed to render. By the way, you have received no illumination this morning, have you?"

"I never do, sir, when I am in the company of one whose conversation I find supremely interesting. But you were telling me about Bridgeford: I live hundreds of miles from Bridgeford, and have never understood the suddenness, and completeness, with which men like Professors Hanky and Panky and Dr. Downie changed front. Do they believe as you and I do, or did they merely go with the times? I spent a couple of hours with Hanky and Panky only two evenings ago, and was not so much impressed as I could have wished with the depth of their religious fervour."

"They are sincere now—more especially Hanky—but I cannot think I am judging them harshly, if I say that they were not so at first. Even now, I fear, that they are more carnally than spiritually minded. See how they have fought for the aggrandisement of their own order. It is mainly their doing that the Musical Banks have usurped the spiritual authority formerly exercised by the straighteners."

"But the straighteners," said my father, "could not co-exist with Sunchildism, and it is hard to see how the claims of the Banks can be reasonably gainsaid."

"Perhaps; and after all the Banks are our main bulwark against the evils that I fear will follow from the repeal of the laws against machinery. This has already led to the development of a materialism which minimizes the miraculous element in the Sunchild's ascent, as our own people minimize the material means that were the necessary prologue to the miraculous."

Thus did they converse; but I will not pursue their conversation further. It will be enough to say that in further floods of talk Mr. Balmy confirmed what George had said about the Banks having lost their hold upon the masses. That hold was weak even in the time of my father's first visit; but when the people saw the hostility of the Banks to a movement which far the greater number of them accepted, it seemed as though both Bridgeford and the Banks were doomed, for Bridgeford was heart and soul with the Banks. Hanky, it appeared, though under thirty, and not yet a Professor, grasped the situation, and saw that Bridgeford must either move with the times, or go. He consulted some of the most sagacious Heads of Houses and Professors, with the result that a committee of enquiry was appointed, which in due course reported that the evidence for the Sunchild's having been the only child of the sun was conclusive. It was about this time—that is to say some three years after his ascent—that "Higgism," as it had been hitherto called, became "Sunchildism," and "Higgs" the "Sunchild."

My father also learned the King's fury at his escape (for he would call it nothing else) with my mother. This was so great that though he had hitherto been, and had ever since proved himself to be, a humane ruler, he ordered the instant execution of all who had been concerned in making either the gas or the balloon; and his cruel orders were carried out within a couple of hours. At the same time he ordered the destruction by fire of the Queen's workshops, and of all remnants of any materials used in making the balloon. It is said the Queen was so much grieved and outraged (for it was her doing that the material groundwork, so to speak, had been provided for the miracle) that she wept night and day without ceasing three whole months, and never again allowed her husband to embrace her, till he had also embraced Sunchildism.

When the rain came, public indignation at the King's action was raised almost to revolution pitch, and the King was frightened at once by the arrival of the promised downfall and the displeasure of his subjects. But he still held out, and it was only after concessions on the part of the Bridgeford committee, that he at last consented to the absorption of Sunchildism into the Musical Bank system, and to its establishment as the religion of the country. The far-reaching changes in Erewhonian institutions with which the reader is already acquainted followed as a matter of course.

"I know the difficulty," said my father presently, "with which the King was persuaded to allow the way in which the Sunchild's dress should be worn to be a matter of opinion, not dogma. I see we have adopted different fashions. Have you any decided opinions upon the subject?"

"I have; but I will ask you not to press me for them. Let this matter remain as the King has left it."

My father thought that he might now venture on a shot. So he said, "I have always understood, too, that the King forced the repeal of the laws against machinery on the Bridgeford committee, as another condition of his assent?"

"Certainly. He insisted on this, partly to gratify the Queen, who had not yet forgiven him, and who had set her heart on having a watch, and partly because he expected that a development of the country's resources, in consequence of a freer use of machinery, would bring more money into his exchequer. Bridgeford fought hard and wisely here, but they had gained so much by the Musical Bank Managers being recognised as the authorised exponents of Sunchildism, that they thought it wise to yield—apparently with a good grace—and thus gild the pill which his Majesty was about to swallow. But even then they feared the consequences that are already beginning to appear, and which, if I mistake not, will assume far more serious proportions in the future."

"See," said my father suddenly, "we are coming to another procession, and they have got some banners; let us walk a little quicker and overtake it."

"Horrible!" replied Mr. Balmy fiercely. "You must be short-sighted, or you could never have called my attention to it. Let us get it behind us as fast as possible, and not so much as look at it."

"Oh, yes, yes," said my father, "it is indeed horrible, I had not seen what it was."

He had not the faintest idea what the matter was, but he let Mr. Balmy walk a little ahead of him, so that he could see the banners, the most important of which he found to display a balloon pure and simple, with one figure in the car. True, at the top of the banner there was a smudge which might be taken for a little chariot, and some very little horses, but the balloon was the only thing insisted on. As for the procession, it consisted entirely of men, whom a smaller banner announced to be workmen from the Fairmead iron and steel works. There was a third banner, which said, "Science as well as Sunchildism."

CHAPTER XV

THE TEMPLE IS DEDICATED TO MY FATHER, AND CERTAIN EXTRACTS ARE READ FROM HIS SUPPOSED SAYINGS

"IT IS ENOUGH to break one's heart," said Mr. Balmy when he had outstripped the procession, and my father was again beside him. " 'As well as,' indeed! We know what that means. Wherever there is a factory there is a hot-bed of unbelief. 'As well as'! Why it is a defiance."

"What, I wonder," said my father innocently, "must the Sunchild's feelings be, as he looks down on this procession. For there can be little doubt that he is doing so."

"There can be no doubt at all," replied Mr. Balmy, "that he is taking note of it, and of all else that is happening this day in Erewhon. Heaven grant that he be not so angered as to chastise the innocent as well as the guilty."

"I doubt," said my father, "his being so angry even with this procession, as you think he is."

Here, fearing an outburst of indignation, he found an excuse for rapidly changing the conversation. Moreover he was angry with himself for playing upon this poor good creature. He had not done so of malice prepense; he had begun to deceive him, because he believed himself to be in danger if he spoke the truth; and though he knew the part to be an unworthy one, he could not escape from continuing to play it, if he was to discover things that he was not likely to discover otherwise.

Often, however, he had checked himself. It had been on the tip of his tongue to be illuminated with the words,

> Sukoh and Sukop were two pretty men,
> They lay in bed till the clock struck ten,

and to follow it up with,

> Now with the drops of this most Yknarc time
> My love looks fresh,

in order to see how Mr. Balmy would interpret the assertion here made about the Professors, and what statement he would connect with his own Erewhonian name; but he had restrained himself.

The more he saw, and the more he heard, the more shocked he was at the mischief he had done. See how he had unsettled the little mind this poor, dear, good gentleman had ever had, till he was now a mere slave to preconception. And how many more had he not in like manner brought to the verge of idiocy? How many again had he not made more corrupt than they were before, even though he had not deceived them—as for example, Hanky and Panky. And the young? how could such a lie as that a chariot and four horses came down out of the clouds enter seriously into the life of any one, without distorting his mental vision, if not ruining it?

And yet, the more he reflected, the more he also saw that he could do no good by saying who he was. Matters had gone so far that though he spoke with the tongues of men and angels he would not be listened to; and even if he were, it might easily prove that he had added harm to that which he had done already. No. As soon as he had heard Hanky's sermon, he would begin to work his way back, and if the Professors had not yet removed their purchase, he would recover it; but he would pin a bag containing about five pounds worth of nuggets on to the tree in which they had hidden it, and, if possible, he would find some way of sending the rest to George.

He let Mr. Balmy continue talking, glad that this gentleman required little more than monosyllabic answers, and still more glad, in spite of some agitation, to see that they were now nearing Sunch'ston, towards which a great concourse of people was hurrying from Clearwater, and more distant towns on the main road. Many whole families were coming,—the fathers and mothers carrying the smaller children, and also their own shoes and stockings, which they would put on when nearing the town. Most of the pilgrims brought provisions with them. All wore European costumes, but only a few of them wore it reversed, and these were almost invariably of higher social status than the great body of the people, who were mainly peasants.

When they reached the town, my father was relieved at finding that Mr. Balmy had friends on whom he wished to call before going to the temple. He asked my father to come with him, but my father said that he too had friends, and would leave him for the present, while hoping to meet him again later in the day. The two, therefore, shook hands with great effusion, and went their several ways. My father's way took him first into a confectioner's shop, where he bought a couple of Sunchild buns, which he put into his pocket, and refreshed himself with a bottle of Sunchild cordial and water. All shops except those dealing in refreshments were closed, and the town was gaily decorated with flags and flowers, often festooned into words or emblems proper for the occasion.

My father, it being now a quarter to eleven, made his way towards the temple, and his heart was clouded with care as he walked along. Not only was his heart clouded, but his brain also was oppressed, and he reeled so much on leaving the confectioner's shop, that he had to catch hold of some railings till the faintness and giddiness left him. He knew the feeling to be the same as what he had felt on the Friday evening, but he had no idea of the cause, and as soon as the giddiness left him he thought there was nothing the matter with him.

Turning down a side street that led into the main square of the town, he found himself opposite the south end of the temple, with its two lofty towers that flanked the richly decorated main entrance. I will not attempt to describe the architecture, for my father could give me little information on this point. He saw only the south front for two or three minutes, and was not impressed by it, save in so far as it was richly ornamented—evidently at great expense—and very large. Even if he had had a longer look, I doubt whether I should have got more out of him, for he knew nothing of architecture, and I fear his test whether a building was good or bad, was whether it looked old and weather-beaten or no. No matter what a building was, if it was three or four hundred years old he liked it, whereas, if it was new, he would look to nothing but whether it kept the rain out. Indeed I have heard him say that the mediæval sculpture on some of our great cathedrals often only pleases us because time and weather have set their seals upon it, and that if we could see it as it was when it left the mason's hands, we would find it no better than much that is now turned out in the Euston Road.

The ground plan here given will help the reader to understand the few following pages more easily.

The building was led up to by a flight of steps (M), and on entering it my father found it to consist of a spacious nave, with two aisles and an apse which was raised some three feet above the nave and aisles. There were no transepts. In the apse there was the table (a), with the two bowls of Musical Bank money mentioned on an earlier page, as also the alms-box in front of it.

At some little distance in front of the table stood the President's chair (c), or I might almost call it throne. It was so placed that his back would be turned towards the table, which fact again shows that the table was not regarded as having any greater sanctity than the rest of the temple.

Behind the table, the picture already spoken of was raised aloft. There was no balloon; some clouds that hung about the lower part of the chariot served to conceal the fact that the painter was uncertain whether it ought to have wheels or no. The horses were without driver, and my father thought that some one ought to have had them in hand, for they were in far too excited a state to be left safely to themselves. They had hardly any harness, but what little there was

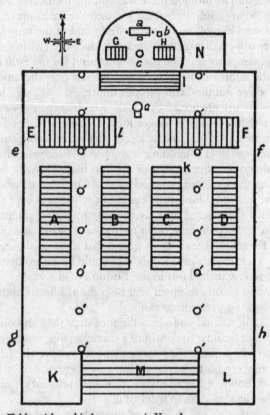

- *a.* Table with cashier's seat on either side, and alms-box in front. The picture is behind it.
- *b.* The reliquary.
- *c.* The President's chair.
- *d.* Pulpit and lectern.
- *e.*
  f. ⎱
  g. ⎰ Side doors.
  h.
- *i.* Yram's seat.
- *k.* Seats of George and the Sun-child.
- *o'* Pillars.
- *A, B, C, D, E, F, G, H,* blocks of seats.
- *l.* Steps leading from the apse to the nave.
- *K* and *L.* Towers.
- *M.* Steps and main entrance.
- *N.* Robing-room.

was enriched with gold bosses. My mother was in Erewhonian costume, my father in European, but he wore his clothes reversed. Both he and my mother seemed to be bowing graciously to an unseen crowd beneath them, and in the distance, near the bottom of the picture, was a fairly accurate representation of the Sunch'ston new temple. High up, on the right hand, was a disc, raised and gilt, to represent the sun; on it, in low relief, there was an indication of a gorgeous palace, in which, no doubt, the sun was supposed to live; though how they made it all out my father could not conceive.

On the right of the table there was a reliquary (*b*) of glass, much adorned with gold, or more probably gilding, for gold was so scarce in Erewhon that gilding would be as expensive as a thin plate of gold would be in Europe: but there is no knowing. The reliquary was attached to a portable stand some five feet high, and inside it was the relic already referred to. The crowd was so great that my father could not get near enough to see what it contained, but I may say here, that when, two days later, circumstances compelled him to have a close look at it, he saw that it consisted of about a dozen fine coprolites, deposited by some antediluvian creature or creatures, which, whatever else they may have been, were certainly not horses.

In the apse there were a few cross benches (G and H) on either side, with an open space between them, which was partly occupied by the President's seat already mentioned. Those on the right, as one looked towards the apse, were for the Managers and Cashiers of the Bank, while those on the left were for their wives and daughters.

In the centre of the nave, only a few feet in front of the steps leading to the apse, was a handsome pulpit and lectern (*d*). The pulpit was raised some feet above the ground, and was so roomy that the preacher could walk about in it. On either side of it there were cross benches with backs (E and F); those on the right were reserved for the Mayor, civic functionaries, and distinguished visitors, while those on the left were for their wives and daughters.

Benches with backs (A, B, C, D) were placed about half-way down both nave and aisles—those in the nave being divided so as to allow a free passage between them. The rest of the temple was open space, about which people might walk at their will. There were side doors (*e*, *g*, and *f*, *h*) at the upper and lower end of each aisle. Over the main entrance was a gallery in which singers were placed.

As my father was worming his way among the crowd, which was now very dense, he was startled at finding himself tapped lightly on the shoulder, and turning round in alarm was confronted by the beaming face of George.

"How do you do, Professor Panky?" said the youth—who had decided thus to address him. "What are you doing here among the common people? Why have you not taken your place in one of the seats reserved for our distinguished visitors? I am afraid they must be all full by this time, but I will see what I can do for you. Come with me."

"Thank you," said my father. His heart beat so fast that this was all he could say, and he followed meek as a lamb.

With some difficulty the two made their way to the right-hand corner seats of block C, for every seat in the reserved block was taken. The places which George wanted for my father and for himself were already occupied by two young men of about eighteen and nineteen, both of them well-grown, and of prepossessing appearance. My father saw by the truncheons they carried that they were special constables; but he took no notice of this, for there were many others scattered about the crowd. George whispered a few words to one of them, and to my father's surprise they both gave up their seats, which appear on the plan as (*k*).

It afterwards transpired that these two young men were George's brothers, who by his desire had taken the seats some hours ago, for it was here that George had determined to place himself and my father if he could find him. He chose these places because they would be near enough to let his mother (who was at *i*, in the middle of the front row of block E, to the left of the pulpit) see my father without being so near as to embarrass him; he could also see and be seen by Hanky, and hear every word of his sermon; but perhaps his chief reason had been the fact that they were not far from the side-door at the upper end of the right-hand aisle, while there was no barrier to interrupt rapid egress should this prove necessary,

It was now high time that they should sit down, which they accordingly did. George sat at the end of the bench, and thus had my father on his left. My father was rather uncomfortable at seeing the young men whom they had turned out, standing against a column close by, but George said that this was how it was to be, and there was nothing to be done but to submit. The young men seemed quite happy, which puzzled my father, who of course had no idea that their action was preconcerted.

Panky was in the first row of block F, so that my father could not see his face except sometimes when he turned round. He was sitting on the Mayor's right hand, while Dr. Downie was on his left; he looked at my father once or twice in a puzzled way, as though he

·ought to have known him, but my father did not think he recognised him. Hanky was still with President Gurgoyle and others in the robing-room, N; Yram had already taken her seat; my father knew her in a moment, though he pretended not to do so when George pointed her out to him. Their eyes met for a second; Yram turned hers quickly away, and my father could not see a trace of recognition in her face. At no time during the whole ceremony did he catch her looking at him again.

"Why, you stupid man," she said to him later on in the day with a quick, kindly smile, "I was looking at you all the time. As soon as the President or Hanky began to talk about you I knew you would stare at him, and then I could look. As soon as they left off talking about you I knew you would be looking at me, unless you went to sleep—and as I did not know which you might be doing, I waited till they began to talk about you again."

My father had hardly taken note of his surroundings when the choir began singing, accompanied by a few feeble flutes and lutes, or whatever the name of the instrument should be, but with no violins, for he knew nothing of the violin, and had not been able to teach the Erewhonians anything about it. The voices were all in unison, and the tune they sang was one which my father had taught Yram to sing; but he could not catch the words.

As soon as the singing began, a procession, headed by the venerable Dr. Gurgoyle, President of the Musical Banks of the province, began to issue from the robing-room, and move towards the middle of the apse. The President was sumptuously dressed, but he wore no mitre, nor anything to suggest an English or European Bishop. The Vice-President, Head Manager, Vice-Manager, and some Cashiers of the Bank, now ranged themselves on either side of him, and formed an impressive group as they stood, gorgeously arrayed, at the top of the steps leading from the apse to the nave. Here they waited till the singers left off singing.

When the litany, or hymn, or whatever it should be called, was over, the Head Manager left the President's side and came down to the lectern in the nave, where he announced himself as about to read some passages from the Sunchild's Sayings. Perhaps because it was the first day of the year according to their new calendar, the reading began with the first chapter, the whole of which was read. My father told me that he quite well remembered having said the last verse, which he still held as true; hardly a word of the rest was ever spoken by him, though he recognised his own influence in almost all of it.

The reader paused, with good effect, for about five seconds between each paragraph, and read slowly and very clearly. The chapter was as follows:—

"These are the words of the Sunchild about God and man. He said—

1. God is the baseless basis of all thoughts, things, and deeds.

2. So that those who say that there is a God, lie, unless they also mean that there is no God; and those who say that there is no God, lie, unless they also mean that there is a God.

3. It is very true to say that man is made after the likeness of God; and yet it is very untrue to say this.

4. God lives and moves in every atom throughout the universe. Therefore it is wrong to think of Him as 'Him' and 'He,' save as by the clutching of a drowning man at a straw.

5. God is God to us only so long as we cannot see him. When we are near to seeing Him He vanishes, and we behold Nature in His stead.

6. We approach Him most nearly when we think of Him as our expression for Man's highest conception, of goodness, wisdom, and power. But we cannot rise to Him above the level of our own highest selves.

7. We remove ourselves most far from Him when we invest Him with human form and attributes.

8. My father the sun, the earth, the moon, and all planets that roll round my father, are to God but as a single cell in our bodies to ourselves.

9. He is as much above my father, as my father is above men and women.

10. The universe is instinct with the mind of God. The mind of God is in all that has mind throughout all worlds. There is no God but the Universe, and man, in this world is His prophet.

11. God's conscious life, nascent, so far as this world is concerned, in the infusoria, adolescent in the higher mammals, approaches maturity on this earth in man. All these living beings are members one of another, and of God.

12. Therefore, as man cannot live without God in the world, so neither can God live in this world without mankind.

13. If we speak ill of God in our ignorance it may be forgiven us; but if we speak ill of His Holy Spirit indwelling in good men and women it may not be forgiven us."

The Head Manager now resumed his place by President Gurgoyle's side, and the President in the name of his Majesty the King declared the temple to be hereby dedicated to the contemplation of the Sunchild and the better exposition of his teaching. This was all that was said. The reliquary was then brought forward and placed at the top of the steps leading from the apse to the nave; but the original intention of carrying it round the temple was abandoned for fear of accidents through the pressure round it of the enormous multitudes who were assembled. More singing followed of a simple but impressive kind; during this I am afraid I must own that my father, tired with his walk, dropped off into a refreshing slumber, from which he did not wake till George nudged him and told him not to snore, just as the Vice-Manager was going towards the lectern to read another chapter of the Sunchild's Sayings—which was as follows:—

The Sunchild also spoke to us a parable about the unwisdom of the children yet unborn, who though they know so much, yet do not know as much as they think they do.

He said:—

"The unborn have knowledge of one another so long as they are unborn, and this without impediment from walls or material obstacles. The unborn children in any city form a population apart, who talk with one another and tell each other about their developmental progress.

"They have no knowledge, and cannot even conceive the existence of anything that is not such as they are themselves. Those who have been born are to them what the dead are to us. They can see no life in them, and know no more about them than they do of any stage in their own past development other than the one through which they are passing at the moment. They do not even know that their mothers are alive—much less that their mothers were once as they now are. To an embryo, its mother is simply the environment, and is looked upon much as our inorganic surroundings are by ourselves.

"The great terror of their lives is the fear of birth,—that they shall have to leave the only thing that they can think of as life, and enter upon a dark unknown which is to them tantamount to annihilation.

"Some, indeed, among them have maintained that birth is not the death which they commonly deem it, but that there is a life beyond the womb of which they as yet know nothing, and which is a million fold more truly life than anything they have yet been able even to imagine. But the greater number shake their yet unfashioned heads and say they have no evidence for this that will stand a moment's examination.

"'Nay,' answer the others, 'so much work, so elaborate, so wondrous as that whereon we are now so busily engaged must have a purpose, though the purpose is beyond our grasp.'

" 'Never,' reply the first speakers; 'our pleasure in the work is sufficient justification for it. Who has ever partaken of this life you speak of, and re-entered into the womb to tell us of it? Granted that some few have pretended to have done this, but how completely have their stories broken down when subjected to the tests of sober criticism. No. When we are born we are born, and there is an end of us.'

"But in the hour of birth, when they can no longer reenter the womb and tell the others, Behold! they find that it is not so."

Here the reader again closed his book and resumed his place in the apse.

CHAPTER XVI

PROFESSOR HANKY PREACHES A SERMON, IN THE COURSE OF WHICH MY FATHER DECLARES HIMSELF TO BE THE SUNCHILD

PROFESSOR HANKY THEN went up into the pulpit, richly but soberly robed in vestments the exact nature of which I cannot determine. His carriage was dignified, and the harsh lines on his face gave it a strong individuality, which, though it did not attract, conveyed an impression of power that could not fail to interest. As soon as he had given attention time to fix itself upon him, he began his sermon without text or preliminary matter of any kind, and apparently without notes.

He spoke clearly and very quietly, especially at the beginning; he used action whenever it could point his meaning, or give life and colour, but there was no approach to staginess or even oratorical display. In fact, he spoke as one who meant what he was saying, and desired that his hearers should accept his meaning, fully confident in his good faith. His use of pause was effective. After the word "mistake," at the end of the opening sentence, he held up his half-bent hand and paused for full three seconds, looking intently at his audience as he did so. Every one felt the idea to be here enounced that was to dominate the sermon.

The sermon—so much of it as I can find room for—was as follows:—

"My friends, let there be no mistake. At such a time, as this, it is well we should look back upon the path by which we have travelled, and forward to the goal towards which we are tending. As it was necessary that the material foundations of this building should be so sure that there shall be no subsidence in the superstructure, so is it not less necessary to ensure that there shall be no subsidence in the immaterial structure that we have raised in consequence of the Sunchild's sojourn among us. Therefore, my friends, I again say, 'Let there be no mistake.' Each stone that goes towards the uprearing of this visible fane, each human soul that does its part in building the invisible temple of our national faith, is bearing witness to, and lending its support to, that which is either the truth of truths, or the baseless fabric of a dream.

"My friends, this is the only possible alternative. He in whose name we are here assembled, is either worthy of more reverential honour than we can ever pay him, or he is worthy of no more honour than any other honourable man among ourselves. There can be no halting between these two opinions. The question of questions is, was he the child of the tutelary god of this world—the sun, and is it to the palace of the sun that he returned when he left us, or was he, as some amongst us still do not hesitate to maintain, a mere man, escaping by unusual but strictly natural means to some part of this earth with which we are unacquainted. My friends, either we are on a right path or on a very wrong one, and in a matter of such supreme importance—there must be no mistake.

"I need not remind those of you whose privilege it is to live in Sunch'ston, of the charm attendant on the Sunchild's personal presence and conversation, not of his quick sympathy, his keen intellect, his readiness to adapt himself to the capacities of all those who came to see him while he was in prison. He adored children, and it was on them that some of his most conspicuous miracles were performed. Many a time when a child had fallen and hurt itself, was he known to make the place well by simply kissing it. Nor need I recall to your minds the spotless purity of his life—so spotless that not one breath of slander has ever dared to visit it. I was one of the not very many who had the privilege of being admitted to the inner circle of his friends during the later weeks that he was amongst us. I loved him dearly, and it will ever be the proudest recollection of my life that he deigned to return me no small measure of affection."

My father, furious as he was at finding himself dragged into complicity with this man's imposture, could not resist a smile at the effrontery with which he lowered his tone here, and appeared unwilling to dwell on an incident which he could not recall without being affected almost to tears, and mere allusion to which had involved an apparent self-display that was above all things repugnant to him. What a difference between the Hanky of Thursday evening with its "never set eyes on him and hope I never shall," and the Hanky of Sunday morning, who now looked as modest as Cleopatra might have done had she been standing godmother to a little blue-eyed girl—Bellerophon's first-born baby.

Having recovered from his natural, but promptly repressed, emotion, the Professor continued:—

"I need not remind you of the purpose for which so many of us, from so many parts of our kingdom, are here assembled. We know what we have come hither to do: we are come each one of us to sign and seal by his presence the bond of his assent to those momentous changes, which have found their first great material expression in the temple that you see around you.

"You all know how, in accordance with the expressed will of the Sunchild, the Presidents and Vice-Presidents of the Musical Banks began as soon as he had left us to examine, patiently, carefully, earnestly, and without bias of any kind, firstly the evidences in support of the Sunchild's claim to be the son of the tutelar deity of this world, and secondly the precise nature of his instructions as regards the future position and authority of the Musical Banks.

"My friends, it is easy to understand why the Sunchild should have given us these instructions. With that foresight which is the special characteristic of divine, as compared with human, wisdom, he desired that the evidences in support of his superhuman character should be collected, sifted, and placed on record, before anything was either lost through the death of those who could alone substantiate it, or unduly supplied through the enthusiasm of over-zealous visionaries. The greater any true miracle has been, the more certainly will false ones accrete round it; here, then, we find the explanation of the command the Sunchild gave to us to gather, verify, and record, the facts of his sojourn here in Erewhon. For above all things he held it necessary to ensure that there should be neither mistake, nor even possibility of mistake.

"Consider for a moment what differences of opinion would infallibly have arisen, if the evidences for the miraculous character of the Sunchild's mission had been conflicting—if they had rested on versions each claiming to be equally authoritative, but each hopelessly irreconcilable on vital points with every single other. What would future generations have said in answer to those who bade them fling all human experience to the winds, on the strength of records written they knew not certainly by whom, nor how long after the marvels that they recorded, and of which all that could be certainly said was that no two of them told the same story?

"Who that believes either in God or man—who with any self-respect, or respect for the gift of reason with which God had endowed him, either would, or could, believe that a chariot and four horses had come down from heaven, and gone back again with human or quasi-human occupants, unless the evidences for the fact left no loophole for escape? If a single loophole were left him, he would be unpardonable, not for disbelieving the story, but for believing it. The sin against God would lie not in want of faith, but in faith.

"My friends, there are two sins in matters of belief. There is that of believing on too little evidence, and that of requiring too much before we are convinced. The guilt of the latter is incurred, alas! by not a few amongst us at the present day, but if the testimony to the truth of the wondrous event so faithfully depicted on the picture that confronts you had been less contemporaneous, less authoritative, less unanimous, future generations—and it is for them that we should now provide—would be guilty of the first-named, and not less heinous sin if they believed at all.

"Small wonder, then, that the Sunchild, having come amongst us for our advantage, not his own, would not permit his beneficent designs to be endangered by the discrepancies, mythical developments, idiosyncrasies, and a hundred other defects inevitably attendant on amateur and irresponsible recording. Small wonder, then, that he should have chosen the officials of the Musical Banks, from the Presidents and Vice-Presidents downwards to be the authoritative exponents of his teaching, the depositaries of his traditions, and his representatives here on earth till he shall again see fit to visit us. For he will come. Nay it is even possible that he may be here amongst us at this very moment, disguised so that none may know him, and intent only on watching our devotion towards him. If this be so, let me implore him, in the name of the sun his father, to reveal himself."

Now Hanky had already given my father more than one look that had made him uneasy. He had evidently recognised him as the supposed ranger of last Thursday evening. Twice he had run his eye like a searchlight over the front benches opposite to him, and when the beam had reached my father there had been no more searching. It was beginning to dawn upon my father that George might have discovered that he was not Professor Panky; was it for this reason that these two young special constables, though they gave up their places, still kept so close to him? Was George only waiting his opportunity to arrest him—not of course even suspecting who he was—but as a foreign devil who had tried to pass himself off as Professor Panky? Had this been the meaning of his having followed him to Fairmead? And should he have to be thrown into the Blue Pool by George after all? "It would serve me," said he to himself, "richly right."

These fears which had been taking shape for some few minutes were turned almost to certainties by the half-contemptuous glance Hanky threw towards him as he uttered what was obviously intended as a challenge. He saw that all was over, and was starting to his feet to declare himself, and thus fall into the trap that Hanky was laying for him, when George gripped him tightly by the knee and whispered, "Don't—you are in great danger." And he smiled kindly as he spoke.

My father sank back dumbfounded. "You know me?" he whispered in reply.

"Perfectly. So does Hanky, so does my mother; say no more," and he again smiled.

George, as my father afterwards learned, had hoped that he would reveal himself, and had determined in spite of his mother's instructions, to give him an opportunity of doing so. It was for this reason that he had not arrested him quietly, as he could very well have done, before the service began. He wished to discover what manner of man his father was, and was quite happy as soon as he saw that he would have spoken out if he had not been checked. He had not yet caught Hanky's motive in trying to goad my father, but on seeing that he was trying to do this, he knew that a trap was being laid, and that my father must not be allowed to speak.

Almost immediately, however, he perceived that while his eyes had been turned on Hanky, two burly vergers had wormed their way through the crowd and had taken their stand close to his two brothers. Then he understood, and understood also how to frustrate.

As for my father, George's ascendancy over him—quite felt by George—was so absolute that he could think of nothing now but the exceeding great joy of finding his fears groundless, and of delivering himself up to his son's guidance in the assurance that the void in his heart was filled, and that his wager not only would be held as won, but was being already paid. How they had found out, why he was not to speak as he would assuredly have done—for he was in a white heat of fury—what did it all matter now that he had found that which he had feared he should fail to find? He gave George a puzzled smile, and composed himself as best he could to hear the continuation of Hanky's sermon, which was as follows:—

"Who could the Sunchild have chosen, even though he had been gifted with no more than human sagacity, but the body of men whom he selected? It becomes me but ill to speak so warmly in favour of that body of whom I am the least worthy member, but what other is there in Erewhon so above all suspicion of slovenliness, self-seeking, preconceived bias, or bad faith? If there was one set of qualities more essential than another for the conduct of the investigations entrusted to us by the Sunchild, it was those that turn on meekness and freedom from all spiritual pride. I believe I can say quite truly that these are the qualities for which Bridgeford is more especially renowned. The readiness of her Professors to learn even from those who at first sight may seem least able to instruct them—the gentleness with which they correct an opponent if they feel it incumbent upon them to do so, the promptitude with which they acknowledge error when it is pointed out to them and quit a position no matter how deeply they have been committed to it, at the first moment in which they see that they cannot hold it righteously, their delicate sense of honour, their utter immunity from what the Sunchild used to call log-rolling or intrigue, the scorn with which they regard anything like hitting below the belt—these I believe I may truly say are the virtues for which Bridgeford is pre-eminently renowned."

The Professor went on to say a great deal more about the fitness of Bridgeford and the Musical Bank managers for the task imposed on them by the Sunchild, but here my father's attention flagged—nor, on looking at the verbatim report of the sermon that appeared next morning in the leading Sunch'ston journal, do I see reason to reproduce Hanky's words on this head. It was all to show that there had been no possibility of mistake.

Meanwhile George was writing on a scrap of paper as though he was taking notes of the sermon. Presently he slipped this into my father's hand. It ran:—

"You see those vergers standing near my brothers, who gave up their seats to us. Hanky tried to goad you into speaking that they might arrest you, and get you into the Bank prisons. If you fall into their hands you are lost. I must arrest you instantly on a charge of poaching on the King's preserves, and make you my prisoner. Let those vergers catch sight of the warrant which I shall now give you. Read it and return it to me. Come with me quietly after service. I think you had better not reveal yourself at all."

As soon as he had given my father time to read the foregoing, George took a warrant out of his pocket. My father pretended to read it and returned it. George then laid his hand on his shoulder, and in an undertone arrested him. He then wrote on another scrap of paper and passed it on to the elder of his two brothers. It was to the effect that he had now arrested my father, and that if the vergers attempted in any way to interfere between him and his prisoner, his brothers were to arrest both of them, which, as special constables, they had power to do.

Yram had noted Hanky's attempt to goad my father, and had not been prepared for his stealing a march upon her by trying to get my father arrested by Musical Bank officials, rather than by her son. On the preceding evening this last plan had been arranged on; and she knew nothing of the note that Hanky had sent an hour or two later to the Manager of the temple—the substance of which the reader can sufficiently guess. When she had heard Hanky's words and saw the vergers, she was for a few minutes seriously alarmed, but she was reassured when she saw George give my father the warrant, and her two sons evidently explaining the position to the vergers.

Hanky had by this time changed his theme, and was warning his hearers of the dangers that would follow on the legalization of the medical profession, and the repeal of the edicts against machines. Space forbids me to give his picture of the horrible tortures that future generations would be put to by medical men, if these were not duly kept in check by the influence of the Musical Banks; the horrors of the inquisition in the middle ages are nothing to what he depicted as certain to ensue if medical men were ever to have much money at their command. The only people in whose hands money might be trusted safely were those who presided over the Musical Banks. This tirade was followed by one not less alarming about she growth of materialistic tendencies among the artisans employed in the production of mechanical inventions. My father, though his eyes had been somewhat opened by the second of the two processions he had seen on his way to Sunch'ston, was not prepared to find that in spite of the superficially almost universal acceptance of the new faith, there was a powerful, and it would seem growing, undercurrent of scepticism, with a desire to reduce his escape with my mother to a purely natural occurrence.

"It is not enough," said Hanky, "that the Sunchild should have ensured the preparation of authoritative evidence of his supernatural character. The evidences happily exist in overwhelming strength, but they must be brought home to minds that as yet have stubbornly refused to receive them. During the last five years there has been an enormous increase in the number of those whose occupation in the manufacture of machines inclines them to a materialistic explanation even of the most obviously miraculous events, and the growth of this class in our midst constituted, and still constitutes, a grave danger to the state.

"It was to meet this that the society was formed on behalf of which I appeal fearlessly to your generosity. It is called, as most of you doubtless know, the Sunchild Evidence Society; and his Majesty the King graciously consented to become its Patron. This society not only collects additional evidences—indeed it is entirely due to its labours that the precious relic now in this temple was discovered—but it is its beneficent purpose to lay those that have been authoritatively investigated before men who, if left to themselves, would either neglect them altogether, or worse still reject them.

"For the first year or two the efforts of the society met with but little success among those for whose benefit they were more particularly intended, but during the present year the working classes in some cities and towns (stimulated very much by the lectures of my illustrious friend Professor Panky) have shown a most remarkable and zealous interest in Sunchild evidences, and have formed themselves into local branches for the study and defence of Sunchild truth.

"Yet in spite of all this need—of all this patient labour and really very gratifying success—the subscriptions to the society no longer furnish it with its former very modest income—an income which is deplorably insufficient if the organization is to be kept effective, and the work adequately performed. In spite of the most rigid economy, the committee have been compelled to part with a considerable portion of their small reserve fund (provided by a legacy) to tide over difficulties. But this method of balancing expenditure and income is very unsatisfactory, and cannot be long continued.

"I am led to plead for the society with especial insistence at the present time, inasmuch as more than one of those whose unblemished life has made them fitting recipients of such a signal favour, have recently had visions informing them that the Sunchild will again shortly visit us. We know not when he will come, but when he comes, my friends, let him not find us unmindful of, nor ungrateful for, the inestimable services he has rendered us. For come he surely will. Either in winter, what time icicles hang by the wall and milk comes frozen home in the pail—or in summer when days are at their longest and the mowing grass is about—there will be an hour, either at morn, or eve, or in the middle day, when he will again surely come. May it be mine to be among those who are then present to receive him."

Here he again glared at my father, whose blood was boiling. George had not positively forbidden him to speak out; he therefore sprang to his feet, "You lying hound," he cried, "I am the Sunchild, and you know it."

George, who knew that he had my father in his own hands, made no attempt to stop him, and was delighted that he should have declared himself though he had felt it his duty to tell him not to do so. Yram turned pale. Hanky roared out, "Tear him in pieces—leave not a single limb on his body. Take him out and burn him alive." The vergers made a dash for him—but George's brothers seized them. The crowd seemed for a moment inclined to do as Hanky bade them, but Yram rose from her place, and held up her hand as one who claimed attention. She advanced towards George and my father as unconcernedly as though she were merely walking out of church, but she still held her hand uplifted. All eyes were turned on her, as well as on George and my father, and the icy calm of her self-possession chilled those who were inclined for the moment to take Hanky's words literally. There was not a trace of fluster in her gait, action, or words, as she said—

"My friends, this temple, and this day, must not be profaned with blood. My son will take this poor madman to the prison. Let him be judged and punished according to law. Make room, that he and my son may pass."

Then, turning to my father, she said, "Go quietly with the Ranger."

Having so spoken, she returned to her seat as unconcernedly as she had left it.

Hanky for a time continued to foam at the mouth and roar out, "Tear him to pieces! burn him alive!" but when he saw that there was no further hope of getting the people to obey him, he collapsed on to a seat in the pulpit, mopped his bald head, and consoled himself with a great pinch of powder which corresponds very closely to our own snuff.

George led my father out by the side door at the north end of the western aisle; the people eyed him intently, but made way for him without demonstration. One voice alone was heard to cry out, "Yes, he is the Sunchild!" My father glanced at the speaker, and saw that he was the interpreter who had taught him the Erewhonian language when he was in prison.

George, seeing a special constable close by, told him to bid his brothers release the vergers, and let them arrest the interpreter—this the vergers, foiled as they had been in the matter of my father's arrest, were very glad to do. So the poor interpreter, to his dismay, was lodged at once in one of the Bank prison-cells, where he could do no further harm.

CHAPTER XVII

GEORGE TAKES HIS FATHER TO PRISON, AND THERE OBTAINS SOME USEFUL INFORMATION

BY THIS TIME George had gotten my father into the open square, where he was surprised to find that a large bonfire had been made and lighted. There had been nothing of the kind an hour before; the wood, therefore, must have been piled and lighted while people had been in church. He had no time at the moment to enquire why this had been done, but later on he discovered that on the Sunday morning the Manager of the new temple had obtained leave from the Mayor to have the wood piled in the square, representing that this was Professor Hanky's contribution to the festivities of the day. There had, it seemed, been no intention of lighting it until nightfall; but it had accidently caught fire through the carelessness of a workman, much about the time when Hanky began to preach. No one for a moment believed that there had been any sinister intention, or that Professor Hanky when he urged the crowd to burn my father alive, even knew that there was a pile of wood in the square at all—much less that it had been lighted—for he could hardly have supposed that the wood had been got together so soon. Nevertheless both George and my father, when they knew all that had passed, congratulated themselves on the fact that my father had not fallen into the hands of the vergers, who would probably have tried to utilise the accidental fire, though in no case is it likely they would have succeeded.

As soon as they were inside the gaol, the old Master recognised my father. "Bless my heart—what? You here, again, Mr. Higgs? Why, I thought you were in the palace of the sun your father."

"I wish I was," answered my father, shaking hands with him, but he could say no more.

"You are as safe here as if you were," said George laughing, "and safer." Then turning to his grandfather, he said, "You have the record of Mr. Higgs's marks and measurements? I know you have: take him to his old cell; it is the best in the prison; and then please bring me the record."

The old man took George and my father to the cell which he had occupied twenty years earlier—but I cannot stay to describe his feelings on finding himself again within it. The moment his grandfather's back was turned, George said to my father, "And now shake hands also with your son."

As he spoke he took my father's hand and pressed it warmly between both his own.

"Then you know you are my son," said my father as steadily as the strong emotion that mastered him would permit.

"Certainly."

"But you did not know this when I was walking with you on Friday?"

"Of course not. I thought you were Professor Panky; if I had not taken you for one of the two persons named in your permit, I should have questioned you closely, and probably ended by throwing you into the Blue Pool." He shuddered as he said this.

"But you knew who I was when you called me Panky in the temple?"

"Quite so. My mother told me everything on Friday evening."

"And that is why you tried to find me at Fairmead?"

"Yes, but where in the world were you?"

"I was inside the Musical Bank of the town, resting and reading." George laughed, and said, "On purpose to hide?"

"Oh no; pure chance. But on Friday evening? How could your mother have found out by that time that I was in Erewhon? Am I on my head or my heels?"

"On your heels, my father, which shall take you back to your own country as soon as we can get you out of this."

"What have I done to deserve so much good-will? I have done you nothing but harm." Again he was quite overcome.

George patted him gently on the hand, and said, "You made a bet and you won it. During the very short time that we can be together, you shall be paid in full, and may heaven protect us both."

As soon as my father could speak he said, "But how did your mother find out that I was in Erewhon?"

"Hanky and Panky were dining with her, and they told her some things that she thought strange. She cross-questioned them, put two and two together, learned that you had got their permit out of them, saw that you intended to return on Friday, and concluded that you would be sleeping in Sunch'ston. She sent for me, told me all, bade me scour Sunch'ston to find you, intending that you should be at once escorted safely over the preserves by me. I found your inn, but you had given us the slip. I tried first Fairmead and then Clearwater, but did not find you till this morning. For reasons too long to repeat, my mother warned Hanky and Panky that you would be in the temple; whereon Hanky tried to get you into his clutches. Happily he failed, but if I had known what he was doing I should have arrested you before the service. I ought to have done this, but I wanted you to win your wager, and I shall get you safely away in spite of them. My mother will not like my having let you hear Hanky's sermon and declare yourself."

"You half told me not to say who I was."

"Yes, but I was delighted when you disobeyed me."

"I did it very badly. I never rise to great occasions, I always fall to them, but these things must come as they come."

"You did it as well as it could be done, and good will come of it."

"And now," he continued, "describe exactly all that passed between you and the Professors. On which side of Panky did Hanky sit, and did they sit north and south or east and west? How did you get—oh, yes, I know that—you told them it would be of no further use to them. Tell me all else you can."

My father said that the Professors were sitting pretty well east and west, so that Hanky, who was on the east side, nearest the mountains, had Panky, who was on the Sunch'ston side, on his right hand. George made a note of this. My father then told what the reader already knows, but when he came to the measurement of the boots, George said, "Take your boots off," and began taking off his own. "Foot for foot," he said, "we are not father and son, but brothers. Yours will fit me; they are less worn than mine, but I daresay you will not mind that."

On this George *ex abundanti cautelâ* knocked a nail out of the right boot that he had been wearing and changed boots with my father; but he thought it more plausible not to knock out exactly the same nail that was missing on my father's boot. When the change was made, each found—or said he found—the other's boots quite comfortable.

My father all the time felt as though he were a basket given to a dog. The dog had got him, was proud of him, and no one must try to take him away. The promptitude with which George took to him, the obvious pleasure he had in "running" him, his quick judgment, verging as it should towards rashness, his confidence that my father trusted him without reserve, the conviction of perfect openness that was conveyed by the way in which his eyes never budged from my father's when he spoke to him, his genial, kindly manner, perfect physical health, and the air he had of being on the best possible terms with himself and every one else—the combination of all this so overmastered my poor father (who indeed had been sufficiently mastered before he had been five minutes in George's company) that he resigned himself as gratefully to being a basket, as George had cheerfully undertaken the task of carrying him.

In passing I may say that George could never get his own boots back again, though he tried more than once to do so. My father always made some excuse. They were the only memento of George that he brought home with him; I wonder that he did not ask for a lock of his hair, but he did not. He had the boots put against a wall in his bedroom, where he could see them from his bed, and during his illness, while consciousness yet remained with him, I saw his eyes continually turn towards them. George, in fact, dominated him as long as anything in this world could do so. Nor do I wonder; on the contrary, I love his memory the better; for I too, as will appear later, have seen George, and whatever little jealousy I may have felt, vanished on my finding him almost instantaneously gain the same ascendancy over me his brother, that he had gained over his and my father. But of this no more at present. Let me return to the gaol in Sunch'ston.

"Tell me more," said George, "about the Professors."

My father told him about the nuggets, the sale of his kit, the receipt he had given for the money, and how he had got the nuggets back from a tree, the position of which he described.

"I know the tree; have you got the nuggets here?"

"Here they are, with the receipt, and the pocket handkerchief marked with Hanky's name. The pocket handkerchief was found wrapped round some dried leaves that we call tea, but I have not got these with me." As he spoke he gave everything to George, who showed the utmost delight in getting possession of them.

"I suppose the blanket and the rest of the kit are still in the tree?"

"Unless Hanky and Panky have got them away, or some one has found them."

"This is not likely. I will now go to my office, but I will come back very shortly. My grandfather shall bring you something to eat at once. I will tell him to send enough for two"—which he accordingly did.

On reaching the office, he told his next brother (whom he had made an under-ranger) to go to the tree he described, and bring back the bundle he should find concealed therein. "You can go there and back," he said, "in an hour and a half, and I shall want the bundle by that time."

The brother, whose name I never rightly caught, set out at once. As soon as he was gone, George took from a drawer the feathers and bones of quails, that he had shown my father on the morning when he met him. He divided them in half, and made them into two bundles, one of which he docketed, "Bones of quails eaten, XIX. xii. 29, by Professor Hanky, P.O. W.W., &c." And he labelled Panky's quail bones in like fashion.

Having done this he returned to the gaol, but on his way he looked in at the Mayor's, and left a note saying that he should be at the gaol, where any message would reach him, but that he did not wish to meet Professors Hanky and Panky for another couple of hours. It was now about half-past twelve, and he caught sight of a crowd coming quietly out of the temple, whereby he knew that Hanky would soon be at the Mayor's house.

Dinner was brought in almost at the moment when George returned to the gaol. As soon as it was over George said:—

"Are you quite sure you have made no mistake about the way in which you got the permit out of the Professors?"

"Quite sure. I told them they would not want it, and said I could save them trouble if they gave it me. They never suspected why I wanted it. Where do you think I may be mistaken?"

"You sold your nuggets for rather less than a twentieth part of their value, and you threw in some curiosities, that would have fetched about half as much as you got for the nuggets. You say you did this because you wanted money to keep you going till you could sell some of your nuggets. This sounds well at first, but the sacrifice is too great to be plausible when considered. It looks more like a case of good honest manly straightforward corruption."

"But surely you believe me?"

"Of course I do. I believe every syllable that comes from your mouth, but I shall not be able to make out that the story was as it was not, unless I am quite certain what it really was."

"It was exactly as I have told you."

"That is enough. And now, may I tell my mother that you will put yourself in her, and the Mayor's, and my, hands, and will do whatever we tell you?"

"I will be obedience itself—but you will not ask me to do anything that will make your mother or you think less well of me?"

"If we tell you what you are to do, we shall not think any the worse of you for doing it. Then I may say to my mother that you will be good and give no trouble—not even though we bid you shake hands with Hanky and Parky?"

"I will embrace them and kiss them on both cheeks, if you and she tell me to do so. But what about the Mayor?"

"He has known everything, and condoned everything, these last twenty years. He will leave everything to my mother and me."

"Shall I have to see him?"

"Certainly. You must be brought up before him to-morrow morning."

"How can I look him in the face?"

"As you would me, or any one else. It is understood among us that nothing happened. Things may have looked as though they had happened, but they did not happen."

"And you are not yet quite twenty?"

"No, but I am son to my mother—and," he added, "to one who can stretch a point or two in the way of honesty as well as other people."

Having said this with a laugh, he again took my father's hand between both his, and went back to his office—where he set himself to think out the course he intended to take when dealing with the Professors.

CHAPTER XVIII

YRAM INVITES DR. DOWNIE AND MRS. HUMDRUM TO LUNCHEON—A PASSAGE AT ARMS BETWEEN HER AND HANKY IS AMICABLY ARRANGED

THE DISTURBANCE CAUSED by my father's outbreak was quickly suppressed, for George got him out of the temple almost immediately; it was bruited about, however, that the Sunchild had come down from the palace of the sun, but had disappeared as soon as any one had tried to touch him. In vain did Hanky try to put fresh life into his sermon; its back had been broken, and large numbers left the church to see what they could hear outside, or failing information, to discourse more freely with one another.

Hanky did his best to quiet his hearers when he found that he could not infuriate them,—

"This poor man," he said, "is already known to me, as one of those who have deluded themselves into believing that they are the Sunchild. I have known of his so declaring himself, more than once, in the neighbourhood of Bridgeford, and others have not infrequently done the same; I did not at first recognise him, and regret that the shock of horror his words occasioned me should have prompted me to suggest violence against him. Let this unfortunate affair pass from your minds, and let me again urge upon you the claims of the Sunchild Evidence Society."

The audience on hearing that they were to be told more about the Sunchild Evidence Society melted away even more rapidly than before, and the sermon fizzled out to an ignominious end quite unworthy of its occasion.

About half-past twelve, the service ended, and Hanky went to the robing-room to take off his vestments. Yram, the Mayor, and Panky, waited for him at the door opposite to that through which my father had been taken; while waiting, Yram scribbled off two notes in pencil, one to Dr. Downie, and another to Mrs. Humdrum, begging them to come to lunch at once—for it would be one o'clock before they could reach the Mayor's. She gave these notes to the Mayor, and bade him bring both the invited guests along with him.

The Mayor left just as Hanky was coming towards her. "This, Mayoress," he said with some asperity, "is a very serious business. It has ruined my collection. Half the people left the temple without giving anything at all. You seem," he added in a tone the significance of which could not be mistaken, "to be very fond, Mayoress, of this Mr. Higgs."

"Yes," said Yram, "I am: I always liked him, and I am sorry for him; but he is not the person I am most sorry for at this moment—— he, poor man, is not going to be horsewhipped within the next twenty minutes." And she spoke the "he" in italics.

"I do not understand you, Mayoress."

"My husband will explain, as soon as I have seen him."

"Hanky," said Panky, "you must withdraw, and apologise at once."

Hanky was not slow to do this, and when he had disavowed everything, withdrawn everything, apologised for everything, and eaten humble pie to Yram's satisfaction, she smiled graciously, and held out her hand, which Hanky was obliged to take.

"And now, Professor," she said, "let me return to your remark that this is a very serious business, and let me also claim a woman's privilege of being listened to whenever she chooses to speak. I propose, then, that we say nothing further about this matter till after luncheon. I have asked Dr. Downie and Mrs. Humdrum to join us——"

"Why Mrs. Humdrum?" interrupted Hanky none too pleasantly, for he was still furious about the duel that had just taken place between himself and his hostess.

"My dear Professor," said Yram good-humouredly, "pray say all you have to say and I will continue."

Hanky was silent.

"I have asked," resumed Yram, "Dr. Downie and Mrs. Humdrum to join us, and after luncheon we can discuss the situation or no as you may think proper. Till then let us say no more. Luncheon will be over by two o'clock or soon after, and the banquet will not begin till seven, so we shall have plenty of time."

Hanky looked black and said nothing. As for Panky he was morally in a state of collapse, and did not count.

Hardly had they reached the Mayor's house when the Mayor also arrived with Dr. Downie and Mrs. Humdrum, both of whom had seen and recognised my father in spite of his having dyed his hair. Dr. Downie had met him at supper at Mr. Thims's rooms when he had visited Bridgeford, and naturally enough had observed him closely. Mrs. Humdrum, as I have already said, had seen him more than once when he was in prison. She and Dr. Downie were talking earnestly over the strange reappearance of one whom they had believed long since dead, but Yram imposed on them the same silence that she had already imposed on the Professors.

"Professor Hanky," said she to Mrs. Humdrum, in Hanky's hearing, "is a little alarmed at my having asked you to join our secret conclave. He is not married, and does not know how well a woman can hold her tongue when she chooses. I should have told you all that passed, for I mean to follow your advice, so I thought you had better hear everything yourself."

Hanky still looked black, but he said nothing. Luncheon was promptly served, and done justice to in spite of much preoccupation; for if there is one thing that gives a better appetite than another, it is a Sunday morning's service with a charity sermon to follow. As the guests might not talk on the subject they wanted to talk about, and were in no humour to speak of anything else, they gave their whole attention to the good things that were before them, without so much as a thought about reserving themselves for the evening's banquet. Nevertheless, when luncheon was over, the Professors were in no more genial, manageable, state of mind than they had been when it began.

When the servants had left the room, Yram said to Hanky, "You saw the prisoner, and he was the man you met on Thursday night?"

"Certainly, he was wearing the forbidden dress and he had many quails in his possession. There is no doubt also that he was a foreign devil."

At this point, it being now nearly half-past two, George came in, and took a seat next to Mrs. Humdrum—between her and his mother—who of course sat at the head of the table with the Mayor opposite to her. On one side of the table sat the Professors, and on the other Dr. Downie, Mrs. Humdrum, and George, who had heard the last few words that Hanky had spoken.

CHAPTER XIX

A COUNCIL IS HELD AT THE MAYOR'S, IN THE COURSE OF WHICH GEORGE TURNS THE TABLES ON THE PROFESSORS

"NOW WHO," SAID Yram, "is this unfortunate creature to be, when he is brought up to-morrow morning, on the charge of poaching?"

"It is not necessary," said Hanky severely, "that he should be brought up for poaching. He is a foreign devil, and as such your son is bound to fling him without trial into the Blue Pool. Why bring a smaller charge when you must inflict the death penalty on a more serious one? I have already told you that I shall feel it my duty to report the matter at headquarters, unless I am satisfied that the death penalty has been inflicted."

"Of course," said George, "we must all of us do our duty, and I shall not shrink from mine—but I have arrested this man on a charge of poaching, and must give my reasons; the case cannot be dropped, and it must be heard in public. Am I, or am I not, to have the sworn depositions of both you gentlemen to the fact that the prisoner is the man you saw with quails in his possession? If you can depose to this he will be convicted, for there can be no doubt he killed the birds himself. The least penalty my father can inflict is twelve months' imprisonment with hard labour; and he must undergo this sentence before I can Blue-Pool him.

"Then comes the question whether or no he is a foreign devil. I may decide this in private, but I must have depositions on oath before I do so, and at present I have nothing but hearsay. Perhaps you gentlemen can give me the evidence I shall require, but the case is one of such importance that were the prisoner proved never so clearly to be a foreign devil, I should not Blue-Pool him till I had taken the King's pleasure concerning him. I shall rejoice, therefore, if you gentlemen can help me to sustain the charge of poaching, and thus give me legal standing-ground for deferring action which the King might regret, and which once taken cannot be recalled."

Here Yram interposed. "These points," she said, "are details. Should we not first settle, not what, but who, we shall allow the prisoner to be, when he is brought up to-morrow morning? Settle this, and the rest will settle itself. He has declared himself to be the Sunchild, and will probably do so again. I am prepared to identify him, so is Dr. Downie, so is Mrs. Humdrum, the interpreter, and doubtless my father. Others of known respectability will also do so, and his marks and measurements are sure to correspond quite sufficiently. The question is, whether all this is to be allowed to appear on evidence, or whether it is to be established, as it easily may, if we give our minds to it, that he is not the Sunchild."

"Whatever else he is," said Hanky, "he must not be the Sunchild. He must, if the charge of poaching cannot be dropped, be a poacher and a foreign devil. I was doubtless too hasty when I said that I believed I recognised the man as one who had more than once declared himself to be the Sunchild——"

"But, Hanky," interrupted Panky, "are you sure that you can swear to this man's being the man we met on Thursday night? We only saw him by firelight, and I doubt whether I should feel justified in swearing to him."

"Well, well: on second thoughts I am not sure, Panky, but what you may be right after all; it is possible that he may be what I said he was in my sermon."

"I rejoice to hear you say so," said George, "for in this case the charge of poaching will fall through. There will be no evidence against the prisoner. And I rejoice also to think that I shall have nothing to warrant me in believing him to be a foreign devil. For if he is not to be the Sunchild, and not to be your poacher, he becomes a mere monomaniac. If he apologises for having made a disturbance in the temple, and promises not to offend again, a fine, and a few days' imprisonment, will meet the case, and he may be discharged."

"I see, I see," said Hanky very angrily. "You are determined to get this man off if you can."

"I shall act," said George, "in accordance with sworn evidence, and not otherwise. Choose whether you will have the prisoner to be your poacher or no: give me your sworn depositions one way or the other, and I shall know how to act. If you depose on oath to the identity of the prisoner and your poacher, he will be convicted and imprisoned. As to his being a foreign devil, if he is the Sunchild, of course he is one; but otherwise I cannot Blue-Pool him even when his sentence is expired, without testimony deposed to me on oath in private, though no open trial is required. A case for suspicion was made out in my hearing last night, but I must have depositions on oath to all the leading facts before I can decide what my duty is. What will you swear to?"

"All this," said Hanky, in a voice husky with passion, "shall be reported to the King."

"I intend to report every word of it; but that is not the point: the question is what you gentlemen will swear to?"

"Very well. I will settle it thus. We will swear that the prisoner is the poacher we met on Thursday night, and that he is also a foreign devil: his wearing the forbidden dress; his foreign accent; the foot-tracks we found in the snow, as of one coming over from the other side; his obvious ignorance of the Afforesting Act, as shown by his having lit a fire and making no effort to conceal his quails till our permit showed him his blunder; the cock-and-bull story he told us about your orders, and that other story about his having killed a foreign devil—if these facts do not satisfy you, they will satisfy the King that the prisoner is a foreign devil as well as a poacher."

"Some of these facts," answered George, "are new to me. How do you know that the foot-tracks were made by the prisoner?"

Panky brought out his note-book and read the details he had noted.

"Did you examine the man's boots?"

"One of them, the right foot; this, with the measurements, was quite enough."

"Hardly. Please to look at both soles of my own boots; you will find that those tracks were mine. I will have the prisoner's boots examined; in the meantime let me tell you that I was up at the statues on Thursday morning, walked three or four hundred yards beyond them, over ground where there was less snow, returned over the snow, and went two or three times round them, as it is the Ranger's duty to do once a year in order to see that none of them are beginning to lean."

He showed the soles of his boots, and the Professors were obliged to admit that the tracks were his. He cautioned them as to the rest of the points on which they relied. Might they not be as mistaken, as they had just proved to be about the tracks? He could not, however, stir them from sticking to it that there was enough evidence to prove my father to be a foreign devil, and declaring their readiness to depose to the facts on oath. In the end Hanky again fiercely accused him of trying to shield the prisoner.

"You are quite right," said George, "and you will see my reasons shortly."

"I have no doubt," said Hanky significantly, "that they are such as would weigh with any man of ordinary feeling."

"I understand, then," said George, appearing to take no notice of Hanky's innuendo, "that you will swear to the facts as you have above stated them?"

"Certainly."

"Then kindly wait while I write them on the form that I have brought with me; the Mayor can administer the oath and sign your depositions. I shall then be able to leave you, and proceed with getting up the case against the prisoner."

So saying, he went to a writing-table in another part of the room, and made out the depositions.

Meanwhile the Mayor, Mrs. Humdrum, and Dr. Downie (who had each of them more than once vainly tried to take part in the above discussion) conversed eagerly in an undertone among themselves. Hanky was blind with rage, for he had a sense that he was going to be outwitted; the Mayor, Yram and Mrs. Humdrum had already seen that George thought he had all the trumps in his own hand but they did not know more. Dr. Downie was frightened, and Panky so muddled as to be *hors de combat*.

George now rejoined the Professors, and read the depositions: the Mayor administered the oath according to Erewhonian custom; the Professors signed without a word, and George then handed the document to his father to countersign.

The Mayor examined it, and almost immediately said, "My dear George, you have made a mistake; these depositions are on a form reserved for deponents who are on the point of death."

"Alas!" answered George, "there is no help for it. I did my utmost to prevent their signing. I knew that those depositions were their own death warrant, and that is why, though I was satisfied that the prisoner is a foreign devil, I had hoped to be able to shut my eyes. I can now no longer do so, and as the inevitable consequence, I must Blue-Pool both the Professors before midnight. What man of ordinary feeling would not under these circumstances have tried to dissuade them from deposing as they have done?"

By this time the Professors had started to their feet, and there was a look of horrified astonishment on the faces of all present, save that of George, who seemed quite happy.

"What monstrous absurdity is this?" shouted Hanky; "do you mean to murder us?"

"Certainly not. But you have insisted that I should do my duty, and I mean to do it. You gentlemen have now been proved to my satisfaction to have had traffic with a foreign devil; and under section 37 of the Afforesting Act, I must at once Blue-Pool any such persons without public trial."

"Nonsense, nonsense, there was nothing of the kind on our permit, and as for trafficking with this foreign devil, we spoke to him, but we neither bought nor sold. Where is the Act?"

"Here. On your permit you were referred to certain other clauses not set out therein, which might be seen at the Mayor's office. Clause 37 is as follows:—

"It is furthermore enacted that should any of his Majesty's subjects be found, after examination by the Head Ranger, to have had traffic of any kind by way of sale or barter with any foreign devil, the said Ranger, on being satisfied that such traffic has taken place, shall forthwith, with or without the assistance of his under-rangers, convey such subjects of his Majesty to the Blue-Pool, bind them, weight them, and fling them into it, without the formality of a trial, and shall report the circumstances of the case to his Majesty."

"But we never bought anything from the prisoner. What evidence can you have of this but the word of a foreign devil in such straits that he would swear to anything?"

"The prisoner has nothing to do with it. I am convinced by this receipt in Professor Panky's handwriting which states that he and you jointly purchased his kit from the prisoner, and also this bag of gold nuggets worth about £100 in silver, for the absurdly small sum of £4, 10s. in silver. I am further convinced by this handkerchief marked with Professor Hanky's name, in which was found a broken packet of dried leaves that are now at my office with the rest of the prisoner's kit."

"Then we were watched and dogged," said Hanky, "on Thursday evening."

"That, sir," replied George, "is my business, not yours."

Here Panky laid his arms on the table, buried his head in them, and burst into tears. Every one seemed aghast, but the Mayor, Yram, and Mrs. Humdrum saw that George was enjoying it all far too keenly to be serious. Dr. Downie was still frightened (for George's surface manner was Rhadamanthine) and did his utmost to console Panky. George pounded away ruthlessly at his case.

"I say nothing about your having bought quails from the prisoner and eaten them. As you justly remarked just now, there is no object in preferring a smaller charge when one must inflict the death penalty on a more serious one. Still, Professor Hanky, these are bones of the quails you ate as you sate opposite the prisoner on the side of the fire nearest Sunch'ston; these are Professor Panky's bones, with which I need not disturb him. This is your permit, which was found upon the prisoner, and which there can be no doubt you sold him, having been bribed by the offer of the nuggets for——"

"Monstrous, montrous! Infamous falsehood! Who will believe such a childish trumped-up story!"

"Who, sir, will believe anything else? You will hardly contend that you did not know the nuggets were gold, and no one will believe you mean enough to have tried to get this poor man's property out of him for a song—you knowing its value, and he not knowing the same. No one will believe that you did not know the man to be a foreign devil, or that he could hoodwink two such learned Professors so cleverly as to get their permit out of them. Obviously he seduced you into selling him your permit, and—I presume because he wanted a little of our money—he made you pay him for his kit. I am satisfied that you have not only had traffic with a foreign devil, but traffic of a singularly atrocious kind, and this being so, I shall Blue-Pool both of you as soon as I can get you up to the Pool itself. The sooner we start the better. I shall gag you, and drive you up in a close carriage as far as the road goes; from that point you can walk up, or be dragged up as you may prefer, but you will probably find walking more comfortable."

"But," said Hanky, "come what may, I must be at the banquet. I am set down to speak."

"The Mayor will explain that you have been taken somewhat suddenly unwell."

Here Yram, who had been talking quietly with her husband, Dr. Downie, and Mrs. Humdrum, motioned her son to silence.

"I feared," she said, "that difficulties might arise, though I did not foresee how seriously they would affect my guests. Let Mrs. Humdrum on our side, and Dr. Downie on that of the Professors, go into the next room and talk the matter quietly over; let us then see whether we cannot agree to be bound by their decision. I do not doubt but they will find some means of averting any catastrophe more serious—No, Professor Hanky, the doors are locked—than a little perjury in which we shall all share and share alike."

"Do what you like," said Hanky, looking for all the world like a rat caught in a trap. As he spoke he seized a knife from the table, whereupon George pulled a pair of handcuffs from his pocket and slipped them on to his wrists before he well knew what was being done to him.

"George," said the Mayor, "this is going too far. Do you mean to Blue-Pool the Professors or no?"

"Not if they will compromise. If they will be reasonable, they will not be Blue-Pooled; if they think they can have everything their own way, the eels will be at them before morning."

A voice was heard from the head of Panky which he had buried in his arms upon the table. "Co—co—co—co—compromise," it said; and the effect was so comic that every one except Hanky smiled. Meanwhile Yram had conducted Dr. Downie and Mrs. Humdrum into an adjoining room.

CHAPTER XX

MRS. HUMDRUM AND DR. DOWNIE PROPOSE A COMPROMISE, WHICH, AFTER AN AMENDMENT BY GEORGE, IS CARRIED *NEM CON.*

THEY RETURNED IN about ten minutes, and Dr. Downie asked Mrs. Humdrum to say what they had agreed to recommend.

"We think," said she very demurely, "that the strict course would be to drop the charge of poaching, and Blue-Pool both the Professors and the prisoner without delay.

"We also think that the proper thing would be to place on record that the prisoner is the Sunchild—about which neither Dr. Downie nor I have a shadow of doubt.

"These measures we hold to be the only legal ones, but at the same time we do not recommend them. We think it would offend the public conscience if it came to be known, as it certainly would, that the Sunchild was violently killed, on the very day that had seen us dedicate a temple in his honour, and perhaps at the very hour when laudatory speeches were being made about him at the Mayor's banquet; we think also that we should strain a good many points rather than Blue-Pool the Professors.

"Nothing is perfect, and Truth makes her mistakes like other people; when she goes wrong and reduces herself to such an absurdity as she has here done, those who love her must save her from herself, correct her, and rehabilitate her.

"Our conclusion, therefore, is this:—

"The prisoner must recant on oath his statement that he is the Sunchild. The interpreter must be squared, or convinced of his mistake. The Mayoress, Dr. Downie, I, and the gaoler (with the interpreter if we can manage him), must depose on oath that the prisoner is not Higgs. This must be our contribution to the rehabilitation of Truth.

"The Professors must contribute as follows: They must swear that the prisoner is not the man they met with quails in his possession on Thursday night. They must further swear that they have one or both of them known him, off and on, for many years past, as a monomaniac with Sunchildism on the brain but otherwise harmless. If they will do this, no proceedings are to be taken against them.

"The Mayor's contribution shall be to reprimand the prisoner, and order him to repeat his recantation in the new temple before the Manager and Head Cashier, and to confirm his statement on oath by kissing the reliquary containing the newly found relic.

"The Ranger and the Master of the Gaol must contribute that the prisoner's measurements, and the marks found on his body, negative all possibility of his identity with the Sunchild, and that all the hair on the covered as well as the uncovered parts of his body was found to be jet black.

"We advise further that the prisoner should have his nuggets and his kit returned to him, and that the receipt given by the Professors together with Professor Hanky's handkerchief be given back to the Professors.

"Furthermore, seeing that we should all of us like to have a quiet evening with the prisoner, we should petition the Mayor and Mayoress to ask him to meet all here present at dinner to-morrow evening, after his discharge, on the plea that Professors Hanky and Panky and Dr. Downie may give him counsel, convince him of his folly, and if possible free him henceforth from the monomania under which he now suffers.

"The prisoner shall give his word of honour, never to return to Erewhon, nor to encourage any of his countrymen to do so. After the dinner to which we hope the Mayoress will invite us, the Ranger, if the night is fair, shall escort the prisoner as far as the statues, whence he will find his own way home.

"Those who are in favour of this compromise hold up their hands."

The Mayor and Yram held up theirs. "Will you hold up yours, Professor Hanky," said George, "if I release you?"

"Yes," said Hanky with a gruff laugh, whereon George released him and he held up both his hands.

Panky did not hold up his, whereon Hanky said, "Hold up your hands, Panky, can't you? We are really very well out of it."

Panky, hardly lifting his head sobbed out, "I think we ought to have our f-f-fo-fo-four pounds ten returned to us."

"I am afraid, sir," said George, "that the prisoner must have spent the greater part of this money."

Every one smiled; indeed it was all George could do to prevent himself from laughing outright. The Mayor brought out his purse, counted the money, and handed it good-humouredly to Panky, who gratefully received it, and said he would divide it with Hanky. He then held up his hands, "But," he added, turning to his brother Professor, "so long as I live, Hanky, I will never go out anywhere again with you."

George then turned to Hanky and said, "I am afraid I must now trouble you and Professor Panky to depose on oath to the facts which Mrs. Humdrum and Dr. Downie propose you should swear to in open court to-morrow. I knew you would do so, and have brought an ordinary form, duly filled up, which declares that the prisoner is not the poacher you met on Thursday; and also, that he has been long known to both of you as a harmless monomaniac."

As he spoke he brought out depositions to the above effect which he had just written in his office; he showed the Professors that the form was this time an innocent one, whereon they made no demur to signing and swearing in the presence of the Mayor, who attested.

"The former depositions," said Hanky, "had better be destroyed at once."

"That," said George, "may hardly be, but so long as you stick to what you have just sworn to, they will not be used against you."

Hanky scowled, but knew that he was powerless and said no more.

The knowledge of what ensued did not reach me from my father. George and his mother, seeing how ill he looked, and what a shock the events of the last few days had given him, resolved that he should not know of the risk that George was about to run; they therefore said nothing to him about it. What I shall now tell, I learned on the occasion already referred to when I had the happiness to meet George. I am in some doubt whether it is more fitly told here, or when I come to the interview between him and me; on the whole, however, I suppose chronological order is least outraged by dealing with it here.

As soon as the Professors had signed the second depositions, George said, "I have not yet held up my hands, but I will hold them up if Mrs. Humdrum and Dr. Downie will approve of what I propose. Their compromise does not go far enough, for swear as we may, it is sure to get noised abroad, with the usual exaggerations, that the Sunchild has been here, and that he has been spirited away either by us, or by the sun his father. For one person whom we know of as having identified him, there will be five, of whom we know nothing, and whom we cannot square. Reports will reach the King sooner or later, and I shall be sent for. Meanwhile the Professors will be living in fear of intrigue on my part, and I, however unreasonably, shall fear the like on theirs. This should not be. I mean, therefore, on the day following my return from escorting the prisoner, to set out for the capital, see the King, and make a clean breast of the whole matter. To this end I must have the nuggets, the prisoner's kit, his receipt, Professor Hanky's handkerchief, and, of course, the two depositions just sworn to by the Professors. I hope and think that the King will pardon us all round; but whatever he may do I shall tell him everything."

Hanky was up in arms at once. "Sheer madness," he exclaimed. Yram and the Mayor looked anxious; Dr. Downie eyed George as though he were some curious creature, which he heard of but had never seen, and was rather disposed to like. Mrs. Humdrum nodded her head approvingly.

"Quite right, George," said she, "tell his Majesty everything."

Dr. Downie then said, "Your son, Mayoress, is a very sensible fellow. I will go with him, and with the Professors—for they had better come too; each will hear what the other says, and we will tell the truth, the whole truth, and nothing but the truth. I am, as you know, a *persona grata* at Court; I will say that I advised your son's action. The King has liked him ever since he was a boy, and I am not much afraid about what he will do. In public, no doubt we had better hush things up, but in private the King must be told."

Hanky fought hard for some time, but George told him that it did not matter whether he agreed or no. "You can come," he said, "or stop away, just as you please. If you come, you can hear and speak; if you do not, you will not hear, but these two depositions will speak for you. Please yourself."

"Very well," he said at last, "I suppose we had better go."

Every one having now understood what his or her part was to be, Yram said they had better shake hands all round and take a couple of hours' rest before getting ready for the banquet. George said that the Professors did not shake hands with him very cordially, but the farce was gone through. When the handshaking was over, Dr. Downie and Mrs. Humdrum left the house, and the Professors retired grumpily to their own room.

I will say here that no harm happened either to George or the Professors in consequence of his having told the King, but will reserve particulars for my concluding chapter.

CHAPTER XXI

YRAM, ON GETTING RID OF HER GUESTS, GOES TO THE PRISON TO SEE MY FATHER

YRAM DID NOT take the advice she had given her guests, but set about preparing a basket of the best cold dainties she could find, including a bottle of choice wine that she knew my father would like; thus loaded she went to the gaol, which she entered by her father's private entrance.

It was now about half-past four, so that much more must have been said and done after luncheon at the Mayor's than ever reached my father. The wonder is that he was able to collect so much. He, poor man, as soon as George left him, flung himself on to the bed that was in his cell and lay there wakeful, but not unquiet, till near the time when Yram reached the gaol.

The old gaoler came to tell him that she had come and would be glad to see him; much as he dreaded the meeting there was no avoiding it, and in a few minutes Yram stood before him.

Both were agitated, but Yram betrayed less of what she felt than my father. He could only bow his head and cover his face with his hands. Yram said, "We are old friends; take your hands from your face and let me see you. There! That is well."

She took his right hand between both hers, looked at him with eyes full of kindness, and said softly—

"You are not much changed, but you look haggard, worn, and ill; I am uneasy about you. Remember, you are among friends, who will see that no harm befalls you. There is a look in your eyes that frightens me."

As she spoke she took the wine out of her basket, and poured him out a glass, but rather to give him some little thing to distract his attention, than because she expected him to drink it—which he could not do.

She never asked him whether he found her altered, or turned the conversation ever such a little on to herself; all was for him; to soothe and comfort him, not in words alone, but in look, manner, and voice. My father knew that he could thank her best by controlling himself, and letting himself be soothed and comforted—at any rate so far as he could seem to be.

Up to this time they had been standing, but now Yram, seeing my father calmer, said, "Enough, let us sit down."

So saying she seated herself at one end of the small table that was in the cell, and motioned my father to sit opposite to her. "The light hurts you?" she said, for the sun was coming into the room. "Change places with me, I am a sun worshipper. No, we can move the table, and we can then see each other better."

This done, she said, still very softly, "And now tell me what it is all about. Why have you come here?"

"Tell me first," said my father, "what befell you after I had been taken away. Why did you not send me word when you found what had happened? or come after me? You know I should have married you at once, unless they bound me in fetters."

"I know you would; but you remember Mrs. Humdrum? Yes, I see you do. I told her everything; it was she who saved me. We thought of you, but she saw that it would not do. As I was to marry Mr. Strong, the more you were lost sight of the better, but with George ever with me I have not been able to forget you. I might have been very happy with you, but I could not have been happier than I have been ever since that short dreadful time was over. George must tell you the rest. I cannot do so. All is well. I love my husband with my whole heart and soul, and he loves me with his. As between him and me, he knows everything; George is his son, not yours; we have settled it so, though we both know otherwise; as between you and me, for this one hour, here, there is no use in pretending that you are not George's father. I have said all I need say. Now, tell me what I asked you—Why are you here?"

"I fear," said my father, set at rest by the sweetness of Yram's voice and manner—he told me he had never seen any one to compare with her except my mother—"I fear, to do as much harm now as I did before, and with as little wish to do any harm at all."

He then told her all that the reader knows, and explained how he had thought he could have gone about the country as a peasant, and seen how she herself had fared, without her, or any one, even suspecting that he was in the country.

"You say your wife is dead, and that she left you with a son—is he like George?"

"In mind and disposition, wonderfully; in appearance, no; he is dark and takes after his mother, and though he is handsome, he is not so good-looking as George."

"No one," said George's mother, "ever was, or ever will be, and he is as good as he looks."

"I should not have believed you if you had said he was not."

"That is right. I am glad you are proud of him. He irradiates the lives of every one of us."

"And the mere knowledge that he exists will irradiate the rest of mine."

"Long may it do so. Let us now talk about this morning—did you mean to declare yourself?"

"I do not know what I meant; what I most cared about was the doing what I thought George would wish to see his father do."

"You did that; but he says he told you not to say who you were."

"So he did, but I knew what he would think right. He was uppermost in my thoughts all the time."

Yram smiled, and said, "George is a dangerous person; you were both of you very foolish; one as bad as the other."

"I do not know. I do not know anything. It is beyond me; but I am at peace about it, and hope I shall do the like again to-morrow before the Mayor."

"I heartily hope you will do nothing of the kind. George tells me you have promised him to be good and to do as we bid you."

"So I will; but he will not tell me to say that I am not what I am."

"Yes, he will, and I will tell you why. If we permit you to be Higgs the Sunchild, he must either throw his own father into the Blue Pool—which he will not do—or run great risk of being thrown into it himself, for not having Blue-Pooled a foreigner. I am afraid we shall have to make you do a good deal that neither you nor we shall like."

She then told him briefly of what had passed after luncheon at her house, and what it had been settled to do, leaving George to tell the details while escorting him towards the statues on the following evening. She said that every one would be so completely in every one else's power that there was no fear of any one's turning traitor. But she said nothing about George's intention of setting out for the capital on Wednesday morning to tell the whole story to the King.

"Now," she said, when she had told him as much as was necessary, "be good, and do as you said you would."

"I will. I will deny myself, not once, nor twice, but as often as is necessary. I will kiss the reliquary, and when I meet Hanky and Panky at your table, I will be sworn brother to them—so long, that is, as George is out of hearing; for I cannot lie well to them when he is listening."

"Oh yes, you can. He will understand all about it; he enjoys falsehood as well as we all do, and has the nicest sense of when to lie and when not to do so."

"What gift can be more invaluable?"

My father, knowing that he might not have another chance of seeing Yram alone, now changed the conversation.

"I have something," he said, "for George, but he must know nothing about it till after I am gone."

As he spoke, he took from his pockets the nine small bags of nuggets that remained to him.

"But this," said Yram, "being gold, is a large sum: can you indeed spare it, and do you really wish George to have it all?"

"I shall be very unhappy if he does not, but he must know nothing about it till I am out of Erewhon."

My father then explained to her that he was now very rich, and would have brought ten times as much, if he had known of George's existence.

"Then," said Yram, musing, "if you are rich, I accept and thank you heartily on his behalf. I can see a reason for his not knowing what you are giving him at present, but it is too long to tell."

The reason was, that if George knew of this gold before he saw the King, he would be sure to tell him of it, and the King might claim it, for George would never explain that it was a gift from father to son; whereas if the King had once pardoned him, he would not be so squeamish as to open up the whole thing again with a postscript to his confession. But of this she said not a word.

My father then told her of the box of sovereigns that he had left in his saddle-bags. "They are coined," he said, "and George will have to melt them down, but he will find some way of doing this. They will be worth rather more than these nine bags of nuggets."

"The difficulty will be to get him to go down and fetch them, for it is against his oath to go far beyond the statues. If you could be taken faint and say you wanted help, he would see you to your camping ground without a word, but he would be angry if he found he had been tricked into breaking his oath in order that money might be given him. It would never do. Besides, there would not be time, for he must be back here on Tuesday night. No; if he breaks his oath he must do it with his eyes open—and he will do it later on—or I will go and fetch the money for him myself. He is in love with a grand-daughter of Mrs. Humdrum's, and this sum, together with what you are now leaving with me, will make him a well-to-do man. I have always been unhappy about his having any of the Mayor's money, and his salary was not quite enough for him to marry on. What can I say to thank you?"

"Tell me, please, about Mrs. Humdrum's grand-daughter. You like her as a wife for George?"

"Absolutely. She is just such another as her grandmother must have been. She and George have been sworn lovers ever since he was ten, and she eight. The only drawback is that her mother, Mrs. Humdrum's second daughter, married for love, and there are many children, so that there will be no money with her; but what you are leaving will make everything quite easy, for he will sell the gold at once. I am so glad about it."

"Can you ask Mrs. Humdrum to bring her grand-daughter with her to-morrow evening?"

"I am afraid not, for we shall want to talk freely at dinner, and she must not know that you are the Sunchild; she shall come to my house in the afternoon and you can see her then. You will be quite happy about her, but of course she must not know that you are her father-in-law that is to be."

"One thing more. As George must know nothing about the sovereigns, I must tell you how I will hide them. They are in a silver box, which I will bind to the bough of some trees close to my camp; or if I can find a tree with a hole in it I will drop the box into the hole. He cannot miss my camp; he has only to follow the stream that runs down from the pass till it gets near a large river, and on a small triangular patch of flat ground, he will see the ashes of my camp fire, a few yards away from the stream on his right hand as he descends. In whatever tree I may hide the box, I will strew wood ashes for some yards in a straight line towards it. I will then light another fire underneath, and glaze the tree with a knife that I have left at my camping ground. He is sure to find it."

Yram again thanked him, and then my father, to change the conversation, asked whether she thought that George really would have Blue-Pooled the Professors.

"There is no knowing," said Yram. "He is the gentlest creature living till some great provocation rouses him, and I never saw him hate and despise any one as he does the Professors. Much of what he said was merely put on, for he knew the Professors must yield. I do not like his ever having to throw any one into that horrid place, no more does he, but the Rangership is exactly the sort of thing to suit him, and the opening was too good to lose. I must now leave you, and get ready for the Mayor's banquet. We shall meet again to-morrow evening. Try and eat what I have brought you in this basket. I hope you will like the wine." She put out her hand, which my father took, and in another moment she was gone, for she saw a look in his face as though he would fain have asked her to let him once more press his lips to hers. Had he done this, without thinking about it, it is likely enough she would not have been ill pleased. But who can say?

For the rest of the evening my father was left very much to his own not too comfortable reflections. He spent part of it in posting up the notes from which, as well as from his own mouth, my story is in great part taken. The good things that Yram had left with him, and his pipe, which she had told him he might smoke quite freely, occupied another part, and by ten o'clock he went to bed.

CHAPTER XXII

MAINLY OCCUPIED WITH A VERACIOUS EXTRACT FROM A SUNCH'STONIAN JOURNAL

WHILE MY FATHER was thus wiling away the hours in his cell, the whole town was being illuminated in his honour, and not more than a couple of hundred yards off, at the Mayor's banquet, he was being extolled as a superhuman being.

The banquet, which was at the town hall, was indeed a very brilliant affair, but the little space that is left me forbids my saying more than that Hanky made what was considered the speech of the evening, and betrayed no sign of ill effects from the bad quarter of an hour which he had spent so recently. Not a trace was to be seen of any desire on his part to change his tone as regards Sunchildism—as, for example, to minimize the importance of the relic, or to remind his hearers that though the chariot and horses had undoubtedly come down from the sky and carried away my father and mother, yet that the earlier stage of the ascent had been made in a balloon. It almost seemed, so George told my father, as though he had resolved that he would speak lies, all lies, and nothing but lies.

Panky, who was also to have spoken, was excused by the Mayor on the ground that the great heat and the excitement of the day's proceedings had quite robbed him of his voice.

Dr. Downie had a jumping cat before his mental vision. He spoke quietly and sensibly, dwelling chiefly on the benefits that had already accrued to the kingdom through the abolition of the edicts against machinery, and the great developments which he foresaw as probable in the near future. He held up the Sunchild's example, and his ethical teaching, to the imitation and admiration of his hearers, but he said nothing about the miraculous element in my father's career, on which he declared that his friend Professor Hanky had already so eloquently enlarged as to make further allusion to it superfluous.

The reader knows what was to happen on the following morning. The programme concerted at the Mayor's was strictly adhered to. The following account, however, which appeared in the Sunch'ston bi-weekly newspaper two days after my father had left, was given me by George a year later, on the occasion of that interview to which I have already more than once referred. There were other accounts in other papers, but the one I am giving departs the least widely from the facts. It ran:—

"*The close of a disagreeable incident.*—Our readers will remember that on Sunday last during the solemn inauguration of the temple now dedicated to the Sunchild, an individual on the front bench of those set apart for the public suddenly interrupted Professor Hanky's eloquent sermon by declaring himself to be the Sunchild, and saying that he had come down from the sun to sanctify by his presence the glorious fane which the piety of our fellow-citizens and others has erected in his honour.

"Wild rumours obtained credence throughout the congregation to the effect that this person was none other than the Sunchild himself, and in spite of the fact that his complexion and the colour of his hair showed this to be impossible, more than one person was carried away by the excitement of the moment, and by some few points of resemblance between the stranger and the Sunchild, Under the influence of this belief, they were preparing to give him the honour which they supposed justly due to him, when to the surprise of every one he was taken into custody by the deservedly popular Ranger of the King's preserves, and in the course of the afternoon it became generally known that he had been arrested on the charge of being one of a gang of poachers who have been known for some time past to be making such havoc among the quails on the preserves.

"This offence, at all times deplored by those who desire that his Majesty shall enjoy good sport when he honours us with a visit, is doubly deplorable during the season when, on the higher parts of the preserves, the young birds are not yet able to shift for themselves; the Ranger, therefore, is indefatigable in his efforts to break up the gang, and with this end in view, for the last fortnight has been out night and day on the remoter sections of the forest—little suspecting that the marauders would venture so near Sunch'ston as it now seems they have done. It is to his extreme anxiety to detect and punish these miscreants that we must ascribe the arrest of a man, who, however foolish, and indeed guilty, he is in other respects, is innocent of the particular crime imputed to him. The circumstances that led to his arrest have reached us from an exceptionally well-informed source, and are as follows:—

"Our distinguished guests, Professors Hanky and Panky, both of them justly celebrated archæologists, had availed themselves of the opportunity afforded them by their visit to Sunch'ston, to inspect the mysterious statues at the head of the stream that comes down near this city, and which have hitherto baffled all those who have tried to ascertain their date and purpose.

"On their descent after a fatiguing day the Professors were benighted, and lost their way. Seeing the light of a small fire among some trees near them, they made towards it, hoping to be directed rightly, and found a man, respectably dressed, sitting by the fire with several brace of quails beside him, some of them plucked. Believing that in spite of his appearance, which would not have led them to suppose that he was a poacher, he must unquestionably be one, they hurriedly enquired their way, intending to leave him as soon as they had got their answer; he, however, attacked them, or made as though he would do so, and said he would show them a way which they should be in no fear of losing, whereon Professor Hanky, with a well-directed blow, felled him to the ground. The two Professors, fearing that other poachers might come to his assistance, made off as nearly as they could guess in the direction of Sunch'ston. When they had gone a mile or two onward at haphazard, they sat down under a large tree, and waited till day began to break; they then resumed their journey, and before long struck a path which led them to a spot from which they could see the towers of the new temple.

"Fatigued though they were, they waited before taking the rest of which they stood much in need, till they had reported their adventure at the Ranger's office. The Ranger was still out on the preserves, but immediately on his return on Saturday morning he read the description of the poacher's appearance and dress, about which last, however, the only remarkable feature was that it was better than a poacher might be expected to possess, and gave an air of respectability to the wearer that might easily disarm suspicion.

"The Ranger made enquiries at all the inns in Sunch'ston, and at length succeeded in hearing of a stranger who appeared to correspond with the poacher whom the Professors had seen; but the man had already left, and though the Ranger did his best to trace him he did not succeed. On Sunday morning, however, he observed the prisoner, and found that he answered the description given by the Professors; he therefore arrested him quietly in the temple, but told him that he should not take him to prison till the service was over. The man said he would come quietly inasmuch as he should easily be able to prove his innocence. In the meantime, however, he professed the utmost anxiety to hear Professor Hanky's sermon, which he said he believed would concern him nearly. The Ranger paid no attention to this, and was as much astounded as the rest of the congregation were, when immediately after one of Professor Hanky's most eloquent passages, the man started up and declared himself to be the Sunchild. On this the Ranger took him away at once, and for the man's own protection hurried him off to prison.

"Professor Hanky was so much shocked at such outrageous conduct, that for the moment he failed to recognise the offender; after a few seconds, however, he grasped the situation, and knew him to be one who on previous occasions, near Bridgeford, had done what he was now doing. It seems that he is notorious in the neighbourhood of Bridgeford, as a monomaniac who is so deeply impressed with the beauty of the Sunchild's character—and we presume also of his own—as to believe that he is himself the Sunchild.

"Recovering almost instantly from the shock the interruption had given him, the learned Professor calmed his hearers by acquainting them with the facts of the case, and continued his sermon to the delight of all who heard it. We should say, however, that the gentleman who twenty years ago instructed the Sunchild in the Erewhonian language, was so struck with some few points of resemblance between the stranger and his former pupil, that he acclaimed him, and was removed forcibly by the vergers.

"On Monday morning the prisoner was brought up before the Mayor. We cannot say whether it was the sobering effect of prison walls, or whether he had been drinking before he entered the temple, and had now had time enough to recover himself—at any rate for some reason or other he was abjectly penitent when his case came on for hearing. The charge of poaching was first gone into, but was immediately disposed of by the evidence of the two Professors, who stated that the prisoner bore no resemblance to the poacher they had seen, save that he was about the same height and age, and was respectably dressed.

"The charge of disturbing the congregation by declaring himself the Sunchild was then proceeded with, and unnecessary as it may appear to be, it was thought advisable to prevent all possibility of the man's assertion being accepted by the ignorant as true, at some later date, when those who could prove its falsehood were no longer living. The prisoner, therefore, was removed to his cell, and there measured by the Master of the Gaol, and the Ranger in the presence of the Mayor, who attested the accuracy of the measurements. Not one single one of them corresponded with those recorded of the Sunchild himself, and a few marks such as moles, and permanent scars on the Sunchild's body were not found on the prisoner's.

Furthermore the prisoner was shaggy-breasted, with much coarse jet black hair on the fore-arms and from the knees downwards, whereas the Sunchild had little hair save on his head, and what little there was, was fine, and very light in colour.

"Confronted with these discrepancies, the gentleman who had taught the Sunchild our language was convinced of his mistake, though he still maintained that there was some superficial likeness between his former pupil and the prisoner. Here he was confirmed by the Master of the Gaol, the Mayoress, Mrs. Humdrum, and Professors Hanky and Panky, who all of them could see what the interpreter meant, but denied that the prisoner could be mistaken for the Sunchild for more than a few seconds. No doubt the prisoner's unhappy delusion has been fostered, if not entirely caused, by his having been repeatedly told that he was like the Sunchild. The celebrated Dr. Downie, who well remembers the Sunchild, was also examined, and gave his evidence with so much convincing detail as to make it unnecessary to call further witnesses.

"It having been thus once for all officially and authoritatively placed on record that the prisoner was not the Sunchild, Professors Hanky and Panky then identified him as a well known monomaniac on the subject of Sunchildism, who in other respects was harmless. We withhold his name and place of abode, out of consideration for the well known and highly respectable family to which he belongs. The prisoner admitted with much contrition that he had made a disturbance in the temple, but pleaded that he had been carried away by the eloquence of Professor Hanky; he promised to avoid all like offence in future, and threw himself on the mercy of the court.

"The Mayor, unwilling that Sunday's memorable ceremony should be the occasion of a serious punishment to any of those who took part in it, reprimanded the prisoner in a few severe but not unkindly words, inflicted a fine of forty shillings, and ordered that the prisoner should be taken directly to the temple, where he should confess his folly to the Manager and Head Cashier, and confirm his words by kissing the reliquary in which the newly found relic has been placed. The prisoner being unable to pay the fine, some of the ladies and gentlemen in court kindly raised the amount amongst them, in pity for the poor creature's obvious contrition, rather than see him sent to prison for a month in default of payment.

"The prisoner was then conducted to the temple, followed by a considerable number of people. Strange to say, in spite of the overwhelming evidence that they had just heard, some few among the followers, whose love of the marvellous overpowered their reason, still maintained that the prisoner was the Sunchild. Nothing could be more decorous than the prisoner's behaviour when, after hearing the recantation that was read out to him by the Manager, he signed the document with his name and address, which we again withhold, and kissed the reliquary in confirmation of his words.

"The Mayor then declared the prisoner to be at liberty. When he had done so he said, 'I strongly urge you to place yourself under my protection for the present, that you may be freed from the impertinent folly and curiosity of some whose infatuation might lead you from that better mind to which I believe you are now happily restored. I wish you to remain for some few hours secluded in the privacy of my own study, where Dr. Downie and the two excellent Professors will administer that ghostly counsel to you, which will be likely to protect you from any return of your unhappy delusion.'

"The man humbly bowed assent, and was taken by the Mayor's younger sons to the Mayor's own house, where he was duly cared for. About midnight, when all was quiet, he was conducted to the outskirts of the town towards Clearwater, and furnished with enough money to provide for his more pressing necessities till he could reach some relatives who reside three or four days' walk down on the road towards the capital. He desired the man who accompanied him to repeat to the Mayor his heartfelt thanks for the forbearance and generosity with which he had been treated. The remembrance of this, he said, should be ever present with him, and he was confident would protect him if his unhappy monomania showed any signs of returning.

"Let us now, however, remind our readers that the poacher who threatened Professors Hanky and Panky's life on Thursday evening last is still at large. He is evidently a man of desperate character, and it is to be hoped that our fellow-citizens will give immediate information at the Ranger's office if they see any stranger in the neighbourhood of the preserves whom they may have reasonable grounds for suspecting.

"*P.S.*—As we are on the point of going to press we learn that a dangerous lunatic, who has been for some years confined in the Clearwater asylum, succeeded in escaping on the night of Wednesday last, and it is surmised with much probability, that this was the man who threatened the two Professors on Thursday evening. His being alone, his having dared to light a fire, probably to cook quails which he had been driven to kill from stress of hunger, the respectability of his dress, and the fury with which he would have attacked the two Professors single-handed, but for Professor Hanky's presence of mind in giving him a knock-down blow, all point in the direction of thinking that he was no true poacher, but—what is even more dangerous—a madman at large. We have not received any particulars as to the man's appearance, nor the clothes he was wearing, but we have little doubt that these will confirm the surmise to which we now give publicity. If it is correct it becomes doubly incumbent on all our fellow-citizens to be both on the watch, and on their guard.

"We may add that the man was fully believed to have taken the direction towards the capital; hence no attempts were made to look for him in the neighbourhood of Sunch'ston, until news of the threatened attack on the Professors led the keeper of the asylum to feel confident that he had hitherto been on a wrong scent."

CHAPTER XXIII

MY FATHER IS ESCORTED TO THE MAYOR'S HOUSE, AND IS INTRODUCED TO A FUTURE DAUGHTER-IN-LAW

MY FATHER SAID he was followed to the Mayor's house by a good many people, whom the Mayor's sons in vain tried to get rid of. One or two of these still persisted in saying he was the Sunchild—whereon another said, "But his hair is black."

"Yes," was the answer, "but a man can dye his hair, can he not? look at his blue eyes and his eye-lashes?"

My father was doubting whether he ought not to again deny his identity out of loyalty to the Mayor and Yram, when George's next brother said, "Pay no attention to them, but step out as fast as you can." This settled the matter, and in a few minutes they were at the Mayor's, where the young men took him into the study; the elder said with a smile, "We should like to stay and talk to you, but my mother said we were not to do so." Whereon they left him much to his regret, but he gathered rightly that they had not been officially told who he was, and were to be left to think what they liked, at any rate for the present.

In a few minutes the Mayor entered, and going straight up to my father shook him cordially by the hand.

"I have brought you this morning's paper," said he. "You will find a full report of Professor Hanky's sermon, and of the speeches at last night's banquet. You see they pass over your little interruption with hardly a word, but I dare say they will have made up their minds about it all by Thursday's issue."

He laughed as he produced the paper—which my father brought home with him, and without which I should not have been able to report Hanky's sermon as fully as I have done. But my father could not let things pass over thus lightly.

"I thank you," he said, "but I have much more to thank you for, and know not how to do it."

"Can you not trust me to take everything as said?"

"Yes, but I cannot trust myself not to be haunted if I do not say—or at any rate try to say—some part of what I ought to say."

"Very well; then I will say something myself. I have a small joke, the only one I ever made, which I inflict periodically upon my wife. You, and I suppose George, are the only two other people in the world to whom it can ever be told; let me see, then, if I cannot break the ice with it. It is this. Some men have twin sons; George in this topsy turvey world of ours has twin fathers—you by luck, and me by cunning. I see you smile; give me your hand."

My father took the Mayor's hand between both his own. "Had I been in your place," he said, "I should be glad to hope that I might have done as you did."

"And I," said the Mayor, more readily than might have been expected of him, "fear that if I had been in yours—I should have made it the proper thing for you to do. There! The ice is well broken, and now for business. You will lunch with us, and dine in the evening. I have given it out that you are of good family, so there is nothing odd in this. At lunch you will not be the Sunchild, for my younger children will be there; at dinner all present will know who you are, so we shall be free as soon as the servants are out of the room.

"I am sorry, but I must send you away with George as soon as the streets are empty—say at midnight—for the excitement is too great to allow of your staying longer. We must keep your rug and the things you cook with, but my wife will find you what will serve your turn. There is no moon, so you and George will camp out as soon as you get well on to the preserves; the weather is hot, and you will neither of you take any harm. To-morrow by mid-day you will be at the statues, where George must bid you good-bye, for he must be at Sunch'ston to-morrow night. You will doubtless get safely home; I wish with all my heart that I could hear of your having done so, but this, I fear, may not be."

"So be it," replied my father, "but there is something I should yet say. The Mayoress has no doubt told you of some gold, coined and uncoined, that I am leaving for George. She will also have told you that I am rich; this being so, I should have brought him much more, if I had known that there was any such person. You have other children; if you leave him anything, you will be taking it away from your own flesh and blood; if you leave him nothing, it will be a slur upon him. I must therefore send you enough gold to provide for George as your other children will be provided for; you can settle it upon him at once, and make it clear that the settlement is instead of provision for him by will. The difficulty is in the getting the gold into Erewhon, and until it is actually here, he must know nothing about it."

I have no space for the discussion that followed. In the end it was settled that George was to have £2000 in gold, which the Mayor declared to be too much, and my father too little. Both, however, were agreed that Erewhon would before long be compelled to enter into relations with foreign countries, in which case the value of gold would decline so much as to make £2000 worth little more than it would be in England. The Mayor proposed to buy land with it, which he would hand over to George as a gift from himself, and this my father at once acceded to. All sorts of questions such as will occur to the reader were raised and settled, but I must beg him to be content with knowing that everything was arranged with the good sense that two such men were sure to bring to bear upon it.

The getting the gold into Erewhon was to be managed thus. George was to know nothing, but a promise was to be got from him that at noon on the following New Year's day, or whatever day might be agreed upon, he would be at the statues, where either my father or myself would meet him, spend a couple of hours with him, and then return. Whoever met George was to bring the gold as though it were for the Mayor, and George could be trusted to be human enough to bring it down, when he saw that it would be left where it was if he did not do so.

"He will kick a good deal," said the Mayor, "at first, but he will come round in the end."

Luncheon was now announced. My father was feeling faint and ill; more than once during the forenoon he had a return of the strange giddiness and momentary loss of memory which had already twice attacked him, but he had recovered in each case so quickly that no one had seen he was unwell. He, poor man, did not yet know what serious brain exhaustion these attacks betokened, and finding himself in his usual health as soon as they passed away, set them down as simply effects of fatigue and undue excitement.

George did not lunch with the others. Yram explained that he had to draw up a report which would occupy him till dinner time. Her three other sons, and her three lovely daughters, were there. My father was delighted with all of them, for they made friends with him at once. He had feared that he would have been disgraced in their eyes, by his having just come from prison, but whatever they may have thought, no trace of anything but a little engaging timidity on the girls' part was to be seen. The two elder boys—or rather young men, for they seemed fully grown, though, like George, not yet bearded—treated him as already an old acquaintance, while the youngest, a lad of fourteen, walked straight up to him, put out his hand, and said, "How do you do, sir?" with a pretty blush that went straight to my father's heart.

"These boys," he said to Yram aside, "who have nothing to blush for—see how the blood mantles into their young cheeks, while I, who should blush at being spoken to by them, cannot do so."

"Do not talk nonsense," said Yram, with mock severity.

But it was no nonsense to my poor father. He was awed at the goodness and beauty with which he found himself surrounded. His thoughts were too full of what had been, what was, and what was yet to be, to let him devote himself to these young people as he would dearly have liked to do. He could only look at them, wonder at them, fall in love with them, and thank heaven that George had been brought up in such a household.

When luncheon was over, Yram said, "I will now send you to a room where you can lie down and go to sleep for a few hours. You will be out late tonight, and had better rest while you can. Do you remember the drink you taught us to make of corn parched and ground? You used to say you liked it. A cup shall be brought to your room at about five, for you must try and sleep till then. If you notice a little box on the dressing-table of your room, you will open it or no as you like. About half-past five there will be a visitor, whose name you can guess, but I shall not let her stay long with you. Here comes the servant to take you to your room." On this she smiled, and turned somewhat hurriedly away.

My father on reaching his room went to the dressing-table, where he saw a small unpretending box, which he immediately opened. On the top was a paper with the words, "Look—say nothing—forget." Beneath this was some cotton wool, and then—the two buttons and the lock of his own hair, that he had given Yram when he said good-bye to her.

The ghost of the lock that Yram had then given him rose from the dead, and smote him as with a whip across the face. On what dust-heap had it not been thrown how many long years ago? Then she had never forgotten him? to have been remembered all these years by such a woman as that, and never to have heeded it—never to have found out what she was though he had seen her day after day for months. Ah! but she was then still budding. That was no excuse. If a lovable woman—aye, or any woman—has loved a man, even though he cannot marry her, or even wish to do so, at any rate let him not forget her—and he had forgotten Yram as completely until the last few days, as though he had never seen her. He took her little missive, and under "Look," he wrote, "I have;" under "Say nothing," "I will;" under "forget," "never." "And I never shall," he said to himself, as he replaced the box upon the table. He then lay down to rest upon the bed, but he could get no sleep.

When the servant brought him his imitation coffee—an imitation so successful that Yram made him a packet of it to replace the tea that he must leave behind him—he rose and presently came downstairs into the drawing-room, where he found Yram and Mrs. Humdrum's grand-daughter, of whom I will say nothing, for I have never seen her, and know nothing about her, except that my father found her a sweet-looking girl, of graceful figure and very attractive expression. He was quite happy about her, but she was too young and shy to make it possible for him to do more than admire her appearance, and take Yram's word for it that she was as good as she looked.

CHAPTER XXIV

AFTER DINNER, DR. DOWNIE AND THE PROFESSORS WOULD BE GLAD TO KNOW WHAT IS TO BE DONE ABOUT SUNCHILDISM

IT WAS ABOUT six when George's *fiancée* left the house, and as soon as she had done so, Yram began to see about the rug and the best substitutes she could find for the billy and pannikin. She had a basket packed with all that my father and George would want to eat and drink while on the preserves, and enough of everything, except meat, to keep my father going till he could reach the shepherd's hut of which I have already spoken. Meat would not keep, and my father could get plenty of flappers—*i.e.* ducks that cannot yet fly—when he was on the river-bed down below.

The above preparations had not been made very long before Mrs. Humdrum arrived, followed presently by Dr. Downie and in due course by the Professors, who were still staying in the house. My father remembered Mrs. Humdrum's good honest face, but could not bring Dr. Downie to his recollection till the Doctor told him when and where they had met, and then he could only very uncertainly recall him, though he vowed that he could now do so perfectly well.

"At any rate," said Hanky, advancing towards him with his best Bridgeford manner, "you will not have forgotten meeting my brother Professor and myself."

"It has been rather a forgetting sort of a morning," said my father demurely, "but I can remember that much, and am delighted to renew my acquaintance with both of you."

As he spoke he shook hands with both Professors.

George was a little late, but when he came, dinner was announced. My father sat on Yram's right-hand, Dr. Downie on her left. George was next my father, with Mrs. Humdrum opposite to him. The Professors sat one on either side of the Mayor. During dinner the conversation turned almost entirely on my father's flight, his narrow escape from drowning, and his adventures on his return to England; about these last my father was very reticent, for he said nothing about his book, and antedated his accession of wealth by some fifteen years, but as he walked up towards the statues with George he told him everything.

My father repeatedly tried to turn the conversation from himself, but Mrs. Humdrum and Yram wanted to know about Nna Haras, as they persisted in calling my mother—how she endured her terrible experiences in the balloon, when she and my father were married, all about my unworthy self, and England generally. No matter how often he began to ask questions about the Nosnibors and other old acquaintances, both the ladies soon went back to his own adventures. He succeeded, however, in learning that Mr. Nosnibor was dead, and Zulora, an old maid of the most unattractive kind, who had persistently refused to accept Sunchildism, while Mrs. Nosnibor was the recipient of honours hardly inferior to those conferred by the people at large on my father and mother, with whom, indeed, she believed herself to have frequent interviews by way of visionary revelations. So intolerable were these revelations to Zulora, that a separate establishment had been provided for her. George said to my father quietly—"Do you know I begin to think that Zulora must be rather a nice person."

"Perhaps," said my father grimly, "but my wife and I did not find it out."

When the ladies left the room, Dr. Downie took Yram's seat, and Hanky Dr. Downie's; the Mayor took Mrs. Humdrum's, leaving my father, George, and Panky, in their old places. Almost immediately, Dr. Downie said, "And now, Mr. Higgs, tell us, as a man of the world, what we are to do about Sunchildism?"

My father smiled at this. "You know, my dear sir, as well as I do, that the proper thing would be to put me back in prison, and keep me there till you can send me down to the capital. You should eat your oaths of this morning, as I would eat mine; tell every one here who I am; let them see that my hair has been dyed; get all who knew me when I was here before to come and see me; appoint an unimpeachable committee to examine the record of my marks and measurements, and compare it with those of my own body. You should let me be seen in every town at which I lodged on my way down, and tell people that you had made a mistake. When you get to the capital, hand me over to the King's tender mercies and say that our oaths were only taken this morning to prevent a ferment in the town. I will play my part very willingly. The King can only kill me, and I should die like a gentleman."

"They will not do it," said George quietly to my father, "and I am glad of it."

He was right. "This," said Dr. Downie, "is a counsel of perfection. Things have gone too far, and we are flesh and blood. What would those who in your country come nearest to us Musical Bank Managers do if they found they had made such a mistake as we have, and dared not own it?"

"Do not ask me," said my father; "the story is too long, and too terrible."

"At any rate, then, tell us what you would have us do that is within our reach."

"I have done you harm enough, and if I preach, as likely as not I shall do more."

Seeing, however, that Dr. Downie was anxious to hear what he thought, my father said—

"Then I must tell you. Our religion sets before us an ideal which we all cordially accept, but it also tells us of marvels like your chariot and horses, which we most of us reject. Our best teachers insist on the ideal, and keep the marvels in the background. If they could say outright that our age has outgrown them, they would say so, but this they may not do; nevertheless they contrive to let their opinions be sufficiently well known, and their hearers are content with this.

"We have others who take a very different course, but of these I will not speak. Roughly, then, if you cannot abolish me altogether, make me a peg on which to hang all your own best ethical and spiritual conceptions. If you will do this, and wriggle out of that wretched relic, with that not less wretched picture—if you will make me out to be much better and abler than I was, or ever shall be, Sunchildism may serve your turn for many a long year to come. Otherwise it will tumble about your heads before you think it will.

"Am I to go on or stop?"

"Go on," said George softly. That was enough for my father, so on he went.

"You are already doing part of what I wish. I was delighted with the two passages I heard on Sunday, from what you call the Sunchild's Sayings. I never said a word of either passage; I wish I had; I wish I could say anything half so good. And I have read a pamphlet by President Gurgoyle, which I liked extremely; but I never said what he says I did. Again, I wish I had. Keep to this sort of thing, and I will be as good a Sunchildist as any of you. But you must bribe some thief to steal that relic, and break it up to mend the roads with; and——for I believe that here as elsewhere fires sometimes get lighted through the carelessness of a workman—set the most careless workman you can find to do a plumbing job near that picture."

Hanky looked black at this, and George trod lightly on my father's toe, but he told me that my father's face was innocence itself.

"These are hard sayings," said Dr. Downie.

"I know they are." replied my father, "and I do not like saying them, but there is no royal road to unlearning, and you have much to unlearn. Still, you Musical Bank people bear witness to the fact that beyond the kingdoms of this world there is another, within which the writs of this world's kingdoms do not run. This is the great service which our church does for us in England, and hence many of us uphold it, though we have no sympathy with the party now dominant within it. 'Better,' we think, 'a corrupt church than none at all.' Moreover, those who in my country would step into the church's shoes are as corrupt as the church, and more exacting. They are also more dangerous, for the masses distrust the church, and are on their guard against aggression, whereas they do not suspect the doctrinaires and faddists, who, if they could, would interfere in every concern of our lives.

"Let me return to yourselves. You Musical Bank Managers are very much such a body of men as your country needs—but when I was here before you had no figurehead; I have unwittingly supplied you with one, and it is perhaps because you saw this, that you good people of Bridgeford took up with me. Sunchildism is still young and plastic; if you will let the cock-and-bull stories about me tacitly drop, and invent no new ones, beyond saying what a delightful person I was, I really cannot see why I should not do for you as well as any one else.

"There. What I have said is nine-tenths of it rotten and wrong, but it is the most practicable rotten and wrong that I can suggest, seeing into what a rotten and wrong state of things you have drifted. And now, Mr. Mayor, do you not think we may join the Mayoress and Mrs. Humdrum?"

"As you please, Mr. Higgs," answered the Mayor.

"Then let us go, for I have said too much already, and your son George tells me that we must be starting shortly."

As they were leaving the room Panky sidled up to my father and said, "There is a point, Mr. Higgs, which you can settle for me, though I feel pretty certain how you will settle it. I think that a corruption has crept into the text of the very beautiful—"

At this moment, as my father, who saw what was coming, was wondering what in the world he could say, George came up to him and said, "Mr. Higgs, my mother wishes me to take you down into the storeroom, to make sure that she has put everything for you as you would like it." On this my father said he would return directly and answer what he knew would be Panky's question.

When Yram had shown what she had prepared—all of it, of course, faultless—she said, "And now, Mr. Higgs, about our leave-taking. Of course we shall both of us feel much. I shall; I know you will; George will have a few more hours with you than the rest of us, but his time to say good-bye will come, and it will be painful to both of you. I am glad you came—I am glad you have seen George, and George you, and that you took to one another. I am glad my husband has seen you; he has spoken to me about you very warmly, for he has taken to you much as George did. I am very, very glad to have seen you myself, and to have learned what became of you—and of your wife. I know you wish well to all of us; be sure that we all of us wish most heartily well to you and yours. I sent for you and George, because I could not say all this unless we were alone; it is all I can do," she said, with a smile, "to say it now."

Indeed it was, for the tears were in her eyes all the time, as they were also in my father's.

"Let this," continued Yram, "be our leave-taking—for we must have nothing like a scene upstairs. Just shake hands with us all, say the usual conventional things, and make it as short as you can; but I could not bear to send you away without a few warmer words than I could have said when others were in the room."

"May heaven bless you and yours," said my father, "for ever and ever."

"That will do," said George gently. "Now, both of you shake hands, and come upstairs with me."

————

When all three of them had got calm, for George had been moved almost as much as his father and mother, they went upstairs, and Panky came for his answer. "You are very possibly right," said my father—"the version you hold to be corrupt is the one in common use amongst ourselves, but it is only a translation, and very possibly only a translation of a translation, so that it may perhaps have been corrupted before it reached us."

"That," said Panky, "will explain everything," and he went contentedly away.

My father talked a little aside with Mrs. Humdrum about her grand-daughter and George, for Yram had told him that she knew all about the attachment, and then George, who saw that my father found the greatest difficulty in maintaining an outward calm, said, "Mr. Higgs, the streets are empty; we had better go."

My father did as Yram had told him; shook hands with every one, said all that was usual and proper as briefly as he could, and followed George out of the room. The Mayor saw them to the door, and saved my father from embarrassment by saying, "Mr. Higgs, you and I understand one another too well to make it necessary for us to say so. Good-bye to you, and may no ill befall you ere you get home."

My father grasped his hand in both his own. "Again," he said, "I can say no more than that I thank you from the bottom of my heart."

As he spoke he bowed his head, and went out with George into the night.

CHAPTER XXV

GEORGE ESCORTS MY FATHER TO THE STATUES; THE TWO THEN PART

THE STREETS WERE quite deserted as George had said they would be, and very dark, save for an occasional oil lamp.

"As soon as we can get within the preserves," said George, "we had better wait till morning. I have a rug for myself as well as for you."

"I saw you had two," answered my father; "you must let me carry them both; the provisions are much the heavier load."

George fought as hard as a dog would do, till my father said that they must not quarrel during the very short time they had to be together. On this George gave up one rug meekly enough, and my father yielded about the basket and the other rug.

It was about half-past eleven when they started, and it was after one before they reached the preserves. For the first mile from the town they were not much hindered by the darkness, and my father told George about his book and many another matter; he also promised George to say nothing about this second visit. Then the road became more rough, and when it dwindled away to be a mere lane—becoming presently only a foot track—they had to mind their footsteps, and got on but slowly. The night was starlit, and warm, considering that they were more than three thousand feet above the sea, but it was very dark, so that my father was well enough pleased when George showed him the white stones that marked the boundary, and said they had better soon make themselves as comfortable as they could till morning.

"We can stay here," he said, "till half-past three, there will be a little daylight then; we will rest half an hour for breakfast at about five, and by noon we shall be at the statues, where we will dine."

This being settled, George rolled himself up in his rug, and in a few minutes went comfortably off to sleep. Not so my poor father. He wound up his watch, wrapped his rug round him, and lay down; but he could get no sleep. After such a day, and such an evening, how could any one have slept?

About three the first signs of dawn began to show, and half an hour later my father could see the sleeping face of his son—whom it went to his heart to wake. Nevertheless he woke him, and in a few minutes the two were on their way—George as fresh as a lark—my poor father intent on nothing so much as on hiding from George how ill and unsound in body and mind he was feeling.

They walked on, saying but little, till at five by my father's watch George proposed a halt for breakfast. The spot he chose was a grassy oasis among the trees, carpeted with subalpine flowers, now in their fullest beauty, and close to a small stream that here came down from a side valley. The freshness of the morning air, the extreme beauty of the place, the lovely birds that flitted from tree to tree, the exquisite shapes and colours of the flowers, still dew-bespangled, and above all, the tenderness with which George treated him, soothed my father, and when he and George had lit a fire and made some hot corn-coffee—with a view to which Yram had put up a bottle of milk—he felt so much restored as to look forward to the rest of his journey without alarm. Moreover he had nothing to carry, for George had left his own rug at the place where they had slept, knowing that he should find it on his return; he had therefore insisted on carrying my father's. My father fought as long as he could, but he had to give in.

"Now tell me," said George, glad to change the subject, "what will those three men do about what you said to them last night? Will they pay any attention to it?"

My father laughed. "My dear George, what a question—I do not know them well enough."

"Oh, yes, you do. At any rate say what you think most likely."

"Very well. I think Dr. Downie will do much as I said. He will not throw the whole thing over, through fear of schism, loyalty to a party from which he cannot well detach himself, and because he does not think that the public is quite tired enough of its toy. He will neither preach nor write against it, but he will live lukewarmly against it, and this is what the Hankys hate. They can stand either hot or cold, but they are afraid of lukewarm. In England Dr. Downie would be a Broad Churchman."

"Do you think we shall ever get rid of Sunchildism altogether?"

"If they stick to the cock-and-bull stories they are telling now, and rub them in, as Hanky did on Sunday, it may go, and go soon. It has taken root too quickly and easily; and its top is too heavy for its roots; still there are so many chances in its favour that it may last a long time."

"And how about Hanky?"

"He will brazen it out, relic, chariot, and all: and he will welcome more relics and more cock-and-bull stories; his single eye will be upon his own aggrandisement and that of his order. Plausible, unscrupulous, heartless scoundrel that he is, he will play for the queen and the women of the court, as Dr. Downie will play for the king and the men. He and his party will sleep neither night nor day, but they will have one redeeming feature—whoever they may deceive, they will not deceive themselves. They believe every one else to be as bad as they are, and see no reason why they should not push their own wares in the way of business. Hanky is everything that we in England rightly or wrongly believe a typical Jesuit to be."

"And Panky—what about him?"

"Panky must persuade himself of his own lies, before he is quite comfortable about telling them to other people. Hanky keeps Hanky well out of it; Panky must have a base of operations in Panky. Hanky will lead him by the nose, bit by bit, for his is the master spirit. In England Panky would be what we call an extreme ritualist."

"Then the real battle will be between Hanky and Dr. Downie. Which will carry the day?"

"For the present, probably Hanky. He is the more vigilant and energetic; in this case Sunchildism will have to go, and I am afraid your whole Musical Bank system will be swept away along with it."

"And why not?"

"Because, my dear boy, though false in the letter, if good counsels prevail, it may be made true enough in spirit. If it were to go, its place would be soon filled by men who would be as false in letter as the others were, and much more false in spirit. You want a heart to check your head, and a head to check your heart. As in our English body politic there are two parties opposed to one another, neither of which can thrive if the other is unduly weakened, so in our spiritual and intellectual world two parties more or less antagonistic are equally necessary. Those who are at the head of science provide us with the one party; those whom we call our churchmen are the other. Both are corrupt, but we can spare neither, for each checks as far as it can the corruptions of the other."

"Then you would have us uphold Sunchildism, knowing it to be untrue?"

"Do what you will, you will not get perfect truth. And if you can follow the lead which I believe Dr. Downie will give you, that is to say, get rid of cock-and-bull stories, idealise my unworthy self, and, as I said last night, make me a peg on which to hang your own best thoughts—Sunchildism will be as near truth as anything you are likely to get. But if Hankyism triumphs, come what may you must get rid of it, for he and his school will tamper with the one sure and everlasting word of God revealed to us by human experience. He who plays fast and loose with this is as one who would forge God's signature to a cheque drawn on God's own bank."

"Are we to foster the belief that it was indeed the Sunchild who interrupted Hanky's sermon?"

"Yes, where you safely can, but not otherwise; and commit the facts to writing as soon as you can find time. Do nothing to jeopardise your own safety; you can do more by perfunctory acquiescence than by open dissent. And tell those friends whom you can trust, what these my parting words to you have been. But above all I charge you solemnly, do nothing to jeopardise your own safety; you cannot play into Hanky's hands more certainly than by risking this. Think how he and Panky would rejoice, and how Dr. Downie would grieve. Be wise and wary; bide your time; do what you prudently can, and you will find you can do much; try to do more, and you will do nothing. Be guided by the Mayor, by your mother—and by that dear old lady whose grandson you will—"

"Then they have told you," interrupted the youth, blushing scarlet.

"My dearest boy, of course they have, and I have seen her, and am head over ears in love with her myself."

He was all smiles and blushes, and vowed for a few minutes that it was a shame of them to tell me, but presently he said—

"Then you like her?"

"Rather!" said my father vehemently, and shaking George by the hand. But he said nothing about the nuggets and the sovereigns, knowing that Yram did not wish him to do so. Neither did George say anything about his determination to start for the capital in the morning, and make a clean breast of everything to the King. So soon does it become necessary even for those who are most cordially attached to hide things from one another. My father, however, was made comfortable by receiving a promise from the youth that he would take no step of which the persons he had named would disapprove.

When once Mrs. Humdrum's grand-daughter had been introduced there was no more talking about Hanky and Panky; for George began to bubble over with the subject that was nearest his heart, and how much he feared that it would be some time yet before he could be married. Many a story did he tell of his early attachment and of its course for the last ten years, but my space will not allow me to inflict one of them on the reader. My father saw that the more he listened and sympathised and encouraged, the fonder George became of him, and this was all he cared about.

Thus did they converse hour after hour. They passed the Blue Pool, without seeing it or even talking about it for more than a minute. George kept an eye on the quails and declared them fairly plentiful and strong on the wing, but nothing now could keep him from pouring out his whole heart about Mrs. Humdrum's grand-daughter, until towards noon they caught sight of the statues, and a halt was made which gave my father the first pang he had felt that morning, for he knew that the statues would be the beginning of the end.

There was no need to light a fire, for Yram had packed for them two bottles of a delicious white wine, something like White Capri, which went admirably with the many more solid good things that she had provided for them. As soon as they had finished a hearty meal my father said to George, "You must have my watch for a keepsake; I see you are not wearing my boots. I fear you did not find them comfortable, but I am glad you have not got them on, for I have set my heart on keeping yours."

"Let us settle about the boots first. I rather fancied that that was why you put me off when I wanted to get my own back again; and then I thought I should like yours for a keepsake, so I put on another pair last night, and they are nothing like so comfortable as yours were."

"Now I wonder," said my father to me, "whether this was true, or whether it was only that dear fellow's pretty invention; but true or false I was as delighted as he meant me to be."

I asked George about this when I saw him, and he confessed with an ingenuous blush that my father's boots had hurt him, and that he had never thought of making a keepsake of them, till my father's words stimulated his invention.

As for the watch, which was only a silver one, but of the best make, George protested for a time, but when he had yielded, my father could see that he was overjoyed at getting it; for watches, though now permitted, were expensive and not in common use.

Having thus bribed him, my father broached the possibility of his meeting him at the statues on that day twelvemonth, but of course saying nothing about why he was so anxious that he should come.

"I will come," said my father, "not a yard farther than the statues, and if I cannot come I will send your brother. And I will come at noon; but it is possible that the river down below may be in fresh, and I may not be able to hit off the day, though I will move heaven and earth to do so. Therefore if I do not meet you on the day appointed, do your best to come also at noon on the following day. I know how inconvenient this will be for you, and will come true to the day if it is possible."

To my father's surprise, George did not raise so many difficulties as he had expected. He said it might be done, if neither he nor my father were to go beyond the statues. "And difficult as it will be for you," said George, "you had better come a second day if necessary, as I will, for who can tell what might happen to make the first day impossible?"

"Then," said my father, "we shall be spared that horrible feeling that we are parting without hope of seeing each other again. I find it hard enough to say good-bye even now, but I do not know how I could have faced it if you had not agreed to our meeting again."

"The day fixed upon will be our XXI. i. 3, and the hour noon as near as may be?"

"So. Let me write it down: 'XXI. i. 3, *i.e.* our December 9, 1891, I am to meet George at the statues, at twelve o'clock, and if he does not come, I am to be there again on the following day.' "

In like manner, George wrote down what he was to do: "XXI. i. 3, or failing this XXI. i. 4. Statues. Noon."

"This," he said, "is a solemn covenant, is it not?"

"Yes," said my father, "and may all good omens attend it!"

The words were not out of his mouth before a mountain bird, something like our jackdaw, but smaller and of a bluer black, flew out of the hollow mouth of one of the statues, and with a hearty chuckle perched on the ground at his feet, attracted doubtless by the scraps of food that were lying about. With the fearlessness of birds in that country, it looked up at him and George, gave another hearty chuckle, and flew back to its statue with the largest fragment it could find.

They settled that this was an omen so propitious that they could part in good hope. "Let us finish the wine," said my father, "and then, do what must be done."

They finished the wine to each other's good health; George drank also to mine, and said he hoped my father would bring me with him, while my father drank to Yram, the Mayor, their children, Mrs. Humdrum, and above all to Mrs. Humdrum's grand-daughter. They then re-packed all that could be taken away; my father rolled his rug to his liking, slung it over his shoulder, gripped George's hand, and said, "My dearest boy, when we have each turned our backs upon one another, let us walk our several ways as fast as we can, and try not to look behind us."

So saying he loosed his grip of George's hand, bared his head, lowered it, and turned away.

George burst into tears, and followed him after he had gone two paces; he threw his arms round him, hugged him, kissed him on his lips, cheeks, and forehead, and then turning round, strode full speed towards Sunch'ston. My father never took his eyes off him till he was out of sight, but the boy did not look round. When he could see him no more, my father with faltering gait, and feeling as though a prop had suddenly been taken from under him, began to follow the stream down towards his old camp.

CHAPTER XXVI

MY FATHER REACHES HOME, AND DIES NOT LONG AFTERWARDS

My FATHER COULD walk but slowly, for George's boots had blistered his feet, and it seemed to him that the river-bed, of which he caught glimpses now and again, never got any nearer; but all things come to an end, and by seven o'clock on the night of Tuesday, he was on the spot which he had left on the preceding Friday morning. Three entire days had intervened, but he felt that something, he knew not what, had seized him, and that whereas before these three days life had been one thing, what little might follow them, would be another—and a very different one.

He soon caught sight of his horse which had strayed a mile lower down the river-bed, and in spite of his hobbles had crossed one ugly stream that my father dared not ford on foot. Tired though he was, he went after him, bridle in hand, and when the friendly creature saw him, it recrossed the stream, and came to him of its own accord—either tired of his own company, or tempted by some bread my father held out towards him. My father took off the hobbles, and rode him bare-backed to the camping ground, where he rewarded him with more bread and biscuit, and then hobbled him again for the night.

"It was here," he said to me on one of the first days after his return, "that I first knew myself to be a broken man. As for meeting George again, I felt sure that it would be all I could do to meet his brother; and though George was always in my thoughts, it was for you and not him that I was now yearning. When I gave George my watch, how glad I was that I had left my gold one at home, for that is yours, and I could not have brought myself to give it him."

"Never mind that, my dear father," said I, "but tell me how you got down the river, and thence home again."

"My very dear boy," he said, "I can hardly remember, and I had no energy to make any more notes. I remember putting a scrap of paper into the box of sovereigns, merely sending George my love along with the money; I remember also dropping the box into a hole in a tree, which I blazed, and towards which I drew a line of wood-ashes. I seem to see a poor unhinged creature gazing moodily for hours into a fire which he heaps up now and again with wood. There is not a breath of air; Nature sleeps so calmly that she dares not even breathe for fear of waking; the very river has hushed its flow. Without, the starlit calm of a summer's night in a great wilderness; within, a hurricane of wild and incoherent thoughts battling with one another in their fury to fall upon him and rend him—and on the other side the great wall of mountain, thousands of children praying at their mother's knee to this poor dazed thing. I suppose this half delirious wretch must have been myself. But I must have been more ill when I left England than I thought I was, or Erewhon would not have broken me down as it did."

No doubt he was right. Indeed it was because Mr. Cathie and his doctor saw that he was out of health and in urgent need of change, that they left off opposing his wish to travel. There is no use, however, in talking about this now.

I never got from him how he managed to reach the shepherd's hut, but I learned some little from the shepherd, when I stayed with him both on going towards Erewhon and on returning.

"He did not seem to have drink in him," said the shepherd, "when he first came here; but he must have been pretty full of it, or he must have had some bottles in his saddle-bags; for he was awful when he came back. He had got them worse than any man I ever saw, only that he was not awkward. He said there was a bird flying out of a giant's mouth and laughing at him, and he kept muttering about a blue pool, and hanky-panky of all sorts, and he said he knew it was all hanky-panky, at least I thought he said so, but it was no use trying to follow him, for it was all nothing but horrors. He said I was to stop the people from trying to worship him. Then he said the sky opened and he could see the angels going about and singing 'Hallelujah.' "

"How long did he stay with you?" I asked.

"About ten days, but the last three he was himself again, only too weak to move. He thought he was cured except for weakness."

"Do you know how he had been spending the last two days or so before he got down to your hut?"

I said two days, because this was the time I supposed he would take to descend the river.

"I should say drinking all the time. He said he had fallen off his horse two or three times, till he took to leading him. If he had had any other horse than old Doctor he would have been a dead man. Bless you, I have known that horse ever since he was foaled, and I never saw one like him for sense. He would pick fords better than that gentleman could, I know, and if the gentleman fell off him he would just stay stock still. He was badly bruised, poor man, when he got here. I saw him through the gorge when he left me, and he gave me a sovereign; he said he had only one other left to take him down to the port, or he would have made it more."

"He was my father," said I, "and he is dead, but before he died he told me to give you five pounds which I have brought you. I think you are wrong in saying that he had been drinking."

"That is what they all say; but I take it very kind of him to have thought of me."

My father's illness for the first three weeks after his return played with him as a cat plays with a mouse; now and again it would let him have a day or two's run, during which he was so cheerful and unclouded that his doctor was quite hopeful about him. At various times on these occasions I got from him that when he left the shepherd's hut, he thought his illness had run itself out, and that he should now reach the port from which he was to sail for S. Francisco without misadventure. This he did, and he was able to do all he had to do at the port, though frequently attacked with passing fits of giddiness. I need not dwell upon his voyage to S. Francisco, and thence home; it is enough to say that he was able to travel by himself in spite of gradually, but continually, increasing failure.

"When," he said, "I reached the port, I telegraphed, as you know, for more money. How puzzled you must have been. I sold my horse to the man from whom I bought it, at a loss of only about £10, and I left with him my saddle, saddle-bags, small hatchet, my hobbles, and in fact everything that I had taken with me, except what they had impounded in Erewhon. Yram's rug I dropped into the river when I knew that I should no longer need it—as also her substitutes for my billy and pannikin; and I burned her basket. The shepherd would have asked me questions. You will find an order to deliver everything up to bearer. You need therefore take nothing from England."

At another time he said, "When you go, for it is plain I cannot, and go one or other of us must, try and get the horse I had: he will be nine years old, and he knows all about the rivers: if you leave everything to him, you may shut your eyes, but do not interfere with him. Give the shepherd what I said and he will attend to you, but go a day or two too soon, for the margin of one day was not enough to allow in case of a fresh in the river; if the water is discoloured you must not cross it—not even with Doctor. I could not ask George to come up three days running from Sunch'ston to the statues and back."

Here he became exhausted. Almost the last coherent string of sentences I got from him was as follows:—

"About George's money if I send him £2000 you will still have nearly £150,000 left, and Mr. Cathie will not let you try to make it more. I know you would give him four or five thousand, but the Mayor and I talked it over, and settled that £2000 in gold would make him a rich man. Consult our good friend Alfred" (meaning, of course, Mr. Cathie) "about the best way of taking the money. I am afraid there is nothing for it but gold, and this will be a great weight for you to carry—about, I believe, 36 lbs. Can you do this? I really think that if you lead your horse you . . . no—there will be the getting him down again———"

"Don't worry about it, my dear father," said I, "I can do it easily if I stow the load rightly, and I will see to this. I shall have nothing else to carry, for I shall camp down below both morning and evening. But would you not like to send some present to the Mayor, Yram, their other children, and Mrs. Humdrum's granddaughter?"

"Do what you can," said my father. And these were the last instructions he gave me about those adventures with which alone this work is concerned.

The day before he died, he had a little flicker of intelligence, but all of a sudden his face became clouded as with great anxiety; he seemed to see some horrible chasm in front of him which he had to cross, or which he feared that I must cross, for he gasped out words, which, as near as I could catch them, were, "Look out! John! Leap! Leap! Le . . ." but he could not say all that he was trying to say and closed his eyes, having, as I then deemed, seen that he was on the brink of that gulf which lies between life and death; I took it that in reality he died at that moment; for there was neither struggle nor hardly movement of any kind afterwards—nothing but a pulse which for the next several hours grew fainter and fainter so gradually, that it was not till some time after it had ceased to beat that we were certain of its having done so.

CHAPTER XXVII

I MEET MY BROTHER GEORGE AT THE STATUES, ON THE TOP OF THE PASS INTO EREWHON

THIS BOOK HAS already become longer than I intended, but I will ask the reader to have patience while I tell him briefly of my own visit to the threshold of that strange country of which I fear that he may be already beginning to tire.

The winding-up of my father's estate was a very simple matter, and by the beginning of September 1891 I should have been free to start; but about that time I became engaged, and naturally enough I did not want to be longer away than was necessary. I should not have gone at all if I could have helped it. I left, however, a fortnight later than my father had done.

Before starting I bought a handsome gold repeater for the Mayor, and a brooch for Yram, of pearls and diamonds set in gold, for which I paid £200. For Yram's three daughters and for Mrs. Humdrum's grand-daughter I took four brooches each of which cost about £15, 15s., and for the boys I got three ten-guinea silver watches. For George I only took a strong English knife of the best make, and the two thousand pounds' worth of uncoined gold, which for convenience' sake I had had made into small bars. I also had a knapsack made that would hold these and nothing else—each bar being strongly sewn into its place, so that none of them could shift. Whenever I went on board ship, or went on shore, I put this on my back, so that no one handled it except myself—and I can assure the reader that I did not find it a light weight to handle. I ought to have taken something for old Mrs. Humdrum, but I am ashamed to say that I forgot her.

I went as directly as I could to the port of which my father had told me, and reached it on November 27, one day later than he had done in the preceding year.

On the following day, which was a Saturday, I went to the livery stables from which my father had bought his horse, and found to my great delight that Doctor could be at my disposal, for, as it seemed to me, the very reasonable price of fifteen shillings a day. I showed the owner of the stables my father's order, and all the articles he had left were immediately delivered to me. I was still wearing crape round one arm, and the horse-dealer, whose name was Baker, said he was afraid the other gentleman might be dead.

"Indeed, he is so," said I, "and a great grief it is to me; he was my father."

"Dear, dear," answered Mr. Baker, "that is a very serious thing for the poor gentleman. He seemed quite unfit to travel alone, and I feared he was not long for this world, but he was bent on going."

I had nothing now to do but to buy a blanket, pannikin, and billy, with some tea, tobacco, two bottles of brandy, some ship's biscuits, and whatever other few items were down on the list of requisites which my father had dictated to me. Mr. Baker, seeing that I was what he called a new chum, showed me how to pack my horse, but I kept my knapsack full of gold on my back, and though I could see that it puzzled him, he asked no questions. There was no reason why I should not set out at once for the principal town of the colony, which was some ten miles inland; I, therefore, arranged at my hotel that the greater part of my luggage should await my return, and set out to climb the high hills that back the port. From the top of these I had a magnificent view of the plains that I should have to cross, and of the long range of distant mountains which bounded them north and south as far as the eye could reach. On some of the mountains I could still see streaks of snow, but my father had explained to me that the ranges I should here see were not those dividing the English colony from Erewhon. I also saw, some nine miles or so out upon the plains, the more prominent buildings of a large town which seemed to be embosomed in trees, and this I reached in about an hour and a half; for I had to descend at a foot's pace, and Doctor's many virtues did not comprise a willingness to go beyond an amble.

At the town above referred to I spent the night, and began to strike across the plains on the following morning. I might have crossed these in three days at twenty-five miles a day, but I had too much time on my hands, and my load of gold was so uncomfortable that I was glad to stay at one accommodation house after another, averaging about eighteen miles a day. I have no doubt that if I had taken advice, I could have stowed my load more conveniently, but I could not unpack it, and made the best of it as it was.

On the evening of Wednesday, December 2, I reached the river which I should have to follow up; it was here nearing the gorge through which it had to pass before the country opened out again at the back of the front range. I came upon it quite suddenly on reaching the brink of a great terrace, the bank of which sloped almost precipitously down towards it, but was covered with grass. The terrace was some three hundred feet above the river, and faced another similar one, which was from a mile and a half to two miles distant. At the bottom of this huge yawning chasm rolled the mighty river, and I shuddered at the thought of having to cross and recross it. For it was angry, muddy, evidently in heavy fresh, and filled bank and bank for nearly a mile with a flood of seething waters.

I followed along the northern edge of the terrace, till I reached the last accommodation house that could be said to be on the plains—which, by the way, were here some eight or nine hundred feet above sea level. When I reached this house, I was glad to learn that the river was not likely to remain high for more than a day or two, and that if what was called a Southerly Burster came up, as it might be expected to do at any moment, it would be quite low again before three days were over.

At this house I stayed the night, and in the course of the evening a stray dog—a retriever, hardly full grown, and evidently very much down on his luck—took up with me; when I inquired about him, and asked if I might take him with me, the landlord said he wished I would, for he knew nothing about him and was trying to drive him from the house. Knowing what a boon the companionship of this poor beast would be to me when I was camping out alone, I encouraged him, and next morning he followed me as a matter of course.

In the night the Southerly Burster which my host anticipated had come up, cold and blustering, but invigorating after the hot, dry wind that had been blowing hard during the daytime as I had crossed the plains. A mile or two higher up I passed a large sheep-station, but did not stay there. One or two men looked at me with surprise, and asked me where I was going, whereon I said I was in search of rare plants and birds for the Museum of the town at which I had slept the night after my arrival. This satisfied their curiosity, and I ambled on accompanied by the dog. In passing I may say that I found Doctor not to excel at any pace except an amble, but for a long journey, especially for one who is carrying a heavy, awkward load, there is no pace so comfortable; and he ambled fairly fast.

I followed the horse track which had been cut through the gorge, and in many places I disliked it extremely, for the river, still in fresh, was raging furiously; twice, for some few yards, where the gorge was wider and the stream less rapid, it covered the track, and I had no confidence that it might not have washed it away; on these occasions Doctor pricked his ears towards the water, and was evidently thinking exactly what his rider was. He decided, however, that all would be sound, and took to the water without any urging on my part. Seeing his opinion, I remembered my father's advice, and let him do what he liked, but in one place for three or four yards the water came nearly up to his belly, and I was in great fear for the watches that were in my saddle-bags. As for the dog, I feared I had lost him, but after a time he rejoined me, though how he contrived to do so I cannot say.

Nothing could be grander than the sight of this great river pent into a narrow compass, and occasionally becoming more like an immense waterfall than a river, but I was in continual fear of coming to more places where the water would be over the track, and perhaps of finding myself unable to get any farther. I therefore failed to enjoy what was really far the most impressive sight in its way that I had ever seen. "Give me," I said to myself, "the Thames at Richmond," and right thankful was I, when at about two o'clock I found that I was through the gorge and in a wide valley, the greater part of which, however, was still covered by the river. It was here that I heard for the first time the curious sound of boulders knocking against each other underneath the great body of water that kept rolling them round and round.

I now halted, and lit a fire, for there was much dead scrub standing that had remained after the ground had been burned for the first time some years previously. I made myself some tea, and turned Doctor out for a couple of hours to feed. I did not hobble him, for my father had told me that he would always come for bread. When I had dined, and smoked, and slept for a couple of hours or so, I reloaded Doctor and resumed my journey towards the shepherd's hut, which I caught sight of about a mile before I reached it. When nearly half a mile off it, I dismounted, and made a written note of the exact spot at which I did so. I then turned for a couple of hundred yards to my right, at right angles to the track, where some huge rocks were lying—fallen ages since from the mountain that flanked this side of the valley. Here I deposited my knapsack in a hollow underneath some of the rocks, and put a good sized stone in front of it, for I meant spending a couple of days with the shepherd to let the river go down. Moreover, as it was now only December 3, I had too much time on my hands, but I had not dared to cut things finer.

I reached the hut at about six o'clock, and introduced myself to the shepherd, who was a nice, kind old man, commonly called Harris, but his real name he told me was Horace—Horace Taylor. I had the conversation with him of which I have already told the reader, adding that my father had been unable to give a coherent account of what he had seen, and that I had been sent to get the information he had failed to furnish.

The old man said that I must certainly wait a couple of days before I went higher up the river. He had made himself a nice garden, in which he took the greatest pride, and which supplied him with plenty of vegetables. He was very glad to have company, and to receive the newspapers which I had taken care to bring him. He had a real genius for simple cookery, and fed me excellently. My father's £5, and the ration of brandy which I nightly gave him, made me a welcome guest, and though I was longing to be at any rate as far as the foot of the pass into Erewhon, I amused myself very well in an abundance of ways with which I need not trouble the reader.

One of the first things that Harris said to me was, "I wish I knew what your father did with the nice red blanket he had with him when he went up the river. He had none when he came down again; I have no horse here, but I borrowed one from a man who came up one day from down below, and rode to a place where I found what I am sure were the ashes of the last fire he made, but I could find neither the blanket nor the billy and pannikin he took away with him. He said he supposed he must have left the things there, but he could remember nothing about it."

"I am afraid," said I, "that I cannot help you."

"At any rate," continued the shepherd, "I did not have my ride for nothing, for as I was coming back I found this rug half covered with sand on the river-bed."

As he spoke he pointed to an excellent warm rug, on the spare bunk in his hut. "It is none of our make," said he; "I suppose some foreign digger has come over from the next river down south and got drowned, for it had not been very long where I found it, at least I think not, for it was not much fly-blown, and no one had passed here to go up the river since your father."

I knew what it was, but I held my tongue beyond saying that the rug was a very good one.

The next day, December 4, was lovely, after a night that had been clear and cold, with frost towards early morning. When the shepherd had gone for some three hours in the forenoon to see his sheep (that were now lambing), I walked down to the place where I had left my knapsack, and carried it a good mile above the hut, where I again hid it. I could see the great range from one place, and the thick new fallen snow assured me that the river would be quite normal shortly. Indeed, by evening it was hardly at all discoloured, but I waited another day, and set out on the morning of Sunday, December 6. The river was now almost as low as in winter, and Harris assured me that if I used my eyes I could not miss finding a ford over one stream or another every half mile or so. I had the greatest difficulty in preventing him from accompanying me on foot for some little distance, but I got rid of him in the end; he came with me beyond the place where I had hidden my knapsack, but when he had left me long enough, I rode back and got it.

I see I am dwelling too long upon my own small adventures. Suffice it that, accompanied by my dog, I followed the north bank of the river till I found I must cross one stream before I could get any farther. This place would not do, and I had to ride half a mile back before I found one that seemed as if it might be safe. I fancy my father must have done just the same thing, for Doctor seemed to know the ground, and took to the water the moment I brought him to it. It never reached his belly, but I confess I did not like it. By and by I had to recross, and so on, off and on, till at noon I camped for dinner. Here the dog found me a nest of young ducks, nearly fledged, from which the parent birds tried with great success to decoy me. I fully thought I was going to catch them, but the dog knew better and made straight for the nest, from which he returned immediately with a fine young duck in his mouth, which he laid at my feet, wagging his tail and barking. I took another from the nest and left two for the old birds.

The afternoon was much as the morning and towards seven I reached a place which suggested itself as a good camping ground. I had hardly fixed on it and halted before I saw a few pieces of charred wood, and felt sure that my father must have camped at this very place before me. I hobbled Doctor, unloaded, plucked and singed a duck, and gave the dog some of the meat with which Harris had furnished me; I made tea, laid my duck on the embers till it was cooked, smoked, gave myself a nightcap of brandy and water, and by and by rolled myself round in my blanket, with the dog curled up beside me. I will not dwell upon the strangeness of my feelings— nor the extreme beauty of the night. But for the dog, and Doctor, I should have been frightened, but I knew there were no savage creatures or venomous snakes in the country, and both the dog and Doctor were such good companionable creatures, that I did not feel so much oppressed by the solitude as I had feared I should be. But the night was cold, and my blanket was not enough to keep me comfortably warm.

The following day was delightfully warm as soon as the sun got to the bottom of the valley, and the fresh fallen snow disappeared so fast from the snowy range that I was afraid it would raise the river—which, indeed, rose in the afternoon and became slightly discoloured, but it cannot have been more than three or four inches deeper, for it never reached the bottom of my saddle-bags. I believe Doctor knew exactly where I was going, for he wanted no guidance. I halted again at mid-day, got two more ducks, crossed and recrossed the river, or some of its streams, several times, and at about six, caught sight, after a bend in the valley, of the glacier descending on to the river bed. This I knew to be close to the point at which I was to camp for the night, and from which I was to ascend the mountain. After another hour's slow progress over the increasing roughness of the river-bed, I saw the triangular delta of which my father had told me, and the stream that had formed it, bounding down the mountain side. Doctor went right up to the place where my father's fire had been, and I again found many pieces of charred wood and ashes.

As soon as I had unloaded Doctor and hobbled him, I went to a tree hard by, on which I could see the mark of a blaze, and towards which I thought I could see a line of wood ashes running. There I found a hole in which some bird had evidently been wont to build, and surmised correctly that it must be the one in which my father had hidden his box of sovereigns. There was no box in the hole now, and I began to feel that I was at last within measureable distance of Erewhon and the Erewhonians.

I camped for the night here, and again found my single blanket insufficient. The next day, i.e. Tuesday, December 8, I had to pass as I best could, and it occurred to me that as I should find the gold a great weight, I had better take it some three hours up the mountain side and leave it there, so as to make the following day less fatiguing, and this I did, returning to my camp for dinner; but I was panic-stricken all the rest of the day lest I should not have hidden it safely, or lest I should be unable to find it next day—conjuring up a hundred absurd fancies as to what might befall it. And after all, heavy though it was, I could have carried it all the way. In the afternoon I saddled Doctor and rode him up to the glaciers, which were indeed magnificent, and then I made the few notes of my journey from which this chapter has been taken. I made excuses for turning in early, and at daybreak rekindled my fire and got my breakfast. All the time the companionship of the dog was an unspeakable comfort to me.

It is now the day my father had fixed for my meeting with George, and my excitement (with which I have not yet troubled the reader, though it had been consuming me ever since I had left Harris's hut) was beyond all bounds, so much so that I almost feared I was in a fever which would prevent my completing the little that remained of my task; in fact, I was in as great a panic as I had been about the gold that I had left. My hands trembled as I took the watches and the brooches for Yram and her daughters from my saddle-bags, which I then hung, probably on the very bough on which my father had hung them. Needless to say, I also hung my saddle and bridle along with the saddle-bags.

It was nearly seven before I started, and about ten before I reached the hiding-place of my knapsack. I found it, of course, quite easily, shouldered it, and toiled on towards the statues. At a quarter before twelve I reached them, and almost beside myself as I was, could not refrain from some disappointment at finding them a good deal smaller than I expected. My father, correcting the measurement he had given in his book, said he thought that they were about four or five times the size of life; but really I do not think they were more than twenty feet high, any one of them. In other respects my father's description of them is quite accurate. There was no wind, and as a matter of course, therefore, they were not chanting. I wiled away the quarter of an hour before the time when George became due, with wondering at them, and in a way admiring them, hideous though they were; but all the time I kept looking towards the part from which George should come.

At last my watch pointed to noon, but there was no George. A quarter past twelve, but no George. Half-past, still no George. One o'clock, and all the quarters till three o'clock, but still no George. I tried to eat some of the ship's biscuits I had brought with me, but I could not. My disappointment was now as great as my excitement had been all the forenoon; at three o'clock I fairly cried, and for half an hour could only fling myself on the ground and give way to all the unreasonable spleen that extreme vexation could suggest. True, I kept telling myself that for aught I knew George might be dead, or down with the fever; but this would not do; for in this last case he should have sent one of his brothers to meet me, and it was not likely that he was dead. I am afraid I thought it most probable that he had been casual—of which unworthy suspicion I have long since been heartily ashamed.

I put the brooches inside my knapsack, and hid it in a place where I was sure no one would find it; then, with a heavy heart, I trudged down again to my camp—broken in spirit, and hopeless for the morrow.

I camped again, but it was some hours before I got a wink of sleep; and when sleep came it was accompanied by a strange dream. I dreamed that I was by my father's bedside, watching his last flicker of intelligence, and vainly trying to catch the words that he was not less vainly trying to utter. All of a sudden the bed seemed to be at my camping ground, and the largest of the statues appeared, quite small, high up the mountain side, but striding down like a giant in seven league boots till it stood over me and my father, and shouted out "Leap, John, leap." In the horror of this vision I woke with a loud cry that woke my dog also and made him show such evident signs of fear, that it seemed to me as though he too must have shared my dream.

Shivering with cold I started up in a frenzy, but there was nothing, save a night of such singular beauty that I did not even try to go to sleep again. Naturally enough, on trying to keep awake I dropped asleep before many minutes were over.

In the morning I again climbed up to the statues, without, to my surprise, being depressed with the idea that George would again fail to meet me. On the contrary, without rhyme or reason, I had a strong presentiment that he would come. And sure enough, as soon as I caught sight of the statues, which I did about a quarter to twelve, I saw a youth coming towards me, with a quick step, and a beaming face that had only to be seen to be fallen in love with.

"You are my brother," said he to me. "Is my father with you?"

I pointed to the crape on my arm, and to the ground, but said nothing.

He understood me, and bared his head. Then he flung his arms about me and kissed my forehead according to Erewhonian custom. I was a little surprised at his saying nothing to me about the way in which he had disappointed me on the preceding day; I resolved, however, to wait for the explanation that I felt sure he would give me presently.

CHAPTER XXVIII

GEORGE AND I SPEND A FEW HOURS TOGETHER AT THE STATUES, AND THEN PART—I REACH HOME— POSTSCRIPT

I HAVE SAID on an earlier page that George gained an immediate ascendancy over me, but ascendancy is not the word—he took me by storm; how, or why, I neither know nor want to know, but before I had been with him more than a few minutes I felt as though I had known and loved him all my life. And the dog fawned upon him as though he felt just as I did.

"Come to the statues," said he, as soon as he had somewhat recovered from the shock of the news I had given him. "We can sit down there on the very stone on which our father and I sat a year ago. I have brought a basket, which my mother packed for—for—him and me. Did he talk to you about me?"

"He talked of nothing so much, and he thought of nothing so much. He had your boots put where he could see them from his bed until he died."

Then followed the explanation about these boots, of which the reader has already been told. This made us both laugh, and from that moment we were cheerful.

I say nothing about our enjoyment of the luncheon with which Yram had provided us, and if I were to detail all that I told George about my father, and all the additional information that I got from him—(many a point did he clear up for me that I had not fully understood)—I should fill several chapters, whereas I have left myself only one. Luncheon being over I said—

"And are you married?"

"Yes" (with a blush), "and are you?"

I could not blush. Why should I? And yet young people—especially the most ingenious among them—are apt to flush up on being asked if they are, or are going to be, married. If I could have blushed, I would. As it was I could only say that I was engaged and should marry as soon as I got back.

"Then you have come all this way for me, when you were wanting to get married?"

"Of course I have. My father on his death-bed told me to do so, and to bring you something that I have brought you."

"What trouble I have given! How can I thank you?"

"Shake hands with me."

Whereon he gave my hand a stronger grip than I had quite bargained for.

"And now," said I, "before I tell you what I have brought, you must promise me to accept it. Your father said I was not to leave you till you had done so, and I was to say that he sent it with his dying blessing."

After due demur George gave his promise, and I took him to the place where I had hidden my knapsack.

"I brought it up yesterday," said I.

"Yesterday? but why?"

"Because yesterday—was it not?—was the first of the two days agreed upon between you and our father?"

"No—surely to-day is the first day—I was to come XXI. i. 3, which would be your December 9."

"But yesterday was December 9 with us—to-day is December 10."

"Strange! What day of the week do you make it?"

"To-day is Thursday, December 10."

"This is still stranger—we make it Wednesday; yesterday was Tuesday."

Then I saw it. The year XX. had been a leap year with the Erewhonians, and 1891 in England had not. This, then, was what had crossed my father's brain in his dying hours, and what he had vainly tried to tell me. It was also what my unconscious self had been struggling to tell my conscious one during the past night, but which my conscious self had been too stupid to understand. And yet my conscious self had caught it in an imperfect sort of a way after all, for from the moment that my dream had left me I had been composed, and easy in my mind that all would be well. I wish some one would write a book about dreams and parthenogenesis—for that the two are part and parcel of the same story—a brood of folly without father bred—I cannot doubt.

I did not trouble George with any of this rubbish, but only showed him how the mistake had arisen. When we had laughed sufficiently over my mistake—for it was I who had come up on the wrong day, not he—I fished my knapsack out of its hiding-place.

"Do not unpack it," said I, "beyond taking out the brooches, or you will not be able to pack it so well; but you can see the ends of the bars of gold, and you can feel the weight; my father sent them for you. The pearl brooch is for your mother, the smaller brooches are for your sisters, and your wife."

I then told him how much gold there was, and from my pockets brought out the watches and the English knife.

"This last," I said, "is the only thing that I am giving you; the rest is all from our father. I have many many times as much gold myself, and this is legally your property as much as mine is mine."

George was aghast, but he was powerless alike to express his feelings, or to refuse the gold.

"Do you mean to say that my father left me this by his will?"

"Certainly he did," said I, inventing a pious fraud.

"It is all against my oath," said he, looking grave.

"Your oath be hanged," said I. "You must give the gold to the Mayor, who knows that it was coming, and it will appear to the world as though he were giving it you now instead of leaving you anything."

"But it is ever so much too much!"

"It is not half enough. You and the Mayor must settle all that between you. He and our father talked it all over, and this was what they settled."

"And our father planned all this without saying a word to me about it while we were on our way up here?"

"Yes. There might have been some hitch in the gold's coming. Besides the Mayor told him not to tell you."

"And he never said anything about the other money he left for me—which enabled me to marry at once? Why was this?"

"Your mother said he was not to do so."

"Bless my heart, how they have duped me all round. But why would not my mother let your father tell me? Oh yes—she was afraid I should tell the King about it, as I certainly should, when I told him all the rest."

"Tell the King?" said I, "what have you been telling the King?"

"Everything; except about the nuggets and the sovereigns, of which I knew nothing; and I have felt myself a blackguard ever since for not telling him about these when he came up here last autumn—but I let the Mayor and my mother talk me over, as I am afraid they will do again."

"When did you tell the King?"

Then followed all the details that I have told in the latter part of Chapter XXI. When I asked how the King took the confession, George said—

"He was so much flattered at being treated like a reasonable being, and Dr. Downie, who was chief spokesman, played his part so discreetly, without attempting to obscure even the most compromising issues, that though his Majesty made some show of displeasure at first, it was plain that he was heartily enjoying the whole story.

"Dr. Downie showed very well. He took on himself the onus of having advised our action, and he gave me all the credit of having proposed that we should make a clean breast of everything.

"The King, too, behaved with truly royal politeness; he was on the point of asking why I had not taken our father to the Blue Pool at once, and flung him into it on the Sunday afternoon, when something seemed to strike him; he gave me a searching look, on which he said in an undertone, 'Oh yes,' and did not go on with his question. He never blamed me for anything, and when I begged him to accept my resignation of the Rangership, he said—

"'No. Stay where you are till I lose confidence in you, which will not, I think, be very soon. I will come and have a few days' shooting about the middle of March, and if I have good sport I shall order your salary to be increased. If any more foreign devils come over, do not Blue-Pool them; send them down to me, and I will see what I think of them; I am much disposed to encourage a few of them to settle here.'

"I am sure," continued George, "that he said this because he knew I was half a foreign devil myself. Indeed he won my heart not only by the delicacy of his consideration, but by the obvious good will he bore me. I do not know what he did with the nuggets, but he gave orders that the blanket and the rest of my father's kit should be put in the great Erewhonian Museum. As regards my father's receipt, and the Professors' two depositions, he said he would have them carefully preserved in his secret archives. 'A document,' he said somewhat enigmatically, 'is a document—but, Professor Hanky, you can have this'—and as he spoke he handed him back his pocket-handkerchief.

"Hanky during the whole interview was furious, at having to play so undignified a part, but even more so, because the King while he paid marked attention to Dr. Downie, and even to myself, treated him with amused disdain. Nevertheless, angry though he was, he was impenitent, unabashed, and brazened it out at Bridgeford, that the King had received him with open arms, and had snubbed Dr. Downie and myself. But for his (Hanky's) intercession, I should have been dismissed then and there from the Rangership. And so forth. Panky never opened his mouth.

"Returning to the King, his Majesty said to Dr. Downie, 'I am afraid I shall not be able to canonise any of you gentlemen just yet. We must let this affair blow over. Indeed I am in half a mind to have this Sunchild bubble pricked; I never liked it, and am getting tired of it; you Musical Bank gentlemen are overdoing it. I will talk it over with her Majesty. As for Professor Hanky, I do not see how I can keep one who has been so successfully hoodwinked, as my Professor of Worldly Wisdom; but I will consult her Majesty about this point also. Perhaps I can find another post for him. If I decide on having Sunchildism pricked, he shall apply the pin. You may go.'

"And glad enough," said George, "we all of us were to do so."

"But did he," I asked, "try to prick the bubble of Sunchildism?"

"Oh no. As soon as he said he would talk it over with her Majesty, I knew the whole thing would end in smoke, as indeed to all outward appearance it shortly did; for Dr. Downie advised him not to be in too great a hurry, and whatever he did to do it gradually. He therefore took no further action than to show marked favour to practical engineers and mechanicians. Moreover he started an aëronautical society, which made Bridgeford furious; but so far, I am afraid it has done us no good, for the first ascent was disastrous, involving the death of the poor fellow who made it, and since then no one has ventured to ascend. I am afraid we do not get on very fast."

"Did the King," I asked, "increase your salary?"

"Yes. He doubled it."

"And what do they say in Sunch'ston about our father's second visit?"

George laughed, and showed me the newspaper extract which I have already given. I asked who wrote it.

"I did," said he, with a demure smile; "I wrote it at night after I returned home, and before starting for the capital next morning. I called myself 'the deservedly popular Ranger,' to avert suspicion. No one found me out; you can keep the extract; I brought it here on purpose."

"It does you great credit. Was there ever any lunatic, and was he found?"

"Oh, yes. That part was true, except that he had never been up our way."

"Then the poacher is still at large?"

"It is to be feared so."

"And were Dr. Downie and the Professors canonised after all?"

"Not yet; but the Professors will be next month—for Hanky is still Professor. Dr. Downie backed out of it. He said it was enough to be a Sunchildist without being a Sunchild Saint. He worships the jumping cat as much as the others, but he keeps his eye better on the cat, and sees sooner both when it will jump, and where it will jump to. Then, without disturbing any one, he insinuates himself into the place which will be best when the jump is over. Some say that the cat knows him and follows him; at all events when he makes a move the cat generally jumps towards him soon afterwards."

"You give him a very high character."

"Yes, but I have my doubts about his doing much in this matter; he is getting old, and Hanky burrows like a mole night and day. There is no knowing how it will all end."

"And the people at Sunch'ston? Has it got well about among them, in spite of your admirable article, that it was the Sunchild himself who interrupted Hanky?"

"It has, and it has not. Many of us know the truth, but a story came down from Bridgeford that it was an evil spirit who had assumed the Sunchild's form, intending to make people sceptical about Sunchildism; Hanky and Panky cowed this spirit, otherwise it would never have recanted. Many people swallow this."

"But Hanky and Panky swore that they knew the man."

"That does not matter."

"And now, please, how long have you been married?"

"About ten months."

"Any family?"

"One boy about a fortnight old. Do come down to Sunch'ston and see him—he is your own nephew. You speak Erewhonian so perfectly that no human being would suspect you were a foreigner, and you look one of us from head to foot. I can smuggle you through quite easily, and my mother would so like to see you."

I should dearly have liked to have gone, but it was out of the question. I had nothing with me but the clothes I stood in; moreover I was longing to be back in England, and when once I was in Erewhon there was no knowing when I should be able to get away again; but George fought hard before he gave in.

It was now nearing the time when this strange meeting between two brothers—as strange a one as the statues can ever have looked down upon—must come to an end. I showed George what the repeater would do, and what it would expect of its possessor. I gave him six good photographs, of my father and myself—three of each. He had never seen a photograph, and could hardly believe his eyes as he looked at those I showed him. I also gave him three envelopes addressed to myself, care of Alfred Emery Cathie, Esq., 15 Clifford's Inn, London, and implored him to write to me if he could ever find means of getting a letter over the range as far as the shepherd's hut. At this he shook his head, but he promised to write if he could. I also told him that I had written a full account of my father's second visit to Erewhon, but that it should never be published till I heard from him—at which he again shook his head, but added, "And yet who can tell? For the King may have the country opened up to foreigners some day after all."

Then he thanked me a thousand times over, shouldered the knapsack, embraced me as he had my father, and caressed the dog, embraced me again, and made no attempt to hide the tears that ran down his cheeks.

"There," he said; "I shall wait here till you are out of sight."

I turned away, and did not look back till I reached the place at which I knew that I should lose the statues. I then turned round, waved my hand—as also did George, and went down the mountain side, full of sad thoughts, but thankful that my task had been so happily accomplished, and aware that my life henceforward had been enriched by something that I could never lose.

For I had never seen, and felt as though I never could see, George's equal. His absolute unconsciousness of self, the unhesitating way in which he took me to his heart, his fearless frankness, the happy genial expression that played on his face, and the extreme sweetness of his smile—these were the things that made me say to myself that the "blazon of beauty's best" could tell me nothing better than what I had found and lost within the last three hours. How small, too, I felt by comparison! If for no other cause, yet for this, that I, who had wept so bitterly over my own disappointment the day before, could meet this dear fellow's tears with no tear of my own.

But let this pass. I got back to Harris's hut without adventure. When there, in the course of the evening, I told Harris that I had a fancy for the rug he had found on the river-bed, and that if he would let me have it, I would give him my red one and ten shillings to boot. The exchange was so obviously to his advantage that he made no demur, and next morning I strapped Yram's rug on to my horse, and took it gladly home to England, where I keep it on my own bed next to the counterpane, so that with care it may last me out my life. I wanted him to take the dog and make a home for him, but he had two collies already, and said that a retriever would be of no use to him. So I took the poor beast on with me to the port, where I was glad to find that Mr. Baker liked him and accepted him from me, though he was not mine to give. He had been such an unspeakable comfort to me when I was alone, that he would have haunted me unless I had been able to provide for him where I knew he would be well cared for. As for Doctor, I was sorry to leave him, but I knew he was in good hands.

"I see you have not brought your knapsack back, sir," said Mr. Baker.

"No," said I, "and very thankful was I when I had handed it over to those for whom it was intended."

"I have no doubt you were, sir, for I could see it was a desperate heavy load for you."

"Indeed it was." But at this point I brought the discussion to a close.

Two days later I sailed, and reached home early in February 1892. I was married three weeks later, and when the honeymoon was over, set about making the necessary, and some, I fear, unnecessary additions to this book—by far the greater part of which had been written, as I have already said, many months earlier. I now leave it, at any rate for the present, April 22, 1892.

Postscript.—On the last day of November 1900, I received a letter addressed in Mr. Alfred Cathie's familiar handwriting, and on opening it found that it contained another, addressed to me in my own, and unstamped. For the moment I was puzzled, but immediately knew that it must be from George. I tore it open, and found eight closely written pages, which I devoured as I have seldom indeed devoured so long a letter. It was dated XXIX. vii. I, and, as nearly as I can translate it, was as follows:—

"Twice, my dearest brother, have I written to you, and twice in successive days in successive years, have I been up to the statues on the chance that you could meet me, as I proposed in my letters. Do not think I went all the way back to Sunch'ston—there is a ranger's shelter now only an hour and a half below the statues, and here I passed the night. I knew you had got neither of my letters, for if you had got them and could not come yourself, you would have sent some one whom you could trust with a letter. I know you would, though I do not know how you would have contrived to do it.

"I sent both letters through Bishop Kahabuka (or, as his inferior clergy call him, 'Chowbok'), head of the Christian Mission to Erewhemos, which, as your father has doubtless told you, is the country adjoining Erewhon, but inhabited by a coloured race having no affinity with our own. Bishop Kahabuka has penetrated at times into Erewhon, and the King, wishing to be on good terms with his neighbours, has permitted him to establish two or three mission stations in the western part of Erewhon. Among the missionaries are some few of your own countrymen. None of us like them, but one of them is teaching me English, which I find quite easy.

"As I wrote in the letters that have never reached you, I am no longer Ranger. The King, after some few years (in the course of which I told him of your visit, and what you had brought me), declared that I was the only one of his servants whom he could trust, and found high office for me, which kept me in close confidential communication with himself.

"About three years ago, on the death of his Prime Minister, he appointed me to fill his place; and it was on this, that so many possibilities occurred to me concerning which I dearly longed for your opinion, that I wrote and asked you, if you could, to meet me personally or by proxy at the statues, which I could reach on the occasion of my annual visit to my mother—yes—and father—at Sunch'ston.

"I sent both letters by way of Erewhemos, confiding them to Bishop Kahabuka, who is just such another as St. Hanky. He tells me that our father was a very old and dear friend of his—but of course I did not say anything about his being my own father. I only inquired about a Mr. Higgs, who was now worshipped in Erewhon as a supernatural being. The Bishop said it was, 'Oh, so very dreadful,' and he felt it all the more keenly, for the reason that he had himself been the means of my father's going to Erewhon, by giving him the information that enabled him to find the pass over the range that bounded the country.

"I did not like the man, but I thought I could trust him with a letter, which it now seems I could not do. This third letter I have given him with a promise of a hundred pounds in silver for his new Cathedral, to be paid as soon as I get an answer from you.

"We are all well at Sunch'ston; so are my wife and eight children—five sons and three daughters—but the country is at sixes and sevens. St. Panky is dead, but his son Pocus is worse. Dr. Downie has become very lethargic. I can do less against St. Hankyism than when I was a private man. A little indiscretion on my part would plunge the country in civil war. Our engineers and so-called men of science are sturdily begging for endowments, and steadily claiming to have a hand in every pie that is baked from one end of the country to the other. The missionaries are buying up all our silver, and a change in the relative values of gold and silver is in progress of which none of us foresee the end.

"The King and I both think that annexation by England, or a British Protectorate, would be the saving of us, for we have no army worth the name, and if you do not take us over some one else soon will. The King has urged me to send for you. If you come (do! do! do!) you had better come by way of Erewhemos, which is now in monthly communication with Southampton. If you will write me that you are coming I will meet you at the port, and bring you with me to our own capital, where the King will be overjoyed to see you."

The rest of the letter was filled with all sorts of news which interested me, but would require chapters of explanation before they could become interesting to the reader.

The letter wound up:—

"You may publish now whatever you like, whenever you like.

"Write to me by way of Erewhemos, care of the Right Reverend the Lord Bishop, and say which way you will come. If you prefer the old road, we are bound to be in the neighbourhood of the statues by the beginning of March. My next brother is now Ranger, and could meet you at the statues with permit and luncheon, and more of that white wine than ever you will be able to drink. Only let me know what you will do.

"I should tell you that the old railway which used to run from Clearwater to the capital, and which, as you know, was allowed to go to ruin, has been reconstructed at an outlay far less than might have been expected—for the bridges have been maintained for ordinary carriage traffic. The journey, therefore, from Sunch'ston to the capital can now be done in less than forty hours. On the whole, however, I recommend you to come by way of Erewhemos. If you start, as I think possible, without writing from England, Bishop Kahabuka's palace is only eight miles from the port, and he will give you every information about your further journey—a distance of less than a couple of hundred miles. But I should prefer to meet you myself.

"My dearest brother, I charge you by the memory of our common father, and even more by that of those three hours that linked you to me for ever, and which I would fain hope linked me also to yourself—come over, if by any means you can do so—come over and help us.

"GEORGE STRONG."

"My dear," said I to my wife who was at the other end of the breakfast table, "I shall have to translate this letter to you, and then you will have to help me to begin packing; for I have none too much time. I must see Alfred, and give him a power of attorney. He will arrange with some publisher about my book, and you can correct the press. Break the news gently to the children; and get along without me, my dear, for six months as well as you can."

.   .   .   .   .   .

I write this at Southampton, from which port I sail to-morrow—*i.e.* November 15, 1900—for Erewhemos.